PRAISE FOR

"The characters are [...] chemistry is magic. It's [...]"
—A[...], bestselling author of *Same Time Next Summer*

"A pure delight! Has all the elements of a perfect story: small island setting, a feisty yet vulnerable heroine, and a nerdy hero who stole my heart."
—Jennifer Probst, *New York Times* bestselling author of *The Secret Love Letters of Olivia Moretti*

"McKinlay writes sexy, funny romances!"
—Jill Shalvis, *New York Times* bestselling author of *The Sweetheart List*

"A playful, breezy read that I couldn't put down!"
—Abby Jimenez, *New York Times* bestselling author of *Yours Truly*

"I devoured this clever novel in one sitting!"
—Lori Nelson Spielman, *New York Times* bestselling author of *The Star-Crossed Sisters of Tuscany*

"With lovable characters and swoonworthy moments, this heartwarming tale has it all." —*Woman's World*

"This flawless rom-com is sure to delight."
—*Publishers Weekly* (starred review)

"With McKinlay's zingy prose and effervescent wit . . . she deftly pivots from moments of comic absurdity to heartfelt emotion without missing a beat." —*Booklist* (starred review)

TITLES BY JENN MCKINLAY

Witches of Dubious Origin

Paris Is Always a Good Idea
Wait For It
Summer Reading
Love at First Book

HAPPILY EVER AFTER ROMANCES

The Good Ones
The Christmas Keeper

BLUFF POINT ROMANCES

About a Dog
Barking Up the Wrong Tree
Every Dog Has His Day

CUPCAKE BAKERY MYSTERIES

Sprinkle with Murder
Buttercream Bump Off
Death by the Dozen
Red Velvet Revenge
Going, Going, Ganache
Sugar and Iced
Dark Chocolate Demise
Vanilla Beaned
Caramel Crush
Wedding Cake Crumble
Dying for Devil's Food
Pumpkin Spice Peril
For Batter or Worse
Strawberried Alive
Sugar Plum Poisoned
Fondant Fumble

LIBRARY LOVER'S MYSTERIES

Books Can Be Deceiving
Due or Die
Book, Line, and Sinker
Read It and Weep
On Borrowed Time
A Likely Story
Better Late Than Never
Death in the Stacks
Hitting the Books
Word to the Wise
One for the Books
Killer Research
The Plot and the Pendulum
Fatal First Edition
A Merry Little Murder Plot

HAT SHOP MYSTERIES

Cloche and Dagger
Death of a Mad Hatter
At the Drop of a Hat
Copy Cap Murder
Assault and Beret
Buried to the Brim
Fatal Fascinator

Witches of Dubious Origin

Jenn McKinlay

ACE
NEW YORK

ACE
Published by Berkley
An imprint of Penguin Random House LLC
1745 Broadway, New York, NY 10019
penguinrandomhouse.com

Copyright © 2025 by Jennifer McKinlay
Excerpt from *Love at First Book* by Jenn McKinlay copyright © 2024 by Jennifer McKinlay
Penguin Random House values and supports copyright. Copyright fuels creativity, encourages diverse voices, promotes free speech, and creates a vibrant culture. Thank you for buying an authorized edition of this book and for complying with copyright laws by not reproducing, scanning, or distributing any part of it in any form without permission. You are supporting writers and allowing Penguin Random House to continue to publish books for every reader. Please note that no part of this book may be used or reproduced in any manner for the purpose of training artificial intelligence technologies or systems.

ACE is a registered trademark, and the A colophon is a trademark of
Penguin Random House LLC.

Book design by Kristin del Rosario
Interior art: title page frame © denisik11/Shutterstock; books
© Nikolaenko Ekaterina/Shutterstock

Library of Congress Cataloging-in-Publication Data

Names: McKinlay, Jenn author
Title: Witches of dubious origin / Jenn McKinlay.
Description: New York: Ace, 2025.
Identifiers: LCCN 2025018409 (print) | LCCN 2025018410 (ebook) |
ISBN 9780593819753 trade paperback | ISBN 9780593819760 ebook
Subjects: LCGFT: Fantasy fiction | Witch fiction | Novels
Classification: LCC PS3612.A948 W58 2025 (print) | LCC PS3612.A948
(ebook) | DDC 813/.6—dc23/eng/20250423
LC record available at https://lccn.loc.gov/2025018409
LC ebook record available at https://lccn.loc.gov/2025018410

First Edition: October 2025

Printed in the United States of America
1st Printing

The authorized representative in the EU for product safety and compliance is
Penguin Random House Ireland, Morrison Chambers, 32 Nassau Street,
Dublin D02 YH68, Ireland, https://eu-contact.penguin.ie.

For my amazing editor, Kate Seaver.
No matter what genre I write in,
you always make my work infinitely better.
Thank you for your wisdom, support, encouragement,
and endless patience.
This book is as much yours as it is mine.
I couldn't do any of this without you
and look forward to seeing what we conjure up next.

Witches of Dubious Origin

1

"Package for you, Zoe." Bill Reed, my coworker at the Wessex Public Library, dropped a thick padded envelope, clearly holding a book, onto my desk. I glanced up at him. I was the reference librarian. He was acquisitions. Generally, book purchases went right to him.

Bill shrugged at the confusion on my face. "I know, but it's addressed to you and stamped *Personal*."

I glanced at the brown envelope. Sure enough, there was the stamp in an imperative shade of red right above the handwritten name *Zoanne Ziakas*—my name—and the library's address. Weirdly, there was no postmark or stamps or anything to indicate it had been delivered the usual way through the post office.

"Be careful opening it." Bill's eyes narrowed behind his wire-framed glasses. "It could be—"

He paused. Clearly his imagination had run out or he was hesitant to say *bomb* or *poison* or whatever nefarious thing could possibly be stuffed into a nine-by-twelve-inch padded envelope. Bill had the pasty complexion of a man who'd spent his adult life under fluorescent lighting. He was in his fifties, happily married to his wife, Meredith, of thirty years. They had two kids in college and spent most of their time dreaming about retirement. There wasn't much that disturbed Bill, so I was surprised by his unusual caution.

"Could be what?" I prodded.

"I don't know." He ran a hand over his thinning hair in a self-soothing gesture. "I just have a bad feeling about it."

"It's probably a catalog from a publisher or a library supply company that got misdirected to me," I said. Although, when I studied the loopy script of my name written in felt-tip pen, I felt the hair on the back of my neck prickle, and a flutter of alarm tickled my insides. I knew this handwriting. It was my mother's.

No, it couldn't be. My mother had passed away a month ago. There was no way she could have addressed this envelope from beyond the grave. It was just an unfortunate coincidence. Shaking off the unsettling feeling, I grabbed my scissors and sliced the envelope open. It didn't explode. No plume of poisonous smoke was emitted. Instead, out fell a thick black book encircled with a half-inch metal band that was engraved with a series of interlocking lines similar to a Celtic knot. The band latched into a decorative hexagon on the front cover. Fancy.

"Well, that underwhelms," Bill said. He appeared visibly relieved. "Looks like a journal of some sort. You were right. It's probably a promo item from a publisher."

I set the book down and glanced into the envelope. There was no note explaining what the book was, no flyer, nothing. I put the envelope aside and picked up the book. I pressed on the hexagon, thinking that might open the band. It didn't work. I tried turning the hexagon. It didn't budge.

"It's a pretty pricey item for a promo," I said. "Especially since I can't open it."

"Do you want me to try?" he offered.

"Go for it." I handed him the book.

Bill did the same pressing and twisting that I had. He tried to tug on the band but it was secured too tightly to give him any leverage. He handed it back and I returned it to its envelope for safekeeping.

"What we have here is a very decorative paperweight," he concluded.

I laughed. I opened my desk's bottom drawer and dropped the book inside. "I'll look at it later."

Bill headed back to his office, and I returned to my weekly report, forgetting all about the strange black book.

October was my favorite month, when the sticky humidity of summer departed and jeans-and-sweater weather returned. As I walked the half mile from the library to my cottage, I reveled in the chilly temperatures, the scent of wood fires on the air, and the satisfying crunch of leaves under my feet.

The village of Wessex, where I lived and worked, was nestled between the Appalachian Trail and the Housatonic River, in the northwestern corner of Connecticut. It was a small community known for the private boarding school that resided on the west side of the river. I had attended that school before leaving to go to university in New Haven and then doubling back here to the only place that had ever felt like home.

As soon as I stepped inside my cottage, I slipped into my pajamas while I microwaved a big bowl of mac and cheese. I flicked on the television and scrolled through the streaming channels until I found a mystery series I had yet to watch. I preferred the British ones because I loved that the actors and actresses in them looked like real people, as opposed to American television shows, where everyone looks like a supermodel pretending to be a real person.

I was halfway through my bowl of cheesy goodness and a third of the way through the first episode when I heard a thump on my front porch. I paused the show and stopped chewing, listening intently. Living in Wessex, where everyone knew everyone, I wasn't as worried about crime as I was about a neighbor dropping by to chat. It wasn't that bad things didn't happen here—of course they did—it was just that it was very rare, and usually the person who did the crime was known for having a dented moral compass, so it wasn't a big surprise.

Thump!

The noise sounded again, only more forcefully. Putting my bowl down on the coffee table, I shoved my chenille throw aside and crossed the room to the front door, switching on the outside light. I peered out the side window that looked onto the porch before opening the door. If it was a rabid raccoon looking for food, I didn't want to get into it with him. The porch was empty.

Just to be certain everything was all right, I opened the door and poked my head out. I glanced from side to side, seeing only my large potted geranium on one side and my small wicker table and two chairs on the other. Satisfied, I went to close the door and glanced down at the doormat. I gasped. Placed on the center of the mat was the same envelope that Bill had delivered to me at work. But I knew I had left it in my desk drawer. What the hell was it doing here?

I glanced around the porch to see if someone was lurking in the shadows, playing a prank on me. It wasn't really Bill's style—he was more of a dad-joke type of guy—but he was the only person who knew about the book, so logic dictated it had to be him.

"Not funny, Bill!" I called into the darkening evening. There was no answer. No one was there.

I picked up the envelope and pulled the book out, experiencing the same twinge of unease I'd felt before. A flash of green lit the porch as the envelope was immediately engulfed in emerald flames. I yelped and dropped it. In seconds the envelope was gone, leaving no ash or smoke behind. I examined my hand and noted that the weird neon fire hadn't even felt hot.

I glanced out at the street, making certain no one had seen what had just happened. Ever since my childhood, unexpected magic had always made me anxious.

I took another look around the porch and yard before I went back inside, then locked the dead bolt. I studied the aged volume more closely. It was a shade of black so matte it seemed to soak up light. The edges of the pages were jagged and uneven. And the book's hexagonal metal latch was rusted from humidity or lack of use, I couldn't tell which. I brought it to the kitchen, thinking I could open it with a knife.

Not wanting to lose a finger, I chose a butter knife. I slid it under the decorative metal band and tried to pry it loose. The metal didn't budge. I tried to pop the hexagon with the blade as well, but it held fast. I set down the utensil and glanced at the door. If it wasn't Bill who had dropped the book off and made the envelope go *poof* . . . nope. I refused to go there.

The pin pricked my finger and blood beaded up out of the wound. I yelped and dropped the pin. Drops of blood dripped from my middle finger and I pressed my thumb to the tip to stop the flow. Had I just stabbed myself with a pin . . . *on purpose*? I blinked. I glanced down, noting that I was wearing my pajamas.

Relief whooshed inside me. It was okay. It was just a dream. An awful, stupid, painful dream. I shook my head, trying to wake myself up. It didn't work. It couldn't . . . because I was already awake.

I glanced down at my kitchen counter, where small splats of blood marred the smooth surface. The battered old book that I had tucked into my shoulder bag earlier sat on the granite beneath my pricked finger.

Shit! I had almost bled on the book. I spun away from the counter and rinsed my finger in the sink. What the hell had just happened? Sleepwalking? Night terrors? Had I actually pricked myself with a pin? *Why?*

Grabbing a paper towel, I wiped the blood off the granite. I rinsed off the pin and returned it to the container I kept in the utility drawer at the end of the counter. I threw the towel in the trash and stood, staring at the book in confusion. What was the book doing on the counter when I was certain I had put it in my bag?

Insistent whispers sounded at the edge of my mind. Like shadows that faded as the sun rose, the words weren't quite loud enough for me to make out, but I knew. I knew without a doubt that those whispers had been in my dreams and that they had instructed me to stab myself with the straight pin. I glanced down. Goose bumps raised on my forearms as I gazed at the black book. I ran an uninjured finger over the cover, half expecting it to be absorbed into the black leather, as if it could pull me in just as it seemed to soak in the light. It didn't and I lifted my hand and noted my fingers were trembling.

I'd had a strange feeling about this mysterious volume from the moment I'd first touched it, and I knew of only one person who might be able to help me.

2

"You think grief is making me lose it," I said.

During the month since my mother had passed away, Agatha Lively—my friend, mentor, and auntie all rolled into one loving yet bossy package—had repeatedly encouraged me to go to grief counseling, even though my mother and I had been estranged for years. I'd refused, feeling that I couldn't grieve a woman I didn't know. In my heart I understood that the only thing I mourned was that any chance at a relationship with my mother was now gone forever. Okay, so maybe some counseling wouldn't have been completely out of order.

"I didn't say that, Zoe." Agatha lifted the crocheted cozy that resembled a fat white goose off the delicate Haviland teapot and poured me a cup of rose hip tea. She was a big believer in its antioxidant properties. "I merely pointed out that you haven't slept properly since your mother's funeral, and this might be because you're sleep-deprived." She gestured at my finger with the Mickey Mouse bandage on it with a pointed look.

"No judgment, please. I am a meagerly paid public servant and these were on sale."

"I don't remember you being a sleepwalker. Is this a new development?" She ignored the explanation of my choice of bandage, which I wouldn't have needed except that the pinprick had been pretty deep. I was relieved to be up on my tetanus vaccination.

"No, as far as I know I've never done anything like this before." I took the teacup she offered. We were seated in the cluttered front parlor of Agatha's house. It was an old Victorian that sat prominently on the Wessex town green and had been in the Lively family for generations. Agatha was the last surviving Lively, and the house was packed to the rafters with her family's odd heirlooms, treasures, and tchotchkes. None of which she would consider parting with despite the collective mess. Having lived with her during my school vacations, I had tried to declutter it to no avail.

Sometimes I worried that Agatha would be done in by a falling stack of books or she'd trip on the variety of small cauldrons that lined the outer edge of the steps on the central staircase or, even more horrifically, she'd be eaten by one of the many sundew plants in the greenhouse. Yes, they were carnivorous and they gave me the heebie-jeebies. Although, to give credit where credit was due, she never seemed to have a problem with insects of any kind.

Agatha was short and curvy, with a deep brown complexion, white hair that fell in orderly ringlets to her shoulders, and professorial dark-rimmed glasses, which she lowered so she could peer at me with her direct deep brown eyes when she asked, "Have you tried taking valerian root?"

"Is it candy?" I met her gaze and she sighed.

"Of course you haven't. How you have survived to almost forty years of age from the nutrition found in a vending machine is beyond me."

I smiled, mostly because it was true. Not only had Agatha been my legal guardian since I was fourteen, she had also been my first boss. Like her, I was a librarian and Agatha had hired me fresh out of library school fifteen years ago when she was the director of the Wessex Public Library.

She had witnessed firsthand how I'd cobbled together my meals of Rice Krispies Treats (breakfast), Cheez-Its (lunch), and Snickers (dinner), preferably with a cola, not diet, on the side. Of course, I ate other stuff, but those were my mainstays.

"Ignoring my poor nutrition for the moment, what do you think of the book?" I asked.

Agatha sipped from her cup as if bracing herself. She set it down on its saucer atop an impressive stack of magazines. I'd sat in this room thousands of times over the years and I still had no idea what the coffee table beneath all the magazines and books looked like.

"You absolutely can't open it?" she asked.

"No. Whatever sort of lock is on it, it's impossible to crack. Believe me, I tried everything." I took the book out of the canvas bag at my feet and handed it to her.

Agatha accepted the book and a delicate shiver rippled through her body. She glanced up at me and said, "October's first chill has arrived."

I glanced through the large picture window at the town square. The leaves were displaying their final burst of color.

My favorites were the vibrant red of the sugar maples before they all fluttered to the ground. The nightly temperature had dropped and the days were crisp like the apples for sale at the local farmers market. Personally, I couldn't wait to spend the next month consuming copious amounts of Halloween candy while working my way through my to-be-read pile.

Agatha turned the book over in her hands. She studied the hexagonal medallion on the cover, tapping it with a pointy purple fingernail. She held it up with both hands as if offering it to the heavens. With a fierce expression of concentration, she stared at the book, and in a low tone, she whispered the words, "Exsolvo liber."

Unsurprisingly—at least to me—nothing happened.

"Your waves of resistance are impeding my powers," Agatha said.

"Sorry." I shrugged. She had been saying this to me since I had arrived on her doorstep at the snarky age of fourteen with a deep-seated fear of magic because of all it had taken from me.

"I have no idea how to open it." Agatha shook her head. "There's no indication from the cover or the engravings about what it is. Do you suppose it's a personal journal that someone wants added to the library collection?"

"Darned if I know." I sipped my tea. It could use some sugar. "No note came with it."

"No key? Nothing?" Agatha asked.

"Not a thing," I confirmed. "There's no place to put a key. The circular center of the medallion is smooth, like a tiny little bowl, not something a key would fit into."

"Strange." Agatha shivered again and quickly put the

book back in the canvas bag. Her mouth turned down at the corners and a frown line appeared between her brows. I knew that look. Something was bothering her.

"What is it?" I glanced at the bag and then back at her face.

She lifted her head and met my gaze. "There is tremendous power in that book."

I put my teacup down and crossed my arms over my chest. Agatha was a self-proclaimed kitchen witch and used cooking as a way to practice her craft, while I refused to practice magic. It was one of the only differences of opinion we had. "How can you tell when you can't open it?"

"Don't take that tone with me." Agatha wagged a finger at me while retrieving her tea with her other hand.

"I didn't have a tone," I protested. I didn't like that I sounded exactly as I had when I was sixteen and she'd busted me for breaking curfew.

"Oh yes you did," Agatha said. "You sounded exactly like your mother when we were teenagers and she was feeling peevish. And then she would deny it, as if I didn't know exactly how my lifelong best friend was feeling. I don't know who she thought she was fooling."

She stared at me until I cracked. "All right, maybe there was a hint of a tone, but you know how I feel about all things woo-woo."

"And now you're going to double down and be disrespectful?" She leaned back and looked me over as if to say, *the audacity*.

"I'm sorry," I said, and I meant it. I knew being a witch was part of her identity, but I saw nothing useful in practicing spells or magic. In my experience, witchcraft left only death and destruction in its wake.

"Zoe, you know your mother was a witch—" Agatha began, but I interrupted.

"I know." I held up my hand. "And you know the promise she asked me to make when she dropped me off at school."

"What she asked of you . . ." Agatha's voice trailed off and she shook her head. "It's not my business."

"It is," I said. "You stepped in and raised me. I think that makes it your business."

"For her to ask you to swear that you would never use your magic, to deny your abilities—it's just not right," Agatha said. "And I believe your mother would have seen that if she'd—"

"Been around for more than an afternoon here and there? Maybe." I shrugged. "But the truth is, I came to the same decision on my own. I'm not interested in magic or in being a witch. I just want to be normal and oblivious to the craft like regular people."

It was my turn to stare at her. Agatha knew I didn't like talking about my mother or my grandmother and their witchcraft. Despite being well into my thirties, I found the entire notion of casting spells and whatnot deeply uncomfortable. I was a librarian and operated in facts. Period. Full stop.

"Thank you for looking at it." I changed the subject. "I suppose I could just toss it out like those moldy books people insist on donating to the library because they're certain they're worth something even though they're water stained or reek of cigarette smoke or mold."

"No!" Agatha cried. "You can't do that. It might be valuable."

I glanced around her house, noting the piles and piles of belongings left behind by her family.

"Don't say it." She shook her head. "Just because I have a problem sorting my family's possessions doesn't mean I'm wrong about this. That book isn't visibly damaged, and it might be an important historical artifact."

"Fine. If I can't throw it away, what do you suggest I do with it?" I asked. "I can't open it without tearing it apart, so what purpose does it serve?"

"We won't know until we can read it." She took a bracing sip of tea.

Obviously, she was much more interested than I was. This wasn't surprising, as I was unsentimental by nature. Compared to her house, the aesthetic of my cottage on the other side of town could best be described as *no one lives here*. I didn't have any pictures on the walls, there were no collections of any kind except for my books—it's not hoarding if it's books—and I firmly believed in a place for everything and everything in its place. I think that was one of the traits that made me such a good librarian.

"If you say so," I said.

"I do." Agatha refilled my teacup and then her own. "Listen, if you really want to know more about the book, you need a professional appraisal. There's only one place that can help you—the Museum of Literature in New York City."

I blanched. This was problematic. I rarely left Wessex and never by choice. I simply did not enjoy leaving my zip code. "I can't go to the city."

"Zoanne Ziakas." Agatha's voice was sharp. "I have never known you to be a coward."

"I'm not," I protested. "It's just that my comfort margin is very narrow and happens to fall inside the border of Wessex."

Agatha tsked and picked up her teacup. "Do you really want to keep having dreams where you prick yourself with a pin?"

"What makes you think it will happen again?" I asked.

"What makes you think it won't?" she countered.

Damn. She made a good point.

"What if next time you wake up to find you've removed your eyeball with a spoon?" she asked.

"*Ergh.*" I blanched. "Way to go to the dark side."

"Clearly something in that book disturbs your unconscious. Who knows what you'll do next?" Agatha shrugged. "My friends at the museum can help you."

"Is this the place where you're on the board of directors?" I asked.

"Yes." She nodded. "It's the only place I've allowed some of the Lively family heirlooms to be on loan. I trust them implicitly."

I knew Agatha was right that the book needed a professional's assessment. Of that there was no question. But the thought of driving to the nearest station and taking the train into New York City was daunting, to put it mildly.

"You can do this, Zoe," she said.

I glanced at the book in the tote bag and then at the bandage on my finger. I hadn't told Agatha about the murmurs I'd heard in my dream before I'd come to my senses. The voice had whispered to me in a language I'd never heard before, and yet, in my dream, I'd understood it perfectly. Had it come from the book? Or was it just my overactive imagination? It had to be me. I refused to believe otherwise. Still, the unsettled feeling persisted.

"I know I *can* do it." I glanced back at Agatha. "It's more a matter of do I want to?"

"Do you have a choice?" she asked.

I glanced at my finger and then at the book. No, I didn't.

3

Manhattan. I stepped out of the Harlem–125th Street train station and was immediately hit by a thousand volts of frenetic human energy. After scoring a seat in the quiet car on the ride into the city, the high frequency of humanity was a jolt to my system. I immediately missed my serene little village.

I opened a directional app on my phone. I knew it would take forty minutes to walk to Museum Mile, where the Museum of Literature was located across the street from the Jacqueline Kennedy Onassis Reservoir in Central Park, but my appointment was in fifteen minutes. I hailed a cab and was fortunate enough to get the third one that cruised by.

Upon hearing the address, my driver took it as a personal challenge to deliver me to my destination as swiftly as possible. As he whipped down Park Avenue, jockeying for position and navigating through the glut of other vehicles, I lowered the window beside me, hoping a blast of cool air in my face would keep the queasiness that was starting to churn in my gut at bay. It helped just enough to keep down my breakfast of a Twix bar and a cup of salted caramel coffee.

With a sharp right, the driver zipped down the one-way street, stopping in the middle of the narrow road with a piercing squeal of his brakes, giving me the opportunity to test the restraining power of the seat belt. When I fell back against my seat, he pointed at a large stone building set back from the street and surrounded by an intimidating iron fence and said, "There."

This was the most conversation we'd had during the entire trip, which was fine with me. I paid him and added a healthy tip for dropping me off in one piece. When the driver behind us lay on his horn, I hurriedly grabbed my leather shoulder bag and stepped onto the curb. I studied the imposing building in front of me and glanced at the time. Five minutes until my meeting.

I waited for a break in the traffic and dashed across the street. My high heels protested at the uneven pavers that made up the herringbone pattern in front of the building, but I soldiered on. A security guard in a tailored black wool coat over a white shirt and black pants stood to the left of two ornate bronze doors. As I approached, she gave me a quick once-over.

"I have an appointment," I said. "With Director Carpenter."

"That's fine. The museum is open to the public. I'm just here to tase anyone who misbehaves." She smiled, showing a lot of teeth. I did not find this terribly reassuring, but I smiled back anyway, not wanting to be rude and risk a possible tasing. I glanced at her name tag. It read *Tina*.

A brisk breeze from the reservoir tugged the loose end of my dark red cashmere scarf and the hem of my long black wool coat. Agatha had advised me to wear my job-interview best, as the museum was run by a socialite from the Upper East Side. Naturally, I had done a quick background check on her.

Claire Carpenter was her name, and she'd been in charge of the museum for years. Under her leadership, they'd expanded their education program, acquired numerous invaluable additions to the collection, and won the coveted Museum and Heritage Permanent Exhibition of the Year award among many other accolades and achievements. To say I was in awe of her was an understatement.

Tina pulled open one of the massive doors and I stepped inside. I walked up a short flight of stone steps and found myself in a vast entryway. In front of me was an impressively large wooden staircase and on my left was a library, my happy place. Naturally, I chose to go to the library.

It was not the industrial-carpet-and-steel-shelves library of my daily existence in Wessex. This room boasted a teak parquet floor and freestanding oak bookcases that ran the length of the enormous space. If that weren't breathtaking enough, on a pedestal in the center of the room perched a larger-than-life bronze statue of Athena, Greek goddess of knowledge. Wow, just wow.

The smell of the place, paper and leather and cloth bindings, was the same as any other library and one that comforted. I studied the shelf nearest me and noted that most of the volumes appeared to be very old but in excellent condition, which made sense given that I was technically in a museum. I glanced around the space and noted that several of the study tables beyond the statue were occupied—by scholars, I assumed—and there was an information desk. It was as ornately carved as the rest of the interior but tucked unobtrusively into an alcove to the left of the entrance.

A twentysomething woman with purple hair and a septum piercing slipped out from behind the desk. She wore stylish black low-heeled ankle boots, black tights, a black-and-red-plaid miniskirt, and a red turtleneck sweater that clashed spectacularly with her hair. She held a slip of paper in her hand and was walking toward the stacks. She smiled at me in a friendly way and said, "Hi. I have to grab a book for one of the researchers. I'll be right back."

"Of course," I said.

I glanced around the area, looking for another staff person who could direct me. I didn't see anyone and considered, just for a moment, abandoning my mission and hurrying back to my safe little village.

A tall man wearing jeans and a white dress shirt appeared from behind a nearby bookcase and paused at the sight of me. One of his eyebrows ticked up ever so slightly and his gaze dropped to my shoulder bag. Instinctively, I clutched the straps more tightly.

He walked toward me, his stride long and cautious, as if I were a wild animal and he didn't want to startle me. I wasn't sure how I felt about that. He carried an old leather-bound book in one large hand and moved with the careless self-assurance of someone who was at home in this space. I assumed he must work here.

As he drew closer, I noted his startlingly handsome face—

square jaw, long nose, arching black brows, and full lips. His chin-length wavy black hair swung forward as he moved, and I noted the unusual shade of his pale blue eyes as he watched me intently with his head tipped slightly to the side.

"May I help you find something?" His voice was deep, as if it came from the bottom of a well, and his accent was very, very British. Because his exterior packaging wasn't perfect enough?

Still, he'd offered assistance, which I appreciated, and I nodded. When I didn't speak, he leaned forward a bit and lifted both eyebrows in unspoken encouragement.

"Oh, right, sorry." I glanced away, trying to pull it together. "I have an appointment with Claire Carpenter, but I'm not sure where to find her."

"The director's office is on the third floor. I'm happy to show you the way." He gestured to the doorway.

"I don't want to trouble you." I shook my head. "You can just point me in the right direction."

"It's no bother," he said. "I'm headed that way myself."

"Oh, all right." I wondered if I sounded as reluctant as I felt. It wasn't personal. I just wasn't very good at small talk and now I was going to have to engage in it, which I was certain was going to be extremely painful for both of us. I held back a sigh.

I glanced around the room, taking in the tall arched windows, the paneled wainscoting, and the elaborately stenciled frieze that decorated the walls at ceiling height.

"This is quite the place you have here." See? I was a queen of inanity if ever there was one. But honestly, my librarian heart did feel a pang of jealousy at the sheer beauty of this place.

"It is something, isn't it? A Gilded Age mansion built by the steel industrialist Thomas Stewart for his wife, Mabel. Upon her passing, she donated the building specifically for the preservation of books and literature, consequently creating the Museum of Literature. That was back when being a power couple actually meant something." He grinned at me—a slash of white teeth bracketed by two deep dimples, loaded with charm. It was the most natural thing in the world to smile back.

"I'm Zoe Ziakas." I held out my hand, feeling quite bold.

"Jasper Griffin." I tried not to notice how warm his palm was around my cold fingers, but it was impossible when he gently squeezed my hand before releasing it.

"This way, Zoe." Jasper led the way out of the library and I followed.

We strode across the massive entry hall. It was a dark space and I glanced up to admire the coffered oak ceiling and paneled oak woodwork along the walls. The carved pieces, stunning in their detail, were stained a deep mahogany brown.

"What do you think of it?" Jasper gestured to the woodwork.

"It feels like I'm in a very decorative coffin."

Jasper let out a surprised laugh.

"Sorry, that came out a bit harsh."

"But not inaccurate." He started up the steps.

The grand staircase was more of the same carved dark wood and I was relieved when I could see a glimpse of the upper hallway, which was just as overdone as the floor below but with coved plasterwork on the ceiling featuring grapes and vines and musical instruments that ran the length of the passageway above cheery pale yellow walls.

"If you don't mind my asking, what brings you to the Museum of Literature, Zoe?" Jasper paused one step below the top.

"I don't mind." I glanced over my shoulder at him as I stepped onto the landing, noting we were now the same height.

"But you're not going to enlighten me?" He cradled his book to his chest with one hand while he ran his other hand through his unruly hair. It fell back into place as if it knew exactly how to frame his sharp cheekbones to their best advantage.

"How do I know I can trust you with such top secret information?" I asked. Honestly, I wasn't trying to flirt. I was trying to divert his attention with nonsense because I had no idea how to explain the mysterious book in my bag.

"A secret? Are you on a mission?" He cupped his chin with his hand and narrowed his eyes. "Now I'm intrigued."

His deep voice and direct stare were too much to handle and I felt myself get flustered, which, for the record, never happened to me. I turned away from him to study my surroundings and get my bearings.

Across the landing was an enormous portrait of a man and a woman sitting on a settee with a cocker spaniel at their feet. Judging by their Gilded Age clothing—an off-the-shoulder gown trimmed with lace for her and a black jacket and white shirt, collar points up, held securely by a white bow tie for him—I assumed they must be Thomas and Mabel Stewart. They gazed at each other with such devotion. I found myself wondering if it was true love or if the artist had manufactured their look of affection.

"Mabel was the love of Thomas's life and she was his," Jasper said as he moved to stand beside me.

"I was just wondering if the artist had purposefully enhanced that look between them," I said.

"He had no need to. By all accounts, theirs was a genuine love story." I turned to find a very tall, very curvy, blond woman approaching us. I knew from the pictures I'd seen online with her bio that this was the museum director. She held out her hand. "Hi, I'm Claire Carpenter."

"Zoe Ziakas." I clasped her hand briefly and let go. Claire's hair was up in a neat French twist, accentuating her cheekbones and long neck. She wore a dark gray pencil skirt, spiky black heels, and a flattering silk blouse in a shade of blue that perfectly matched her eyes. If I lived a thousand lifetimes, I would never possess her effortless style.

"Welcome to the museum," she said. "I see you've met Jasper."

"He was kind enough to escort me here." I turned to him. "Thank you."

"It was a . . . pleasure." Jasper looked me up and down as if trying to figure me out. Then he smiled. "I'll look forward to hearing more about your secret mission, Zoe."

Claire glanced between us and I felt my face grow warm. Why was this awkward? There was no reason to feel weird just because this incredibly hot guy was a little flirty with me. He was probably like that with everyone, which made the heat in my face even more mortifying.

"See you at this afternoon's meeting, Claire." He nodded at her and then turned and strode down the hallway.

"Nice to meet you, Zoe." Claire smiled and it lit her

eyes, making it feel genuine. "Agatha has told me so much about you."

Quite intentionally, after an exhausting and overly dramatic childhood, I'd chosen to live a very quiet life, preferring the company of books to people and my home to social events. Given that, I couldn't imagine what Agatha would have told Claire about me that could be longer than a sentence or two, and even that could only be managed if Agatha was embellishing. I assumed Claire was being polite, so I returned her smile.

"Agatha is all the family I have, so she might be a tad biased."

"That doesn't make her wrong." Claire gestured toward the end of the hallway. "Shall we talk in my office? You can show me the book there."

"Thank you," I said. "That's perfect."

I walked beside her. She was several inches taller than me and she glided down the hallway with a confident stride. Since I only wore my spiky heels for annual library board meetings, my gait was not nearly so smooth. More like the galumphing of a seal on land, to be honest, but I did try to step lightly with marginal success.

The double doors we approached were antique paneled glass. One stood open and we entered an anteroom with more decorative plaster and a chandelier overhead. Judging by the second set of fancy doors on the far side of the room, we were in an assistant's office. The desk was vacant, but the space was extremely tidy.

"My assistant, Sebastian, went to fetch us some refreshments," Claire said. She led me through the second set of doors into the coolest office I'd ever seen. It was massive, with arched windows that overlooked the lawn and gardens below, the reservoir and park to the west, and all of Midtown to the south.

Built-in bookshelves lined the other windowless walls, and they were packed. An immense mahogany desk was on the far side of the room while a seating area with a couch and two armchairs was in front of a cold fireplace.

There were two people already there and they stood when we entered. They were both tall like Claire, but where she was robust, they were on the lithe side. The man had untamed pure-white hair, which seemed even more so against his tanned complexion and gave him a mad-scientist vibe. He completed the look with wire-framed glasses, a brown cardigan over a blue-plaid shirt, and khaki pants.

The woman was strikingly pale and dressed all in black, from her turtleneck sweater to her wool pants and pointy suede shoes, which didn't help her unnatural pallor at all. She had a thick mass of dark hair held in a clip at the nape of her neck, and her features were handsome rather than pretty, with a square jaw, high cheekbones, and dark eyes framed by arching eyebrows, one of which had a small scar severing it in two.

"I hope you don't mind," Claire said to me. "I invited our head of Special Collections and one of his staff to join us."

"Not at all," I said. This wasn't entirely accurate, as I found the intense gaze of the woman in black to be unsettling.

"Zoe Ziakas, this is Miles Lowenstein and Olive Prendergast," Claire introduced me.

"Nice to meet you." I shook each of their hands. Miles's long fingers were gentle and Olive's grip was surprisingly warm.

Miles returned my smile with a small one of his own, but Olive's face remained impassive. Okay, then.

"Beverages and snacks have arrived." A man entered the room, pushing a cart with an assortment of food and drink on it. Shorter than everyone else in the room, including me, he had a deep brown complexion and close-cropped black hair and was dressed in a vibrantly purple-and-aqua-patterned shirt, navy pants, and pointy-toed brown loafers.

He parked the cart and Claire introduced us. His full name was Sebastian Hanover, and according to Claire, she couldn't function without him. He smiled, displaying a slash of white teeth, and left us to our meeting, closing the door behind himself.

"All right, let's see the book," Olive said. She glanced at her wristwatch as if she was running late for another meeting.

"Or we could offer our guest a refreshment first," Claire suggested.

"If we must." Olive sank back against the couch.

"We must." Claire turned to me. "Zoe, would you like coffee, tea, or water? We have sparkling and plain."

"Coffee, please." I wasn't thirsty and didn't need more caffeine, but it would give me something to do.

Claire lifted a silver carafe and poured me a cup. She handed it to me, indicating that I should help myself to cream and sugar. She then poured tea for Miles and coffee for Olive, which I noted Olive took black. Of course she did.

Claire poured herself a tall glass of water and leaned back

in her chair. "Agatha told me the book was sent to you at your place of work and then appeared at your house?"

"Yes, it arrived in a padded envelope stamped *Personal* and had my name and the library's address handwritten on it, but there were no stamps or anything that indicated it came through the post office." I picked up the tiny pitcher of milk and added some to my coffee. "My colleague Bill said it was discovered on the circulation desk, but no one saw who dropped it off."

"And then?" Olive gestured with an elegant hand for me to continue.

"It arrived on my doorstep later that day. I heard a noise and went outside to check, and there it was. I didn't see anyone out there, just the book in the envelope it had been delivered in."

"Do you still have the envelope?" Miles asked.

"No," I said. I thought about the green fire that had engulfed it in seconds. How crazy would I sound to these people if I told them about that? I swiftly glanced at their faces, pausing on Olive's. Her barely concealed contempt convinced me to keep that little tidbit to myself for now.

"I asked my colleague about it the next day, but he swore that he didn't drop it off at my house," I said. "I thought he might be pranking me, but that really isn't his style." I set my coffee on a coaster on the low glass table in front of me and opened my shoulder bag. I took the mysterious book out and set it on the center of the table.

As one, they leaned forward to study the book, but no one touched it, which I found odd. How could they inspect it if they didn't pick it up and examine it?

"How did you hurt yourself?" Olive asked.

I didn't want to admit that I'd woken up in my kitchen again last night. This time, I'd nicked my finger with a kitchen knife. Just like the first time, I'd found the book on the counter beneath my hand even though I knew I hadn't left it there. My fresh Mickey Mouse Band-Aid made it impossible to hide the injury.

Olive's dark gaze held mine. The eyebrow with the slice through it arched ever so slightly and I knew there was no way I could prevaricate. She'd read the truth on my face as easily as the time on a clock.

"I nicked my finger with a knife." I cleared my throat. "More accurately, while I was asleep, I heard strange whispers in my dreams. Whispers that I believe came from the book, instructing me to do it."

4

There. I'd said it, admitting the one thing that made me feel vulnerable. But if I wanted their help, I had to tell them everything. After I'd cut myself last night, I'd remembered the voices I'd heard in my dreams . . . again.

The whispers had been clear: I needed to retrieve the book and then make myself bleed. I had no idea why, and in my sleepy state, I'd been unable to fight it until the pain of the cut had brought me back to myself. Needless to say, I was becoming wary of the book, which was also a huge understatement. I was legit scared of it.

I glanced at Claire, Miles, and Olive. No one moved. No one said a word. They simply studied the book. I held my breath. I expected Claire to call security and have my friend Tina with the Taser arrive to escort me out. But she didn't.

Olive and Miles exchanged a side-eye, and Miles nodded as if he'd come to a conclusion.

"That actually explains quite a lot." He glanced at me. "The book is clearly sealed by a blood oath."

I sighed. He sounded like Agatha. I hadn't been exaggerating when I'd told her I had no interest in being a witch. I didn't want anything to do with blood oaths. I was an information specialist who lived by the motto *knowledge is power* and operated on verifiable facts from citable sources. I leaned forward, preparing to leave. There was nothing for me here.

"You can't open the book, can you?" Olive challenged me.

I wanted to retort, *Would I be here if I could?* Instead, I said nothing, but I didn't get up and leave.

"This." Olive tapped the hexagonal medallion on the cover. "This dip is where your blood goes."

It was the tiny circular bowl shape in the center of the hexagon. The same one Agatha had thought a key might open. Now it made sense, I supposed, but blood? *My blood?* Oh hell no.

Suddenly, opening the book seemed like the worst idea ever. I wanted to go home.

"You didn't spill any blood on it, did you?" Olive continued to stare at me. I swear she never blinked.

"No." I shook my head.

"Pity," Olive replied, glancing down at the book.

I felt as if I'd disappointed her and I didn't enjoy the feeling. I was thirty-six years old, a fully realized adult who owned her own home and paid taxes. I did not need the approval of this Morticia Addams wannabe.

"If you're so interested in opening the book, why don't you use your own blood?" I asked.

Olive rolled her eyes as if I'd said the stupidest thing she'd ever heard. Still, she took a small dagger from her black suede shoe—what sort of librarian carried a dagger in their shoe?—and pricked the tip of one of her fingers with it. She held her hand over the hexagon, allowing a few drops to land in the center. We all stared at the book, but nothing happened.

"See? It's not that difficult." Olive turned to Claire, who squirted some antibacterial liquid onto a tissue and wiped Olive's blood off the metal lock. "I can put the book in the vault until another member of the family comes to claim it."

"*My* family? Good luck with that. I'm it. The end of the line on both sides." I picked up my coffee and took a sip. It was delicious, with subtle notes of chocolate and cinnamon. It calmed me.

"Are you quite certain?" Miles asked.

"Yes, my father passed when I was a child and my mother a month ago," I said. "I'm her sole heir. This book couldn't have come from her. I mean, if she'd left it to me, it should have been with her other belongings."

"You would think so, but it isn't a typical item to inherit, is it?" Miles asked. "There's no way of knowing how it found you. It's not exactly like the family china, is it?"

How it found me? I stared at the book. Had it belonged to my mother? The handwriting on the envelope had seemed familiar, but I couldn't know for certain. I'd only seen my mom a handful of times after she'd dropped me off at the boarding school in Wessex twenty-two years ago. At this point in my life, Agatha was more of a mother to me than Juliet Ziakas, which was why my grief was . . . complicated.

"If you're the only remaining member of your family and choose not to try, the book will remain forever closed," Miles said. His expression was aggrieved, as if the book's abandoned fate physically pained him.

"I don't understand," I said. "Why can't someone else bleed on the damn book?"

"Being sealed by a blood oath means only a person who is related by blood to the person who sealed the book can open it," Olive said. "That's assuming the book did come from your mother. It might have nothing to do with your family."

"Really?" I asked. Finally, some good news. "In that case, I feel no need to be the one to unlock the blood curse."

"Oath," Miles corrected me gently. "Blood oath. You did say that the book spoke to you in your dreams. I believe that indicates you are bound to the book."

"But we don't know that for certain," I countered. "I could have been having strawberry-Pop-Tart-midnight-snack nightmares because the book is so creepy. No, as far as I'm concerned, you're welcome to keep the book, the oath, all of it."

Claire was silent, occasionally sipping her water while watching the conversation between the rest of us. Her face was neutral and I couldn't tell what she was thinking, whether she thought I should try to open the book or not. Not that it mattered. I had no intention of doing so.

Olive took a pair of gloves out of her pocket. She slipped them on like she was a crime scene specialist. Miles picked up a box from beside him on the floor. It was an archival box and presumably where the mysterious little black book would live forever and ever, amen.

"All right, then. We'll add it to our inventory," Olive said. She picked up the volume and held it over the open box. "If you're sure."

"I'm positive." I rose to my feet and picked up my shoulder bag. "Absolutely positive."

Olive didn't say a word as she placed the book in the box, but the disapproval that poured off her was palpable—almost as strong as the sudden excruciating pain that split my skull. I staggered and doubled over. I dropped my bag and clapped my hands against my head, half expecting to find an axe lodged in my cranium.

"Zoe, what is it? Are you all right?" Claire set down her water and leapt to her feet. She caught me as I started to slide to the floor.

The pain was so intense I felt tears spring to my eyes. I couldn't catch my breath. I couldn't speak. I tried to point to the book, but before I could lift my hand, I blacked out.

I could hear people talking in hushed tones. As I listened, I gender-identified the voices as belonging to two women and two men. There was an agitated quality to their conversation, but I couldn't make out the words. I blinked and saw a fancy ceiling with swirling plasterwork overhead. That's right. I was in New York City in a meeting at the Museum of Literature.

I forced my eyes fully open and discovered I was lying on the couch, with a man seated in the chair beside me, wafting the fumes from a small handheld diffuser over me. The scents of lavender and vetiver were strong and I assumed he was using them to calm me. It must have worked because my headache was mostly gone.

"Welcome back," he said. He had a soothing Nigerian accent, if I was guessing correctly, and he was very handsome, with a deep brown complexion, warm brown eyes, and a wide smile. He was dressed professionally in a white dress shirt with a blue-striped tie and navy slacks. "My name is Tariq Silver. I work for Miles."

"Awkward to meet you, Tariq." I tried to make light of my embarrassment and his smile widened. "I'm Zoe Ziakas."

"I know." He glanced over his shoulder to where the others were standing at the far side of the room. He raised his voice and said, "She's awake."

Claire immediately started toward us while Tariq helped me to sit up. "Can I get you anything?"

"Not unless you have my dignity in your pocket," I said.

"Sorry, no," Tariq said with a soft laugh.

He switched off the diffuser and set it on the table. I noticed the book was there, out of the box. Olive and Miles followed Claire, who sat down on the couch beside me, leaving the chairs for Miles and Olive. Tariq crossed the room and carried a chair from in front of the windows back to our little circle.

"What happened?" I asked. Although I suspected I knew.

"You fainted," Olive said.

I wasn't sure if I was imagining the judgment in her voice or if she really did find me weak. I sat up straighter.

"I never faint. How could that happen?" I asked. The question was rhetorical, but the expressions on their faces were considering.

They were collectively silent. I suspected they were trying to decide what to tell me. Annoying. They all turned to Miles. He bobbed his head once in acknowledgment, a habit of his that I was beginning to recognize.

"I believe the book is a grimoire," he said. "Are you familiar with the term?"

"Of course, I read *Harry Potter*." Yes, I said it just to see Olive roll her eyes again, which she did. "But I'm also a librarian, so I know that *grimoire* is a word derived from the Old French *grammaire*, which originally referred to any book written in Latin. Grimoires of the Middle Ages favored ceremonial magic and were unsurprisingly written primarily by men who wanted to exact vengeance on their enemies, locate lost treasure, or have the woman they desired forcibly delivered. They also included spells and rituals that advocated animal cruelty, theft, magical rape, and even murder."

I saw Olive's eyebrows lift just the teeniest bit. Was she impressed? Hard to say. I doubled down.

"In later centuries, grimoires became known as handbooks for magic," I said. "And presently, the term is used by Wiccans to refer to their personal spell books, which are more remedy-based to serve their communities."

"You're very knowledgeable," Claire observed.

I shrugged. "I read a lot and I have a good memory for obscure facts and odd details."

"Good?" Claire shook her head. "Agatha said you have an extraordinary memory. She said she'd call it a photographic memory if such a thing existed."

"Which it doesn't," I said.

Miles leaned forward eagerly. "Still, having such a skill must be an invaluable tool in your work."

I shrugged. "It helps with law statutes and sports statistics."

"How do you recall things?" Tariq asked. "Do you see pictures in your head of pages you've read?"

"Not pictures," I said. "It's more like I have all of this information sorted in my brain and I just need to find the right section."

"Like a very large filing cabinet, then?" Claire asked.

I nodded. "That's as good a description as any other."

"What Major League Baseball player won two World Series, had an average of .312, and was only struck out 114 times?" Tariq asked. I stared at him for a beat and he shrugged. "Sorry. Huge baseball fan."

I nodded. I closed my eyes, concentrating on the statistics I had learned during my time as the librarian in charge of acquiring the sports books. The answer popped into my brain just like that. "Joe Sewell."

Tariq gasped.

"What are the only four words in the English language to end in *d-o-u-s*?" Miles asked.

"*Horrendous, stupendous, hazardous,* and . . ." I stared at his nose. "*Tremendous.*"

Miles slapped his knee. "Ask her more questions."

I glanced at Claire. I wasn't here for this. Before she could say anything, Tariq asked, "What is Fermat's Last Theorem?"

I hated math questions, but I couldn't refuse him. I was a librarian. I stared at the ceiling for a moment, trying to bring the formula forward in my brain. "The equation is $a^n = b^n + c^n$ which states there are no positive integers a, b, and c that can satisfy the equation for any integer value of n greater than 2."

Tariq glanced at his phone and his jaw dropped. "She got it."

He and Miles looked giddy.

Olive held up her hand and gave the others a quelling

glance. "Enough. We need to deal with the grimoire at hand before we get sidetracked."

"You're right," Claire said. She gestured for Olive to continue.

"What was your mother's maiden name?" Olive asked me.

"My mother was Juliet Donadieu Ziakas," I said. "She was the only child of Mamie, my grandmother Antoinette Donadieu, who never married and never told my mother who her father was."

"Donadieu?" Olive's eyebrows drew together in a frown. "That's French and is usually used as a surname for orphaned children."

That made sense. I knew Mamie had been raised in an orphanage in France before coming to the United States as a young woman. I didn't share this family factoid, as I was already feeling overexposed.

"It's also the family name of a French coven of witches known for their gift of necromancy," Miles said. It took a moment before his words sank in.

"Get the hell out of here." The words flew out of my mouth before I could stop them.

Olive turned to Miles with a questioning look and he said, "No, you may not."

"Fine." Olive sighed.

"Are you telling me that my grandmother could raise the dead?" I asked. "That's just . . . that's not . . . no, just no."

"Potentially, if this is your family grimoire." Miles gestured to the book. "Whether your grandmother or mother had the gift or knew how to use the book . . . who knows?

Arcane abilities are genetic, much like red hair or brown eyes. The gift skips around."

I had no idea what to make of this. Not to sound *woe is me* or overly dramatic, but my mother essentially abandoned me at the age of fourteen when she dropped me off at boarding school in Wessex and signed over guardianship to Agatha. Prior to that, my mom and I had spent five years constantly moving. If I hadn't known better, I'd have thought we were on the run from the law.

My mother's behavior had been erratic to say the least. All I knew for certain was that at age nine, when my father had been killed in a car crash, I'd lost my mother, who had previously been lovely and kind and full of light, to her guilt and grief, and I'd never gotten her back. Was this book my mother's? Would it explain why she left me? Did I really want to know? Yes, I did.

And yet it involved magic—something I had sworn to avoid, something I *wanted* to avoid.

"What should I do?" I asked.

No one answered me. I suspected they believed I had to decide for myself.

Olive broke the silence. "A grimoire usually begins with who wrote it and for what purpose. If you really want to know if this is your family's book, the answer is likely inside."

I met her dark stare across the table. I was surprised to find the tiniest flicker of compassion in her gaze. She knew this was a monumental decision for me. She glanced down at the book and back up at me. I knew she was right. There was only one choice. And, I rationalized, it wasn't as if I were performing magic and breaking the vow I'd made to my mom to never practice witchcraft. This was merely fulfilling a blood oath—potentially.

Newly resolved, I ripped the bandage off my finger. Last night's wound hadn't completely healed. I squeezed the tip of my finger until a droplet of blood beaded on the tip. I moved my hand toward the book and felt everyone lean in with me.

I hesitated. "Do I need to say an incantation or something?" If I had to say something, that would be crossing the line and breaking my promise.

"That's a Hollywood thing," Olive scoffed. She looked dismissive and I wondered if I'd imagined the sympathy I'd seen moments ago.

"If the grimoire belonged to your family, just your blood should do the trick," Miles said.

I noticed my hand was shaking as I moved it over the hexagonal medallion. I squeezed my finger again and watched as several drops landed right in the circle. It occurred to me then that what I had thought was rust or tarnish on the hexagon had actually been dried blood. *Ew.*

I stared at the hexagon. Was I supposed to twist it? Was there a button to press? Anything? Nothing happened. We all leaned back.

"I guess that's that." I refastened my bandage. "This grimoire clearly didn't belong to my family and whatever this book wants, it isn't from me."

Click. Screech.

I glanced down at the book. The hexagon was rotating all on its own. *Shit.*

5

"It's opening!" Tariq clenched his hands into fists of excitement. "This never gets old."

"Easy," Olive hissed.

Click. The hexagon stopped turning and the engraved metal band that encircled the book popped out of each side of the hexagon. The book appeared to heave a sigh of relief, which I was certain I imagined. Books did not sigh.

I glanced at the others, but they were all staring at the book as if expecting something. Olive glanced at me and gestured impatiently. "Well, open it."

I was half-afraid the book was going to sprout teeth and bite me, but I figured if it did, it was best to do it here, where there were witnesses who could call for medical help. I shook my head. My imagination was running wild.

The cover was thick, made of calf hide that was smooth to the touch. Swallowing past the anxiety that constricted my throat, I gently lifted the cover to reveal the endpapers. They were a weighty parchment in a rich shade of ecru without a mark upon them. I turned the first page and stared at the writing, clearly done by hand, in a deep brown shade of ink or—please, no—*blood*?

Collectively, we hovered over the book to get a closer look. I couldn't read the writing. I flipped through several more pages. The precisely written figures continued line after line, page after page. I mentally sifted through all the ancient languages I had studied over the years, trying to identify it. I couldn't.

Disappointment sucker punched me. This was a cipher I'd never seen. I glanced at the others. The frowns marring their faces indicated they had no idea what any of this meant either. Great, just great.

"It's similar to the *Book of Raziel*." Miles scratched his chin in thought.

"It seems more Code of Hammurabi to me," Olive countered.

"Cuneiform?" Miles considered the book. "No, it's not that linear. What do you think, Tariq?"

"The symbols resemble runes." Tariq drew one in the air with his finger. "Like the Istaby Runestone."

"Whoa, whoa, whoa." I held up my hands. "None of that makes any sense. The *Book of Raziel* is believed to be thirteenth century, and the Code of Hammurabi is seventeenth century BCE, and the Istaby Runestone is from . . . what . . . the year 800?"

"Somewhere between 550 and 790, actually," Tariq said.

"Whatever. This is clearly a bound book." I pointed to it. "Parchment pages, a metal latch, and some sort of cured calf hide for the cover. There is no way it's more than a few centuries old—at best. It's definitely not as old as the Voynich manuscript from the early fifteenth century, which is also indecipherable. In fact, if this is from my family, specifically my mother, it's most likely something she created for her own amusement. You have to understand, my mother had a lot of . . . issues."

I paused, not wanting to share the details of my dysfunctional childhood with a roomful of strangers, and found they were all staring at me. "What?"

"You're very knowledgeable about ancient texts and languages," Miles said.

"Librarian." I pointed to myself, relieved that he was focusing on my knowledge instead my family.

"You know a lot more than the average librarian," Claire said. She sounded impressed.

"The Museum of Literature is always interested in librarians and curators with exceptional abilities," Miles mused.

"That's not me. I took a class on the history of language and writing." I waved my hand dismissively. "It was fascinating, but it has nothing to do with this book, which is likely a . . . hoax."

"I'm sorry," Tariq said. "Did you miss the part where it unlocked when you dripped blood on it?"

I frowned at him. I was not in the mood to be confronted with facts. Agatha's homemade remedies aside, in my experience, magic brought nothing but misery and despair. I'd lost too much in the name of magic, and I was always going to resent what it had taken from me. Plus, I'd made a vow and had managed to keep it for twenty-two years.

"I think it's time for a tour of our department," Miles said. He rose from his seat, indicating that the tour would be now.

"I'm sorry, I can't," I refused. "I have to get back to Wessex."

Olive rose from her seat and stared down at me. I forced myself not to squirm. "Our special collection is called the Books of Dubious Origin, or the BODO for short. Don't you want to know why?"

I did. *Damn it.*

"Fine." I picked up the book, sliding the ends of the metal band back into the hexagon until they clicked, and placed it in my shoulder bag as I stood. "But just a quick tour."

Claire rose from her seat with a warm smile. "I'll leave you in my team's capable hands, then."

"You're not coming with us?" I asked.

"No, I haven't gotten the smell out of my favorite sweater from the last time I visited the BODO," she said. "I'll meet up with you at the end."

This would have sounded ominous, but there was a glint of humor in Claire's eyes that made me think she was teasing. I tried not to worry.

Olive swept out of the office, leaving the rest of us to follow. I found myself between Tariq and Miles, chasing her long-legged stride. They had no problem keeping up, but I had to shift into a higher gear to keep pace in those blasted heels, which had me winded by the time we reached the stairs.

It's not that I was excessively short or out of shape. I was just medium in height and weight and athletic ability. I even had medium-length brown hair. Everything about me, in fact, was a very forgettable medium. If generic was a brand of human, that was me.

"Are you all right?" Olive asked. The eyebrow with the scar arched up as she studied me.

"Just fine," I said. I hoped I didn't sound like a fish out of water, gasping for breath. She nodded once and strode down the staircase.

Back at the main entrance, Olive went in the opposite direction from the library. I glanced over my shoulder to see if Jasper was there. I wanted to see his reaction to my being in the company of the Special Collections staff. If he looked freaked-out, I would take it as a sign to run. Unfortunately, there was no sign of the handsome Brit.

We passed through the opposite side of the building. Ancient books and papyri were on display in thick glass cubes scattered across the enormous room, which I suspected had once been a ballroom. I saw one item out of the corner of my eye and stopped in my tracks. It couldn't be. I approached the glass in wonder. Sitting on a stand and lit from above was a clay disk with a variety of characters engraved on its surface.

"You have the Phaistos Disc?" I asked.

"It's on loan from the Heraklion Archaeological Museum," Miles said. "Our curator Sarah Novak specializes in ancient Greece and Rome. We should introduce you. You'd like her. She had quite the adventure recently."

I wondered what *adventure* was a euphemism for, but I didn't ask. Olive was standing beside an open door at the end of the room. She very pointedly checked the time on her wristwatch again. We hurried to catch up. Well, Tariq and I did. Miles did not seem to feel the same sense of urgency.

The door was made of a heavy metal material. Unlike the ornamental brass doors out front, this one was solid and plain.

Iron, if I was to guess. A cold draft poured out of the opening and I was glad I'd worn my wool coat and scarf.

Olive slipped inside and then Tariq. I followed, leaving Miles to bring up the rear. The lighting was dim, the area illuminated only by softly glowing wall sconces. I registered that I was on a metal landing that led to a spiral staircase that twisted down, down, down. It reminded me of being in a lighthouse. Our footsteps clanged as we wound our way to the landing at the bottom. It was a small space enclosed by three concrete walls and another metal door, but this one had an intricate web of blue lasers shooting across it. Not gonna lie, it was impressive.

Olive stepped up to the lasers and paused. I expected her to shut them off, but she didn't. Instead, she walked into them.

"Ah!" I cried. I fully expected her to be torched like a very large fly in a bug zapper. Instead, she simply disappeared. "What the hell?"

Tariq went next and then Miles crooked his elbow at me. "Take my arm and you'll be all right."

I gave him a doubtful look. "The door behind those lasers looks like it's made of iron or steel or some other very thick metal."

"It's iron," he confirmed. "It's the first line of defense against the supernatural."

Supernatural? Suddenly, I was more alarmed than eager to know what constituted a book of dubious origin. "Why did it look as if Olive and Tariq just melted through it? Is the door an illusion?"

"You could think of it that way," he said. "But more accurately, they magicked through it and we will, too."

"What about the lasers?"

"Just for show." He wagged his elbow at me. "Best get going before Olive comes back through to yell at us."

Enough said. I slipped my hand through his arm, fully expecting to either burn because of the lasers or face-plant against the metal door. But instead, I felt as if I'd been cocooned in a soft, thick blanket. I could hear Miles speaking, but I couldn't make out the words, as my hearing was muffled. It felt as if I were wearing earplugs. We took five steps forward and the cocoon fell away. We were on the other side.

I glanced back. The solid iron door was still there. Miles had said Olive and Tariq had *magicked* their way through, so we must have, too. I wondered if I would have face-planted right into the heavy metal without Miles to escort me through. Despite my resistance to the magical world, I had to acknowledge it was pretty cool.

Olive was tapping her foot and Tariq was smiling and said, "You made it, Zoe."

I nodded. I was too fuzzy to speak. A long curved hallway lined with white subway tiles and lit with track lighting along the concrete floor, walls, and ceiling was revealed. Out of the darkness and into the light we went.

The tunnel ended abruptly at another metal door with the same web of lasers and Olive repeated the same process, disappearing through the metal, then Tariq, followed by Miles and me. It was very disorienting, and when I stepped into the main room, it took me a moment to get my bearings.

I don't know what I expected. Maybe a laboratory type of room where they examined old books under bright fluorescent lights with beakers bubbling all around them. Why beakers would be bubbling I had no idea. My imagination was not that specific. Or perhaps I thought it would be a dank and musty dungeon-like room where the chairs were hard, the room was cold, and they worked by candlelight. This proved inaccurate as well.

Instead, the most beautiful library I had ever seen was spread out before me. We crossed a decorative parquet floor much like the one upstairs. Several wooden worktables piled with books filled the center of the room. Along the walls, three stories of bookcases ran floor to ceiling, with two spiral staircases leading to the upper levels, which were set back behind fancy wrought iron railings. I leaned back to take it all in and noted the glorious domed ceiling overhead. It was painted to resemble the sky, bright blue with fluffy white clouds, giving me the sense of being outside even though we were three stories below ground. My heart swelled in my chest as I immediately fell in love with the place.

"Glorious, isn't it?" Tariq asked.

"It's okay." I shrugged and then sighed. The library deserved better than that and so did Tariq. "Honestly, it's spectacular."

He grinned and then laughed as if he appreciated my honesty.

"Shall we begin?" Miles asked. He gestured for me to follow him. I didn't hesitate. We climbed the spiral staircase to the right. On the upper floor, the items were housed neatly on shelves with a lone papyrus on display in a thick glass case in front of the shelving unit.

"This is our collection of Egyptian papyri," Miles said. "These particular scrolls are considered to be of the dubious sort because they contain rituals and spells and other arcane information."

I glanced through the glass at the papyrus on display. "That's the Egyptian god Set or Seth. Isn't he the master of chaos in the form of storms and war?"

Miles nodded. "Which is exactly why we keep the papyrus down here. We wouldn't want any spells involving such a trickster to get into the wrong hands."

I frowned. As a librarian, I was a hardcore believer in the freedom of information. The only way to combat ignorance was through knowledge, and locking away books, or in this case papyri, was never a solution in my opinion. This was like keeping all tales of folklore out of the public's hands. Wasn't it? Doubt started to seep into my being like smoke under a closed door. I turned away from the papyrus.

The collection was vast and I tried to wrap my head around the idea that over the millennia so many writings had been created that were considered "of dubious origin." There were more papyri, tablets, illuminated manuscripts, and printed folios in a wide array of European languages. We were leaving the third floor when I heard something purr.

"Do you have a cat in here?" I asked.

"No." Miles said. He began to walk down the steps. I started to follow him, but I heard the purring sound again.

I turned to the bookcase beside me, thinking a cat was loose in the shelves. That couldn't be good.

A dark gray volume caught my eye and as I peered closer, a tail dropped from the spine. *What?!* I reached out and tentatively stroked the furry spine of the book with my index finger. The purring became louder.

"Miles!" I stared at the book, watching the tail swish back and forth.

Miles climbed back up the stairs and joined me. "Oh, how nice. You've met Freya."

"It's a book," I said.

"Yes."

"But it purrs."

"Quite loudly," he agreed. He didn't sound nearly as freaked-out as I felt he should. "She likes to have her ears scratched, too."

"Ears?"

"Here." Miles reached forward and gently removed the book from the shelf. "She's usually shy around newcomers. She must approve of you."

It looked like an ordinary book. You know, if books had tails. But when he turned it so the cover was facing up, a cat's face blinked out at me from the center of the book, and the corners of the cover twitched as if they were actually ears. The eyes moved from Miles to me.

"What sort of book is that?" I cried. "I mean, is it a book or is it a cat? And if it's a cat, why is it shelved?" My distress was evident in my voice and the purring stopped and the eyes shut. I glanced at the spine. Sure enough, even the tail had disappeared.

Miles stroked the spine of the book and made soothing sounds. "There, there, Freya. You're all right." He gently shelved the book. He glanced at me and said, "Freya is a rare book of Norse mythology. You can read her if you like. You know, if she lets you, because . . . well . . . cat. Also, it's written in ancient Norse, so you'd need to know that, too."

I shook my head. This went beyond dubious origins and

veered right into weird. "That . . . I . . ." I asked the only question I could formulate. "Is she called Freya because the cat in Norse mythology is the goddess Freya's sacred animal?"

"Precisely." Miles beamed at me. "You really are unusually knowledgeable about all subjects."

I didn't say anything but stared at the dark gray book, wondering if I'd just imagined the purring, the tail, and the cat face.

"No, you didn't imagine it." Miles offered me no more explanation than that and turned to start back down the winding spiral staircase again. I tried to put the strange book out of my mind. I told myself it had to be a novelty item that they shelved in here for fun. But I didn't believe me and I felt something inside me shift that could only be described as an awakening. I tried to clamp it down, but it was like an active child begging to be let out to play. I frowned. I simply wasn't ready to reconsider letting magic into my life and breaking the promise I'd made to my mother.

The first floor was much like the ones above, with bookshelves running along the perimeter of the room. On the sturdy worktables amid the books, I spotted a microscope and a magnifying glass as well as several archival boxes like the one Olive had been about to put my mysterious book into.

"Do you focus on conservation or preservation with the materials you receive?" I asked.

"Because of the nature of our department, we strive to preserve the item exactly as it was when it became part of our collection."

"So if a book's been damaged in a fire, you do nothing?" I asked.

Olive stepped out of a narrow door in between two shelving units. "We consider the damage sustained as part of the object's story."

That seemed an interesting take to me, but I'd never worked with ancient materials before.

"However, if an item's origin is deemed not dubious, then we send it up to the regular collection, where the librarians can determine whether it warrants conservation or not," Tariq added.

He was seated at a table on the far side of the room, with a book in front of him that even from several yards away I could see it was of the Hiberno-Saxon style, much like the Book of Kells from the ninth century. It had elaborate Irish-Celtic initials, which blended beautifully with the Anglo-Saxon zoomorphic interlacing and preference for bright colors. The mere thought that I could be in the same room with a rare tome from the year 800 made me woozy. No wonder I was seeing cats.

"Maybe I've been a public librarian for too long," I said, "but it doesn't feel right to have all of these volumes locked away. I mean, shouldn't people have access to these materials?"

Olive's split eyebrow lifted. The disdain in her gaze almost made me flinch. Almost.

"Follow me." It was an order. She crossed to an alcove on the far side of the room. It was darker than the others even though it had the same overhead lighting. My spine tingled and not in a good way. This shelving unit gave me the same feeling of foreboding as the book that had brought me here.

Olive gestured to the section of books and I noted that many were old, as in hundreds of years old, with unrecognizable symbols on their spines. I was shocked at the malevolence I felt pulsing from the bookcase. It made the hair on the back of my neck prickle.

I scanned the shelves until my gaze was caught by an unprepossessing burgundy volume in the middle of the bookcase. It was shorter than the others and appeared faded and worn. An image came to mind of a frozen heart encased in ice within the book's cracked leather. The withered heart clenched like a fist as if it could punch its way to freedom and unleash a merciless evil upon us all. A shiver rippled through me from head to toe.

Olive's eyes narrowed and she scrutinized my face, her eyes widened slightly in surprise. "You feel *El Corazón*, don't you?"

I didn't answer. The fact that she used the Spanish word for *heart* and described exactly what I'd seen did not help the acute discomfort I was feeling. I tried to shake it off. These were just books. But as I glanced at the small, dark red volume, I knew that this collection and that book in particular were much more than that.

"Whose heart is it?"

"It's a metaphorical heart. It symbolizes a witch's power. In this case, it belonged to a witch called Ariana Darkwood," Miles said. "She was banished from her coven decades ago for practicing black magic."

"Like necromancy?" I felt vulnerable admitting my concerns about what they'd told me about the maternal side of my family, but I had to know.

"No." Miles shook his head. "Necromancy is not black magic when used appropriately."

"*Appropriately*," I repeated. I had a hard time imagining

any circumstance where raising the dead wasn't considered evil. "I still think keeping books locked away is wrong."

"Let me ask you this," Olive said. "Do you think just anyone should be able to utilize these books containing information that we don't yet understand? Are you okay with the worst of humanity having access to texts that instruct them on how to summon a demon, enslave their enemy, and curse a family for seven generations?" She tapped my shoulder bag. "Or raise the dead?"

"Well, when you put it like that . . ." I muttered. I was ready for the conversation to be over, as I really wanted to move away from this section of icky books.

"What Olive is trying to say with her typical sledgehammer finesse is that most of these books are here because we don't yet know their provenance or their intent." Miles pushed his glasses up his nose and tipped his head to the side as he studied me.

"On the upside, those cruel grimoires that you mentioned earlier, Zoe, usually go right upstairs. As they generally have no magic or mystery to them at all," Tariq said with a grin, and I smiled in return.

I glanced around the main room, looking for something more scientific. "How do you authenticate the materials you acquire?"

"So glad you asked," Miles said. "This way."

He crossed the room to another narrow wooden door. He pushed it open and stepped inside, waving me in after him. Olive and Tariq joined us, which surprised me, as I didn't think Olive wanted me to be privy to their secrets. I blinked as I took in the glaringly bright room. This was the laboratory I had been expecting.

"Tariq is our master of radiocarbon dating," Miles said. He gestured for Tariq to take over.

Tariq nodded and crossed the room to a large piece of equipment with coils and wires and tubes. It looked like something out of a science fiction novel.

"This is our accelerated mass spectrometer," he said.

Yup, totally sci-fi. "It feels rather techy for objects of dubious origin," I said.

"Science and the arcane can coexist," Miles assured me. "In fact, it's generally science that reveals the mystical and magical, shining a light on the mysteries we can't solve or comprehend."

I gave him a doubtful look and asked, "How does it work?"

"This machine accelerates negatively charged ions in order to separate the rare carbon-14 atoms from the more common carbon-12 for mass analysis," Tariq explained. "Once we determine the decay of the carbon-14, we can estimate the age of the paper or parchment."

I didn't completely understand, so I asked a follow-up just to be clear. "And we can use this method on my book?"

"Absolutely," Tariq answered at the same time Miles said, "Potentially."

Both Tariq and I turned to face him.

"Potentially?" I asked.

"Zoe, I would like to offer you a position here in the BODO," Miles said.

"What?" Olive and I cried in unison.

"We have a vacancy and I think you would fit in well." Miles held his hands wide to indicate the lab.

"You're giving her Niall's position," Olive said. It wasn't a question, and she didn't sound happy about it.

"He's been gone for two years, Olive," Miles said. His voice was understanding but also firm.

Olive turned and strode to the door, where she leaned against the doorframe, clearly refusing to participate.

"Why me?" I asked. "Surely, you have loads of more-qualified candidates and people in-house who would enjoy this collection much more than I would."

"I've seen your curriculum vitae," Miles said.

"How did you see my CV?" I asked. Miles didn't answer, but I knew. "Agatha."

He didn't confirm or deny, but I knew it was Agatha. She'd always believed I was destined for bigger things than the Wessex Public Library, completely disregarding the fact that Wessex was where I wanted to be.

"You'd bring a unique set of skills to the department," Miles said.

I stared at him. I knew what he was going to say before he said it and I wanted to argue, but the very book I'd brought here would make a liar out of me.

"The Donadieu coven is one of the oldest and most powerful in the world," Miles said. "With that blood in your veins and your family's grimoire, you have the potential to be one of the greatest witches of the modern age."

"*Pfft*," Olive huffed from her place beside the door.

"There are two problems with that," I said. "The first is that I can't read the book and the second is that even if I could, having not practiced any witchcraft since I was a child, I'm likely not powerful enough to manage any magic at all."

I didn't mention my reluctance to examine my abilities. How could I explain to a roomful of strangers what my childhood had been like? That I'd grown up in a household where my mother was an extraordinary witch, so much so that the high priestess of the local coven was threatened by her power. As the members of the local coven frequently turned to my mother instead of the high priestess for help in casting their spells, my father had become concerned that something horrible would happen to my mother because of her ability.

He'd been right. I was never given the specifics, but at a meeting of the coven elders, Mom got into a confrontation with the high priestess. Going against the laws of the coven, the high priestess had attacked, and Mom was severely injured. In my mind, I could still see the jagged wound across my mother's palm inflicted by the high priestess that night. Mom had carried that scar for the rest of her life.

Dad had waited outside the meeting, and when Mom appeared, cradling her wounded hand, he rushed her to the local witch doctor. Unfortunately, it was an icy night outside and Dad lost control of the car and crashed into a tree. He died instantly, while she suffered internal injuries and a concussion. Mom blamed herself and her magic for her husband's death. With the insight of an adult, I knew she had asked me to swear to never use magic to protect me from the same heartbreak she had suffered.

"Are you certain you can't manifest any magic?" Miles asked.

"Yes." There was the tiniest hiccup of doubt in my voice, but I soldiered on, hoping he hadn't noticed. "I appreciate your interest in me, but I don't think I'm a good fit. I studied ancient languages but am by no means an expert. I don't travel well, and I don't practice witchcraft. I am a pragmatic, unimaginative, fact-oriented librarian, and I don't believe I have anything to offer this department."

"Ziakas and I finally agree on something," Olive said. She gestured to the open door. "Here. I'll escort you out."

"I don't think you see yourself as clearly as I do, Zoe. The offer stands," Miles said. "At least consider it. Since the book seems bonded to you and we can't take it from you, if you accept the job, you could make carbon dating and deciphering the grimoire your first project."

I met his gaze. Behind his glasses, his eyes were benevolent and patient, and as he rocked back on his heels with his hands casually stuffed into his pockets, I suspected he was certain I was going to accept. Truly, what librarian wouldn't want to work here? I genuinely felt bad about disappointing him, but there was no way I was going to change my mind.

"Thank you, but I don't need to consider it more. I'm happy right where I am." It was true. I had no intention of ditching my comfortable, stress-free life and I hoped my tone of voice conveyed as much.

Miles considered me for a moment. "If you need us, you know where to find us."

"Thank you." I turned to Tariq and said, "It was a pleasure meeting you and thank you for your help when I blacked out."

"No wahala—it is no problem. My specialty is potions,

which I learned from my grandmother, who was a witch much like yours." Tariq's Nigerian accent made his words as gentle as a hug. "I do hope we meet again, Zoe Ziakas."

I turned and followed Olive, who was already striding across the floor of the main room to the large metal door. Hurrying after her, I felt an insistent tug on my insides, as if the library itself was trying to pull me back, and I wondered for a second, a nanosecond really, if turning down the job was a mistake.

As I stood on the curb, trying to hail a cab, I felt the creepy sensation of being watched. I cast a quick glance over my shoulder at the glorious library behind me, but the windows were barren and even the security guard was absent from her post. It was ridiculous to think that anyone at the Museum of Literature cared if I left or not. Still, the feeling of being observed persisted. I glanced up and spotted a raven perched on the corner of the roof. It met my gaze and I knew it was the reason I'd felt like someone was watching me. Weird.

6

Home. I was so desperately glad to be back at my quiet house in my peaceful village. I parked my car in the driveway and strolled up the walkway, keys in hand. To my surprise, Agatha was sitting on one of the wicker chairs on my front porch.

"I was just about to give up and go home," she said.

"How long have you been waiting?" I asked.

"About an hour."

"I hope you weren't bored."

She held up a paperback novel. "Not a bit."

I smiled. Agatha always had a book on hand, sometimes two in case she finished one and didn't want to be caught without. I climbed the steps, and she rose from her seat and held a paper grocery sack out to me. "Dinner."

"You brought me Twinkies?" I teased.

She snorted. "Lasagna. I suspected today was going to be a long one. How did it go? Were they able to help you?"

"Unfortunately, not with the book," I said. I unlocked the

front door and led the way inside. Agatha followed and I offered her a cup of tea. She accepted and slid onto a stool at the kitchen counter while I fixed the tea, plated some store-bought cookies, and told her all about my meeting, including the blood oath, my supposed family of necromancers, and the job offer.

By the time I finished telling her everything, I was seated on the stool beside hers and we were almost done with the tea and cookies.

"When are you handing in your resignation?" she asked.

"I'm not." I looked at her as if she'd suggested I burn my house down. "I turned them down, obviously."

"You refused a position at the Museum of Literature?" She set her teacup down with a precision that told me she was striving to control her emotions. "Zoe, no one gets offered a job at the museum and never in the Books of Dubious Origin collection. The only reason you were even allowed in there was because I vetted you. Do you have any idea what you've refused?"

"Yes. I'm not working in a place where books are cats or cats are books." I picked up our empty cups and deposited them in the sink.

"Huh?" she asked.

"Miles called her Freya," I said. "It's a book on Norse mythology that looks like a cat."

"Oh, right." Agatha chuckled. "Freya's very affectionate once you get to know her."

I started in surprise. "You've seen the book . . . er . . . cat? You've been in the BODO?"

"Well, I am the BODO liaison on the museum board." She studied me for a moment and said, "I think you could do great things there, Zoe."

"I do great things here," I countered.

"You do, but you have so much untapped potential. Don't you want to use it?" Her voice was measured, as if she was trying very hard not to offend me.

"You know why I can't."

She pressed her lips together as if to keep herself from protesting. I knew Agatha had my best interests at heart. She always did, but I wasn't convinced that embracing the family gift of witchcraft or taking a job at the BODO was right for me.

"You know change isn't easy for me, and all this has come out of nowhere. Plus, it's more than breaking my promise to Mom. The stuff they were saying about Mamie . . ."

"Is this about the necromancy?"

"You knew about that?" I was incredulous.

"Your mother and I were friends for decades." She squeezed my arm in reassurance. "Of course I knew."

"But you never said anything." I couldn't keep the hurt out of my voice. I had thought Agatha was *my* person and that I was hers.

"Juliet asked me not to and as time went by and I saw how you felt about witchcraft and magic, I decided not to mention it, knowing you would reject it." Her gaze was sharp but sympathetic. She was right. I would have absolutely spurned hearing about any of this.

Agatha had been in my life as a child like a long-distance favorite auntie, but she'd been there for me every single day of my life since my mom had dropped me off at the Wessex boarding school when I was fourteen. Agatha was the one I'd spent all my holidays with. She'd helped me pick my dress for prom, attended my graduation, moved me into my dorm, eaten copious amounts of Ben & Jerry's ice cream with me after my first heartbreak, and so on. I was not about to lose her now.

"You're right. I would have," I acknowledged. I lowered my gaze to the countertop for a beat. "There's something I haven't told you."

Agatha leaned forward and rested her chin on her hand. "I'm listening."

"The envelope that the grimoire came in . . ." I hesitated. I knew I should have told her this from the beginning, but I had been in full denial then. I met her gaze and continued, "The handwriting on the envelope. It looked like Mom's."

Agatha gasped and leaned back. "Are you sure?"

"Positive. That's not all," I said. "The envelope disappeared."

"You don't mean it went missing, do you?"

"No. I was holding it in my hand and it was consumed with green fire."

"Was it hot?"

"No."

"Witch fire." Agatha nodded. "And you didn't say anything?"

"De-Nile ain't just a river in Egypt," I quipped. Agatha gave me a stern look. Okay, then. "Do you think it's possible that Mom sent it to me? But if so, how? She's been gone a month. How could it have taken that long to get to me? And why wasn't it with her things from Mystwood Manor?"

Agatha pursed her lips. "You know your mother never told me where she was going when she dropped you off for boarding school."

"I know. She never told me either."

"But do you remember all the times she'd appear over the years?" Agatha asked.

"Always when we least expected it." I nodded.

"And she'd bring you the most extraordinary gifts."

"I remember." I rolled my eyes. "I wanted a flip phone and she'd show up with an antique dollhouse. I wanted a curling wand and she brought me an antique brush and comb set. And how about that last gift? What was it? A crow? No, it was a raven puppet that looked as if it was a century old."

"I do remember." Agatha looked thoughtful. "Didn't she tell you something like *the raven is your friend*?"

"She said she'd had a vision and I should *trust the raven*." I felt a shiver ripple down my spine as I thought of the raven outside the museum.

"Did you ever wonder why?" Agatha asked.

"Because she didn't know me at all?" I picked up a cookie and bit into it with more force than was necessary.

"Possibly, or because the gifts were whatever she could get her hands on *at the time*," Agatha said.

I squinted at her. "What are you saying?"

"I'm just speculating that maybe the reason we could never find your mother was because she wasn't in a *where* but rather a *when*."

"Whoa." I dropped my cookie onto my plate. "Is that even possible?"

"It would take a very powerful witch, and she was one. It's just a theory." Agatha bit into a cookie and made a face. She was not a fan of packaged baked goods. "But I believe your mother most definitely could have conjured a spell that would allow her to move back and forth through time."

"Okay—*whoa*—but okay. Now, here's a question: Why would my mother send me the grimoire when she made me promise to never practice witchcraft?" I asked. "It makes no sense."

"You make a solid point." Agatha finished her cookie. "But we don't know for certain it was your mother who sent you the grimoire."

"Except the handwriting on the envelope looked like hers."

"Easily faked, especially using magic, which could also be why the envelope disappeared. It was likely spelled to leave no trace, and witch fire is the best way to do that," Agatha said. "Listen, I think the universe is handing you an incredible opportunity to expand your talents and embrace your witch heritage."

"Maybe, and that's a very big maybe." It was the most I could offer at the moment. "As for the job offer in *that* library, I need more time to think about it at the very least."

She studied me for a moment as if trying to decide whether to push or not. "If I know Miles, he left the offer open?"

I nodded.

Agatha rose from her seat and stood facing me. "Then take the time it deserves and really think about it, Zoe."

"I want a quiet life, Agatha," I said. "The years between my dad dying and my mom dropping me off in Wessex were, as you know, awful. We were always on the move. We never stayed in one place longer than a season, and we frequently slept in our car. After that, I promised myself that when I was a grown-up, I would live a simple, stress-free life. From what I saw at the museum, the BODO is not that."

"This isn't a quiet life; this is hiding from life. There's a difference," Agatha challenged me.

She was probably right, she usually was, but I wasn't ready to admit it yet. We were at an impasse and we both knew it. Agatha sighed and hugged me. "Just think about it, kiddo."

"I will, but don't get your hopes up."

She pushed the bag she'd brought across the counter. "Reheat the lasagna in the oven, three hundred fifty degrees for thirty minutes. Do not eat it cold."

I laughed because I had absolutely planned to eat it without warming it. "Fine, I'll use the microwave."

She shook her head, her white ringlets bobbing against her shoulders. She refastened her coat and said, "I'll call you tomorrow."

I stood on the porch, watching until she drove off. Again, I had the tingly, uncomfortable sensation of being watched. I scanned the area and gasped. Perched on my mailbox at the end of the driveway was a raven and, again, it was staring at me. I popped back inside and shut the door. It had to be a coincidence, I told myself, even though I didn't believe in coincidences.

The October evening was cool, so I lit a fire in the fireplace and made myself a hot cup of cocoa. I put on my blue-and-black-plaid flannel pajama bottoms with the matching black thermal top and draped my gray chenille throw over my legs as I hunkered into my favorite reading chair and opened my current book. It didn't go well.

Three times I tried to get into the story, but my mind kept bouncing back to the Museum of Literature. Claire had met Olive and me at the museum's exit. Olive had departed with a terse *goodbye*, and Claire had been disappointed to hear that I wasn't interested in a career shift to the museum. For the millionth time—and I would never admit this to Agatha—I wondered if I had done the right thing, which in and of itself was weird because I didn't usually doubt myself.

When I had changed into my jammies, I'd locked my book of dubious origin—the department name was definitely apt—in the small fireproof safe where I kept all my important papers. I was confident, mostly, that it would stay put.

I sipped my cocoa and refocused on the novel. I'd managed to read half a page when I heard a scuffling noise coming from the front porch. I told myself it was the wind and started the next paragraph. The disturbance became louder. I ignored it. Then I heard a tapping noise and decided I needed to investigate what was happening outside.

I put down my novel and shoved my blanket aside. I glanced out the window beside the door. There was no one on the porch. I cautiously opened the door. I checked the walkway to the street. No one was there. I studied the wind chimes hanging on the corner of the porch. They weren't moving, so it hadn't been a breeze. I shifted my gaze to the two wicker chairs to the right. They were empty, but perched on the back of one of them was the raven.

"Ah!" I shouted, startled. Had this uninvited guest been making all that racket? He was the only one here, so it had to have been him. I was equal parts relieved and annoyed. I walked toward the bird. He didn't move. I raised my arms and waved my hands at him. "Shoo!"

He turned his head to the side and stared at me with one beady, pale blue eye, as if assessing my threat level. It was going to be high if he pooped on my furniture.

"Party's over!" I clapped my hands. The sound was loud in the evening quiet. He flapped his wings and flew from the chair to the porch railing. I clapped again. "You don't have to go home, big guy, but you can't stay here."

With a leap, he jumped off the railing and soared out into the darkness. I glanced at the houses on each side of mine. My octogenarian neighbor Mrs. Graham's house was dark. She went to bed promptly at eight every evening. And the Perkins family on the other side of me appeared to be out, since their minivan wasn't in the driveway. Their boys must have had soccer practice. All was quiet. I turned and went back inside, assured that peace had been restored.

I had just settled into my chair and started reading when there was a thumping sound on the porch.

"Oh hell no," I muttered. "We're not doing this all night."

I tossed aside my blanket and crossed to the door. I unlocked it and yanked it open. "I said, *Shoo!*"

But it wasn't the raven. Instead, standing before me was a diminutive, very pale ash-blond woman of a certain age, I was guessing mid- to late fifties. She was wearing a beige wool coat and clutching a stylish handbag, which matched her equally fashionable shoes.

"Can I help you?" I asked.

"I certainly hope so, dear," she said. Her blue eyes crinkled in the corners when she smiled at me. "I'm Eloise Tate, a childhood friend of your grandmother's."

"Excuse me?" I asked. The odds of Mamie coming up in conversation twice in one day had to be a million to one. Years of my life had passed without my grandmother being mentioned and now she'd been mentioned twice. My gut twisted. Something wasn't right.

"Antoinette Donadieu—Toni—she was your grandmother, yes?" Eloise tipped her head to the side as she studied me. "Your resemblance to her is uncanny."

"I'm sorry. I don't want to be rude, but Mamie would be in her eighties now. There's no way you're old enough to have been a childhood friend of hers."

"Oh, but I was," Eloise said. "Sadly, I passed away when I was fifty-two."

"Passed away?" I choked the words out.

"Yes, but dear Toni brought me back and I was her faithful companion right up until the day she died. Now I need you, Zoe, to send me on."

"Send you on?" I repeated. There was a buzzing in my ears, probably panic, which made it hard to hear her.

"Yes, you have the grimoire from your mother, right? Which means you have the spell to send me across the veil to the other side." She beamed and I noticed a fleck of pink lipstick on her teeth.

"You're telling me you're dead." I looked her over. She was clearly *not* dead. So . . . what the actual fuck was going on here?

"Oh, I can assure you, I'm very much deceased." She nodded. "Toni planned to return me before she passed away, but the grimoire was stolen and Toni was murdered before she had the chance."

"*Murdered?*" My chest felt tight. I couldn't get enough air, everything went fuzzy, and I started to see spots. I leaned heavily against the doorjamb. "Who exactly murdered her? Do you know?"

"Why, it was your mother, dear."

7

My knees wobbled. I stared at the wholesome-looking woman standing in front of me. The chilly night air made me shiver as it slipped past me, into my house, as if it had just been waiting for an opening.

"How do you know about—?" I stopped. Should I admit that I had the grimoire to a stranger? Probably not. I only had her word that she was who she said she was, and who she said she was did not seem even remotely possible to me. I took a steadying breath.

Eloise tipped her head to the side and blinked at me. She didn't look dead. Perhaps she was excessively pale, but otherwise, she appeared absolutely normal. Her cheeks were round, her nose pert, and her eyes were kind and filled with understanding. Clearly the strange woman was suffering from something, but being dead wasn't it.

"Why did you say that Mamie was murdered by my mother?" I put aside her claim of being deceased for the moment and focused on the statement that alarmed me the most, as it seemed overly personal.

"I thought it was common knowledge," Eloise said.

"This is the first I'm hearing of it," I said. "And I don't believe you."

"Poor lamb." Eloise lifted her hand as if she would pat my arm, but she paused, neatly clasping her hands in front of her. "I assumed you knew. Oh, I have made a mess of things, haven't I?"

I said nothing. What could I say? It wasn't true. There was no way it could be true. It was an outrageous thing to say. I mean, I would have known if my mom had murdered Mamie, wouldn't I?

Eloise sighed. "In *our* world, everyone believes that Juliet murdered Toni when she stole the grimoire and disappeared."

I felt my heart pound in my chest. I remembered the argument between my mom and Mamie right before my mother insisted we leave my grandmother's house in the middle of the night without saying goodbye. I knew my mom had been furious that Mamie had begun to teach me magic. But murder?

I would deny it completely, except I remembered my mom's erratic behavior during the years when we moved constantly, never staying anywhere longer than a school semester and usually shorter than that. Had she—*we*—been on the run? It would explain so much. I thought of Agatha's guess that my mom had been living in other time periods. Had she been accused of murder? Was she hiding from authorities? Was she hiding the grimoire? But why? Had she left me in Agatha's care to avoid putting me in danger? I thought I was going to be sick.

"Of course, since your mother's death was also a murder—"

"*What?*" I cried. "Why would you say such a thing?"

Eloise's mouth formed an O and her eyes went wide. She didn't answer, as if aware that I was seconds from slamming the door in her face.

"My mother was not murdered." I said the words slowly with extra emphasis. "She died in her sleep at Mystwood Manor, where she was a resident."

"Okay." Eloise's eyebrows lifted, as if she knew better than to argue with me about this.

I felt my anger dissipate as I realized I was standing on my porch in the cold, arguing with a perfect stranger. This was ridiculous.

"How exactly did you find me?" I asked.

Eloise's eyes brightened as if she, too, was relieved by the change of subject. "I've always known where you were, but you didn't have the grimoire, so you couldn't help me."

I swallowed. Had it been this woman my mom had been running from? It seemed improbable, but this hadn't been a typical day, and I really had no idea what to think about anything at the moment.

"Once you opened the book, I sensed it bonding to you just as it did to your mother. Sadly, I could never manage to find her. Very talented your mother was. I'm certain she would have had no trouble with the necromancy spells—both the retrieving and returning of the dead. No matter. Now that you have the Donadieu grimoire, you can send me on." Eloise stared at me hopefully and I felt my face grow warm as I thought about the book in my safe.

I didn't know this woman. I wasn't about to tell her anything. As a librarian and book lover myself, I knew how fanatical people could be about books. I could only imagine what a ruckus a grimoire, readable or not, might cause.

There was no help for it. I needed the input of professionals.

"I'm sorry. I can't help you, but I know some people who can." Before Eloise could say a word, I said, "Come back tomorrow morning at eight and I'll take you to them."

Eloise's eyes narrowed in suspicion just for a moment, but then her congenial smile was back in place, the fleck of pink lipstick still on her teeth. "All right. Sleep well, Zoe."

Relieved that Eloise had agreed to go without a fuss, I stepped back into the house, noting that the raven who'd tapped on my window earlier was again perched on the mailbox. It turned its head to the side and studied me with a sharp gaze from its pale blue eye. Weirdly, it made me feel as if it was watching over me, and I was strangely comforted by that.

I locked the door behind me. It didn't feel like enough protection, so I took one of the wooden chairs from my small dining set and wedged it under the door handle. Yes, Eloise was in her fifties. No, she didn't look as if she worked out. But she also believed she was dead and needed a spell from a grimoire to move on, so I figured better safe than sorry.

I shut off all the lights in the living room and peered out the peephole, which gave me a view of the other side of the front door and the walkway. It was empty. Only the raven on the mailbox remained, ever watchful.

Quietly, I prepped for bed and climbed into my cocoon of blankets. I tucked them tightly around me. It was a habit I'd developed as a kid who'd moved around a lot. I'd always felt as if my bed was my safe space. So long as I was tucked in nice and tight, the monsters couldn't get me. Even in the summer when it was hot, I slept with a light blanket and I never ever let so much as a toe poke out.

Mentally, I ran through my day tomorrow. I was going to have to call out of work . . . again. I didn't like it, but it couldn't be helped.

The grimoire. I'd never heard of it until it had showed up at the library. Yes, I had grown up knowing that Mamie and my mom were witches, but when my mother had left me in Wessex, she'd made me promise to forget all of it. She'd insisted a magical life brought nothing but misery, and as I was abandoned at boarding school, having lost everyone I loved in one way or another, I believed her. I'd shut it all down.

Agatha, to her credit, had never pushed her belief in or practice of the witchy arts onto me—probably because Mom told her not to—so I'd spent the last twenty-two years happily living a quiet nonmagical life in Wessex just like the regular folks. Now it felt as if all my peace was being ripped away from me.

I could feel my anxiety bubbling up inside me. I closed my eyes and tried to breathe through it. I hadn't had a panic attack in years and refused to have one now. Remembering what my mother had taught me when I was little and had nightmares, I visualized myself floating, as light as a flower petal on a warm spring breeze. I could feel the tension seep out of my shoulders and my back. The breeze gently tugged on my hair and clothes as I drifted over rolling green hills with the sounds of happy songbirds in my ears. My lightness of being filled me up and I felt warmed from the inside out. I sighed, relieved to have staved off the anxiety attack.

I slowly opened my eyes and blinked. I was staring at the ceiling, but instead of being eight feet away, it was only one foot. I could reach out and touch the swirling patterns in the paint if I tried. I glanced over my shoulder and saw my bed many feet below. I started and yelped and then I was falling, landing on my bed with a thump. I scrambled up to a seated position, clutching my blankets to my chest.

Had I really just levitated? How? Why? Did Eloise have something to do with this? No, that made no sense. Maybe I was dreaming. I pinched myself. *Ouch!* No, not dreaming. There was simply no denying what had just happened. Somehow I had caused that to happen. But how?

I always did a floating visualization to calm myself down and I had never—not once—actually floated. What had changed? The grimoire.

I was now in possession of a mysterious grimoire, and dead people were showing up at my door, and I was performing magic in my sleep. This was so bad.

Now I had two things to talk to the staff of the BODO about. Eloise and my sudden ability to levitate. Surely, given their extensive collection of the strange, they could help me with both.

Reassured that I had a strategic plan in place, I closed my eyes, willing sleep to come. It didn't. Instead, images from my childhood flitted through my brain like the trailer for a stinker of a movie. Usually I could stuff my memories and my feelings into a little glass jar in my mind and twist the lid until it was nice and tight, but tonight I couldn't. My thoughts were as wild as a can of snakes.

My father. I remembered him as a tall, dark-haired, deep-voiced man who was always cheerfully singing. Whenever he returned home from work, he'd pick me up and swing me around, kissing both my cheeks before setting me back on my feet. My mother would laugh almost as hard as I did, and she would gaze at him with so much love in her eyes.

I felt my throat get tight. I swallowed past the lump. I blinked and mentally pictured stuffing these feeling back into their jar. They wouldn't go.

My brain flitted to another memory I hadn't pondered in years. It was the last night I ever saw Mamie. We had always been close to Mamie and visited her on her island home off the coast of Rhode Island several times a year. Mom and I had stayed with her for a year after my father passed away. My mother had cried all day every day, wouldn't eat, and locked herself in her bedroom, refusing to come out. I was terrified that I was going to lose her, too, and was desperate to help her, but I didn't know how.

Mamie had looked after me, comforting me while I worked through my own sadness, but I felt as if my mother was slipping farther and farther out of reach. To distract me from my mother's emotional absence, Mamie started to teach me things. Namely spells, which I actively forgot—at my mother's insistence—after we left Mamie's house.

One night, while Mamie and I were baking a blueberry pie, my mom appeared in the kitchen. Mamie had taught me how to roll out the pie crust without using my hands. As the rolling pin moved across the dough under my command, she had clapped and cheered and called me her *bright beautiful girl*. I had soaked up every bit of her praise like a sunflower turning its face to the sun.

"What is going on here?" my mother had demanded. She was thin and pale and shaking. She glared at Mamie and yelled, "You are not teaching her magic. We discussed this. I do not want her life burdened by this 'gift.'"

The way Mom said *gift* made it clear she didn't think it was a gift at all. I hadn't seen her use her magic since the night my father died. It was clear to me, even as a child, that she believed Dad's death was her fault. I knew without being told that the guilt was eating her alive.

Mamie glanced at me and then my mom. She tenderly tugged my apron off and turned me toward the door with a gentle push. "Go to your room, mon chaton. I will be up to read to you soon."

I tried to catch my mother's eye, but she was staring at the floor. She was breathing hard and her lips were set in a thin grim line. She was clearly angry, so I scooted up the stairs as fast as I could. I didn't want to be in the blast zone of whatever explosion was about to blow.

They fought for hours. I couldn't make out the words, which was weird because I could usually hear Mamie quite clearly when she called me to breakfast—*mon chaton*, which was French for *my kitten*. But this argument, punctuated by the occasional slam of a door, was muffled. I almost felt as if I had earmuffs on even when I pressed my ear to the wall to hear more clearly.

Mamie didn't come to read to me that night, or if she did, I'd fallen asleep and she chose to leave me be. It was the darker side of dawn when my mother scooped me up, telling me not to make a sound as she carried me out of the house and tucked me into the back seat of our minivan. We drove away as the sun just began to lighten the sky, and my mom never looked back.

My mother didn't tell me about Mamie's death until long after it had happened. Mom never mentioned the specifics of how or when Mamie had passed, and we didn't attend the funeral. Our life became so chaotic, I didn't have much time to think about it. The only thing I knew was that Mamie, the one person who had offered me some stability after my father had died, was gone.

I rubbed my chest with my knuckles. The memory of losing the happy mother I'd known as a child and the grandmother who had cared for me during the worst year of my life actually hurt. I cursed Eloise and the book. I didn't want to remember these things. I had left my family in my rearview mirror years ago and that was where I wanted them to stay. It was well past midnight when I finally fell asleep.

Mercifully, I did not dream that night and when I woke up, I went right to my safe. I popped the latch and the lid lifted. The book was just where I had placed it the evening before. I sighed, relieved that it hadn't moved. Then again, I'd been busy levitating, so perhaps the book had taken the night off, assuming I was busy.

Levitating. I still couldn't wrap my brain around it and I

knew denying what had happened wouldn't do me any good either. There was only one solution. I needed to talk to the staff at the BODO and find out what was happening to me.

I took the book out of the safe and put it in my shoulder bag. Then I went to the kitchen to make a cup of coffee and grab a Rice Krispies Treat out of the pantry. As I overloaded on sugar and caffeine to get my brain back online, I glanced at the clock. Assuming Eloise meant what she'd said last night, she'd be here to go to the Museum of Literature in half an hour. I took my power breakfast into the bedroom to get dressed.

According to the weather app on my phone, it was going to be cool and clear, so I wore black tights and a black wool skirt with a deep purple cashmere sweater over a white collared blouse. I wrestled my hair into a messy bun at the nape of my neck and secured it with several bobby pins. I glanced at my reflection. Functional and professional—it would do.

I returned to the living room, pulled the chair out from under the door handle, and placed it back in its position at the dining table in front of the bay window. In the light of day, it seemed a bit ridiculous to have done that, but in my defense, Eloise had caught me off guard. For a person who hated disorder, I was getting hit hard and fast by an overabundance of mayhem.

I glanced at the door. I wondered if the raven was out there. That was another odd happening, but maybe the bird's appearance in my life really was just a coincidence. Either way, it couldn't hurt to check.

I unlocked the door and pulled it open, bracing myself. It

was unnecessary. No one was there. Even the raven had left my mailbox. I stepped forward and glanced at my wicker chairs, then jumped.

"Good morning, dear." Eloise beamed at me. "Did you have a good sleep?"

8

"Eloise, have you been sitting in that chair all night?" I asked.

"Yes." She nodded.

"You could have frozen to death out here." I stared at her in horror, but she looked exactly as she had the day before, without a hair of her precisely coiffed ash-blond bob out of place.

"No, I wouldn't, silly." She waved a hand at me. "I'm already dead, remember? I don't need to sleep, and I don't feel the cold, or anything, for that matter."

Again with this. I refused to debate whatever she believed about her current state of being. I operated in verifiable facts. "If you don't feel the cold, then why do you wear a coat?" I asked.

"Because people would talk, dear. The key to being undead among the living is to blend in."

I resisted rolling my eyes. Barely. I was certain she'd left last night and had just returned very early this morning. Fine. Whatever.

"Can I get you a cup of coffee?" This was the big test. No one, not even a delusional zombie, could resist a hot cup of coffee in this frigid weather.

"I don't need to eat or drink either." Eloise smiled patiently as if I were thick and she was confident I'd catch on eventually.

"How can you survive without sustenance?" I protested. I braced myself for her to say she drank the blood of naughty children or something else equally horrifying.

Instead, her smile was kind and she said, "Magic."

Naturally. Years of resisting all things otherworldly made me want to dismiss her words, but after opening a book with my own blood, seeing a metaphorical heart encased in a book, and levitating last night, I couldn't. Still, the word *magic* made my skin prickle and I was filled with unease. "I'm just going to finish my coffee and grab my coat and then we can go see those people I mentioned yesterday. I'll be right back."

Eloise nodded and turned to stare at the road in front of my house. I followed her gaze and saw the raven land neatly on my mailbox, where he turned his head and gave me a watchful stare. I found this oddly reassuring, especially since today had turned into take-your-dead-person-to-work day.

The quiet car on the train was full on this trip, so we sat in a different one, which was unfortunate, as Eloise was very chatty during the entire ride. Not with me, but rather with every other passenger in the vicinity. She asked where they'd bought their shoes, what streaming shows they were watching, why they were going to New York City, et cetera. Shockingly, most of the passengers responded politely and only two refused to engage.

A businessman, judging by his suit, got up and moved to another car and a young woman, who was clearly studying, met Eloise's gaze and put large, sound-muffling headphones on. Eloise did not seem offended in the least. Perhaps believing she was dead made her less sensitive to criticism and slights from others.

I hailed a cab—not the same driver as before, which was a pity. This one seemed in no hurry and we meandered through the city streets until we finally arrived at the museum. I nodded a hello at the security guard Tina with the Taser and went to enter, but Eloise stopped to chat, because of course she did.

"Hello, I'm Eloise Tate." She held out her hand.

Tina gave her an assessing look before she shook her hand. "Hi."

"We're just going to pop in for a minute to speak with . . . someone." I didn't say a name because I didn't really know who could help me with this situation.

"I know. The director is expecting you in her office."

I frowned and then nodded. "Of course."

Tina adjusted the utility belt around her waist and patted her Taser. "You'd better get a move on. Sebastian told me to send you up right away."

My eyes went wide. For no discernible reason, this sounded ominous. "Thanks. This way, Eloise."

I turned and entered the building, leaving Eloise to follow. As we stepped inside, I saw the library and briefly remembered meeting the darkly handsome Jasper Griffin. I shook my head, refusing to be distracted from my purpose. I crossed the dark entry and led the way to the staircase. I glanced at Eloise and noted that she was taking in the opulent surroundings with a wide-eyed gaze. I imagined that was exactly what I'd looked like yesterday. Yesterday. Had it only been twenty-four hours since I'd been here? It felt like a week had passed.

At the top of the stairs, the portrait of the Stewarts greeted us. They looked just as in love as I remembered and I felt a little pang in my chest. This museum was dedicated to the preservation of literature and I feared that by bringing in a family grimoire locked by a blood oath and a potentially undead woman, I was committing an affront to all that the couple had built here.

I glanced down the hallway and took a steadying breath. I had to focus on my purpose. If what Eloise had told me was true, then the only people I knew who could help me to help her were the staff members of the BODO. But if Eloise was some deranged prankster, then I was banking on Olive, with her deathly pallor and new-moon-at-midnight fashion sense to frighten Eloise into realizing she was not undead and needed to get over her fixation on my grandmother. Immediately.

We walked to the end of the hallway. One of the glass doors was propped open by a painted iron statue of a mythical faun holding a set of panpipes. I hadn't noticed him yesterday and I wondered at his sudden appearance. I frowned as I entered the office.

"A gift from one of our benefactors," Sebastian explained, correctly interpreting my expression. "I usually keep him hidden in the closet because he looks like he's up to no good." He rose from behind his desk and walked around it to greet us. When I turned to check that Eloise was following me into the office, I saw the faun snap its teeth at her as she passed by. Without breaking her stride, she flicked its ear.

I pressed my cold fingers to my forehead. Everything was fine. Nothing to see here.

"Good to see you again, Ms. Ziakas." Sebastian stopped in front of me.

"Please, call me Zoe." I dropped my hand and forced a smile. "This is . . . uh . . . an acquaintance of mine, Eloise Tate. Eloise, this is Sebastian Hanover."

I gestured to Eloise as she stepped into the office, her gaze darting around the room as she took in the elegant furnishings and Sebastian, who was as well turned out as he'd been yesterday in an olive-and-cream-pin-striped dress shirt over linen pants paired with dark brown leather loafers and a matching belt.

"A pleasure to meet you," she said. "Are you the director of the museum?"

Sebastian laughed. "No, I'm entirely too fainthearted for that sort of work. Our director is Claire Carpenter. She's waiting for you in her office." He gestured to the closed doors behind his desk. "Please, follow me."

After a gentle knock, he opened the doors and we followed Sebastian into Claire's office. She was seated behind her desk in front of the windows. I had a flash of déjà vu as I stepped into the spectacular office, but I shook it off. This was not a repeat of yesterday, as I had Eloise with me.

Claire stood and beamed at the sight of me. It was impossible not to return her smile given the genuine warmth that lit her eyes.

"Zoe, it's good to see you again." She gestured to the love seat. "Won't you and your companion have a seat?"

I noticed that a couple of chairs had been added to the sitting area, confirming that she'd been expecting us. I led the way to the love seat and Eloise followed.

"May I bring you a refreshment?" Sebastian asked.

"No, thank you," Eloise answered. She sank onto the love seat and demurely crossed her legs at the ankles.

Sebastian glanced at me and I shook my head and said, "No, thanks."

"I'm just outside if you change your mind." With a nod to Claire, he left, keeping the door open between their offices.

Claire sat on the armchair beside mine and looked at me expectantly. My manners kicked in and I said, "Right, sorry. Claire Carpenter, this is Eloise Tate."

Claire leaned forward and clasped Eloise's hand warmly in hers. Claire turned back to me and said, "Dare I hope that your return indicates that you've changed your mind about the position?"

"No, I'm afraid not," I said. "But I do need some expert advice from the staff of the BODO."

"Oh, all right." Claire looked disappointed but turned to face the open door.

"I've sent for them," Sebastian said before she could say a word.

"And that's why I can't do without him," Claire said. She glanced back at Eloise and me.

There was a tension in the room, probably because of me,

and I didn't know how to explain that the woman beside me believed she was dead and insisted that my grandmother had brought her back from the other side. Even though I'd been aware of magic all my life, most of it had been Agatha's gentle, comforting kitchen magic or the happy moments when my mom had made me laugh by making flowers dance or changing our dog's fur to colorful polka dots. Even Mamie's magic had been manageable to my child brain: catching rainbows with my hands and fashioning them into hair ribbons. Witchcraft had been fun and warm and lovely and then it had changed.

Unchecked magic had physically and emotionally injured my mother and tangentially killed my father, and the light and joy of it had been extinguished in me like a candle in the wind, leaving only pain and fear in the darkness that followed.

And now I was confronted with this? The witchcraft that Eloise was speaking of—necromancy—was terrifying. Bringing dead people back was next level and I was struggling to understand Mamie doing something like that. Instead, I asked the lesser question that was bothering me.

"Both Tina the security guard and Sebastian seemed to think you were expecting me, but how did you know I was coming today?" I asked.

Claire smiled and reached over to pat my knee. "I was being very optimistic and hoping to manifest your return. And here you are."

Somehow, this did not make me feel any better and I felt like there was something she wasn't telling me, but I let it go for the moment.

"Is there anything I can help with while we wait for the others?" Claire asked.

"I'd rather explain it just once," I said.

"Understandable." Claire nodded.

"You have a lovely museum," Eloise said. "You know, I lived in New York City for a few years back in the sixties and seventies."

"As a child?" Claire asked.

"Oh, no, I was in my twenties," Eloise said. "I lived on Christopher Street in the Village. It was all jazz clubs, shopping for leather bags at Hildegarde's, oh, and getting blessed by Rollerena."

Claire and I stared blankly at her.

Eloise smiled at us. "Rollerena was a man who rollerskated all over the Village in the early seventies, particularly in Washington Square Park. He was a hoot in his white wedding gown and carrying a wand." She glanced at me. "Your grandmother Toni and I got a real kick out of him. Of course, Toni was busy raising your mother, Juliet, so she didn't get to enjoy the city like I did. Pity."

Claire studied Eloise. I could see two frown lines deepening between her brows as she was clearly trying to figure out how Eloise, who didn't look a day over fifty-five, could possibly be old enough to have partied the night away in the sixties and seventies.

Claire looked at me in confusion, but I pressed my lips together and said nothing. This was Eloise's story to tell and I was not going to get more involved than I already was.

The room was silent except for the ticking of the antique pewter clock on the wall. It seemed inordinately loud and I was overly aware of it, as if each tick of the second hand signaled that something ominous was about to happen.

Olive strode into the room. She was dressed in a black tunic sweater and black leggings, over which she wore a crocheted black vest that was so long it almost reached her black Dr. Martens. Her hair was scraped back from her face and braided into a thick plait. The style accentuated her arching brows, deep-set eyes, sharp cheekbones, and square jaw.

Miles and Tariq followed her, looking much as they had the day before. Professionally dressed in dress shirts and pants but not in anything so remarkable that I would be able to remember it an hour from now. Not like Olive.

Olive's glance darted to me as she stood beside a vacant chair. One eyebrow, the one with the slit in it, rose in surprise. "Here to accept the job?"

"Um . . . no." I cleared my throat. What was it about this woman that intimidated me so? The feeling that she could kill me without hesitation and then suck the marrow out of my bones? Yeah, that, definitely that. "I . . . um . . . have an acquaintance I'd like you to meet."

Miles and Tariq looked from me to Eloise to Olive to Claire as if trying to figure out what was happening without any context clues.

"Eloise Tate, this is Olive Prendergast, Miles Lowenstein, and Tariq Silver. They work in— "

Claire shot me a cautionary glance and I remembered that Agatha had said the only reason I'd been allowed in the BODO was because I'd been vetted by her. I nodded before I continued, "—a special collection at the museum."

"How lovely." Eloise took them in one at a time.

Miles and Tariq took two of the available seats, but Olive didn't move. She didn't take her gaze off Eloise. She crossed her arms over her chest and her dark eyes narrowed as she asked, "How long?"

"Excuse me?" Eloise asked. She didn't even flinch under Olive's cold regard, for which I would have given her mad respect at any other time.

"How long have you been undead?" Olive held Eloise's gaze without blinking and I thought I might faint . . . again.

9

"How lovely of you to ask, dear." Eloise beamed at her. "Why, it's been—"

"No!" I cried. "No, no, no, no. This is not a thing. She is not deceased. This"—I paused to gesture at Eloise—"is not real. I brought her here for you to snap her back to reality, not to go along with her delusion."

Olive turned to look at me. She sank gracefully into one of the armchairs and said, "But she *is* dead."

"No, she isn't," I insisted. My teeth were gritted, but I couldn't help it. My jaw was clenched and no amount of deep breathing would loosen it. It was at that moment that I realized how deeply I'd been clinging to the notion that Eloise was a fraud.

Olive turned to Miles. "This confirms our speculation about Toni Donadieu."

"What speculation?" I demanded, even though I knew. They were now convinced that Mamie was a necromancer, with the skill the Donadieu coven was known for. I wanted to squeeze my temples with my fingers to push back the headache that was building.

Miles studied me from behind his glasses and his soft brown eyes were kind. "I imagine this is all a bit of a shock."

"No, it isn't, because she's wrong." I turned to Olive, who looked at me with a bored glance. "Why do you say she's undead? Why would you even think such a thing?"

"I have to admit I'm with Zoe on this," Claire said. "I certainly didn't suspect anything of the kind."

"That's because you have no magical ability," Olive said to Claire. It wasn't said meanly, just factually. Claire nodded, accepting Olive's blunt words without taking offense. "If you look closely, you'll note that Ms. Tate—"

"Oh, do call me Eloise, please." Eloise smiled even as she interrupted Olive. *She. Interrupted. Olive.* She was either very brave or very foolish. I wasn't sure which.

"*Eloise*"—Olive said her name with great emphasis—"is not breathing, for one thing. Living people require oxygen. Her pallor indicates there's no blood pumping through her heart to her extremities, and I suspect if we listen closely, she has no heartbeat. Lastly, there is a peppery smell about her, which indicates a very strong magic is binding her corpse—"

"I prefer *body*," Eloise interrupted again. This time, I decided she was definitely foolish and I was surprised the heat of Olive's glare didn't sear Eloise's hair to the roots. Olive closed her eyes for a moment.

"Of course you do," Olive acknowledged. "But that doesn't make it so. Your . . . vessel?" Olive asked, and Eloise nodded, agreeing to the term. "Your vessel is bound by a magic so strong it allows you to retain the form you had on the day you died."

"Quite right." Eloise turned to me. "Your grandmother was very powerful. It's just a shame she passed before she could return me to the other side."

I slumped forward, bending over my lap so I could stare at my shoes. This was not how this was supposed to go. I wanted to cry or punch something or run from the room as far and as fast as I could. None of these choices were a viable option.

I lifted my head and glanced at Olive and then Miles. "I need your help to send Eloise . . . on."

Miles's expression was one of understanding while Olive looked annoyed and waved her hands at Eloise. "We can't help you with this."

I opened my mouth to protest, but Miles spoke first. "What Olive means is that you're the blood relative of Toni Donadieu, and since she is the one who brought Eloise back from the dead, you are the only one who can return her."

"But I can't," I said. "I don't even know what language the book is written in. I wouldn't even know how to go about decoding it."

"It's a shame there isn't an entire collection of books—a museum, if you will—devoted to the history of the written word nearby that you have access to," Olive said.

I decided right then and there that I did not like Olive Prendergast. I'm sure my feelings were evident in my expression, but she met my stare, clearly not caring what I thought of her.

Olive turned to Eloise. "Is that what you want? To walk on?"

"Is that even in question?" Eloise asked.

"Yes, it is," Olive said. "I've met my share of unfriendly undead and the last thing they wanted was to be sent on."

"I'm not like that," Eloise insisted. She turned to me. "You've known me for half a day. Would you say I'm an unpleasant undead?"

"Not that I've noticed," I admitted reluctantly.

"See?" Eloise asked Olive. "I'm just very, very tired. I've been waiting twenty-six years for someone to help me back through the veil." She turned to me and patted my hand. "I spent several years trying to find Juliet, following the magic of the grimoire, but then the magic just disappeared and so did Juliet, leaving you behind at school. Once you had the grimoire in your possession, I felt its power return, just like when Toni had it."

"Looks like it's up to you." Olive stared at me. Her tone didn't invite dissent.

"No, you don't understand. It *can't* be me." I jumped to my feet. "I made a promise—a vow—that I would never use magic and I won't break it. Not for anyone."

"Who would ask—" Miles began, but I interrupted him.

"I don't want to talk about it."

The entire room went silent while I tried to catch my breath. I could feel their eyes on me while my gaze flitted around the room, avoiding contact with anyone. Suddenly everyone turned to face the doorway just as I sensed someone had entered the room behind me.

I turned and a flush of embarrassment warmed my face as I recognized Jasper Griffin and knew he'd witnessed my mini meltdown. Still, I refused to look away when his light blue gaze locked on mine.

Claire rose from her seat in surprise. "Jasper, when did you get here?"

"Just now. Sorry to interrupt." He didn't look at her but kept his focus on me.

"Good to see you, Griffin," Miles said. "Successful recon last night?"

"Very." He strode across the room toward us, still holding my gaze as he approached.

"Zoe, you remember Jasper Griffin," Claire reintroduced us.

"Of course." I glanced away, finally breaking the connection. "And this is Eloise Tate." I gestured between them. "Jasper Griffin."

"And what do you do here, Mr. Griffin?" Eloise asked as she clasped his hand in hers.

"Jasper is the BODO's field operative in charge of containment," Miles explained.

I let that sink in. "I take that to mean Mr. Griffin is the person you call when everything goes to shit."

Jasper's eyebrows lifted and he chuckled low and deep, his amusement crinkling the corners of his eyes. He did not, however, correct me and I wondered if *I* was now the "shit."

"Do call me Jasper. Good to see you again, Zoe. Nice to meet you, Ms. Tate."

"Eloise, please," Eloise said with a polite smile.

"Eloise it is," Jasper agreed. He turned to me and asked, "Did you get your secret mission sorted, Zoe?"

"More or less. It's not much of a secret now." I gestured to the group.

"Zoe, if it will ease your mind, Tariq can take Eloise for a full medical workup if she agrees to it," Miles suggested.

I turned from Jasper and faced the group, trying to ignore the way his deep, accented voice had said my name. It took me a second to process what Miles had said.

"Yes, please, I think that would be wise." What I didn't say was that I was desperately hoping that Eloise wasn't who or what she said she was. Given the events of the past few days, it was a long shot, no question, but before I broke my vow of no witchcraft, I wanted to know precisely what I was dealing with.

"Would that be all right with you, Ms. Eloise?" Miles asked.

"Just Eloise is fine." She simpered a bit under his regard, but no color filled her cheeks. She was just as pale as she'd been when I'd first met her.

"Will this make you feel better, dear?" Eloise asked me.

I met her gaze and felt like an absolute jerk. She looked so innocent, like a lost little kid just trying to find her family. Still, I nodded, not trusting myself to speak. The librarian in me, who operated in citable sources and verifiable truths, needed proof, otherwise I would always have doubts about going back on my word to my mother.

"All right, then." To her credit, Eloise didn't hesitate.

"If you'll follow me." Tariq gestured to the door. "I promise to make it as quick as possible."

As soon as they left the room, I turned to Olive. Her face was impassive, expressionless per usual, and I had the horrifying thought that perhaps she had recognized Eloise so easily because she was similar. As in, maybe the reason Olive came across as so cold and unfeeling was because she was undead herself. I didn't know how to ask that, so instead I asked, "How certain are you?"

She didn't ask what I was talking about. She just shrugged. Her dark gaze was bored when it met mine. "As I said, I've met my share of undead before. Eloise has the same look about her. If you look closely, you'll notice there's something not quite right."

"Like the lack of actual breathing?" Claire asked. Her voice held the tiniest note of sarcasm, but Olive just bobbed her head in accord.

I felt as if I were being sucked down into quicksand. If this was real, if Eloise was truly undead and Mamie had been the one to bring her back, I didn't know how I could manage to live with breaking my word to my mom. It had taken up a sacred space in my heart as the last thing I'd been able to do for her before she'd left me. Going back on that promise, given her recent death, felt wrong on a soul-deep level. With that thought, I reached into my shoulder bag and retrieved the book.

10

"I want you to keep this," I said. I held out the volume to Claire. She didn't take it. Neither did Miles or Olive when I shifted toward them. "Please."

"This is quite a change in attitude from yesterday, Ziakas," Olive said, addressing me by my last name. She crossed her arms over her chest. "Weren't you determined to sort the situation yourself?"

Miles shot her a chastising glance. "Tell us about meeting Eloise. How did that come about?"

"She knocked on my door," I said. "After I was terrorized by a single-minded raven who would not get off my porch—I swear it was watching me—"

Jasper broke into a fit of coughing, and I paused, waiting for him to be okay before I continued.

"Anyway, when I finally shooed the bird away, there was a thump on the porch, and I opened my door to find Eloise standing there."

Claire took my arm and led me back to the love seat. Olive and Miles resumed their seats in the armchairs, and Jasper took the chair Tariq had vacated. I felt them all watching me expectantly, so I told them everything I'd learned from Eloise the prior evening, from Mamie being the one who had brought Eloise back from the dead to Eloise's belief that Mamie had been murdered. That was where I paused.

"What else, Zoe?" Claire prodded gently. "What else did Eloise tell you?"

I took a deep breath. I could feel their scrutiny and I wondered if they would think I'd gone mad. I glanced down at the book in my hands. I hadn't opened it since my visit yesterday. Perhaps it was my overactive imagination or maybe it was everything I'd learned about the book, but I could swear I felt it thrum low and deep in my hands. Like a cat sitting on the lap of its chosen person, the grimoire had a strange sort of contentment emanating from it. I hastily put it on the table in front of me, wanting to put some distance between me and it.

I spoke slowly, forcing out the words I didn't want to speak. "Eloise said that my mother murdered my grandmother and stole the book and that someone then murdered my mother for the same reason." My throat was tight, my voice rough. I rejected this narrative with every bit of my soul and I knew my voice conveyed as much. "It's not true. My mother didn't murder my grandmother."

"That must have been a lot for you to take in." Claire's voice was kind and I felt my clenched shoulders ease in response to her empathy.

"And now Eloise wants you to send her on," Miles said.

"Yes, but I can't. I can't decipher the book. I have no idea where to begin. Also, I'm not cut out for whatever all this is. Frankly, I don't want to have anything to do with it." I pushed the grimoire across the table. I don't think I imagined that it resisted me like a child digging in its heels, refusing to leave the playground. I stopped pushing and it sat in the center, its silver hexagon and engraved band catching the light against its dark matte cover.

"Forgive me, Zoe." Jasper glanced at me apologetically. "But it seems to me that if Eloise found you, then whoever potentially murdered your mother—assuming that's true—will come looking for you and that grimoire. And I don't think they're going to ask for it nicely."

I glared at him. I decided I didn't like this ridiculously good-looking man with all his well-reasoned arguments.

"Jasper's right," Claire said. "You could be in danger whether you have the book in your possession or not."

I stared at the grimoire. What was I supposed to do? Eloise and the grimoire were tapping into memories and emotions from my childhood that I had tucked away in the *Things Never to Be Dealt With* file and I resented them mightily for it. I stood and backed away from the table until I was standing in between Miles's and Jasper's chairs. I wanted out of there. I wanted to go home, back to my quiet life.

"Please take the book," I pleaded. My voice was low, just above a whisper, when I added, "Burn it, lock it up, put it through a paper shredder. I don't care. I never want to see it again."

I should have been prepared. I wasn't. The headache, when it came, was so swift and fierce it felt as if someone had split my cranium in two. I cried out and clapped my hands to my head. I managed to stagger two steps back before I heard a shout and crumpled into someone's arms.

When I awoke on the couch, I found Tariq seated in the chair beside me with his magical diffuser puffing its aromatic mist over me. His smile widened when I blinked awake, and he said, "We must stop meeting like this, Zoe."

I forced my lips to curve up, but it was an effort.

"How's your headache?" His smile vanished, wiped away by an expression of concern.

"It's better," I said. It was. Lingering stabs darted across my skull, but I could manage them.

I glanced past him at the table. The book was exactly where I'd left it. Surprisingly, I didn't feel any malevolence coming from the tome; rather it felt more like reproach. I glanced away. Despite my love of books, I had never considered them sentient beings, but the bizarre events of the past few days were causing me to rethink that.

I swung my legs off the couch and Tariq helped me sit up. I glanced over my shoulder to see Miles and Olive in the corner in conversation with Eloise while Claire and Jasper hovered nearby, looking as if they'd been watching me. I felt my face get warm. I'd blacked out twice in front of the museum director. In front of a professional woman I admired. It was straight-up humiliating.

"How are you feeling, Zoe?" Claire joined us.

"Mortified." I blew out a breath. "I know I fell on someone and I'm so sorry."

"Not at all," Jasper assured me.

"It was you." Of course it had been Jasper I'd landed on.

Why swooning into the arms of a hot British guy was worse than face-planting on Olive, I couldn't say. It just was. I stood on shaky legs, wishing I could flee the scene, but a wary glance at the book had me reconsidering. "I swear I've never fainted in my life until yesterday. And now today. I'm so embarrassed."

"There's no need." Jasper shook his head. "I'm just glad I was there to break your fall." He glanced from me to the table, his pale blue eyes contemplative. "Clearly, the book has already formed an attachment to you."

I would have scoffed and called that preposterous, but the evidence was damning. Any time I tried to part company with the book, I was hit with a scorching headache and I blacked out. I wondered if my grimoire was going to sprout a tail, eyes, and ears like the Freya book in the BODO. That would certainly make it easier for me to bond with it.

"Zoe, Jasper was right when he said whoever is after that book will come for you," Claire said. "I genuinely believe you're in danger."

I probably should have been scared, but all I felt was irritated. Annoyed that someone was messing with my very calm, very controlled, very orderly life.

"I want to help you." Claire put her hand on my forearm and gave it a gentle squeeze before she let go. "We have several safe places in the city where you can stay until we determine who might come after you and the book."

My eyes went wide. Leave my home in Wessex? My job? My life? Nope. Nuh-uh. I was not doing that. I didn't care who came after me. "There's no need," I said. "If someone comes for the grimoire, I'll—" I stopped talking. I had been about to say that I'd give it to them gladly, but I caught myself. I didn't want to suffer from another brain-crushing headache and I didn't want to faint.

"You'll what?" Jasper raised one arching black brow in question. I suspected he knew what I'd been about to say.

"I'll deal with it," I said. It sounded lame even to me, but really, what else could I say? I was not giving up the peaceful life I loved. No way, no how. Desperately wanting to change the subject, I glanced at Tariq and caught his gaze, then I jutted my chin in the direction of Eloise. "What did you find out?"

I wanted him to say, *She's a fraud. She's as alive as you and me.* But he didn't.

"She is exactly what she says she is." Tariq stood and walked toward us with his mouth set in a grim line. "She's dead—very, very dead. Or undead—very, very undead. However you want to look at it."

I shook my head. "How is that possible?"

"Magic," Claire said.

She, Tariq, and Jasper surveyed me with varying degrees of sympathy. They had expected this outcome. I was the only one who'd been holding out hope for a different answer. I felt a surge of anger rise up inside me and I knew, like most anger, it came from a place of fear. I didn't want to betray the promise I'd made to my mother and I resented that I was being forced to do just that. Frankly, I was terrified of magic and witchcraft and the heartache it had caused in my life. I'd been clinging to the promise I'd made my mother, because it had kept me safe from myself all these years.

"Eloise, tell me the truth," I demanded.

"I have." She held her hands wide as if to show her innocence.

"No, you haven't," I argued. "Why me? Why do *I* have to help you? Why can't you just die again?"

"Because her vessel is bound by magic," Olive said. "She can't die again. I thought we covered this. Just because you don't like something doesn't mean you can deny it out of existence."

"Can't I?" I cried. I noted that both Tariq and Miles looked nervous, but Olive looked even more bored, which was a much bigger insult than if she'd gotten angry.

"Zoe, I found Eloise's obituary." Tariq moved to stand beside me. "It all checks out. She died thirty-four years ago in the same Pennsylvania town she was born in. I printed it out so you could read it. See? She looks just like her picture."

Tariq held out a sheet of paper. I glanced at it. It was a digitized photo of the original newspaper from 1991. I glanced at the entry he pointed to. Sure enough, the same ash-blond bob and guileless smile peered out at me from the paper. The photo next to the name *Eloise Tate* was of the woman standing in front of me.

I glanced up at undead Eloise and said, "I'm sorry, but I can't help you."

Eloise looked crushed and lifted her hand to tuck her hair behind her ear. As I watched, her ear fell off. *Her. Ear. Fell. Off.*

Being the unflappable professional that I was, I screamed as her ear bounced across the carpet to stop at my feet. I stopped shrieking and stared stupidly at the ear on the floor.

"Well, shoot!" Eloise opened her handbag and crouched in front of me. She snatched the ear off the carpet and tucked it into her bag. She stood and smoothed her clothes, as if not having any creases made up for missing an ear.

I swallowed. It went down hard, and I felt myself sway on my feet.

"Steady there." Jasper stepped forward and grasped my elbow, supporting me when I just wanted to slide down to the floor. Suddenly, being unconscious seemed like a lovely state to be in.

I glanced at the faces around us, noting that their expressions ranged from curious to wary but not surprised. "You saw that, right? You saw her ear land on the floor, yes? And there was no blood, no gore, just her *EAR* on the carpet."

"We did." Miles nodded, as if this wasn't the most insane thing that had ever happened.

"I'm so sorry," Eloise said. "I have no idea why this has started happening."

Olive's head snapped in her direction, and she tapped her chin with her index finger as she considered the undead woman. "This has happened before?"

Eloise sighed. She nodded reluctantly and held up her right hand. Her pinkie was missing. How had I not noticed that? Then she held back the hair on the other side of her head. She had no ear on that side of her head either.

"I'm also missing a toe. I started losing body parts shortly after Juliet was mur— Er . . . died," Eloise said.

"Interesting." Miles pushed his glasses up on his nose. He and Olive glanced at each other as if to confirm that they were thinking the same thing. They nodded in unison.

"It's just a theory, but I suspect it's because Juliet didn't have the gift of necromancy, but Ziakas might," Olive said. "While Juliet was alive and the book was in her possession, the spells cast by Toni remained intact because Juliet didn't have the ability to reverse them, but once the book was passed to Ziakas, any spells cast by Toni using the grimoire are now weakening because Ziakas does have the ability." She cast me a doubtful look. "Potentially."

"But why would Mamie's spells weaken because of me?" I asked.

"I don't know for certain, not without more research," Miles said. "But at a guess, I would say Olive's right. Now that the book is in your possession, the magic that your grandmother used to bind Eloise to her vessel is weakening as the book bonds to you. You will have to either recast the spell that brought her back from the beyond or send her on," Miles said.

"I'm going to have to decipher the book, aren't I?" I could feel the panic spiral starting to swirl inside me.

"Yes," Olive said. She made it sound like *duh*. I chose to ignore her.

"What if I can't do it?" I cried. "What if Eloise starts falling apart at a rapid rate and she's just a pile of body parts while I'm flitting around trying to figure out what sort of language the book is written in?"

"Oh, I wouldn't like that." Eloise shook her head. "Not at all."

"We'll help you, Zoe," Miles said. His voice was soft but assured, as if he were talking me back from the edge of a precipice. "You're not alone in this."

Olive shot him a skeptical look, which he ignored.

I raised my hands in exasperation. "I don't even know where to start. I have a job with responsibilities in Wessex and I can't take care of Eloise. I mean, I don't even know how to take care of a dead person. Oh God, I can't believe I just said that." There was a minor note of hysteria in my voice that I was powerless to stop.

Claire cleared her throat. "I think that is my area of expertise."

I glanced at her in doubt. "Handled a lot of ancient grimoires and their accompanying dead people, have you?"

I heard Jasper chuckle but didn't dare turn to look at him. I would not be distracted from my anxiety spinout by a handsome face.

Claire smiled at me. "Amazingly, managing the upper crust of New York is not that different; people are people, dead or otherwise."

I knew she was trying to make me feel better and I desperately wanted to buy in, but I needed some specifics. "What do you propose to do?"

"First, I will speak with your boss in Wessex," Claire said. "We will coordinate a work exchange program, sending one of our librarians to fill your position while you work here. This will give you time and access to all our resources while you translate the book."

I nodded. "That could work."

"Of course it will," Claire said. "In the meantime, we will set Eloise up in one of the safe houses and give her a job in the BODO so she's nearby when you crack the code."

"You're very optimistic about that," I said.

"Confident," Claire corrected me. "I'm very confident."

I wished I were.

"Zoe, I know you said you didn't think a safe house was necessary for you, but I think you should reconsider," Jasper said. "You don't know who might be out there searching for the book."

Tariq nodded. "What he said."

I turned to Eloise. "You said that my mother murdered my grandmother to get the family grimoire and that someone then murdered my mother for the same reason, but you never said who you thought murdered my mother."

"Well, that's because I don't know who," Eloise said. "I assumed she was murdered for the grimoire because of its potential power. There are a lot of witches who wouldn't hesitate to kill for the spells in that book. Of course, they might not have known that they needed a witch from the Donadieu line to be able to open the book and decipher the spells."

"If that's true, then it seems to me that whoever murdered my mother also murdered my grandmother," I said. "Because I know my mother would never ever do such a thing." This was my case-closed voice. If Eloise wanted my help, I would not tolerate any insinuation that my mother was a murderer and a thief.

Eloise studied me for a beat and then nodded. "As you say." Message received.

I glanced at the others and spoke with what I hoped sounded like the voice of authority. "We're making quite an assumption that my grandmother and my mother were murdered.

Until I have solid evidence, I'm going to remain in my house. I'll come here every day, of course, but I'm not giving up my home."

I must have sounded more badass than I thought, because they all slowly nodded and even though Claire looked worried, she didn't argue with me.

11

Claire went to her office to arrange the job swap, and I headed to the Books of Dubious Origin department to start my first day. Miles led me through the magicked doors while Jasper escorted Eloise. Tariq and Olive entered on their own.

"If you become a permanent member of our team, I'll teach you the way of the doors," Miles said as we entered the special collection.

I dropped his arm and turned to face him. "Is that a bribe?"

"Would it work?"

I smiled. "No."

"Then it's just a fact." His expression was chagrined.

"What if I only have basic abilities?" I asked. "Meaning, what if I'm not necromancer-level powerful?"

Miles shook his head. "Like calls to like, Zoe. The grimoire found you precisely because of your power."

"Did it?" I frowned "Or was it delivered to me purposefully?"

"It opened for you." Miles's tone was decisive, as if that was the end of the discussion for him. It was just as well since, having woken up eight inches from my ceiling, I had no rebuttal.

"Are you ready to radiocarbon-date your book?" Tariq asked me.

I blinked in surprise. "Just like that?"

Tariq shrugged. "It might help you sort out where to begin with the translating."

"Good point."

"Jasper, we need to discuss your current project," Miles said. There was a slight hesitation before he said *project*, and I wondered if he was choosing his words more carefully since Eloise and I were present.

"Right. Lots to report." Jasper's gaze lingered on me, and I would have thought he was referring to me, but that would be ridiculous. Miles had said he was a field operative in charge of containment. Other than the arrival of Eloise on my doorstep, which I felt I had managed just fine all things considered, there wasn't much to contain.

"That leaves you with me," Olive said to Eloise. I saw Eloise shift on her feet and found it oddly comforting that even a woman who'd been dead for more than thirty years found Olive intimidating. "This way."

Eloise shot us a nervous glance and Tariq said, "Don't worry. She doesn't bite unless you give her a reason to."

Eloise's eyes went wide and Olive snapped over her shoulder, "I can hear you, Silver."

"I know," Tariq chirped, looking unrepentant.

As Eloise followed Olive, I turned to Tariq, keeping my

voice low. "Baiting Olive? Do you also play with matches and run with scissors?"

"I can hear you, too, Ziakas," Olive cried.

I jumped and Tariq chuckled. "You'll get used to her."

He turned and led the way to the lab, sparing me from having to correct him. I was positive that even if I came back from the dead like Eloise, I would never not be afraid of Olive.

The lab was empty when Tariq and I entered. I took the book out of my bag. It felt solid in my hands. I had no idea what Tariq would have to do to it and I felt a pang of protectiveness toward the grimoire. I frowned. No, no, no. I wasn't concerned with this particular book. I was a librarian by trade. I would have felt this mindful about any book in my charge.

"What do you have to do to date it?" I tried to sound professional, but my voice slid up in pitch, revealing my concern.

Tariq smiled and reached over to pat my shoulder. "Don't worry. I only need a tiny sample, about five millimeters in size. When you open it, we can look for a dried-out fragment that's loose. I promise I will not harm your family's grimoire."

"It's not—" I began, but Tariq interrupted me.

"Zoe." His voice was gently chiding. "Whatever we discover, it's going to be all right, yes?"

"Okay." I put the book on the steel table, feeling as if I were offering up my child for circumcision.

"Everything getting sorted in here?" Jasper strode into the room, pausing beside me at the steel table. I didn't think I imagined that the cold room was suddenly warmer and smaller than it had been just moments before.

"Yes. In fact, you're just in time," Tariq said. "Zoe is about to open the book."

Jasper's eyes glinted with interest. "Brilliant. Miles told me it was rather dramatic."

"Speaking of Miles, I thought you were in a meeting with him." It wasn't that I didn't want Jasper there . . . Well, truthfully, it was exactly that I didn't want him there.

"I was," Jasper said. "But he received a call that required privacy, so here I am."

I nodded. Of course. Because I wasn't already nervous enough, now I had to open the book with him watching me with those startlingly pale eyes from beneath those perfectly arched brows. Fabulous.

"Go ahead, Zoe. I'll prepare my equipment." Tariq handed me a first aid kit before crossing the room to his mass spectrometer.

The small metal box had a surgical needle in it. It was packaged, which I assumed meant it was sterilized. This was actually welcome, as the nick on my finger had just started to heal and I didn't want to pick the scab to draw blood.

I blew out a breath, thinking how appropriate it was that an inherited artifact was making me bleed. It was the cherry on top of the three-scoop sundae of neglect, family secrets, and emotional distance that had made up my familial relations over the last two decades.

Overly aware of Jasper watching me, I used my thumb to press my middle finger until it was red, then I stabbed it. I felt him wince in sympathy, but I didn't look away from my purpose. The blood beaded up immediately and I moved my finger over the hexagonal lock. I let three drops land in the center before I moved my thumb over the pinprick, pressing on it to stop the bleeding.

I waited. Just as before, right when I thought nothing was going to happen, the medallion began to turn and the metal bands popped out.

"Bloody hell," Jasper muttered, and I couldn't have agreed more.

Again, I had the sensation of the book sighing in relief and I did, too.

"May I?" Jasper gestured to my hand. I nodded and he gently dabbed an antiseptic wipe from the first aid kit on the tip of my injured finger and then put a bandage securely around it.

"Thank you." My voice sounded stilted. I wasn't used to people helping me. It felt . . . odd.

In an effort to escape his perceptive gaze, I turned my attention to the book. I opened the cover, letting it lie flat. I flicked through the pages. I still didn't recognize the symbols. I had no idea what the dark brown ink was made of. I supposed it depended on how old the book was. I did note that the parchment in the beginning of the book felt very different from the pages in the middle and the end. They had a different weight and texture to them.

Jasper lowered his tall frame so that his elbows rested on the steel table. He didn't touch the book, but I glanced at him and saw his eyes scanning the page as if looking for something, anything, that he might recognize. His frown deepened and I knew he was just as stumped as the rest of us.

"We need to collect any loose fragments," I said. "Just five millimeters in size for the carbon dating."

"Seems simple enough," Jasper said. He grabbed a pair of tweezers and an empty vial out of the first aid kit. "Lead on."

This seemed like a terrible idea, since I had no idea what I was doing. I glanced back at the book. Unlike yesterday, when I had been completely freaked-out, today I felt as if I was finally seeing the book for what it was. A mysterious little tome, full of strange symbols on a variety of parchment and paper types. This made me pause.

Why would the creator of the grimoire have used different materials? I picked up the book and studied the hand stitching at the top of the spine. Several tiny bits of dried parchment fluttered to the tabletop.

"Well done, Zoe. That certainly made it easy," Jasper said.

I watched as he carefully tweezed the little bits and dropped them into the vial. I could feel the heat of him as his side was pressed against mine. It was a welcome warmth in the cold lab, but I refused to be distracted by it or him.

I put the book down and examined the cover. The calfskin and the Celtic-style lock seemed newer than the painfully fragile parchment used in the beginning of the book. It occurred to me that if what everyone believed was true and this was a family grimoire, then it could have been handed down through the ages, and perhaps whoever had bound it together had done so decades, potentially centuries, after the first pages had been written.

I flipped the pages. The ink changed color halfway through, the brown turning into black and remaining that color until the end. Despite this change, the pages were still handwritten and consistently used the same symbols, but it was definitely a different hand doing the writing. Several different hands, I suspected. I wondered how many Donadieu witches had contributed to the book. Had it been passed mother to daughter? Or grandmother to granddaughter?

"Oh, there's another one." Jasper tweezed up another fragment. This one was larger than the others and I felt my anxiety spike. I didn't want the book to crumble under my inexperienced hands.

"It's all right," Jasper's deep voice crooned. "You're doing just fine."

I tried to ignore the flash of awareness I felt. I was certain every woman alive between the age of nineteen and ninety would feel the same thing in his presence. It meant nothing.

I studied the book as a whole. There was a feminine energy about it. Maybe it was the precise way the cipher was written, like a handwritten recipe card for carrot cake you'd get from your favorite aunt. The symbols were softened with little flourishes and embellishments and what looked like notes in the margins—exactly like if an aunt had added little bits of wisdom to her recipe. Interesting.

"Any luck finding a fragment?" Tariq asked as he returned to the table.

"We found several," Jasper said. "There were loose bits in every segment of the book."

"Excellent." Tariq beamed. "Which one do you want to use?"

"All of them," I said.

His eyebrows rose in surprise.

"After looking more closely at it, I suspect this grimoire was bound centuries after the first pages were written," I explained. "Judging by the difference in the feel of the pages, the ink, and the handwriting, I think these were recipes handed down for generations."

"I'm sorry, did you say *recipes*?" Jasper asked.

"You know what I mean." I waved a dismissive hand at him, focusing on Tariq, who looked as if he was trying not to smile.

"Spells?" Jasper asked. "Don't tell me you can't say the word, Zoe."

"I can," I protested. Never mind that hearing him say my name in that deep voice of his with his delicious British accent made my brain fuzzy. I blinked, trying to focus. "I'm just more comfortable not saying it."

"Why not?" he asked. "It's a grimoire; that's what they're composed of—spells."

"It makes me uncomfortable." I knew my expression was pained, as if I was an introvert—not wrong—being forced to participate in a group activity and I just couldn't bear it—also not wrong. Technically, I could, I supposed, but that didn't mean I'd enjoy it.

"Why?" Jasper's eyebrows rose in surprise.

In that moment, I could have told them about the vow I'd made to my mother when I was fourteen, promising I would never practice magic, but the thought of sharing such a personal story made me cringe. I simply wasn't ready for that yet. Instead, I diverted.

"It's a long story, but I have a question for you both," I said.

Jasper inclined his head and Tariq nodded. "Go ahead."

"Have you ever heard of someone, hypothetically speaking of course, manifesting a visualization?"

Tariq cupped his chin with his hand. "Can you give me an example?"

I drummed my fingers on the steel tabletop as I considered what to say. "What if a person used a relaxing meditation where they pictured their body floating and then, when they opened their eyes, they discovered they were many feet up in the air?"

"You levitated on a simple visualization?" Tariq's eyes went wide and he dropped his hand from his chin.

"I didn't say it was me."

Tariq and Jasper exchanged a look.

"How could that happen to a person who's never had anything out of the ordinary happen to them before?" I persisted.

"Meaning no previous evidence of any special magical abilities?" Tariq asked.

I nodded. I didn't include my memories of the things Mamie had taught me, because I honestly didn't know if those magical moments had been Mamie or me.

"How to explain . . ." Tariq blew out a breath.

"If you'll allow me?" Jasper asked.

Tariq waved his hand in acquiescence.

"Simply put," Jasper said, "it comes down to belief."

"I'm not following." I turned toward him, realized we were entirely too close for comfort, and scooted myself back a few inches.

"Think of magic as a living thing," he said. "All living things need sustenance."

I nodded. "Okay."

"Belief is the fuel required for magic to exist." He tapped the grimoire on the table. "Nothing written in here can manifest unless the witch using it believes it."

I pondered his words. "You mean magic is like getting gifts from Santa Claus. You have to believe to receive."

Tariq blinked and then laughed. "You are something, Zoe Ziakas. And yes, it's exactly like that."

Jasper huffed a laugh, but then his voice lowered and he said, "It would seem that whoever levitated during a visualization believes."

Maybe it was my childhood memories being dredged up or the fact that I was in possession of a book that opened all by itself when I bled on it, but yeah, there was no question. I believed. Damn it.

"How long will it take to date the samples?" I asked, wanting to change the subject.

"It'll take a few hours in the machine for each one." Tariq lifted the glass vial and studied the bits and pieces inside. "But then I have to do a data analysis, which could get complicated depending on what compounds we discover. I won't have a comprehensive report for you for a couple of days."

I sighed. I was not the most patient person and waiting a few days for an analysis of the grimoire was frustrating because there was nothing I could do—no research rabbit hole to jump in—to move it along.

"Come on, then." Jasper nudged me with his elbow. "I want to show you something."

I glanced at the volume on the table. Should I leave it

here? Take it with me? If I left the room, would I get a vicious headache and black out again?

"No one will touch the book," Tariq promised. "You can leave it in my care."

"All right." I stepped back from the table and the cover of the book slammed shut, making me jump. The metal bands locked into place in the hexagon as if the book were an old lady, primly tightening the belt on her bathrobe. Well, hell, what did that mean?

I glanced at Tariq and Jasper. They wore matching expressions of surprise. I was glad it wasn't just me. I cleared my throat and leaned down over the book. There was no way I could mask the awkwardness in my voice when I said, "I'll be right back. You don't have to blast me with a headache, okay?"

The latch on the book didn't move and I couldn't feel any emotion coming from it. Of course, it wasn't as if I expected it to do anything, but I suddenly appreciated the clear communication that came from Freya the cat-book or book-cat, however it identified itself. I hesitated.

Tariq met my gaze across the table. "You won't know unless you go."

I leaned down again. "I'll only be a minute. Seriously, you won't even miss me."

Again I felt nothing. Wait. That was exactly what I felt. Nothing. But not the nothing of no feeling; rather, it was the nothing from being shut out.

Straightening up, I said, "I think it's shunning me."

"Meaning you can go, but it's going to sulk when you return," Jasper said. "Sounds like a woman I once dated."

Tariq laughed, but I was a bit too freaked-out to find humor in the fact that I was talking to a book, having a sort of relationship with a book that went beyond reading it. This was bizarre on so many levels.

Jasper turned on his heel and led the way to the door. I glanced at Tariq, who made a shooing gesture with his hand. "Go. It'll be fine."

I turned and followed the well-muscled Brit, half expecting to be struck by cranial pain at any moment, but nothing happened. We stepped through the door into the main BODO library and I paused. I was fine. No headache. No blackout. It felt like a win.

Jasper was striding across the room toward one of the spiral staircases. I hurried after him, wondering what he could possibly plan to show me that would rival a book that had just shut and locked itself.

There were three stories in the BODO library and when we reached the top one, I found I was winded. Exercise had never been high on my list of priorities. Given the choice between jogging several miles or reading half a book, I'd choose the book every time. I realized I was going to have to recalibrate my thinking. If I had to climb these stairs every day while I worked on deciphering the book, I was going to get into shape whether I liked it or not.

"All right?" Jasper asked.

"Fine," I fibbed. I could hear the rasping of my breath in the stillness of the library and I attempted to stifle it, taking smaller, shallower breaths and trying to look as if I weren't about to keel over while I caught my breath.

Jasper's smile was a slash of white teeth. He was clearly

amused by my attempt to hide my lack of fitness. "If you're going to work here, you'll likely have to start using the gym on the premises. Some of our assignments require peak athleticism."

"I'm not going to work here." I shook my head. "This is a temporary job swap until I can figure out what happened to my mother and grandmother, decode the book, and send Eloise on."

"Why temporary?" he asked. "Why don't you want to work here?"

Good question. It was getting harder to answer with each passing day, so I went for the simple nonanswer. "It's complicated."

"So you've mentioned." He raised one eyebrow, inviting me to share more. I didn't.

"You wanted to show me something?"

"Quite right." He turned away, filling my vision with his broad shoulders, slim waist, and— I forced my gaze away. Just because they didn't grow them like this back at my public library didn't mean I had an excuse to ogle.

He turned in to one of the many alcoves made by the bookcases. "Miles filled me in on the theory about your grandmother being born into the famous Donadieu coven in France. I thought this section might be of interest to you."

He gestured to the shelf that was at eye level. My gaze narrowed. "These books are in French."

"Précisément." He bowed his head and I suspected he was testing me to see if I read French, which of course I did.

I turned and scanned the spines of the books. They reminded me of the grimoire I had left with Tariq, minus the metal bands and funky lock. I pulled one from the shelf. It was old and handwritten. There was a date at the top in the European style of day, month, year, with the month spelled out.

I scanned a random passage. My French was rusty but not so much that I didn't know what I was reading. I turned to Jasper and asked, "Was there a specific reason you felt I needed to research spells to enhance a man's virility?"

12

Jasper barked a laugh at my pointed glance. "It does not say that."

I held the book out to him, but he didn't take it. Instead, he leaned forward and read the passage over my shoulder. "Raw quail eggs and fermented pig's bollocks?"

"Don't forget the salt."

He made a gagging sound, which made me laugh. I turned to face him and found, again, that we were standing entirely too close. I took a not very subtle side step away from him. He tipped his head, watching me as if trying to determine the cause of my discomfort.

"Apologies if I crowded you," he said. "Sometimes I forget how big I am. I didn't mean to loom."

"No, it's fine." There was absolutely no way I was going to admit that it wasn't his height and broad shoulders so much as my awareness of *him* that had me stepping away. I wasn't accustomed to being in close proximity with men around my age. The most constant male in my life being my coworker Bill, and he was more like a funcle—a fun uncle.

Living in a small town didn't offer me a very large dating pool and when I considered it, I realized I hadn't dated in months and months, possibly over a year. I suspected my libido had been dormant until yesterday, when this freaking guy rolled into my orbit.

I shook the thought away and turned back to the bookshelf. "And you're showing me these books because?"

"This is our French collection of grimoires, journals, and histories, which includes several volumes about the Donadieu coven. I thought you might find these books helpful in your research. Maybe there's something that can assist your translation of your book." He tapped the volume in my hands. "Of course, if you need to use that spell on your boyfriend—"

It was my turn to laugh. It was as loud and jarring as gunfire. I cleared my throat. "Sorry, but there is no boyfriend."

"*Reeeeally?*" He drew out the one-word question as if savoring the information.

One thing became glaringly apparent, at least to me, and that was that this guy was so far out of my league I had no idea if he was flirting with me or not. Given our disparate levels of attractiveness, it seemed unlikely, but I was really bad at reading people, so the potential for embarrassment was at an all-time high.

I studied the glint in his pale blue eyes and the small smile that played on his lips. Flirting or friendly? I had no idea. Give me an entire calculus textbook to memorize—no problem. Ask me what my calculus professor was thinking judging by the expression on their face and I'd suffer a full-on brain hemorrhage.

I turned back to the bookcase—because books I understood—and began to pull volumes that I thought might be helpful. Since Mamie was a Donadieu and from France, I agreed with Jasper that the best place to start my quest to crack the code of the grimoire was with contextual and historical research centered on the Donadieu coven. Then I would have to do a symbol analysis of the code used, comparing it to known alphabets and historical systems.

These French books would hopefully give me the cultural clues I was seeking. Somewhere there had to be a reference to the point of origin for the symbols used in the Donadieu grimoire, and I was going to find it. The familiar old thrill of researching a particularly thorny information request filled my soul and I left the stacks with a decided bounce in my step.

Cradling my armful, I turned toward the stairs. Jasper stood in my path and when I went to walk around him, he plucked the books out of my arms and turned to lead the way.

Unsure of what to do with my hands, I tucked them into my pockets until we reached the spiral staircase and I grabbed the railing. As we walked by what I now recognized as the ancient Norse section, I looked for the fuzzy gray book, but there was no sign of Freya. Was someone using her or had she left on her own? She was a book with catitude, so I assumed the latter.

When we reached the bottom floor, I saw a movement out of the corner of my eye. It was Eloise standing in front of the collection of horrible books Olive had shown me the day before.

She was holding her hands clasped in front of her chest. I wondered if she was praying. I certainly couldn't blame her if the malevolence coming from the books caused that response.

I remembered the vision I'd had of a beating heart encased in ice trying to punch its way out of the book Olive had called *El Corazón*. Was Eloise having a similar vision? Did she feel the same tendrils of evil reaching out from the books as if trying to find purchase outside their cloth and leather bindings? In Eloise's undead state, could she feel it, too?

"It's quite the collection, isn't it?" I stopped beside her.

She turned to me. Not a hair of her ash-blond bob was out of place, but her eyes were wide. Her lipstick was the same pink as the night I'd met her, but when she smiled tentatively, there was no trace of it on her teeth. For the first time, it struck me how desperate she must have been to knock on the door of a stranger and ask them to help her move forward from the undead trap she'd been stuck in for decades.

"There are so many overpowering emotions coming from these books," she whispered, as though she didn't want the books themselves to overhear. "And yet, I find it difficult to move away."

I blew out a breath. I knew exactly what she meant. My entire life, books had been my safe space, my sanctuary, my area of temporary refuge. And now I was in a library filled with books whose purpose and provenance were dubious at best and evil at worst, and I had no idea what to make of it all.

Jasper deposited my stack of books on a nearby table. He joined us, staring at the shelves. I saw his mouth tighten, as if this section made him as uncomfortable as it did me. I turned back to Eloise, and keeping my voice low, I asked, "Does this section frighten you?"

The books unnerved me, but I didn't say so. I supposed I was hoping Eloise would say they alarmed her, too, so I wouldn't feel alone in my unease, but she didn't.

"No, it doesn't." She shook her head. "I'm already dead, after all. What could any of these books possibly do to me?"

Decrypting a cipher was likely not everyone's idea of a good time, but for me, a person who lived for the Sunday crossword and had never met a puzzle I could resist, it was fascinating. I thought about the symbols in the grimoire when brushing my teeth, riding the train, and searching the museum's collection for any books that might help me understand it.

Sitting at a table in the main room of the BODO, I had the stack of French witchcraft books Jasper had shown me as well as *The Black Pullet*, an eighteenth-century French grimoire full of magical symbols and diagrams—because it seemed logical to start researching the source materials from the region of France where my family had originated. I'd also reached farther back into the collection to examine *The Picatrix*, an ancient Arabic grimoire also known as *Ghayat Al-Hakim*, but was disappointed to find that none of the symbols on its pages matched the ones in Mamie's grimoire.

I brought the grimoire home with me every day, afraid that if I tried to leave it at the museum overnight, I would suffer another blackout. At first, I felt as if I were being held captive by the book, but as I studied its pages while curled up in my bed every night, my feelings changed.

Oh, the book still freaked me out, especially since I had to offer the hexagonal lock a few drops of blood every time I opened it, but I started to think of it as a strange sort of textbook that I was using for an intensive course in code breaking, or maybe that's what I told myself so I could mentally manage the situation.

I tried not to get discouraged, but after a week spent trying to match the symbols in the grimoire to anything in the BODO's collection or on the wonderful world of the Internet, I was becoming frustrated. I had made no progress—as in zero, nothing, nada, nil. Miles and Tariq remained optimistic, suggesting different avenues of research—such as the incredible online archive of witchcraft at Cornell University—while Olive looked vindicated, as if she had never expected me to be able to decipher the book. I was surprised by how much that stung.

Tariq finished the carbon dating of the grimoire and confirmed what I'd suspected. The early pages of the book were made of a parchment he determined to be several centuries old, while the newer pages were unable to be dated as they were less than a few decades old and didn't have enough broken-down carbon molecules to be measurable. Given how recent the final entries in the grimoire were, I believed they must be from Mamie, and I was more motivated than ever to crack the code.

With no other recourse, I decided my next step was to catalog each symbol in the grimoire. Scrounging a large legal pad and some pencils from the office supply cupboard, I copied every symbol and noted its frequency of use. When I had captured them all, I started to look for patterns. If symbols were placed together frequently, I copied those patterns down, too.

As I flipped through the pages, I felt the book emit a hum of satisfaction, as if it were pleased to have its contents examined, and I wondered how many witches had contributed to it. What were their personal stories? Was I worthy to be entrusted with a resource such as this?

The memory of my promise to my mother weighed heavily upon me. I could recall the intensity of that moment as clearly today as it had been twenty-two years ago. It was early autumn and we were standing on the front steps of the Wessex boarding school while Agatha waited nearby. Mom cupped my face and met my gaze. Her eyes had a fierce light in them and her mouth was tight, as if holding back emotion. When she spoke, her voice held an urgency that made me squirm.

"Promise me, Zoanne," she said. "Promise me that you will forget everything Mamie taught you, you will forget about being a witch and the craft, and you will never practice magic again. Promise me."

"But I've only used it a little bit since we left Mamie," I protested. Even at fourteen, the promise she was asking of me didn't sit right.

"Please, Zoe. I have to leave." She squeezed my shoulders with her thin fingers until it hurt. I pushed her hands off me.

"Fine, I promise." I glared at her.

"Thank you." My mother pulled me into a hug even though I resisted. She kissed my forehead and said, "I know you don't understand, but you have to trust me. I'm doing this to protect you."

Before I could ask what she was protecting me from, she climbed back into her car and drove away as if the police were after her. I saw her only a handful of times after that and for only a few hours at most. As time went on, I assumed she'd meant she was protecting me from using magic because of her guilt over my father's death. Still, I had kept my promise—it suited me and the quiet life I longed for—and I hadn't practiced magic since.

I glanced down at the open grimoire. Centuries of ancestors and their spells were carefully archived in the volume in front of me. Had I gotten it wrong? Had my mother been protecting me from something or someone? If what Eloise had said was true and someone had murdered both Mamie and my mom, I had to consider the possibility that my mother had been running from something that neither Agatha nor I knew anything about. The thought gutted me.

I dropped my pencil onto the table and leaned close to the book. "I need a minute."

I expected the book to slam shut in a huff, but instead, its cover gently closed and the metal bands locked into place with a soft click. I paused to do a vibe check and felt sympathy coming from the small black book. I resisted the urge to pat its cover as I pushed back my chair and rose from my seat.

I climbed the nearest spiral staircase all the way to the top and walked along the upper level until I reached a quiet alcove. We were in the basement of the museum. There were no windows here and for the first time since I'd started working in the BODO, I felt claustrophobic. I sat on the floor, leaned my back against the wall, and pulled my legs into my chest. I lowered my forehead to my knees and sighed.

What was I going to do? I was no closer to translating the book than I'd been the first time I'd opened it. Eloise was going to run out of smaller body parts soon, and what was she going to do if she lost an arm or a leg? I swallowed. I felt sick to my stomach.

But my upset wasn't just about Eloise. Every day I spent in the BODO researching witches and witchcraft was another day I was confronted with my past. More and more memories resurfaced from my visits with Mamie at her home on Hagshill Isle and the memory of the simple spells she'd taught me tempted me. I wanted to try them out and see if I still had the magic that Mamie had seen in me when I was her chaton.

It occurred to me then that if I could decode the grimoire, I could call Mamie and my mom back across the veil. I could see them again. The mere thought of it was almost beyond my comprehension and I felt jittery and off-kilter with a mix of happiness and trepidation, as if I'd had way too much caffeine on an empty stomach.

If I could see them again, ask them what had happened and why my mother had felt the need to leave me, maybe I could find closure on so many unanswered questions about my life. I thought of my mother as I remembered her best—the happy woman who had loved me so damn much—and I knew that version of my mother would want me to have that peace even if it meant using magic to get it.

I closed my eyes. Jasper had said belief was the key to magic. Okay, then. I hadn't attempted to do anything since the night I'd levitated, but here in the quiet, I thought, *Why not try it just to see?* If I could float my entire body, surely I could manage to float a book off the shelf.

I cleared my mind, pushing away all the negativity and self-doubt. I focused on the books in the stacks beside me. In my mind, I gently lifted one off the shelf and visualized it floating in the air. I felt the same pulse of peaceful energy that I'd felt while I'd been levitating fill me with a warm glow, as if I had embers gently burning in my core. This was magic. I recognized it as the same feeling I'd had as a child when Mamie would teach me simple spells of practical magic.

Deep in my visualization, I knew it was the moment of truth. If all went well, when I opened my eyes, I expected the book would be hanging in the air right there in front of me. Simple enough, right?

"Bloody hell! Freya, are you flying?" Jasper's voice, normally so deep and calm, sounded agitated.

I opened my eyes just in time to see Freya fall into Jasper's outstretched hands. Her tail was at peak terrified floof and he cradled the book against his chest and stroked her spine until her trembling stopped and her tail disappeared inside the book.

"There, there, you're all right, love," he said. "Now, off you pop." He let go of the furry gray book and she drifted through the air into an open slot on the bookcase. It was the first time I'd seen magic actively used by anyone at the BODO and it weirdly felt absolutely normal.

"Sorry, Freya," I said. There was no response from the book-cat, not that I had expected any.

"She'll be all right." Jasper crouched down in front of me.

I turned my head and met his gaze. A small smile played

upon his full lips and I realized I hadn't seen him in days and I'd missed him.

"She's never going to forgive me for that." I sighed.

"Freya? Not to worry. She doesn't hold grudges, otherwise she'd never forgive Tariq for turning her into a hat."

"He did not." I laughed at the image despite my doubt.

"He most certainly did," Jasper insisted. "He wore poor Freya all winter while he tried to figure out how to reverse the spell."

"Is everyone at the museum a witch?" I asked.

Jasper pursed his lips as he considered the question. "Not the museum, no. Here in the BODO, however, I suppose the simplest answer is yes, we all have our own talents. Claire, who does not possess any magic, has chosen us each for our different skill sets."

"She's created a department of witches to deal with the dubious books."

"Technically, women are called *witches* whilst men are referred to as *mages*. Because of the nature of our work for the museum, we tend to think of ourselves as academics first. Our mission is to be good stewards for the collection that Mabel left in our care."

"Mabel Stewart, Thomas's wife, the woman in the portrait in the hallway outside Claire's office?" I glanced out at the many shelves of the collection and then back at him. "Was she a witch?"

"She was," he said. "And she made it her mission to collect as much information as she could because she feared it was a dying art. She wanted to provide a place where witches and mages in future generations would be able to learn their craft but also to contain those materials that could be dangerous if they fell into the wrong hands. The Books of Dubious Origin collection was built for people like you and me, Zoe."

I felt the crushing burden of unmet expectations flatten me. I was failing spectacularly and was quite certain Mabel Stewart would be woefully disappointed in me.

"I'm making no progress." My voice sounded positively defeated.

"I wouldn't say that," Jasper said. "You managed to bring Freya to you."

"Against her will, no doubt," I said.

"An even bigger achievement." His eyes twinkled. "Your first intentional magic?"

"Not my first, but it's been a really long time." I squinted at him. "What I meant was I'm having no luck translating the grimoire."

Jasper nodded. "Miles told me."

I dropped my chin to my knees. I felt like such a fraud. Why couldn't I crack this code?

"If you're done beating yourself up, I'd like to show you something."

"I'm not . . . That's not what I was doing." It totally was and clearly he knew it.

"Of course it was," he said. "I expect you're not used to being unable to find the answers you seek, and that has to be a bit of a blow to your ego."

"This has nothing to do with my ego," I protested. Although, truthfully, it positively chafed that I couldn't figure out the meaning of the symbols in the grimoire. "I'm merely upset that I can't help Eloise."

"Zoe, it's not just on you," Jasper said. "We're a team here. We're *all* trying to help her."

Miles and Tariq had said as much, but I wasn't a group project sort of person, so I was adjusting to that as well.

"Is that why you've been gone?" I asked.

He nodded. "I was trying to track down an obscure text at the Bodleian that Miles thought would be helpful. Sadly, it's on loan to a scholar in Sweden."

"The Bodleian? As in the library at Oxford?" I asked. My inner librarian started to geek out so hard.

"Is there another?" he asked.

"I didn't realize. I mean, I knew Tariq was calculating the age of the book, but I didn't know you were working on it, too."

"As I said, we're a team, and that includes you."

"I don't think Olive sees it that way."

His lips curved up. "Perhaps not, but she doesn't view any of us that way."

That surprised a huff of amusement out of me.

"Come on." He patted my arm and stood.

Reluctantly, I followed. I'd sat there for so long my body had gotten stiff and my first few steps were painful as the blood moved back into my limbs.

"Where are we going?" I asked as I fell into step beside him.

"You'll see." He headed for the back. It was quiet, as the sounds from the open library below were muffled by the volume of books.

Jasper turned down a narrow passageway and stopped in the corner. The narrow bit of wall that was visible was done in decorative plaster much like the domed ceiling of the upper hallway in the museum above us. The plaster here was shaped to resemble a large pillar with a grapevine twining around it. Jasper stopped in front of it and pressed on one of the grapes. There was a click, and a narrow door swung open and revealed a dimly lit staircase.

I glanced at him in surprise. "Where does it go?"

"Out," he said. "You didn't think the main entrance to the BODO is our only way of coming and going, did you?"

"Didn't really think about it, to be honest."

Jasper turned sideways to fit his broad shoulders into the narrow passageway. The stairs were steep, almost a vertical climb. I didn't hesitate as I ducked inside and followed.

My thighs burned from the incline and I recommitted to getting in better shape if I was going to work in this staircase-infested facility. We passed two doors on our ascent, but Jasper didn't stop until we reached the door at the top. It was plain, with a round brass knob. Jasper turned it and pushed the door open.

Bright sunlight and a cold breeze greeted us. Jasper led the way, stepping outside onto the flat roof of the museum. I gawked. Despite the arrival of autumn, we were standing in what was clearly an immense garden. Most of the raised beds were now barren, but a large greenhouse was on the north side of the roof and I could see that it was full of greenery.

Amid the long raised beds, small café tables and chairs had been scattered, as if inviting visitors to linger. At one of the tables, Miles and Tariq sat with a pot of tea and an empty two-tiered plate between them.

"Glad you could join us, Zoe," Miles said. He gestured to

the vacant seats at their table in silent invitation. Tariq poured tea into two mugs and pushed them toward us, indicating the little pitcher of milk and the sugar on the table.

"A bit early for tea, isn't it?" I asked Jasper.

"It's four o'clock somewhere." His lips curved up on one side and he winked at me.

We sat down and I gratefully cupped the hot beverage in my hands. A stiff breeze blew across the roof from the reservoir and I shivered. Without saying a word, Jasper shrugged his jacket off and draped it over my shoulders.

"Thank you." I tried to sound normal, as if hot guys offered me their coats all the time, when I was certain that this had never happened to me—not once—in my thirty-six years of existence. I refused to be weird about it—at least on the outside.

"This is an amazing space," I said. "It must be beautiful in the spring."

Tariq beamed. "It was my idea. I take full credit."

Miles and Jasper sent him amused glances as if they'd heard him say this before.

"What inspired it?" I asked.

"I was homesick." Tariq's expression was bleak for just a heartbeat, but then his usual smile appeared, beaming like the sun. "I grew up outside Abuja near Zuma Rock. Nigeria is in a tropical climate, you know, and I missed the vegetation—I use so much of it in my potions—so I asked to put in a greenhouse and Claire agreed."

"Then other librarians and curators wanted garden beds, and the kitchen staff felt they needed one, too, and the next thing we knew, the rooftop garden came to be." Miles held his arms wide. "It has been a boost for everyone's mental health to be able to get a little fresh air and take a plant break during the workday."

"I can see why." I took a deep breath, and even with all my anxiety about Eloise and the mystery surrounding my mother and grandmother, I felt myself relax a smidge. I glanced at the now-dormant beds and noticed that one of them had a short wrought iron fence around it, and it wasn't in alignment with the others but rather was off to the side, isolated.

Tariq followed the line of my gaze. "I wouldn't go near that one. That's Olive's poison garden."

13

I turned to confirm that he was teasing me, but he wasn't smiling and his warm brown eyes were deadly serious.

"Olive has a poison garden. That tracks." I nodded and pulled Jasper's coat tighter around me.

"Which is why she's absolved from bringing anything to our potluck lunches—ever," Jasper said.

A laugh burst out of me before I could soften it. I was so loud, in fact, that I startled a bird off the roof of a nearby gardening shed. As it propelled itself into the air with its powerful wings, I noted it was a raven. I watched as it circled the rooftop before flying away toward Central Park.

"Beautiful birds, ravens," Jasper observed.

"If you say so." I shuddered.

"You don't think so?"

"No." I shook my head. "I've had a particularly pesky one sitting outside my house on my mailbox for the past week. It's a bit too Edgar Allan Poe for me. He's always skulking around."

Jasper frowned and looked about to protest, but both Miles

and Tariq began to cough as if trying not to laugh. He glared at them, and I wondered what inside joke I was missing.

Before I could ask, Miles turned to me and said, "Have I told you that I once worked with your grandmother?"

"No." I straightened up.

"It was decades ago." Miles held out the empty two-tiered plate to me. "Sweet is on the top, savory the bottom. Tap either plate three times."

I tapped the top one, naturally. Three perfect petit fours appeared as if they'd mushroomed out of the plate.

Tariq handed me a small plate to put them on. I picked up the pink one with the white frosting ribbon and sniffed it. It smelled of vanilla and strawberry and yum.

I glanced at Miles. "How?"

"It's an enchanted plate," he said. "From Versailles, during the reign of the Sun King, so it can only conjure the foods Louis XIV enjoyed."

I took a small bite. It was delicious. "Wow."

Miles passed the plate to Jasper, who tapped the lower plate three times. In a blink, three meat-filled pastries materialized. Jasper let out a low rumble of approval and set them on his own plate.

"You were saying about my grandmother?" I reminded Miles. The petit fours were drool-worthy and the magic plate a showstopper, but I wanted to hear his memories of Mamie.

"We were young, both still apprentices of the craft, but there was a dark witch terrorizing the covens of the Northeast, so an alliance was formed to rid the region of her."

"How was she terrorizing the covens?" I asked.

"She was using dark magic to steal the powers of prominent witches and mages," Miles said. "It was a very scary time."

"I remember hearing about it from my mother," Jasper said. "Ariana Darkwood was one of the reasons she didn't want me to come work in the States."

"My family as well," Tariq said. "She took the powers of twenty-seven witches and mages."

"Wait," I said. "Ariana Darkwood? Isn't she the one whose heart is trapped inside the book *El Corazón* in the BODO?"

"She's the one." Miles sipped his tea. "And that's all thanks to your grandmother Toni. She set a trap for Ariana, pretending to be a much more powerful witch than she was at the time. She was absolutely fearless." The admiration in Miles's voice made me feel a surge of pride for Mamie. "When Ariana stepped into her trap, a group of us bound Ariana with a spell while Toni used *El Corazón* to lock Ariana's own powers into the book, which is that book's intended purpose."

"When I first saw *El Corazón* on the shelf, I envisioned a beating heart encased in ice." I picked at the yellow frosting flower on the top of a chocolate petit four, not wanting to make eye contact with anyone if I was completely off base.

"Because witchcraft comes from the heart, that is the form her power took when sealed inside the book," Miles said. "The book was crafted by a dark mage with the intent of stealing his wife's power."

"Sounds like a swell guy." I ate the chocolate pastry in one bite.

"He was jealous that she was more talented than he was,"

Tariq said. "The story goes that he gifted her with the book to write her spells in, but when she did, the book stole her spells and her magic, leaving her powerless."

"This sounds like a horrible fairy tale," I said.

"Don't blame the Fae for that spineless troll," Olive said as she strode across the rooftop toward us. Per usual, she was all in black. Today it was a black-herringbone wool blazer with a thick fur collar over a black turtleneck sweater and pants. Her shoes were pointy-toed black loafers that made no sound as she glided across the gravel-strewn garden floor toward us. How did she manage to be soundless on gravel? This was not a skill that a normal person developed.

The Fae? Olive had said it as if she was defending the Fae. Was Olive a faerie? Yeah, there was absolutely no way I was asking her.

"I'm sure Zoe didn't mean it like that," Jasper said, casting me a meaningful glance.

"No, of course not. Um . . . did Ariana die?" I asked. While I was all for Mamie stopping the dark witch from stealing others' powers, I wasn't so hot to discover she'd committed murder.

"No, Ariana was merely rendered powerless. The alliance banished her to a ghost town—an old mining town in Pennsylvania where the abandoned mine had been burning for over fifty years—where there was not a vestige of magic to sustain her. She died twenty-seven years ago."

"The same year as Mamie." The idea of a dark witch stealing powers was chilling. I hunkered deeper into Jasper's coat and took a bracing sip of hot tea. It occurred to me that this was exactly the sort of thing my mother had been talking about when she'd said she was trying to protect me. That, too, felt like a gut punch.

"Quite a coincidence." As Olive came closer, I noticed that long, curved claws were visible on the ends of the fur wrap she wore. I shivered, but it wasn't from the cold.

"Olive, I haven't seen you up here since the last of your autumn crocuses bloomed," Miles said.

"And you won't see me again until it's time to plant the datura."

I was about to ask when that was when I noticed that her fur moved. No, it didn't just move. It climbed, tightening about her shoulders until a little head with a short snout and two round eyes popped up and peered at us from behind her back. Olive's fur was actually a sloth!

"Well, hello, Sir Napsalot the Sage," Miles said. "I didn't think he ever left the greenhouse when the weather got chilly."

"He doesn't," Olive said. She reached back and lifted the creature off her back, setting him on the ground. "But one of his powers is to bring tranquility, which I was in need of a few moments ago."

She nodded at the sloth, and he studied our group. When his gaze met mine, I could have sworn he could see into my very soul, which would have been alarming except I could swear he was smiling at me. A feeling of peacefulness passed over me and I felt myself relax.

"All right, that's enough, Napsalot," Olive said. "Back to the greenhouse with you."

He turned away from us and started to drag himself the thirty feet to the greenhouse. With an impatient huff, Olive scooped him up and carried him the rest of the way. We watched as she placed him on a low-lying branch of one of the many tall trees in the greenhouse.

"Just to be clear," I said, "Olive's familiar is a sloth?"

"Yes, but I'd strongly advise you not to take the mickey out of her about it," Jasper said.

"She's a bit prickly in regard to him," Tariq agreed. "Plus, we all love Sir Napsalot. He's good for her."

"You called him *the sage*," I said to Miles.

"One of his many gifts is divination," he said. "Along with time disorder and secret keeping." He looked as if he'd say more, but Olive was striding back toward us and we all grew silent.

"What did you need tranquility for?" Miles asked.

Olive turned to me. "Because someone managed to summon Freya and she appeared in my office ten minutes ago and has been yowling nonstop ever since. I had to summon Naps just to calm her down."

"That was me," I confessed.

Jasper sent me a sympathetic glance, while Miles and Tariq appeared surprised. Olive, per usual, looked annoyed.

"Not to press you," Miles said, "but I was under the impression that you had made a vow not to practice magic."

It was moment-of-truth time. I didn't want pity, so I kept it short and sweet and just the facts. "When my mother dropped me off at boarding school when I was fourteen, she made me promise to never use magic or witchcraft again. She said she was doing it to protect me."

I kept my gaze fixed on the magical plate. I didn't want to

see their expressions. "She blamed herself and her witchcraft for my father's death. She wanted to spare me that sort of heartache, so I made the promise and I've never done any magic until today, when I managed to call Freya to me."

They were all silent. In fact, they were quiet for so long, I was forced to glance up from the plate to see what they were thinking. Miles rubbed his chin thoughtfully, Tariq and Jasper looked empathetic to my plight, but Olive—once again—looked annoyed.

"Well, it's clear to me that the reason you have been unable to translate your own family's grimoire is because your witchcraft has been woefully neglected and your ability stunted." Olive turned toward the building, calling over her shoulder, "Report to my office first thing tomorrow morning."

"Okay. But . . . why?" I raised my voice to be heard as she was striding away. She paused and turned to face me.

"Tomorrow, we start your magical training. Miles will teach you magical theory and safety protocols, Tariq potions, Jasper energy manipulation, and I will cover the basic spells." She spun on her heel and with a wave of her arm, the door opened, she stepped through it, and it slammed shut after her.

I had to give it to her; it was an impressive exit.

Having managed to float Freya and myself without any particular effort, I thought learning to use my magic would be like cleaning out a closet. Open boxes, sort the contents, and learn how to use things I'd shoved to the back. It was nothing like that.

Potentially, it was my nerves, but I found I couldn't concentrate when someone—Olive—was watching me. Frankly, I had performance anxiety.

"Again, Ziakas," Olive ordered. We were standing in her office, which was as austere as her wardrobe. The furniture was black leather; the bookcases were oak stained a deep walnut brown. There were no art pieces or photos. In fact, it felt exactly like a dark version of my own home. I would have thought this would make me comfortable. It did not.

"I can feel the magic in you, Ziakas." Olive frowned. She was holding a blue orb of light in her palm. She'd been trying to teach me how to create a ball of light for more than an hour. I was tired, hungry, and grumpy. "This is the most basic of spells. Children are taught this before their third birthday. We've been at this for days. Why are you struggling?"

"If I knew the answer to that, I likely wouldn't be struggling," I said. She closed her fist and the light orb disappeared into nothing.

"Cup your hands together as if you're packing a snowball." She demonstrated the position, and I mirrored her.

"Relax your shoulders; you can't call the craft if you're tense."

"I'm always tense."

She ignored me. "Close your eyes. Picture the light you want to manifest, imagine it filling your palms."

I did as I was told. I felt the warmth inside me answer my call. I could feel the magic shoot down my arms and into my hands. I kept the vision of the light orb firmly in my mind. I was certain that this time I'd nailed it. I opened my eyes and unclasped my hands. A squiggle of light the size of a polliwog wriggled off my palm, did two loop the loops, and shot straight up to the ceiling, where it disappeared with a splat.

Olive heaved a beleaguered sigh while I stared at the ceiling, wondering what I'd done wrong.

"Ahem." Miles stood in the open doorway. He'd clearly seen the whole thing. "Sorry to interrupt, but Zoe is due for her magical theory lesson."

"Take her. She is beyond my help." Olive dismissed me with a wave of her long-fingered hand.

"Olive." Miles's tone was chiding, but she turned her back on us. As I watched, she held out her arms and suddenly Sir Napsalot appeared, hanging on her like she was a tree. Clearly, she felt she needed his calming influence. I scuttled out of her room, feeling like an utter failure.

"Don't take Olive's words to heart," Miles said as we strode down the hallway to his workspace.

"I'm not, but even I know she isn't wrong," I said. "I can feel the pull of the magic. I know it's in me, but I can't get it to manifest the way I want."

"You're potentially blocked by the vow you made to your mother. You've carried it for over two decades. That's not something that can be set aside by a few classes," Miles said. "Perhaps our sessions on magical theory will help you embrace your heritage."

"Maybe, but I'm concerned that I'm not working on decrypting the grimoire as much as I should be," I fretted.

"A better understanding of exactly what witchcraft and magic are might give you some insights."

I nodded. Truthfully, the two lessons I enjoyed most during the day were magical theory with Miles and potion making with Tariq. Olive was simply terrifying, and Jasper—well, energy manipulation required a lot of focus, which was nearly impossible with him in my orbit.

Miles's office was cluttered much like Agatha's house, which was likely why I felt at home there. I had to clear a stack of books off one of the armchairs in order to sit while he conjured a silver carafe of hot coffee with a mismatched sugar bowl, a pitcher of milk, and two mugs.

I looked at him in question and asked, "Any chance you can manifest a chocolate bar?"

He smiled. "The carafe only makes coffee—tea if it's sulking—but that's it."

"Another magical object."

"They're everywhere; most people just don't recognize them."

"How do they exist?" I asked.

"A witch or mage bespells them," he answered.

"Did you bespell this carafe?"

"Me? No, it was my mother's. Normally, the spell would fade from the object once the witch who cast the spell passed away, but because I'm a mage and the witch was my mother, the magic is strong in this little pot."

"Like the grimoire with me," I said.

"Precisely." He poured a mug and handed it to me.

"Thank you." I added milk and sugar. "What will I be learning today?"

"We've covered magic as a natural force powered by the universe, like gravity or electricity," he said. "Are you comfortable with all that?"

"I think so." I sipped my coffee. "I mean, I can feel the magic in me and it feels—for lack of a better word—organic."

"Good word," Miles agreed. "Let's move along to spell structure."

This felt promising. I leaned forward in my seat.

"When you found yourself levitating or when you called Freya to you, what do you remember?" He leaned back in his seat and cradled his mug in his hands.

"Feeling a warmth in my core and being hyperfocused on what I was visualizing in my mind."

"We call that *intent*." Miles sipped from his mug. "It's the most important part of any spell. The clarity of your will shapes the outcome of the spell."

"Which was why I found myself levitating." I nodded. "Do you think my clarity of will isn't that strong when I'm studying the grimoire? Is that why I can't understand it?"

"Perhaps, but given that none of us can interpret it, I think it's more complicated than that."

"How can I make my intent clearer?"

"Incantations, spoken or thought, can help a witch or mage to focus. Hand gestures, like the one Olive was trying to teach you, strengthen the intent, and sometimes it helps to have a focus object."

"Like a wand? Because that would be cool," I said.

Miles chuckled. "They're a bit out of fashion these days, as they appear more like a bit of cosplay and draw unwanted attention, but crystals are popular. I might suggest Olive use a labradorite crystal—known as a magical concentrator—with you."

I knew nothing about crystals except that they were not as bitchin' as wands. Still, I was willing to try anything. We talked about spell structure for another half hour. Talking to Miles was like talking to an encyclopedia of magic. He seemed to have the entire history of witches and mages committed to memory.

"Do you come from a long line of mages?" I asked.

Miles pushed his glasses up on his nose. I realized I had crossed over into personal territory, which was rude at best and incredibly insensitive at worst.

"I'm sorry, it's not my business," I said.

"No, it's all right," he said. "You are entrusting us with your abilities. It's only right for you to ask about our credentials." He paused, looking over my shoulder as if the past were somewhere in his piles of stuff. "My father was a mage and my mother a witch, both from magical families of many generations. They were young and happy and in love, married just a few years and with a baby—me—the first of what they hoped would be many children, but the Nazis put an end to that. I was smuggled out of Germany with friends of my parents' while they stayed, hoping they could use their gifts to fight. Instead, they were betrayed, captured, tortured, and murdered."

My heart felt as if it had turned to stone. "I'm so sorry, Miles."

"It was a long time ago." He waved his hand dismissively, but I saw the sheen of moisture in his eyes. "That's why we keep our abilities out of the public eye if at all possible. Less than one percent of the world's population has magical abilities. To say that regular people don't understand us is—"

"Woefully ignorant? Criminally understated? A mistake that could cost you your life?" I asked.

"All of that." Abruptly, Miles looked every minute of his eighty-something years.

"Why me?" The question came out of my mouth before I knew it was festering inside me.

"Why you what?" Miles frowned.

"Why did you offer me a job at the BODO? I know it wasn't because I have a good memory and am well read." I crossed my arms over my chest, letting him know I was prepared to wait for the answer.

"Honestly, because I believe you are a necromancer, and that is a skill that none of us have," Miles said. "Frankly, we need you, Zoe."

It took me a moment to process his words. I was about to say something encouraging, I hoped, when there was a knock on the door. Tariq poked his head in and said, "My turn."

I put my half-finished coffee on the table and rose to my feet.

"Let me end today with this, Zoe. Be careful. Tomorrow, we'll discuss the magical laws of the world and the one that is most imperative—the law of balance. Always remember, every magical action has a consequence."

Potions with Tariq was a welcome changeup. Tariq talked about being born into a family of witches and mages in Nigeria. The culture of his homeland both revered and feared anyone considered to be magical, much like the rest of the world, and so his family also kept their gifts close.

"What potion shall we brew today?" Tariq asked.

"Can you make chocolate in that?" I pointed to the silver

cauldron he had on a stand above a Bunsen burner—definitely a different aesthetic than a potbellied woodstove or an open fireplace.

Tariq cupped his chin with one hand as he considered and then a grin spread over his face. The next hour was spent measuring, grinding bits of this and that with a mortar and pestle—you'd think there'd be a magical food processor, but no—and then stirring and stirring and stirring some more. Seriously, no KitchenAid mixer either.

By the time my session with Tariq was winding down, I doubted we had accomplished anything. It was then that he magicked some brussels sprout, probably from the greenhouse on the roof. To my mind, there was no worse vegetable in the history of vegetables, so my enthusiasm was nonexistent when he told me to dip one into our steaming cauldron.

I held the base between my fingers and dipped the bitter ball of yuck into the potion. When I pulled it out, it looked exactly the same. I'd rather been expecting it to transform into a chocolate truffle, but no. Clearly, I had failed.

"Oh, man, I swear I did everything you said." My voice came out in a whine that annoyed even me.

"Taste it." Tariq gestured to the sprout. I frowned and he said, "Trust the process."

I resisted the urge to hold my nose as I lifted the sprout to my lips. I opened my mouth reluctantly, as if he'd asked me to eat a cockroach. I expected to chomp through the hard, bitter little leaves, but instead, it was like biting into a luscious, creamy bonbon of dark chocolate filled with mousse.

I covered my mouth with my free hand while the chocolate melted in my mouth. "Are you kidding me?"

"That's how my gran got me to eat my vegetables." His eyes twinkled and his laugh was pure joy.

"What am I missing?" Jasper asked as he entered the room.

"Tariq is being an alchemist and turning vegetables into something better than gold." I finished my first sprout and reached for another.

"Have you made your chocolate masking potion again?" Jasper asked.

"It is my specialty," Tariq said.

Jasper turned to me. "He makes it every year for the Christmas party. It's essentially the best fondue ever."

"I'll say." I held out a sprout to him. Jasper didn't hesitate and immediately dipped his sprout in the potion and popped it into his mouth. The three of us decimated the small pile of sprouts in no time.

I sighed when they were all gone, thinking I could have easily eaten another half dozen. Then I had a terrible thought. "Miles said that he was going to talk to me tomorrow about the laws of magic. He said there is a law of balance and that every magical act has a consequence. What would be the consequence here?"

Tariq gestured to the empty bowl where the sprouts had been. "That you will eat too much and get really sick."

That made sense. I nodded and said, "Totally worth it."

We left Tariq to his work, and Jasper and I grabbed our coats and trudged up the stairs to the rooftop. Because he was a field operative, he didn't have an official office in the BODO, so he'd decided the roof was the safest place for me to practice energy manipulation.

When we arrived at the top of the narrow steps, I was

pleased I wasn't gasping for breath as per usual. The late-autumn wind was bitterly cold and whipping across the roof. To my relief, Jasper gestured to the greenhouse. "Let's practice in there."

We scurried across the roof, closing the glass door behind us. Jasper shrugged out of his coat and draped it over a wooden bench beside the entrance. I did the same with mine.

"Let's practice some deep breathing," Jasper said. "You want to quiet your mind as much as possible before we begin."

Meditation. I was not a fan. I found it difficult to be still and even more challenging to keep my brain from shouting out random thoughts like *It's hot in here. I'm going to start sweating. Is he sweating? No, he's just hot. Stop it, Ziakas! Unprofessional.* And so on. It seemed the harder I tried to clear my mind, the louder it shouted.

"Come on now, Zoe," Jasper said. "The same thing we did yesterday. Close your eyes and breathe in for eight, hold for four, and out for eight."

I did this three times and opened my eyes. "It's as clear as it's going to get in here." I tapped my temple with a finger.

"Excellent," Jasper said. "As you know, our objective with energy manipulation is to build up your magical sensitivity and help you draw the power into yourself so you can harness it for your desired outcome."

"Because magic is based on energy," I said, repeating what he had told me the day before. "And energy is in everything. I get it in theory. I just don't know how to tap into it."

"I'll show you." Jasper approached a large potted orange tree. It was loaded with fruit that was still green. Jasper cupped one of the oranges and narrowed his gaze as he focused on it. While I watched, the fruit swelled, filling his hand, and turned a vibrant shade of orange. He plucked it and handed it to me.

"How?" I raised it to my nose and inhaled its sweet citrus scent.

"It's simple but does require a clear mind and lots of practice," he said. "Care to give it a go?"

I tucked the orange into my pants pocket and stepped toward the tree. I chose one of the larger oranges, thinking it wouldn't take as much concentration to ripen it. As Jasper had done, I stared at the fruit while trying to find that well of magic inside myself. It felt like an empty closet. After a few moments, I dropped the fruit and tipped my head back.

"I've got nothing," I said.

"You have something," Jasper corrected me. "I can feel it." He held out his hand as if feeling the air around me and I flinched. Why? What did I think he was going to do? He dropped his hand.

"Sorry," we said at the same time. There was an awkward beat of silence and I knew the weirdness was all mine. I turned back to the tree and cupped the same orange. This time, I closed my eyes, determined to make this stupid fruit ripen if it was the last thing I did.

I felt it then. Not the warmth I usually felt when I reached for my own magic. No, this was different. This was coming from the orange, its leaves, the branch, the entire tree itself. It rolled through me in a gentle wave of power. It called to my own magic, which rose inside me to meet it.

I kept my eyes closed. I felt a smile curve my lips as I embraced the energy from the tree and then returned it to the fruit. I felt it swell in my hand as I pictured it ripening to a luscious orange hue in my mind.

"That's it, love, you're doing it!" Jasper sounded thrilled, and I felt a rush of pride swoop through me. "Uh, Zoe, you should probably—"

Whatever he was about to say was interrupted by the wet, meaty sound of an orange exploding right before I was sprayed with juice, pulp, and rind. I blinked my eyes open and turned to see Jasper also covered in bits and blobs of orange. And he was still ludicrously good-looking. How was that even possible?

"On the upside, you did manage to ripen it." His eyes glinted and his mouth curved up.

I licked a bit of orange off my lips and debated chucking myself into the koi pond at the end of the greenhouse. There was no need. With a sweep of his hands, Jasper wiped us both clean of the orange detritus, and then in a tone as bossy as Olive's, he said, "Again."

There were no more magical breakthroughs for me in any of my other lessons and I felt as if I was losing time on decoding the grimoire. To make it up, I spent the evening in my pajamas, eating chips and dip while sitting on the floor beside the fire studying my notes on the symbols in the book. The grimoire was open on the floor beside me. I felt as if it was patiently waiting for me to unlock its secrets and I muttered, "Me, too, book. Me, too."

I turned to a random page at the back of the grimoire and traced the symbols with my fingers. It occurred to me that it looked like a ledger, the neat symbols flowing down the page in two columns.

What would a grimoire belonging to a family of witches known for necromancy need a ledger for? Was it the names of the dead people who had been raised? Why would they need a list unless it was to keep track of them? Would I find Eloise's name on this list?

My fingers stilled. I studied the most recent entries. The ink was black and the handwriting tight and precise. It reminded me of Mamie's. I was certain she had made these notations. I checked the last page, hoping to see my mother's loopy handwriting, but it wasn't there. Mamie had been the last witch to write in the book.

I leaned back. A sharp pang of disappointment stabbed my chest. I had been hoping to find some sort of connection to my mother. It was ridiculous given that she had dropped me off and moved on, but the girl inside me who'd been left behind still longed for her mom. I glanced at the mug of tea on the hearth and desperately wished it were whiskey.

I picked up the grimoire and flipped to the very first page. I placed my palm on the parchment and closed my eyes. Given that the grimoire was a magical artifact and that magic was made up of energy, I wondered if there was a way I could call the grimoire's magic into myself so that I could understand the book in a sort of magical osmosis. It was a long shot, but what did I have to lose?

I sat there for a long time, feeling the heat of the fire at my back and the fragile paper beneath my fingers. I was about to quit when I felt something, a low hum like an electrical current coursing through the book and into me. Or was it from me into the book? I couldn't tell. Then the whispers started. Just like the first few nights when the book had talked to me in my sleep, I could hear the voices murmuring. I felt my heart pound in my chest as I strained to make out the words.

I swallowed past my unease and willed myself to concentrate on the book. The hum of energies and the whispers were reaching an apex when I heard a ruckus on my front porch. If it was that damn raven again, I was going to get a cat—a very large cat. I ignored the scuffling noise outside. Surely, the bird would realize I was not letting it into the house or offering it any food and go away.

I had just found the hum of energy between me and the grimoire again when the scuffle outside became a thunderous pounding on my door. It was the distinct sound of a fist repeatedly hammering the thick wood.

That was no bird. Wessex was a small village and if it was anyone I knew, they would have called out a greeting. The angry banging stopped and I snatched up my phone as I rose to my feet. A boom sounded against the door as if the person on the other side was trying to kick it open. I grabbed the poker from the fireplace while unlocking my phone. Another boom sounded and the door bent inward. I scuttled into the corner.

I managed to press a nine and a one just as my front door exploded.

14

The wood cracked in half from top to bottom, shaking the entire wall. One half of the door fell inside the house with a crash while the other dangled from its damaged hinges like a drunk clinging to the doorframe. A man shouldered his way inside and I felt my heart stop. Clutched in one meaty fist was the raven. The man had it around the neck and the poor bird hung limply from his grasp.

Was that what the scuffling had been about? Had the raven been trying to warn me? I drew in a shaky breath. Was the poor bird dead because of me? As I stared, the bird's eye opened, meeting my gaze. I didn't hesitate. With a panicked cry that probably sounded like a rabbit screeching, I lifted the poker over my head and charged out of the shadows, straight at the strange man. He flung the bird away as I brought the poker down with all my might. I saw the bird fly out the broken door, but I couldn't spare a second for relief. The man blocked my strike with a forearm and the impact sent reverberations up my arms.

The man bellowed at me and I yelped and darted away,

putting the sofa between us. He spoke in a language I didn't understand. The words sounded Scandinavian but not like any Swedish or Norwegian I had ever heard. He stomped forward and I took in his muscled arms and strange clothes. His dark blond hair was cut in a fringe that fell over his eyes but was short in the back in a sort of reverse mullet, and his beard was thick but neatly trimmed. He looked like he'd just escaped a Renaissance festival via Sweden.

He balled his hands into fists and bellowed, "Bók!"

That word I knew. It was Old Norse for *book*. My heart was pounding in my chest as my mind raced. Out went my first inclination—that he was here to commit sexual assault and murder. As a single woman who lived alone and watched entirely too much true crime, that was the first place my brain went. But the word *bók* was a big tell, and I knew the only book I had of any interest to anyone was my family's grimoire.

He looked past me at my bookcase. He strode forward and I ran around the sofa, keeping it between us. He began to snatch books off the shelves, turning them over in his hands and then hurling them to the ground with enough force to crack their spines.

"Hey!" I cried. It was one thing to barge into my house and terrify me with the threat of bodily harm, but going after my books . . . well, now we had a problem. As my childhood copy of *Anne of Green Gables* flew past my head, I didn't think—I reacted. I lunged forward and brought the iron poker down on his shoulder. He went still.

I backed up, realizing two things simultaneously. First, he

was massive and the top of my head barely reached his shoulders. Second, I was an idiot.

He turned slowly to face me. The intense light in his brown eyes flared through the fringe of hair that covered his forehead and blasted me like a winter wind. I stood frozen in place, overly aware of my faux lambskin–lined slippers, flannel pajama bottoms, and thermal top. These were not fighting clothes. His upper lip curled and terror turned my legs into useless noodles. I watched as he reached forward and plucked the poker out of my hand as if it were no more substantial than a freshly cut flower. He flung it across the room and I heard it smash something. I dared not look behind me even as I fervently hoped it wasn't my coffee maker. Then he leaned forward until his face was just inches from mine and he bellowed, "Bók!"

The stench of his breath gave me my first inkling that I was not dealing with some random person who happened to be scouring my house for the Donadieu family's magical textbook. No, this man's breath smelled like death and I had to swallow against the gag reflex that kicked in as the fetid stench washed over me in a nose-wrinkling, vomit-inducing, malodorous fug.

I knew in that moment that no matter what, I couldn't let him get his big beefy meat hooks on the grimoire. I glanced around the room, frantically searching for a weapon. This was where my minimalist decor was detrimental. There was not even one decorative tchotchke to be weaponized. Damn it!

I grabbed a throw pillow and hurled it at him. He swatted it away as if it were a pesky fly. I used his distraction to bend low and snatch up the grimoire with one hand while I grabbed another pillow with the other. I was about to hurl it right in his face when an arm looped about my waist and hauled me backward toward the door.

"A pillow fight? That's your go-to when a deranged Viking breaks into your house?"

I whipped my head around to find Jasper behind me. He was winded and disheveled, as if he had run all the way from New York. I was about to ask him what he was doing there when my uninvited dead guest raised his arms and shook his fists in peak frustration. Then he saw the book in my hand.

He advanced on us while he roared, "Bók!"

"How's your cardio?" Jasper released my waist and grabbed my free hand in his.

"Terrible." It didn't feel like an appropriate time to lie.

"That's a shame because we need to run. Now!"

Jasper dragged me through the open half of the door, down the steps and walkway, to the street. I glanced back once to see undead Erik the Red ripping the remaining half of my door off its hinges and throwing it across my lawn. How was I ever going to explain this to the neighbors?

"Let's go, love, knees to chest!" Jasper ordered. He didn't have to tell me twice.

I matched my stride to his, which was long, and we bolted down the street, putting distance between us and the undead Viking, who had just started running—as if he had forgotten how and it was taking him a moment to get all the parts in working order.

"Is there a cemetery nearby?" Jasper panted.

I scanned my rattled brain. "Yes. A quarter of a mile from

here, around the corner to the left. Why?" The absolute last place I wanted to go right now was a graveyard, as I felt it would be a bit too convenient for our pursuer to end us there.

"We're going to lead Hairy, Scary, and Dead into a tomb and bind him there until you learn how to send him back to the afterlife," Jasper said. The street was empty, as if the residents knew better than to venture outside with an undead Viking on the loose.

"Bind him in a tomb?" The words hissed out of my mouth as my lungs started to burn. "There's no other way to get rid of him?"

"We could try to light him on fire and let him burn to ash, but it smells ghastly and it's quite messy. Also, he might still come back," Jasper said.

"Tomb it is!" I sprinted around the corner, hoping my inappropriate footwear of fuzzy slippers didn't disintegrate before we got there.

My relief when I saw Eternal Shade Cemetery up ahead was short-lived, as I could hear the Viking's feet pounding the ground behind us. When I went to look, Jasper ordered, "Don't turn around. Focus on finding an accessible mausoleum."

"I know which one we can use," I panted. Then I hoped Agatha would forgive me for sticking an undead Viking in the Lively family tomb. "We need to get to the top of the hill and go to the largest family mausoleum."

"Lead on," Jasper grunted, and gestured with his hand.

The pavement became a dirt road as we turned into the cemetery. The headstones were barely illuminated by the light of the quarter moon, but that was fine. I knew exactly where I was going.

We had only gone a few hundred yards when I stumbled and Jasper grabbed my hand and pulled me off the path and into a copse of trees. He pressed his finger to his lips, indicating quiet, which was no small feat, as my lungs were sucking in oxygen like a starved man devoured food.

I bent over, hugging the grimoire to my chest, and tried to slow my heart rate and control my breathing. I felt light-headed and a little fuzzy, but just then our unexpected Viking ran through the cemetery gate and I realized that Jasper had saved us from being caught.

Jasper grabbed my arm and pulled me down behind several tall headstones. He gestured for me to lie flat and I didn't hesitate. The Viking halted. He lifted his face to the air as if he could smell our scent. I flattened myself even closer to the damp, leaf-strewn earth.

Our pursuer tossed his head, moving aside the fringe that covered his eyes. Then he crept along the side of the road, scanning the headstones as if he knew we were hiding among them. My heart was beating so loudly I was certain he could hear it, and when he stopped and tipped his head as if listening, I was sure of it. I braced myself for him to come at us, but instead he crept by as slowly as Sir Napsalot crossing a road.

I didn't dare move for fear of making a sound that might draw his attention. Now that he was farther into the graveyard than we were, how were we supposed to lure him anywhere? Jasper must have read my expression in the faint moonlight. He leaned close, placing his mouth against my ear, and whispered so quietly it was almost as if he were breathing the words instead of speaking them.

"We're going to split up. I will run him around the cemetery, giving you a chance to make certain the door to the tomb is open."

"How are we going to get him inside?" I whispered, trying to be as quiet as him, but panic made my voice seem thunderous in my own head.

"No idea," he admitted. "We're making it up as we go along."

This did not instill confidence. My stomach dropped. We were going to die. Our heads would likely be ripped right off our necks and tossed aside with our bodies to be found tomorrow. Everyone would think it was a murder-suicide and wonder why two people who barely knew each other decided to end their lives so gruesomely.

"Zoe." Jasper grabbed my hand with his and gave my fingers a quick squeeze, bringing me out of my panic spiral. "Slip through the headstones, going as quietly as you can, straight to the hill. I'll meet you there."

I watched as he pushed himself off the ground and jogged back to the road. Once there, he shouted, "Oy, you bloody half-wit, we're over here!" Then he took off running in the opposite direction.

Sure enough, the undead Viking turned, and with a roar that echoed throughout the entire cemetery, he ran after Jasper, much faster than he'd done before. I tried to tell myself Jasper could stay ahead of him, but even I didn't believe me.

Something scurried in the underbrush as if it, too, wanted to get away, and I started, breaking out of my terror-induced stupor. I pushed up from the cold, hard ground and made my way through the headstones. It was too dark to see as I hurried along the uneven ground, clutching the grimoire close as I made my way to the top of the hill.

The Lively family tomb was the largest, as Agatha's ancestors had been one of the founding families in Wessex. Eleven generations of Livelys had lived, loved, and died in our small town. The tomb itself was beautifully made, crafted of granite from the local quarry. It had been commissioned by Agatha's great-great-great-grandfather. He'd even gone so far as to have all of the previous deceased Livelys dug up and placed in their own dedicated spots in the mausoleum.

The name LIVELY was engraved above the entrance, which suddenly struck me as funny, since the stone edifice housed a family of deceased people. Perhaps a better name for them would be the Unlivelys. Yup, I was teetering on the brink of hysteria.

Agatha had once shown me where the key to the ornate wrought iron doors was kept. I approached the full-size statue of the late Gerard Lively, in his topcoat and tails and seated on his pedestal at the side of the entrance as if to assess all who dared enter, and gently lifted the lid off the marble box he held in one hand. The hefty skeleton key was inside and I snatched it, replacing the lid.

The sound of approaching footsteps made my hand sweat and fingers shake. I quickly opened the door to the crypt and pocketed the key. I stepped inside, glancing at the large marble sarcophagus holding the corpse of the very first Lively.

"Sorry to interrupt and I apologize for what's to come, but I'm in a bit of a jam and Agatha is my friend, so . . . again, very sorry."

I took in the small, cramped space and wondered how we

were going to trap the Viking in here. He was after the book and he knew I had it. The only way to get him in here was to hide the book outside the tomb and then duck back inside and use myself—pretending to have the book—as bait.

I stepped outside the stone building. I could hear Jasper yelling at the big Viking lummox and I assumed it was his way of warning me that he was headed this way. I scanned the area, looking for a place to hide my book. For a blink, I wondered if it would really be so bad to let the Viking have the grimoire so that I could go back to my peaceful life as a small-town librarian, but then I thought of my mom and Mamie and the questions I had about their deaths and knew I couldn't do it.

I glanced at Gerard and the marble box in his hand. Without overthinking it, I placed the grimoire on top of the marble box, hiding it in plain sight.

"Keep that safe for me, G," I said. Then I darted away from the tomb, standing a few yards in front of it, and yelled, "Jasper, over here."

I had no idea how I was going to clue him in about my plan, but I'd have to trust that he'd catch on when he got here. I tensed, waiting, and then I heard them.

The sound of panting and the scrabble of feet on the dirt road grew louder and louder. I hopped from foot to foot. This had to work. It simply had to. My head filled with doubt, but then they arrived and I knew I had no choice but to go for it.

I raised my hand in the air and waved. "Great night for a run, isn't it?"

"I've had better!" Jasper was full-on sprinting. He reached out a hand and made to grab me but I ducked it.

"Mind the door!" I yelled.

His eyes went wide as I checked to see that the Viking saw me and then I dashed into the tomb.

"Zoe!" Jasper yelled at the same time the Viking bellowed.

I swear I felt the entire tomb shudder as the Viking rammed his big body through the doors after me. He was cursing in Old Norse and I couldn't understand a word, but I didn't need to in order to grasp his fury. I hid behind the first Lively in his raised marble bed, hoping that the Viking believed me to be a witch who had just disappeared.

There was the sound of a bone striking something hard and I knew the Viking had just struck his shin on the pedestal that held the sarcophagus. While he hopped on one foot and spewed a stream of curses, I dropped to my hands and knees and scuttled toward the door.

I was almost there. I was so close. All I had to do was slip through and, with Jasper's help, close the doors and lock the Viking inside. It was then that the key clattered from my pocket. *Shit!*

15

The Viking went still and so did I. His voice was soft when he spoke. Despite the echo effect of the small room, I knew he was standing on the opposite side of the raised coffin from me. I held my breath while I gently patted the ground for the key. I had to find it. If we couldn't lock him in, we wouldn't be able to bind him and keep him here.

The Viking continued muttering and it sounded almost like a prayer. Was he so old that he was praying to Odin or had he been converted to Christianity by King Olaf Haraldsson during his reign in the first and second milleniums? *Gah!* Why was I thinking about Norse history now? Stupid brain! Did it matter which god he prayed to? Not if he got his hands on me it didn't. I continued to pat the ground. I couldn't leave without the key.

Then I heard the rustle of his clothes and the tread of his step. He was coming around the coffin. I had to get out of there, but I needed the key. If I left without it, then this would all have been for nothing. I felt the hysteria rise inside me and I wanted to scream. *If I could just have a fucking sliver of light to see!*

As if I had manifested it out of my panicked need, a bright beam suddenly flared through the small stained glass window at the top of the back wall, and I heard a disembodied voice speak in Old Norse and it said one word in a thunderous command. "Biðja!" *Pray.*

The Viking shouted in surprise and dropped to his knees. He had taken the command to heart. I could tell by the cadence of the words and the fervency in his voice. While he was occupied, I glanced at the floor, looking at the colorful pattern on the marble.

The key! I grabbed it and lurched to my feet, throwing myself at the door. I wasn't coordinated enough in my panic to actually move my limbs, so I rolled out between the iron gates with all the grace of an overheated water buffalo on dry land.

I slammed onto the stone steps, clipping my jaw, but I ignored the pain that lanced through my face. Instead, I spun around and slammed the doors. Then I jammed the key into the lock and twisted it until it clicked.

The light that had been shining through the stained glass window abruptly disappeared and a cry of fear echoed against the marble-lined wall of the chamber. I staggered away from the iron doors just as the Viking launched himself at them. The doors rattled and I yelped. The Viking thrust an arm through them, reaching for me. His fingers were about to close around my arm when I was yanked out of reach.

"Good work, love," Jasper said. He pulled me in for a hug, and even though I wasn't the hugging sort, I let him. After the last few terror-filled minutes, his warmth was as welcome as a weighted blanket and just as comforting.

The doors rattled on their hinges as the Viking shook

them with all his might, bellowing his displeasure. It was terrifying, but I made my voice calm when I said, "I have no doubt that the tomb is sturdy; I just don't know if it's enraged-Viking sturdy."

"Quite right." Jasper let me go. We both ignored the Viking, who was now muttering what ominously sounded like a curse upon our very souls. "Let's get on with the binding. Olive texted the instructions to me."

"Olive knows how to bind an undead person?" Why this information surprised me at this juncture, I had no idea. I supposed I was taken aback that this sort of thing happened frequently enough to have a ready-made binding spell.

"Olive knows a lot of things," Jasper said.

I could only imagine.

He swiped his thumb across his phone and read aloud, "Draw the needle through the captive's hat or shoe and he can't escape."

"What needle?" I asked.

"This one." Jasper pulled a black velvet pouch out of the inside pocket of his coat and retrieved a thin silver needle from inside it.

"What's so great about that needle?" I raised my voice to be heard over our furious tomb guest, who had resumed yelling as he reached through the gate with both arms, trying to grab us.

"It was used to sew the burial attire of a corpse."

"Oh." I stared at the needle that glinted in the moonlight. "That's it? We just pull it through his shoe."

"Yes. Of course, we have to do it with intent so we can focus the magic into our desired outcome."

"It's that belief thing again?" I asked.

"Exactly. Witchcraft is actually a very quiet undertaking, which is why so many people are cursed and they don't even know it."

"You mean when they drop their phone in the toilet, spill coffee all over their best outfit, or miss the last train out of the city? That's not just happenstance?"

"It could be," he said. "But more likely, they've been cursed, especially if all those things happen on the same day."

"Now I have to reassess every moment of my life to date." I crossed my arms over my chest. "Hollywood hasn't gotten the memo on the quiet part."

"Good. I'd hate for real magic to become common knowledge."

I couldn't argue that.

We both glanced at the Viking, strategizing how we were going to manage this. The Viking had his face pressed between the decorative iron bars that made up the doors. He was breathing through his nose, making his nostrils flare, and his eyes blazed with a rage so fierce I was surprised we didn't feel the heat searing our skin.

I glanced down at his shoes and noted they were moccasin-like, with a leather upper that appeared to be soft. It might not be that difficult to get the needle to pass through. Of course, if we stabbed him in the foot, that could cause a problem.

"How's your sewing?" Jasper asked.

"I can manage to fasten a button if required. You?"

"I've sewn up more wounds than I can count, including some of my own."

"You're the seamstress, then," I said. "I'll distract him while you slip the needle through his shoe."

He made a face and I wasn't sure if it was because he didn't trust me to distract the Viking or he didn't want to go near the man's feet. I didn't bother to ask, as our guest was rattling the wrought iron so ferociously I was afraid he really would the rip the door off its hinges.

"Get ready," I said to Jasper. He nodded, slipping his phone into his pocket and holding the needle between his fingers.

I crossed to the statue of Gerard and snatched the grimoire off the marble box in his hand. The Viking went instantly still. His eyes went wide as he looked at me holding the book. I knew I had to keep his attention while Jasper attempted to bind him.

I held the book up high over my head while Jasper crouched low, preparing to approach the tomb. The Viking's eyes locked on the book, tracking it as I twirled in place and chanted nonsense.

When Jasper moved in, I leapt from side to side, raising my face to the sky as if imploring the gods to help me raise the dead. We were in a cemetery. I assumed the Viking would expect nothing less. I kept going and going, hoping Jasper completed his task before I ran out of gibberish.

"Done." Jasper leapt back from the gate. I lowered the book, wondering if such a simple thing as a needle could really hold captive two hundred pounds of furious undead guy.

I watched as the Viking gripped the bars. His gaze still on the book. When he tried to reach through the iron gate to grab it, his hands didn't move. He couldn't let go. He was locked in place. I felt my jaw go slack as the Viking went into a frenzy, rattling the door of his prison.

Jasper didn't seem to notice as he took what looked like a smudging stick out of the same black velvet pouch from his coat and lit the end on fire. Blowing out the flames, the clump of herbs started to smoke. He extended his arm away from his face and said, "Don't breathe this in. It's a strain of nightshade that will vanish you and I don't have the antidote on me."

I yanked my pajama top up over my nose and mouth and stayed upwind. I watched as Jasper circled the tomb, waving the smudging stick up and down. The Viking watched him, too, yelling at him when he passed by the doors. I wasn't sure if I was imagining it, but the Viking's voice grew quieter with each pass and he seemed to fade like an old photograph until I couldn't see or hear him at all. Jasper stopped walking and dropped the stick to the ground, where he extinguished it beneath the heel of his shoe.

"There." Jasper brushed his hands off. "Our work here is done."

"What did you do?" I asked. "How did you get rid of him?"

"Oh, he's still there. That's a masking spell—from Tariq," he said. "That particular smudging stick causes whatever being its used on to be rendered mute in all forms. They can't be seen or heard or smelled."

"So no one coming to the cemetery will know he's there?" I asked.

"Exactly."

I stared at the tomb. There was no sign of the enraged

warrior who had terrified us all evening, but even through the smudging spell, I sensed him. I could feel his malevolent gaze upon us and it shook me to my core. I had no doubt if I ever ran into him again when he was loose, he wouldn't hesitate to kill me.

"Who has access to this tomb?" Jasper asked.

"My friend Agatha Lively," I said. "It belongs to her family."

"You'll need to tell her to stay away from here and to make certain no one else goes near it either, at least until we can get rid of her new tenant," he said.

"All right." I couldn't wait for that conversation.

Jasper tapped a quick text into his phone. "Olive and Miles know what happened. We're all in agreement that you can no longer stay in your house."

"Funny you should mention that." I stared him down in the darkness and asked, "How did you arrive at my house just when I was in need of assistance? And how did you just happen to have a needle that can hold someone captive and a smudging stick that could render them invisible?"

"I don't think that's the right question." He took my arm and directed me to the dirt road that led out of the cemetery.

"What do you mean?" I asked. The sweat I'd produced while racing through the graveyard and being scared out of my wits was now cooling in the frigid night air and I shivered, clutching the grimoire to my chest.

Jasper shrugged out of his coat and slipped it over my shoulders. I started to protest, but he shook his head. "I have a shirt and jumper on while you're in your pajamas." He shook his head again, indicating that was the end of it. Fine.

"What's the right question?" I asked, burrowing into his coat.

"How did that deranged undead Viking find you?" he asked.

"I don't know." I shrugged, but deep down I wondered if I had conjured him. When I'd been concentrating on the page in the grimoire and feeling the magic building between me and it, had I called the Viking into being? It was clearly a big mistake. Huge.

The thought that I might have gotten us killed by calling forth an undead Viking? There was not enough wine in my house to deal with that. I was going to have to break out the whiskey.

"I feel as if you're not telling me something," he said.

I could feel Jasper's gaze on the side of my face, but I didn't turn toward him, not wanting to reveal the self-doubt in my eyes. Instead, I diverted.

"What a coincidence," I replied. "I feel the same way about your sudden appearance here with your pocketful of magic tricks." This time, I did give him a careful side-eye.

He looked me up and down, one of his black eyebrows lifting to mimic mine. "Outrunning an undead Viking, saving your grimoire, and not giving an inch. I think even Olive would be impressed."

I sincerely doubted that. I rolled my eyes and walked out of the cemetery, turning onto the sidewalk that led home. The walk back felt shorter than the run from my house had been. Maybe a freaked-out sprinting panic slowed time in a sort of Zeitraffer phenomenon where the brain's visual perception of motion was altered, causing an illusory sense of slowed motion.

Jasper fell into step beside me. "How about I tell you how I got here so fast and why I happened to have exactly what we needed on my person, and you tell me where you think our friend came from? Deal?"

"All right, you first."

"The black pouch"—he paused and patted his pocket—"was given to me by Olive. She has curated an emergency kit of magical objects that anyone who works for the BODO carries with them at all times. I arrived so quickly because I was already here. Claire asked me to keep an eye on you. She was worried that if Eloise was correct and your mother and grandmother were murdered for the book, then the person or persons responsible would come after you next." He pointed down the street to a nondescript black sedan. "That's one of the museum's cars. I've been parked there every night, keeping watch just in case."

I nodded. Now it all made sense. Despite Claire's potential overreach in having a person—*Jasper!*—stationed on my street staking out my house, I felt protected and, in the case of tonight, grateful. I never could have gotten rid of the undead Viking without his help, and judging by the Viking's hyperfocus on getting the book, I likely wouldn't have survived if I'd tried.

"Thank you." The words came out more stiffly than I would have liked, but at least I'd said them.

"You're welcome." Jasper inclined his head. "Your turn."

"I did tell the truth before; I don't know where the Viking

came from. That being said . . ." I hesitated. I wasn't sure how to explain the connection I'd been establishing with a page of the book. Ah well, Jasper's reaction would be nothing compared to Olive's, so perhaps it was a good practice run.

"Yes?" Jasper prodded.

"It could be that while I was attempting to build a magical bridge between me and the grimoire that I inadvertently conjured the undead Viking," I admitted.

He stopped walking, so I did, too. We stood on the sidewalk with him staring at me in horror as if I'd just admitted that I put dill pickles in my Dr Pepper—I do and it's delicious. I don't care what anyone thinks.

"Wait. You think *you* might have conjured that reverse-mullet Thor?" he asked.

"I can't figure how else he got here," I said. "Unless you know of some other necromancer in the vicinity."

From the look on his face, I knew immediately that there were other necromancers close by. What the hell? Why hadn't anyone told me this before? I could have gone to them for advice or help.

His pale eyes studied my face as if he could read every thought I'd just had. "Not all necromancers are . . . friendly."

"Like I am?" I asked with a dash of sarcasm. *Friendly* was not the first word anyone would use to describe me and we both knew it.

"I know it's a lot to take in, but you clearly have skills, Zoe. That potential is one of the reasons Miles wants you to work at the BODO."

"Does he really? Or does he just want to keep an eye on me and any undead army I might raise?" I teased.

A flicker of a smile crossed his lips. "Unlike general magic, which can be harnessed by anyone with some knowledge and practice, necromancy is a very nuanced sort of gift and the wielder has to be very sure in their purpose or it goes all sorts of wrong."

"Like calling forth an angry Viking?"

"Assuming it was you and not someone else, yes, exactly." He clapped my shoulder with his large hand and gave it a firm squeeze. "Let's hope it was you."

"Why? I don't want to be whatever this is," I protested, waving my hands at my body and no doubt looking like I was having a fit. "I want to go back to my quiet little life where weird shit didn't happen all the time."

"I think you're missing one important point," he said. "If it wasn't you but rather another necromancer, then why did they sic a Viking on you? To take your grimoire or worse? And now that their Viking has failed, what will they do next?"

I gasped. "Are you saying what I think you're saying?"

"What do you think I'm saying?" He'd answered my question with a question like an annoying prophet who refused to commit.

"That whoever sent the Viking murdered my grandmother and my mother to get the grimoire and I'm next." I shook my head. "But that makes no sense. The book is bonded to me and supposedly I'm the only one who can use it. How would killing me and taking the book be of any use to them?"

He pressed his lips into a tight line as if he didn't want to say what he was thinking. I stared intently at him, making it clear he wasn't going to get away with not answering.

"If it's a necromancer, chances are their plan is to kill you and then bring you back, making you their minion to use your grimoire in service of them."

I gasped. I'd be an undead minion. This was completely unacceptable.

"If our speculation is correct, they'll just keep sending undead assassins until they get what they want." He tapped the book I cradled to my chest with his finger.

My knees went a little wobbly and Jasper caught me by the elbow. "Chin up, Zoe. You're not alone. You've got me, Miles, Tariq, Claire, and probably Olive to keep you safe."

"Probably Olive," I repeated, finding an unfamiliar comfort in these new and unexpected friends. Even Olive.

16

We were almost at my house and I noted the lights were out at Mrs. Graham's and the Perkinses' minivan was absent, meaning they were likely grabbing pizza in town after a late soccer practice. *Phew.*

"What I can't figure out is how did you or they or whoever call up a Viking?" Jasper used both hands to sweep his hair away from his face. It fell into thick black waves, landing effortlessly just past his jawline. Annoying. "When historically no Vikings landed, lived, died, or were buried in Connecticut."

"That we know of." I dragged my gaze away. "There is the Maine penny to consider."

"Oh, yes, the Goddard coin, discovered on a beach in 1957. It's the only pre-Columbian artifact of the Old Norse ever found in the United States, which also makes no sense. Leif Erikson's settlement Vinland is said to have been in Canada, Newfoundland to be exact, and the farthest south the Vikings were supposed to have gone is New Brunswick. So why was just one penny discovered and nothing else?"

"Maybe the rest of the items were washed out to sea, or the Norseman who the coin belonged to was a captive, or maybe it was planted there by someone just to cause a stir." I shrugged. "I don't know. Just like I have no idea how an ancient Viking could come back from the dead and barge into my house looking for a book."

"That's right," Jasper said. "He was fixated on the book. But why?"

"Maybe, like Eloise, he wants to walk on." It was as good an answer as any, but given that I would have to be the one to send him, I didn't like it. Also, I could understand my grandmother bringing Eloise back for companionship. But who the heck wanted an ancient Viking to pal around with? No one. Which was another reason I was certain that the Viking's arrival was all my fault.

When we reached my walkway, the teeny-tiny hope, truly just a flicker, that this was all a nightmare evaporated as I saw half of my front door still on my lawn while the other half was on the floor at the entrance.

Jasper scooped up the half door as we walked by. He propped it against the side of the house while I stepped around the other half and went inside. The fire had burned out and the books the Viking had tossed from the bookcase were scattered all over the place.

My nerves were frayed. I crossed to the cabinet where I kept an emergency bottle of whiskey and I poured us each a shot. If Jasper didn't want his, I'd happily drink it myself. I noted my fingers were shaking, so instead of holding his glass out to him, I slid it across the granite counter.

Jasper pushed up the sleeves of his sweater and I noticed

each of his forearms bore a tattoo of a very detailed black raven, which ran from his elbow to his wrist, with different Norse runes tattooed below each.

"Odin's ravens?" I asked. I don't know why I was surprised. Probably because I had assumed he was a product of a posh British prep school and wouldn't have tattoos. How very narrow-minded of me.

"Very good." Jasper looked impressed. "My mother, Christina, is a Swede and she used to caution my siblings and me when she left us on our own to behave because Hugin and Munin see and hear all and they would report back to her."

"So these are a nod to your heritage and your childhood?" I asked.

"Something like that." He grabbed the whiskey I had pushed in his direction and lifted it up in the air, tapping it against mine. "Skål."

"Skål," I repeated the Swedish equivalent for *cheers* before I fired back the whiskey, coughing as it scorched a path down my throat but welcoming the bloom of warmth it unfurled inside me.

"I have a question." I poured myself a second shot.

"Another one?" He held out his glass and I poured him one, too.

"How did you end up working for the BODO?" I asked. "You're not like the others."

"I'm not?"

I stared at him, then tossed back my whiskey. I needed the ethanol to ride through my bloodstream to my brain and give me a dopamine release that would override my common sense and make me bold.

"You're the field operative," I said by way of explanation. I felt this was much better than admitting he was ridiculously hot.

"I am." He downed his drink in one swallow, looking clear-eyed while I felt a bit woozy. Undoubtedly, he could handle the effects of alcohol much better than me.

"How did that come about?" I asked. "I don't suppose you answered an online ad?"

He laughed. "No."

I waited. He looked around my little house as he considered what to say. Finally his gaze met mine and he said, "I was recruited by Miles for the job after I graduated from Cambridge with a degree in mythology."

"Mythology?" I asked. "That doesn't seem like the sort of degree that would lead to an occupation that specializes in cleaning up messes."

"Perhaps." He shrugged. "But the alternatives, teaching or writing, had absolutely no appeal, so I took the job."

"And now you're here being chased around a Connecticut village by an undead Viking," I said.

His mouth curved up on one side and his gaze lingered on mine. "I've had worse days."

A rush of heat hit me low and deep as awareness thrummed between us. I glanced away.

I found it impossible to believe there was something worse than what we'd just been through, but when I remembered how calm he'd been while we were running for our lives, I had to admit he had skills. I sensed there was more, much more, to the story than he was telling me, but given that I had likely just released a centuries-old Viking on the neighborhood, I didn't feel I had a right to badger.

"We'd better get that door fixed." He pushed his empty glass across the counter to me. "I don't suppose you have a random piece of plywood lying about?"

"In the detached garage," I said. "Bought during our last hurricane."

"Tools?"

"On the workbench, also in the garage."

"Brilliant." He left through the gaping hole that had once been my door and I watched him go. It was a moment or two before I realized I was staring stupidly after him. I stoppered the whiskey bottle and glanced around my living room.

The books the Viking had tossed from the bookcase were scattered all over the floor and I hurriedly collected them, relieved that none of them was the worse for wear because of the evening's drama.

While I reshelved my books, Jasper returned with the plywood. He propped it up and paused to take a call. I suspected it was someone from the museum, as he surreptitiously glanced at me before answering. I knew if it was Claire, she was going to insist that I stay in one of their safe houses. I had no intention of doing any such thing.

"Right," Jasper said. "I'll tell her."

He ended the call and looked at me. I met his gaze and went for a preemptive strike. "I'm not going to New York."

"But you're not safe here, love," he protested.

He'd called me that several times now. It made my insides flutter, which I really resented because I suspected he knew full well the endearment, spoken in that growly, sensuous accent, did that to any person with a pulse and it was a consciously deployed weapon in his arsenal. In fact, I knew it was, because I'd heard him call Freya *love* when he'd rescued her from me. Well, I wasn't that easily maneuvered.

"If *I'm* the one who brought the Viking forward, then I'm perfectly safe," I said. "I just won't meditate on the grimoire again—ever."

"And if you're not the one who brought him back, then your life is at risk, and given that Eloise is now dependent upon you to send her on, you really can't stay here."

I considered him for a moment. Usually when I stared at someone with no expression on my face, they got uncomfortable, shifted on their feet, and finally glanced away. Not Jasper. Then man leaned in. *He. Leaned. In.*

"Well, what's it going to be, Zoe? You stay here and I keep watch over you, or you come back to New York and settle into one of the safe houses, which, for the record, are actually very-well-situated apartments."

I tipped my chin up. I would not be cowed. "Neither."

It took a lengthy call to Miles and some time replacing my front door with the plywood before I had a moment to throw some things, including my grimoire, into a duffel bag and leave my house.

Jasper had been invaluable in helping secure the sheet of plywood. He told me he'd arranged for someone to come early the next morning to replace my door, for which I was grateful. I was used to doing all of life's chores and tasks by myself, but the night had been more harrowing than I was used to—dramatic understatement—and I was finding it difficult to process, so the assist was welcome.

We arrived at Agatha's house just before midnight. She was waiting for us with a fresh pot of chamomile tea and two guest bedrooms all made up for us. I was exhausted in body but not in mind, so I accepted the tea, weaving my way around her possessions to one of the armchairs in front of the fireplace, which had a nice blaze going. Jasper took the chair opposite me and Agatha sat on the sofa.

She waited until we were settled and had sipped our tea and relaxed into our seats before she said, "What happened tonight?"

Jasper glanced at me over the rim of his cup, clearly indicating that I should do the telling. Fine.

"Potentially, I called an undead Viking into being and he arrived at my house looking for the grimoire." I sipped my tea, wondering how long it would take the chamomile to soothe my frayed nerves. The whiskey certainly hadn't.

Agatha peered at me over the top of her reading glasses. "That makes no sense. You haven't used any of your abilities since you were a child."

"Actually, I've been studying the craft under the supervision of the BODO staff," I said.

"Zoe, why didn't you tell me?" Agatha put her hand over her heart and looked wounded.

"I just started," I said. I glanced at Jasper for unspoken backup.

"She did," he confirmed.

"Fine," Agatha said, looking somewhat mollified. "But

how could you raise a Viking when you can't even read the book?"

Jasper's head swiveled from Agatha to me as he awaited my answer. I told Agatha the same thing I'd told him about studying my notes and then deciding to meditate on a page in the grimoire. Halfway through the telling, a weird feeling, like a chill in my bones, overcame me.

"Hold on," I said. I put my teacup down on the hearth, as there was no place else to put it, and I hurried to the base of the stairs, where I'd left my duffel bag. I rifled through my meager possessions, looking for the one thing I didn't remember packing. It wasn't there. My heart started to beat double time. I dumped the contents of my bag onto the floor, searching for my notebook. It definitely wasn't there.

"Zoe? What's wrong?"

I turned to find Agatha and Jasper watching me with matching expressions of concern.

"I didn't pack my notebook. It's where I wrote all the grimoire's symbols along with their frequency of use and groupings."

"Do you want to go back and get it?" Jasper offered.

"It's not there." I began stuffing my bag with my things. "I would have grabbed it if it was still on the floor in front of the fire when I picked up the rest of the room."

"Maybe it got kicked under the furniture in the ruckus."

"No, I looked everywhere when I was cleaning up." I met Agatha's fretful gaze. "That means while we were being chased by an undead Viking, someone went into my house and took my notes."

"This is concerning for a variety of reasons." Jasper took

out his phone and stepped back into the living room. "Excuse me, I need to make a call."

I pressed a hand to my forehead, trying to remember the details of the notes I'd made about the grimoire. There was nothing in the notes that would help anyone without access to the source material. It was more that someone had entered my home and taken my work. I was pissed.

Agatha frowned. "One question."

"Yes?"

"Where is your undead Viking? How did you manage to lose him?"

"About that . . ." I rose to my feet and gestured to the kitchen, where I knew she kept the hard stuff. "You might want something stronger to drink than chamomile while I tell you."

All in all, Agatha took the news of an undead Viking trapped in her family's mausoleum fairly well. She agreed to stay away from the tomb, and I handed her the key that was usually kept in the marble box for safekeeping.

When Jasper joined us and explained the magic he'd used to trap the Viking, Agatha released a sigh and reached out to hug me. My second hug of the day when I usually got one hug per year from Agatha on my birthday. I wasn't sure what to do with this overabundance of affection.

When Agatha released me, she cupped my face in her hands and said, "I don't care about the Lively tomb. I'm just glad you're all right."

That made my throat tight and my eyes sting. I nodded,

incapable of speaking, and disappeared into my room with my bag of stuff. I unpacked the grimoire and put it in the top drawer of the dresser on the far side of the room from my bed. When I closed the drawer, I got the feeling it was relieved to be safe. Maybe that was just me.

Shockingly, I slept like the dead—for lack of a better description. I had no dreams that I remembered, and when I awoke, the sun was already shining and the day was that clear, crisp cold that was particular to early November in New England. Most of the leaves had fallen and the bare limbs of the trees looked stark against the vibrant blue of the sky.

I dressed in jeans, lace-up brown boots, and a pale pink cashmere turtleneck sweater. I fastened my thick honey-brown hair in a ponytail at the crown of my head, letting the shorter wisps fall around my face, softening the severity of the hairstyle. With a need to feel a semblance of control, I swiped on some mascara and lip gloss. I wasn't a big one for makeup, but even I knew it gave a woman a smidge of confidence when she wasn't feeling her strongest, and that was certainly me today.

I hurried downstairs, stepping around the Lively family odds and ends that filled the house, and strode for the coffeepot in the kitchen, which was by far my favorite room in Agatha's house. It was the only clutter-free space, because it was Agatha's primary area for practicing her kitchen witch skills.

The quartz counters were a soft white with deep veins of gray. The cupboards were also white and the appliances steel. The flooring was a waterproof, scratchproof, luxury type of vinyl made to look like planks of gray-and-cream wood that would likely outlast us all.

I pushed the swinging door open and abruptly came to a stop. Seated at the large dining table were Olive and Miles. Jasper was leaning against the deep steel sink and Agatha was at the stove, whipping up fluffy blueberry pancakes and crispy bacon.

"Good morning, Zoe." Miles popped up from his seat and came at me with his hands outstretched. He clasped my fingers in his and gave them a reassuring squeeze. "We were just discussing the events of last night."

I glanced past him at Olive, who was sipping her coffee, looking bored. Really? An undead Viking was boring? I shuddered to think what she might consider exciting.

"I'm sorry about bringing forth an undead Viking," I said.

Olive frowned. The eyebrow with the scar lifted ever so slightly. "How exactly do you believe you managed that?"

"Eat first." Agatha's voice did not invite argument, and I thought she might be the only person alive who was not intimidated by Olive. She placed a plate of pancakes in front of me. "I know it's not up to your usual nutritional standards, but today you need something more substantial than Rice Krispies Treats."

"I'll choke them down just for you." I winked at her and Agatha nodded in satisfaction.

I poured a hearty amount of maple syrup over my pancakes and took a seat at the table. Jasper delivered a hot cup of coffee to me and my eyes met his for the briefest moment. I could have sworn I saw sympathy in his gaze. How mad was Olive going to be about having to deal with my undead Erik the Red?

I cleared my throat. "Thank you."

I got through half of my short stack before Olive ran out of patience. "All right, you've had enough to take a break. Explain about raising the dead."

I put down my fork and took a sip of the hot coffee. It washed the sticky syrup residue from my mouth and I dabbed my lips with my paper napkin. "Fine." And then I explained everything from placing my hand on a random page of an old section of the grimoire to feeling a bond form between me and the book. Olive and Miles stared at me while I spoke as if trying to find any subtext that might exist. There wasn't any. I was merely doling out the facts.

"That sounds very hypothetical," Miles said.

"That's all I have right now, a working hypothesis." I shoved another bite of pancake into my mouth.

"But it's predicated on the belief that *you* conjured the Viking," he added.

"And?" I prodded.

"I don't think you did," Miles concluded.

17

I put my fork down and took another clarifying sip of coffee.

"I agree with Miles," Olive chimed in.

No surprise there. Her opinion of me seemed to be one of barely concealed impatience. She found me tiresome and useless and had never made any secret of it.

"But I was bonding with the grimoire. I could feel it and I heard the same voices in my head that spoke to me in my dreams when it first arrived. It can't be a coincidence that suddenly there was an outraged Viking on my porch," I said. "Where else could he have come from?"

Olive rolled her eyes. "You seem to think you're the only necromancer in the area."

I stilled with my fork halfway to my mouth. I glanced at Jasper. He had told me there were others, but I decided to play dumb just to see what Olive and Miles said. "I'm not?"

I felt Jasper watching me, but I ignored him.

"I can think of at least two in the area and five if you include all of New England." Olive tossed her long black hair over her shoulder. On anyone else, it would have been a flirtatious gesture, but from her it was dismissive.

"Why didn't you tell me this before?" I asked.

"You seemed to be struggling to accept your family's affinity for necromancy, so we wanted to give you time to process," Miles said. I noticed he kept giving Agatha a wary glance and I suspected she would read him the riot act for not telling me everything from the get-go.

"All right, assuming there is another necromancer in the area and they raised the Viking, why did they send him to my house and why do they want the book?" I asked, not mentioning that Jasper and I had already discussed the possibilities. I wanted to hear it from them.

Jasper took the seat at the table beside me and leaned forward, resting his elbow on the dark wood and propping his chin in his hand. He looked as tired as I felt. "What she said."

Olive and Miles exchanged a glance. I wondered if they could read each other's minds. It wouldn't have surprised me in the least, to be honest.

Agatha let out an impatient sigh. "Enough with the eyeball communication, you two. Zoe deserves an answer, an honest one."

"Well, we can't be sure," Miles hedged. "It's all speculation at this point, but the signs do point to Zoe's grimoire being deemed very powerful, and someone is clearly determined to acquire it."

"But if I'm the only one who can use it, why would they want it?" I asked.

Miles looked conflicted about answering; Olive did not. She stared at me with her opaque black eyes and said, "If you were under the control of another witch or mage, then they could order you to use the grimoire for their benefit."

Agatha let out a hiss and I felt a chill creep into the marrow of my bones. It was no better hearing it the second time around. To be under the control of another, to do their bidding, no matter what it was—no, just no.

"Tariq is investigating the other known necromancers in the area to find out if any of them are involved or know who is."

"What do we do in the meantime?" Agatha asked. "Zoe is clearly a target for whoever wants the grimoire . . . and her."

Having her say it so plainly was a bit unsettling. Okay, more than a bit. As one, we all turned to Miles. He looked at me and said, "I believe the only way forward is to understand the past. We need to find out what happened to your mother and grandmother, Zoe."

I sighed. I knew he was right, and I wanted to know, I really did. But I also dreaded the many complicated feelings this was going to stir up for me. Frankly, if I had to choose between unresolved family issues and an undead Viking, I'd choose the Viking every time.

I met Miles's sympathetic gaze and asked, "Where do we begin?"

We started with a meeting in the main room of the BODO. Tariq had come back from his necromancer reconnaissance, reporting that no one had sicced an undead Norseman on me.

"How do you know they were telling the truth?" I asked.

"I have a tea that encourages honest communication," Tariq said. "Chamomile for clarity, rosemary for truth, and mint for purity of mind among other things. I also add a bit of lemon to boost the other ingredients."

"It's a truth serum?" I asked.

"More like a truth enhancer." He smiled mischievously and I returned it.

"Excellent. On to phase two, then," Miles announced.

"Which would be what?" I asked.

"As I understand it, your mother was in the Mystwood Manor care facility for the last month of her life, yes?" Miles's voice was gentle and full of empathy.

"Apparently." I nodded. "I . . . we . . ." I gestured to Agatha and then myself. "We didn't know she was in residence there until after she passed away."

"Then we're going to Mystwood to see what we can find out," Olive said. "Jasper, this is your area of expertise, so you'll be in charge of coordinating our visit."

"Our?" Jasper lifted his head.

"Yes, you, me, Eloise, and Zoe," Olive clarified.

"Four of us?" He frowned. "Isn't that a bit overkill?"

Olive stared at him with a look that would have sent me hiding under the table. Jasper just smiled at her until she rolled her eyes.

"You're going with Eloise to tour the facility under the guise of having her admitted," Olive said, "while Zoe and I interview the director about her mother's death. I feel like something isn't quite right."

"What are you saying, Olive?" Agatha had come into New York with me and sat beside me at the meeting, lending me her support, as she knew family stuff was my vulnerable spot.

"Juliet Ziakas was middle-aged and living in a well-appointed rehabilitation facility. It feels a tad convenient that she died of a sudden cardiac arrest, doesn't it?" Olive asked.

I glanced at Agatha. She looked as gutted as I felt. It had never occurred to either of us to question my mother's death. Mom had been gone for decades with only sporadic visits for an afternoon here or there. She'd maintained no contact with Agatha or me in between these abrupt appearances, which had ended five years ago. With no indication that I'd ever see her again, I had started to assume she was dead, because it hurt less than thinking she had abandoned me once and for all.

"Don't beat yourself up, Zoe," Agatha said. "There was no way for us to know that your mother had returned or that she needed care."

"Hmm," I hummed noncommittally. The thing was, I felt as if I should have known. I was her only child, her last living relative. I should have known she was back and about the grimoire, and I should have learned more about our Donadieu family history—all of it. To be left in ignorance hurt almost as much as the fact that she had dumped me off at private school and disappeared as if I were just some unwanted baggage.

The ache in my chest was fierce and it was hard to breathe. I felt Jasper's pale gaze watching me and I forced my expression to go flat, to hide the hurt, to put on the mask I had worn since my mother had left me and my things at the front door of the school, given me a quick hug, made me vow I'd never do magic, and driven off with an expression of grim determination.

I shook my head and cleared my throat. Maybe after all this time, I'd finally get some answers.

I glanced at Olive and asked, "When do we leave?"

We arrived at Mystwood Manor early the next morning. The facility served patients who were receiving postsurgical care or recovering from a variety of ailments, such as heart attack and stroke. When Agatha and I had inquired as to why my mother had been admitted, we were told she had been admitted by a doctor in a Boston emergency room for severe weight loss.

The austere building sat on top of a hill in the suburbs of Boston. I had hoped it would be an overcast and dreary day, matching my mood, but the cheerful sun and bright blue skies mocked me as I strode from the rented SUV Olive had picked up outside the train station toward the large redbrick edifice, which perched on the hill like a castle surveying its kingdom.

Olive wore black sunglasses and a black trench coat over another completely black outfit. I wondered briefly what her closet looked like. I suspected it was like a small black hole. She could reach in and pull out anything, knowing it would match. Maybe she was onto something there.

Eloise followed behind her. She was wearing her camel coat and her ash-blond bob was styled meticulously to cover her missing ears. Tariq had procured a pair of stylish leather gloves for her that filled out her missing finger. I wondered what the gloves were stuffed with, but I didn't ask, as I felt it would be rude.

Jasper strode beside me. I felt his gaze on the side of my face and I knew if I looked at him, I'd see an expression of sympathy. I didn't want that. It would do me no good to acknowledge all the *feelings* that were rocketing through me at being here.

"I have a question for you, Zoe," Jasper said.

I sighed. I didn't want to answer any questions about my mother, my relationship with my mother, or how she'd ended up in this facility without my or Agatha's knowledge. It was all just so sad. It hurt to think about, never mind discuss, and yet . . .

"Go ahead." I braced myself.

He slowed his pace, dropping back from Olive and Eloise. I thought it was sensitive of him not to grill me in front of the others.

"What do I do if Eloise loses a body part—say, a significant part—whilst on the tour?"

Caught off guard, I snapped my head in his direction. There was a mischievous glint in his eye and I realized he was trying to distract me from what he knew had to be a difficult task.

I pursed my lips to keep from smiling and nodded, letting him know I knew what he was doing and that I appreciated it. I also decided to play along, as it would keep me from overthinking what was to come.

"Well, I suppose it depends on how significant," I replied. "Are we talking a leg or an arm?"

"Leg would be tough," he said. "I mean, what if we're walking along and it just drops off? She'd have to hop on one foot for the entire tour. Hard to be nonchalant, carrying a leg tucked under my arm, yeah?"

I huffed a small laugh. "An arm might be easier. You could just stop by the infirmary and borrow a sling."

"Very resourceful." He dipped his head.

"Of course, she could go all Headless Horseman on you."

He looked at me with wide eyes. "You think she could lose her noggin?"

I shrugged. "Just thought you might want to get *ahead* of it."

His laughter was rich and deep and broke through the quiet, causing two birds nearby to take flight.

Olive glanced over her shoulder at us, lowered her sunglasses, and frowned. Jasper and I immediately stifled our amusement and Olive turned back around, stepping on the mat that activated the automatic doors. Eloise hurried after her, completely unaware that she'd been the diversion I needed to get through this morning.

As we followed them into the building, Jasper leaned down and said, "Thanks for the heads-up."

I snorted, not daring to meet his gaze for fear it'd turn into a full-on laugh.

The woman at the reception desk, wearing a name badge that read *Marcy*, glanced up. She was middle-aged, with a round face and glasses perched on her nose. She greeted Olive with a warm smile but was distracted as the phone on her desk rang and another office worker dropped a file on the inbox beside her.

"Welcome to Mystwood Manor, may I help you?" Marcy greeted us.

"Yes, we have a meeting with the director," Olive said. "If you could just instruct us on how to get to the office?"

"Certainly. You want to go to the third floor. Take the passage to the right and the director's office is at the end of the hallway."

"Thank you." Olive looked at me and tipped her head in the direction of the elevators.

I glanced at Eloise and Jasper and mouthed *Good luck* before hurrying after Olive.

We rode up to the third floor in silence. Two health care workers in scrubs joined us on floor two. They were talking animatedly when they entered, but one look at Olive and they both stopped speaking, scrambling over each other to get out ahead of us on the third floor. Olive had that effect on people and I supposed it could be considered a sort of superpower.

As we stepped out of the elevator, Olive led the way in the direction Marcy had indicated. We paused in front of a door with a plaque that read DIRECTOR. Olive rapped on the wood three times. There was no answer. She tipped her head as if considering the situation and then turned the handle and pushed the door open.

There was an empty reception station and another office in a room behind it. The door was open and I could see someone seated at the desk in there. I recognized him immediately.

"That's Mr. Moran, the director," I whispered to Olive. "He was the one who called me when my mother passed and met Agatha and me when we came and retrieved Mom's things."

I steeled myself to talk to him. I had so many questions about my mother's stay, things I never would have thought to ask before this grimoire appeared in my life. I patted my coat. I had tucked the grimoire in an inside pocket, having decided to leave my backpack in the SUV. It felt weird to have it so close to me. I felt as if some sort of bond was forming between me and my mysterious book, but maybe it was just because I believed it had been sent to me by my mother and I was standing in the place where she'd spent her last days.

Olive nodded and walked past the assistant's workspace and into the main office. She paused in the doorway and said, "Let me ask the questions."

"Okay." I raised my hands as if in surrender, but I was actually relieved not to have to pick at the scab that was my mother's death in this place.

"Mr. Moran," Olive greeted him. "We're here for our appointment."

The director rose quickly to his feet. He wobbled a bit but steadied himself with a hand on his desk. He smoothed his thinning dark hair back across his head with a nervous hand. "Of course. Please, come in. How can I help you?"

I followed Olive and we took the two seats in front of his desk. Moran sat and folded his hands on his desktop. His face was blank, as if he didn't recall who I was even though we'd seen each other a little over a month ago when I'd collected my mother's things. I supposed with so many residents it was difficult to keep up with the family members who came and went.

"We came to talk to you about Juliet Ziakas," Olive said.

"Right, just so." Moran fiddled with the stapler on his desk, checking and rechecking its alignment, nudging it a millimeter, and checking it again. I had the urge to slap his hand to get him to glance up, but I suppressed it.

"What can you tell us about Ms. Ziakas's passing?" Olive asked.

Moran didn't look up from his desk. "I don't know what you mean."

"She was rather young to have died of a cardiac arrest without a preexisting condition, wasn't she?" Olive asked.

Moran's gaze darted across his desk as if he was searching for something—anything—to divert his attention. I glanced at Olive and noticed the muscle in her cheek bunching. He was getting on her nerves, too.

"I'm not a doctor." Moran began checking the tips of the pencils in the holder on the side of his desk. He took out each one without a sufficiently sharp tip and lined them up on the desk. For sharpening, I supposed.

"I didn't assume you were." Olive drummed her fingers on the arm of her chair. "However, you are the director of this facility and when one of your residents dies, I would think you'd be familiar with the situation."

"I don't . . . I'm not sure . . ." Mr. Moran glanced at the window. "I should go home. My wife will be wondering where I am."

Olive and I exchanged a look. Olive had been right. There was something off about this situation and about Moran. I couldn't put my finger on it, but he was definitely not all here and he was nothing like the kindly man who had consoled me after the death of my mother.

"Mr. Moran." I thought if I questioned him, we'd have more luck. Maybe he would be more sympathetic to a relative. "I don't know if you remember me. I'm Zoe Ziakas, Juliet's daughter."

This seemed to resonate with him. He turned toward me. He didn't meet my gaze but glanced somewhere behind me.

"I'm sorry for your loss," he said. There was no sincerity in his voice. It was almost as if he was saying something he was preprogrammed to say.

"Thank you." I leaned forward. "But I have questions."

"I can't answer any questions," Moran protested. He glanced at us and his eyes looked scared. "I'm not supposed to be here. I'm d—" He flinched and stopped speaking.

"Where are you supposed to be?" Olive asked.

"Ground—" Again he flinched. "Not here. There. Don't let them—*argh*."

Olive abruptly stood up, knocking her chair back a few feet. Startled, I leaned away from her, afraid of what she might do. It was Olive, after all. She wasn't one for announcing her intentions and this was no different.

She held her hands up in front of her with her palms facing Moran. In a low voice, she spoke in an ancient language that was guttural and sharp, the sort of language in which words of affection sounded like insults. It suited her.

The temperature dropped in the room to a bone-deep coldness that I knew I wasn't imagining, as I could see my breath when I exhaled the air I'd been holding in. I glanced at Olive in equal parts fear and wonder. Her face had become even paler than usual and her dark eyes looked wild, as if some supernatural force lurked inside her. One that she kept a tight leash on except for in this moment when she loosened her grasp, allowing a glimpse of it to peek out through her eyes. She was terrifying.

The words were obviously a spell of some sort and now I desperately wanted to know what sort of witch Olive was. When I'd lived with Agatha as a teen, she had told me about the different types of witches, trying to get me interested in my family history, no doubt. I suspected Olive was one of the more powerful ones, like a storm witch, a blood witch, or possibly the most elusive of all—a Fae witch. At this point, nothing would surprise me.

Olive dropped her hands and Moran watched her, unmoving. It took me a moment to realize that he couldn't move, that whatever she had muttered had rendered him a prisoner in his own body.

"What did you do?" I asked.

"Followed a hunch," she said. "Open the closet door."

A hunch had created the terrifying power I'd seen in her eyes? What the hell?

Still, I knew better than to ask questions. I pushed up from my seat and approached the door. I didn't know why I was suddenly so nervous. My fingers shook as I reached for the knob. I glanced back at Olive. She jerked her chin at the door and said, "Do it."

I took the cold metal in my hand and twisted it. I pulled the door open, and out tumbled a woman with tape over her mouth and her hands secured with zip ties. I ripped the tape off her mouth. But instead of taking a breath and saying thank you, she took one look at Mr. Moran and started screaming.

18

"*He's dead!*" she screamed. "*Dead!*" Her face was shiny as tears streamed down her cheeks. She was shaking and she kept screaming, "*Dead!*"

I glanced over my shoulder at Moran. Did the woman mean what I thought she meant? I snatched a tissue from the holder on the desk and dropped into a crouch in front of her.

"Hi, I'm Zoe and this is my friend Olive." I heard a hiss behind me and realized belatedly that we probably shouldn't give our real names. Oops. "We're here to help."

The woman stopped screaming and blinked at me. She began to cry, rocking back and forth in a self-soothing motion. Her shoulder-length curly brown hair was mussed and shot with gray. She wore a blue-and-pink floral silk blouse with a bow at the neck and a pleated skirt in a matching blue. She was wearing sensible low-heeled brown pumps and looked every inch the part of middle-aged office administrator.

"What's your name?" I asked.

"Shelly. Shelly Dabrowski. I'm the interim director here

because Mr. Moran . . . Mr. Moran . . ." She glanced at the man frozen in place at the desk and started to hyperventilate.

"Don't look at him, Shelly, look at me," I instructed. "What happened to Mr. Moran?"

"He died," she wailed, growing louder with each word. "Two weeks ago he passed away from a surgical complication. I went to his funeral and everything. He's dead, but today he showed up here and tied my hands and taped my mouth and shoved me in the closet!" She started to wail.

Olive let out a put-upon sigh and turned to Shelly. She opened her hand, then closed it into a tight fist. Shelly continued screaming, but no sound came out. This seemed to freak her out even more and her eyes rolled back into her head and she slumped to the floor.

"How did you do that?" I gestured to Moran. "And that?"

Olive stared at me.

I was undaunted. "What sort of witch are you?"

Olive's scarred eyebrow lifted, but she didn't answer me. Can't say I was surprised.

"Well, that's not very helpful." I gestured to Shelly's unconscious form. "I had more questions for her."

Olive shrugged. "I'm not good with screamers." She took her phone out of her pocket, tapped it a few times, and held it up to her ear. "Jasper, we have a situation. Yes, the sooner the better."

She ended the call without another word and I wondered where Jasper was on his tour and how he would manage to get out of it and get here in a time that would satisfy Olive.

I stood up and gestured to Moran. "How did you know he was dead?"

Moran's eyes flitted from me to Olive. It was the only part of his body he could move. I would have felt sorry for him, but he looked almost relieved to be frozen in place. Weird.

"It's a gift," Olive said, which I took as a nonanswer. I resisted the urge to roll my own eyes.

She turned back to Moran. She raised her hands again and this time her incantation was soft, almost like she was crooning a lullaby to a sleepy baby. Moran's shoulders slumped, then his neck wobbled, his spine bent, and he sagged back in his chair.

"Who brought you back?" Olive asked.

He opened his mouth to speak, but no words came out. Olive tipped her head to the side, studying him.

"Did he get blasted with the same spell you used on Shelly?" I asked.

Olive gave me a side-eye. "That would never happen."

"Then why can't he speak?" I countered. "He was fine when we got here."

"Mr. Moran, who brought you back?" Olive asked again.

He tried to form the words, but he started to choke.

Olive spun away from him and sat on the edge of the desk. "Someone is controlling him."

"How can you tell?"

"Because he clearly wants to speak but can't." Olive crossed her arms over her chest.

"Could it be because he's newly dead?" I asked. "Maybe he doesn't have control of his vessel yet."

Olive frowned, considering, then she shook her head. "No, the newly deceased usually have more muscle memory than the more aged dead, which is why I didn't catch on that he was undead right away. According to Dabrowski, he's only been dead for two weeks. He should be able to talk, jog a marathon, or—"

"Choke someone out?" I cried as I grabbed Olive and yanked her away from Moran's outstretched hands. He had lurched to his feet and was reaching for us, clearly with the intent to harm.

Olive immediately raised her hands and repeated the spell that froze Moran in place. The same chill permeated the room, but this time I was ready for it. Reaching across his desk with his hands out, it was clear Moran had been about to strangle one or both of us. His face was a mask of resistance, with teeth clenched and helplessness in his eyes. It was obvious he'd been fighting whoever had compelled him to do harm.

"Someone really has a hold on him," Olive observed. "Thanks for the assist."

"No problem." I was surprised by the surge of pleasure I felt at her thanks. "Do you think someone planted Moran here to try to keep us from finding out what happened to my mother?"

"Potentially, but it seems like a lot of work just to keep us from asking about your mother's death. Still, he's not as malleable as they'd like. I believe they reanimated him for a more nefarious reason."

"Such as?"

"I don't think it was me he was trying to strangle." She gave me a pointed look.

My stomach dropped and I glanced at Moran. Had he been trying to kill me? I didn't like that. Not at all. "Do you think it's the same person who is after the grimoire?"

"Seems likely, as you don't offer much else of value," Olive said.

Ouch! So much for the warm fuzzies I'd felt a moment ago.

"But given the potential power of that grimoire, with spells dating back centuries, I believe there could be more than one person looking for it. And, of course, they'd need you, dead or alive, preferably dead if they're a necromancer, to be able to use the grimoire, as it's spelled to respond only to you."

More than one? This did not reassure me. Shocking, I know.

A knock on the door startled me, while Olive didn't look surprised at all. She probably had the hearing of a bat and knew they were there before they knocked.

Eloise entered, with Jasper right behind her. She took in the scene with wide eyes. "I think you've had a much more adventurous visit than we did."

Jasper glanced from Moran to Shelly. "What do you need me to do?"

Was there anything more attractive than a man offering his services, especially for a chore such as this? No, there was not. Or maybe it was just Jasper, offering assistance in his deep British voice, with his dark hair swept back from his handsome face as his arresting pale eyes assessed the situation with the professional gaze of a person who worked in crisis management.

"Shelly, the interim director"—Olive gestured to the woman still unconscious on the floor—"needs to go to the infirmary where she will recover, believing this was all a really bad dream due to dehydration."

"Right." Jasper crouched down and, with a snap of his fingers, released the zip ties around her wrists. He scooped Shelly up with one arm around her back and the other beneath her knees. "Consider it done."

With that, he departed like a superhero flying an injured person to the hospital.

"He's quite dashing, don't you think?" Eloise asked me.

I felt my face grow warm and hoped I hadn't been staring after him, looking like a middle schooler with her first crush. Mortifying.

"He's all right." I shrugged and turned to Olive. "What do we do with Moran?"

"You're the necromancer," Olive said. "You have to break the hold the other necromancer has on him."

"Oh, sure, no problem," I said. "How do you suppose I do that?"

"If I knew, it would be done already." Olive didn't bother to keep the derision out of her tone.

"I might have a suggestion," Eloise said. "Your grandmother Toni used to recite a spell when she ran into corpses that were in the thrall of another necromancer."

Olive's gaze sharpened. "Do you remember the phrase?"

Eloise scrunched up her nose. I wanted to tell her not to do that for fear that her nose might fall off. I kept my mouth shut, but it was a struggle.

"Not being a necromancer myself, I didn't pay much attention, but I think it went something like Hmm-hm-hmm-hm sat on a wall. Hmm-hm-hmm-hm had a great fall."

"Humpty Dumpty?" I asked. "Mamie recited the Humpty Dumpty rhyme to get rid of reanimated corpses that were not her own?"

Eloise paused, considering. "No, that can't be right."

Olive sat in a chair and propped her feet up on the desk, making herself at home while Eloise thought it through.

"Four score and seven . . . no, that's not it either." Eloise paced around the room. "To be or not to be. Nope."

I wanted to help. I did. But given that I had nothing beyond a foundational knowledge about magic, spells, or necromancy, I needed to be quiet and listen and hope for the best.

"I know!" Eloise snapped her fingers, but the sound was muffled by her gloves. I didn't think she should be taking such a risk with the remaining digits she had left. She spread her arms wide and in a deep voice, she said, "Regressus ad mortem corpus! You try it. You're the necromancer. It should work for you."

"Worth a shot." Olive looked at me.

Was it? Was it really? What if I failed? Wisely, knowing there would be no sympathy from Olive, I did not express my self-doubt aloud.

"Regressus ad mortem corpus," I mumbled, feeling incredibly awkward.

As one, we all glanced at Moran. He didn't move, but his eyes flitted from side to side as if he was saying *no dice* with his eyeballs.

"I think it needs more *oomf*," Eloise said. "You didn't sound as if you meant it."

"Well, he did try to choke us," I said. "If this doesn't work, do we really want him mobile again?"

"Eloise is right," Olive said. "That was half-hearted at best. You know you have to focus just like with the light orb we were working on. Try again and this time, mean it."

"Fine." I sighed. I cleared my throat and shouted, "Regressus ad mortem corpus!" It didn't feel right. I tried saying it backward. "Corpus ad mortem regressus!"

We all stared at Moran. This time, his eyes didn't move, they just looked sad.

"Shoot. I really thought that was it," Eloise said.

"Keep thinking," Olive said. She leaned her head back and closed her eyes. "It'll come to you."

Eloise resumed pacing. I stared at Moran. If I got it right, he'd go back to being dead. Weirdly, he clearly wanted to go. Had life here been so terrible that he wanted to leave? Or was it better on the other side, so to speak, and he wanted to return? I wished I could ask him.

I wondered what the spell could be. The words Eloise had spoken had seemed like they'd do the trick. Was it me? Was I not a necromancer like Mamie? Did I not inherit the ability? Miles had said that witch abilities were genetic and skipped generations. I was surprised by the deep disappointment I felt. I wanted this. I wanted to be able to do this.

"Wait," I said. "Following the rules of modern grammar, shouldn't a declarative sentence be subject, verb, then object?"

"I'm listening." Olive opened her eyes.

"If the words are correct, the order should be *corpus*, meaning *the body*, which is the subject; *regressus*, the verb meaning *returning*; and *ad mortem*, which is *to death*, the object where his body is to return."

Olive waved her hand, gesturing for me to try it. My

stomach clenched. What if I was wrong? I glanced at Moran, still frozen with his arms extended. Could it be worse? If he tried to kill us before he shuffled on, it could be. I decided not to dwell on that.

I turned to face Moran. His gaze was pleading and I gave him a small nod, hoping he understood that I was going to try my best. I held my hands out. It was a poor imitation of Olive, for sure, but somehow it still felt right. I felt the warmth of the magic I was calling unfurl in my chest.

I drew in a steadying breath and with as much emphasis as I could muster, I said, "Corpus regressus ad mortem."

A loud cracking noise sounded as if we were standing on ice that had suddenly split. The room became blindingly bright, but I kept my gaze locked with Moran's. I saw his mouth move ever so slightly and with his last breath, he whispered, "Thank you."

He collapsed to the floor in a heap and the bright light disappeared. I sagged against the desk. Olive jumped to her feet and strode around the desk. She stared down at Moran and then back at me. Both of her eyebrows were raised.

"Is he dead?" I asked.

She didn't answer but crouched down to examine the body. I couldn't look. Not yet. Not until I knew.

Eloise was standing on the far side of the room, looking wide-eyed.

Olive popped back up. "He's gone, undead glamour and all. Good work, Ziakas."

Was that praise? From Olive?

"Of course, it took you long enough to work it out," she added.

There was the Olive I knew. All was right with the world again.

I walked around the desk just to see for myself that Moran had indeed departed his vessel. The smell hit me first. I retched and backed away, pulling the collar of my shirt up over my nose.

"Weeks-old corpses are a nasty business," Olive said.

"But how did he get here?" I asked. "Did someone dig him up and put him here?"

Olive considered me and then nodded. "You're learning your necromancy skills in reverse order. Normally, a necromancer employs a ritual, empowered with an artifact of the deceased, to bring the person's soul and body back, as in the case with Moran. Bringing back just a body is less work, but zombies in bodily or skeletal form tend to be feral and harder to control. Bringing back just the soul doesn't give them a body to inhabit and specters are mercurial without a tether and tend to terrify people."

"A ritual with an artifact and then, what, Moran dug his own way out of his grave?" I asked.

"Most likely whoever brought him back uncovered his coffin and then he climbed out." Olive pointed to Moran's hands. Without the glamour he'd been magicked with, his hands were dirt-encrusted, with scrapes and gashes. He had obviously done exactly that.

"But how?" I asked.

"The undead are preternaturally strong," Olive said. "They are no longer bound by their human limits."

"Whoa." I turned to Eloise and asked, "Would it work on you?"

She blinked at me. "What?"

"The incantation I used on Moran," I said.

"Oh, I don't know." Her eyes were wide as if this hadn't occurred to her.

"Eloise, I'm going to try, okay?" I held up my hands and summoned all the internal focus I could. "Corpus regressus ad mortem."

Eloise stiffened as if bracing herself for the impact of my magic. There was no crack of sound and no bright light. She gave me a sad smile and sighed.

I glanced at Olive and she shrugged. "You can't win them all."

"But why didn't it work?"

"Potentially because the spell you just used was for returning the undead raised by another necromancer. But to whom you have no connection. You have a blood tie to your grandmother, however, so the spell to return Eloise is likely a different one. Magic can be very particular," Olive said.

I dropped my hands. A sudden all-encompassing need to understand everything about the grimoire, my grandmother, my mother, their powers, and what had happened to them surged through me. Gone was all my resistance. I would not rest until I had full control of my abilities.

Olive clapped her hands. "Focus. We have a dead body that we need to remove before someone finds it." She opened the desk and rifled through the contents until she came up with a set of keys. "Follow me."

It never occurred to me to refuse and I followed her out to the hallway, as did Eloise. Olive tried several keys until she found the right one. She locked the office door and pocketed the keys.

She strode down the hallway with her chin held high as if she belonged there, as if we hadn't just unanimated the corpse of the former director of Mystwood Manor. I tried to match her composure but found myself glancing furtively around to see if anyone was chasing us. No one was. The few people we passed were laughing and chatting as if everything were perfectly normal.

How could it be normal when I had just sent a dead man back to his grave—you know, if you didn't quibble about the actual location? I felt lightheaded and put my hand out, steadying myself against the wall as we walked.

I had done a BIG spell. REAL magic. Reverse necromancy. Olive and Eloise walked ahead of me as if everything were status quo, but how could it be? We had a dead body to dispose of. I thought I might be sick.

"Pull it together, Ziakas," Olive ordered.

I stared at her back. She hadn't even turned around. How did she know I was spinning out? I shook myself like a dog coming in from the rain. Fine. I'd freak out later.

"That might be easier if you told us what the plan is," I said. It felt good to punch back a little.

Olive glanced at me over her shoulder. "If you must know, we're borrowing some items."

"What items?" Dread pooled in my stomach.

"Hospital attire, which we'll likely find in the laundry," she said.

That didn't seem too bad, and scrubs would definitely help us blend in.

"And, of course, we'll need a stretcher to move the body," Olive answered.

"We can probably find one near admissions," Eloise suggested.

Olive nodded. "That seems likely."

"And what are we going to do with Moran when we have him on a stretcher?" I asked, not really wanting to know but thinking it was better to be prepared.

"Then we'll borrow an ambulance, naturally." Olive stopped walking and turned to face me. "We have to take him back to his grave."

19

I knew she was right and yet... "Do we? Do we really? No one knows who we are. We could just slip out the side door and fade into the afternoon light."

Olive frowned. "I imagine our containment specialist would disagree."

Damn it. She was right. Jasper would want everything tied up nice and neat with no loose ends, such as a man who'd been dead for weeks being found on the floor of his former office.

"Fine, let's go." My tone was at best grudging.

The laundry room was mercifully deserted and there was a pile of clean scrubs to choose from. Olive commandeered a rolling laundry bin for our street clothes and we quickly pulled on the pale blue scrubs. Of course, we didn't have badges, but Olive didn't seem to think that was a problem.

Olive grabbed a spare set of scrubs for Jasper and texted him that we were on our way to admissions. We got lost three times in the maze that was Mystwood Manor. I wondered if they designed these places on purpose to keep the residents too disoriented to complain.

When we reached admissions, Eloise guided us to the hallway behind the department. Sure enough, three heavy-duty stretchers were parked there, with Jasper standing beside one of them.

"How did it go?" Olive asked him.

"It's sorted, if that's what you're asking," he said.

"I am."

"Shelly is resting comfortably in the infirmary," he said. "I informed the nurse that she appeared to be dehydrated or suffering from low blood sugar, as she was hallucinating about the former director right before she fainted."

"Very truth-adjacent," Olive approved.

"She'll be all right," he said. "And if we can get Moran out of her office before she returns, all the better."

"Agreed." Olive nodded.

"One more thing." Jasper reached into his pocket and removed a flash drive. He glanced at me as he handed it to Olive. "I helped myself to the patient records while the medical team was working with Shelly. Juliet Ziakas's chart is on that. Let's hope it gives us some answers."

"Nicely done." Olive pocketed the drive and pointed to the stretcher closest to the elevator. Jasper wheeled it away, with Olive guiding it after she pushed the rolling laundry bin to me.

Eloise and I fell into step behind them. I tried to maintain a calm facade even as I could feel my heart racing. What would my mother's medical records reveal about her condition while she was here? I was desperate to know. Would we discover that she had been murdered, as Eloise had suggested?

I knew we had to deal with Moran's body, but I really would have preferred to leave the facility immediately to look at the files Jasper had found. As a librarian, I knew research was a lengthy process, but this wasn't just research. It was personal.

Once in the elevator, Olive tossed the scrubs to Jasper. "Change."

Where I would have balked at stripping in front of three people—okay, two people and one former person—of the opposite sex, Jasper didn't even hesitate. He shrugged out of his jacket and began to pull his sweater over his head. As the wool and the T-shirt beneath inched up over his very impressive set of abs, I found myself wondering what the rest of shirtless Jasper looked like.

Olive cleared her throat and stared pointedly at me and then Eloise.

I glanced at Eloise, who seemed unaware that Olive had made any noise. Instead, she was staring at Jasper with her mouth hanging slightly open. I pressed my lips together, hoping I hadn't been doing the same. I reached out and spun Eloise around, facing away from Jasper, as I turned my back on him as well.

"Wait! I'm not done ogling," she said. "What harm could there be in that? I'm undead. Do you know how long it's been since I've seen a handsome man in the buff?"

"It's going to be a bit longer." Olive was already facing the door, clearly the only one of us with any sense of self-control.

I heard the zip of Jasper's pants and stared up at the number display above the door. Surely, we should be on the third floor by now. The sound of clothing rustling seemed awfully loud in the small space and I swallowed, overly aware of the physical act of doing so. I wondered if it was actually possible to choke on my own tongue. There was a ding as the elevator landed and I heard Jasper toss his clothes into the laundry bin with the rest of ours.

I glanced over my shoulder and saw that he was dressed fully in scrubs. Eloise let out a disappointed sigh and I shifted my gaze to her and saw the regretful expression on her face. I knew exactly how she felt.

Olive handed out medical caps and masks and we swiftly donned them while exiting the elevator. Mercifully, the hallway was clear.

The stretcher was remarkably easy to handle and we trundled down the hallway toward the director's office. Olive paused to unlock the door, and a middle-aged woman wearing a purple pullover sweater and plaid wool pants came striding down the hallway with a file under one arm and a fierce expression on her face.

"Who are you? What is the meaning of this?" she demanded. "This is Interim Director Dabrowski's office. If you're looking for a patient, you won't find them in there."

Olive eyed the woman over her mask. Even with her striking features covered, Olive's eyes bored into the other woman's gaze until the woman glanced away.

"Sorry, our orders were to come to the office." Jasper lowered his mask, blasting her with the full view of his handsome face. "If there's been a mix-up, perhaps you could direct us to the correct location, Ms. . . . ."

The woman turned toward him, lured no doubt by his British accent and his broad shoulders. Her body relaxed and she tipped her head to the side in a coquettish posture, tossing her shoulder-length blond hair as she smiled at him.

"Ruth. Ruth Weld, assistant to the director." She blinked. "Of course, I'd be happy to help." She stepped around Olive to get to the door. She grasped the handle and found it locked. "That's odd. I just stepped out for a meeting and Shelly didn't say she'd be leaving."

"Do you have a key?" Olive sounded amused and bored, a contradiction that I would have thought an impossibility, but this was Olive.

"I left it in my desk." Ruth looked like she wanted to stamp her foot. "And I left my cell phone in there as well." She glanced at the four of us, judging our trustworthiness. Jasper smiled at her and that seemed to tip the scales. "Wait here. I'll pop down to security and get the master key."

As one, we all assumed relaxed stances, as if we were relieved to have a few minutes of downtime. This seemed to satisfy Ruth and she trotted down the hallway toward the elevator we had just left.

As soon as the doors closed behind her, Olive unlocked the office door and we hurried inside. The stretcher barely fit through the door and Jasper had to wriggle it a bit to get it in there. Once inside, we passed through what I now knew was Ruth's office to the director's.

The smell hit us like a wave of awful even through our

masks, trapping us in the stench of decay and rot. My gag reflex kicked in and I dry-heaved. Olive grabbed something out of her pocket and held it out to me. "Put some under your nose."

I glanced at the menthol salve and quickly popped off the lid and swabbed some under my nostrils beneath my mask. Jasper held out his hand and I passed it to him. He in turn offered it to Eloise but she shook her head. "I'm fine."

I assumed her sense of smell must be broken. Jasper handed it back to Olive and she dabbed some under her mask as well. "All right, let's get going before our friend returns."

Jasper circled the desk. He didn't hesitate but crouched down beside Moran and hefted him up. He got his torso off the ground, but Moran's lower half dangled. Olive and I moved forward and we each grabbed a leg. It was like trying to carry a very heavy tree trunk whose bark was peeling. We had to grab him by his clothing, which was all that was holding him together. I had no idea how Jasper was able to lift his torso.

We did an awkward crab shuffle to the waiting stretcher. Moran's butt was dragging and we couldn't lift him up high enough. "Let's swing him," Jasper suggested. "And one . . ."

"Two . . ." We rocked Moran back and forth, trying to get enough lift to get him up onto the stretcher as if we were about to hoist him into a pool for a swim.

"Three." We gave one mighty heave and Moran bounced up onto the stretcher. Jasper caught him before he rolled over the other side and Eloise dropped a sheet over his body.

"Excellent," Olive said. "Let's go."

"What about the smell in here?" I was mouth-breathing to keep from vomiting.

"No longer our problem," Olive said.

"As the containment specialist, I have to disagree." Jasper reached into the laundry basket and retrieved the black pouch out of his coat while Olive tapped her foot. We watched as he quickly sprinkled what appeared to be salt in the corners of the room. "That should do it."

Jasper pocketed his pouch and pushed the stretcher back into the hallway, with Olive guiding him, leaving Eloise and me to follow. I dragged the wheeled hamper behind us, hoping no one ran into us or asked any questions.

Naturally, we ran into everyone. A man and woman entered the elevator. Eloise, Jasper, and I positioned ourselves to keep the sheeted body from view. With a glimpse at their badges, I saw they were professional staff, both wearing dress shirts and pants beneath their white coats. We were so screwed. Amazingly, neither of them mentioned the smell. I glanced at Olive. Had she contained it somehow? She must have. I sniffed the air, but the menthol salve blocked everything.

Olive looked them over and in an imperious voice greeted them. "Doctor. Doctor."

They exchanged a look and they both mumbled, "Doctor." They ignored the rest of us and turned their attention to the tablet the man was holding, obviously going over a patient's chart.

They departed on the next floor. In their place came a janitor, pushing a rolling bucket and mop. He was young and skinny with a neck tattoo of a fish—a trout if I was correct—and he glanced at us from beneath the brim of the ball cap he wore. He looked past Jasper and said, "If you need a body bag, they're in the morgue in the basement."

"That's where we're headed," Jasper said.

The janitor looked at him and hit the *B* on the elevator panel. "You weren't, but you are now."

"Thank you." Olive nodded at him.

The elevator opened and he stepped out. A woman in a blue blazer and matching skirt with her auburn hair in loose waves about her face went to step in. Olive blocked her.

"We're going down."

The woman glanced past Olive at the stretcher. "Oh." She stepped back, letting the doors shut.

I sagged against the wall. My nerves were ratcheted to the breaking point. I did not think I could handle one more interaction.

The elevator dinged and we arrived at the basement. The doors slid open and I pushed off the wall, ready to start looking for a body bag, not a task I ever thought I would have to do.

"What the hell are you doing down here?" a voice barked.

The man in front of us looked like someone you'd find if you wandered off the path deep in the woods. He was short and wide with a head like a melon. His jowls flapped when he spoke and his nose sported the broken red capillaries of an alcoholic, making it seem red in appearance. His eyes were narrow slits tucked into the folds of skin that draped over his eyelids. He smelled faintly of tobacco, and despite his small stature, I found him terrifying.

"I think the better question is what are you doing here?" Olive demanded. "I thought your kind wasn't allowed near the dead anymore."

The man barked back a laugh. "This from the likes of you." His gaze narrowed. He sniffed the air like a dog catching a scent. Then his eyes went wide. He stared at Olive with equal parts fear and excitement. "What are you?"

"At the moment? Annoyed." Olive glowered and waved her arm. The man moved aside, but I could have sworn it wasn't of his own free will.

I glanced at Jasper. He didn't seem surprised at all. I then looked at Eloise. Her eyes were as wide as mine. What did Olive mean when she'd said *your kind* to this man? Was he another otherworldly being that was going to give me nightmares?

I braced for the worst when I exited the elevator, still pushing the laundry bin, and moved aside so that Jasper could wheel out the stretcher.

"Body bag, ghoul," Olive ordered.

Ghoul? The man was a ghoul?! My brain raced to remember the origin of ghouls. They were first noted in Arabic folklore as a demon class of jinni. Oh. My. God.

"The name is Malachi," the ghoul said.

"Don't care." Olive crossed her arms over her chest and stared at him.

The man licked his withered lips and said, "What'll you give me for it?"

"More like what I won't do to you so long as you do my bidding," Olive countered.

She lifted her hand and I watched in fascination as the tips of her fingers were suddenly engulfed in blue flames. Eloise gasped and the ghoul, Malachi, blanched.

"All right, fine, you've proven your point." He backed away and I took in the room where we were standing. It looked like an operating room. Sterile, with big steel tables, overhead lights, and lots of equipment. Along one wall I noticed large metal drawers, the sort that stowed bodies. I felt my knees get weak.

Malachi tossed a big black bag at Jasper, who snatched it out of the air with reflexes that seemed almost too fast to track. Almost.

Jasper removed the sheet and Eloise and I assisted him with getting Moran stuffed into the sack. The rot that had been evident upstairs had increased exponentially and I thought I might pass out, except Moran didn't smell as bad as he had before. Maybe my sense of smell had been blown out by the stench. How no one had noticed the effluvium of the corpse in the elevator was a mystery to me. I glanced at Olive. I was certain she had contained it somehow, but I didn't think now was the time to ask.

On the far side of the room, Olive was having a heated conversation with Malachi, which ended with him stomping away from her in a full sulk. To me, pissing off a ghoul—*a ghoul!*—was the stuff of nightmares, but Olive didn't seem to care. She sauntered back just as Jasper finished zipping the body bag.

"Malachi is going to get us transportation," she said. "The four of us and a corpse will never fit in the vehicle we came in. I'll have someone from the rental agency pick up the SUV and deliver it to our hotel."

"Where is Malachi getting this vehicle from?" Jasper asked.

"I don't care so long as we can fit the four of us and our deceased companion in it," she answered.

"Just keep him away from me," Eloise said. "I have enough body parts falling off. I don't need a ghoul helping himself to any others."

A wave of dizziness hit me and I grabbed the edge of the steel table to steady myself. This was an actual conversation. A dead person was announcing that she didn't want to be left alone with a ghoul so he wouldn't make a snack out of her.

"You all right, Zoe?" Jasper asked.

"Nope, not even close," I said. "How is a ghoul working here? Aren't they known for eating the dead?"

"Yes, they are," Olive said. "Usually they stick to cemeteries, but Malachi apparently has some sort of special dispensation from the local witch's council to work here. His father is a very powerful mage."

"Supernatural nepotism?" Jasper asked, but before Olive could answer, she was interrupted by Malachi.

"Here are your keys. Now go."

He threw a set of keys at Olive with, I suspected, the intention of hitting her. Jasper caught them before they had the chance. He handed them to Olive, and she glanced at the tag and smiled. "This will do. Good work, Malachi."

If the ghoul was capable of blushing, I swear he would have been. "Sorry about the . . . er . . . I don't know my own strength."

"Apparently." Olive stared at him until he looked away.

"Where's the service exit?" Jasper asked. He hoisted Moran's body up over his shoulder in a fireman's hold.

"Follow me," Malachi said. He shuffled toward the back of the room and we followed, although Eloise kept a body between him and herself at all times.

Malachi led us up a flight of stairs that opened to the delivery area. No one was there, and he strode across the concrete receiving room to the large metal doors at the back. He pressed a button and the door on the left slowly lifted.

Parked just beyond the loading dock was one of the facility's shuttle buses. It looked like a short school bus but was painted in the same signature teal and purple as the outside of the building.

"I can't be seen with you," Malachi said. He gestured for us to go ahead without him.

Olive looked him over and said, "Just so we're clear, if you cross me, I'll come back for you and you won't like the outcome."

Malachi blanched. "Much as I love your company and your veiled threats, I have a good thing going here. I don't ever want to see you again."

"Then be sure that you don't." Olive gestured for us to go around her and get in the shuttle. Jasper led the way, jogging down the steps. I hurried ahead and opened the back doors for him. He rolled Moran into the space for shopping bags and whatnot. He stepped back and I shut the doors.

"Thanks," he said. The man wasn't even winded.

Jasper turned back around and met Olive at the base of the steps, taking the keys from her. Malachi stood on the loading dock, watching us as the metal door lowered. His eyes met mine, a slow smile curved his lips, and then he pursed his lips and blew me an air-kiss.

My insides shivered with cold. Could ghouls do that or was it my own horror icing my internal organs?

"Ignore him." Olive took my arm and led me onto the shuttle where Eloise was already seated. "Ghouls are the worst."

I fell into a seat and rubbed my temples. Ghouls were real. Dead bodies came back to life. Necromancers existed and I was one apparently. And Olive was . . . I had no idea what Olive was. A witch? Yes, but that seemed too tepid for her. What was more powerful than a witch? A sorceress? Maybe. Okay, I was living in a world where all of this was in-my-face real. Cool, cool, cool.

"Where to?" Jasper asked as he slid into the driver's seat.

"The Newtonian." Olive settled back into the seat behind his.

Jasper raised one eyebrow. "That's rather posh, isn't it?"

"Four-star hotels don't ask questions."

"True enough." He started the engine and pulled out of the lot. The shuttle bus bounced over a speed bump and we all turned to see how Moran's body had fared, as if expecting him to groan or something. He didn't.

"Also," Olive continued, "Moran's grave is in the neighboring town, so this will give us easy access for when you two return him."

"*You two?*" I asked. I hoped Olive didn't mean what I thought she meant. After the deranged Viking episode, I'd made a vow to myself not to spend another night in a cemetery until I was six feet under myself.

"Yes, you and Jasper," Olive clarified. Damn it.

20

"Eloise can't risk losing another body part," Olive said. "And I'll be busy digging through Juliet's medical records, trying to determine what actually happened to her, so that leaves you two to return the body to its place of origin."

I wanted to argue that Juliet was my mother, so if anyone should be looking through her file, it was me. Olive's eyebrows rose as if she expected me to respond that way. If I did, I knew I would have to admit that I had no idea what to look for. I closed my mouth and turned my head to look out the window.

It was late afternoon. The day's earlier clear, crisp weather had turned dreary, more aligned with my mood, for which I was grateful. We got stuck in rush hour traffic and spent more than an hour in one of the tunnels under Boston.

I frequently glanced at the body bag in the back. I had no idea why. Did I expect him to reanimate? Maybe. I certainly had no idea what I was doing, and who knew how Eloise had pulled that incantation or spell or whatever it was out of her Swiss-cheese brain. What if Moran's return to rot was only temporary and he woke up? The thought was terrifying. As I stared at the body bag looking for movement, something bothered me, but I couldn't figure out what.

But then it hit me. "How did you manage to mask his smell?"

"Excuse me?" Olive had been leaning against the windowpane with her eyes closed.

"Why doesn't Moran smell?" I repeated. "I about passed out from the stench of him when he unanimated back into his decaying form. Why doesn't he reek now? Shouldn't he be getting worse and worse?"

I saw Jasper glance at me in the driver's rearview mirror. His gaze left me and moved to Olive, but he didn't say anything.

Olive opened one eye. "I took care of it."

"How?" I asked. Eloise sucked in a breath behind me as if she couldn't believe I was questioning Olive, but I was a librarian and lived for information. There was no way I was settling for less than full disclosure.

"You're a curious one, aren't you?" Olive asked.

I didn't answer. I just stared at her. Maybe it was the drama of the day, but I found I wasn't backing down.

"Fine." Olive reached into her coat pocket and handed me a small vial.

I turned the small brown bottle in my hand around. There was no label. I felt her eyes upon me and defiantly unstoppered the bottle. A familiar scent mingled with something I couldn't identify wafted from the glass vial.

"Lavender?"

Olive nodded. "It masks the scent of decay."

"That's it?" I handed the bottle back.

"No, but it's all you need to know until Tariq teaches you the potion," she said. "I sprinkled Moran's body before we pulled the sheet over him. That's why no one noticed the smell in the elevator."

"Brilliant," Eloise muttered.

Olive pocketed the bottle and tipped her head back, closing her eyes. I couldn't wait to ask Tariq about it.

I felt someone watching me and glanced up, meeting Jasper's gaze in the rearview mirror. The corner of his mouth turned up and I felt myself mirroring the action. I had the feeling he understood my need for answers, which was very validating. The cars ahead started to move and he returned his gaze to the road while I stared at the white tile walls of the tunnel in which we were doing time.

As we left the city, darkness fell and I realized I was starving. I wouldn't have thought I'd ever eat again after being cooped up in a shuttle bus with a dead body, but Olive's masking potion worked so well that I could have eaten my body weight in lasagna or pizza or Chinese food. My stomach growled loud enough that I thought it might rouse Moran.

A chocolate chip granola bar appeared in my line of vision. "Eat."

I took the bar from Olive. "Thanks." I wanted to devour the entire thing at once, but instead, I forced myself to take small bites and chew them thoroughly. After all, who knew when I'd get the chance to eat again?

It took us another hour of stop-and-go traffic to get to our exit. Several miles later, in the heart of a Boston suburb, our bougie hotel appeared. Jasper parked the shuttle in the visitor's lot and Olive hopped out and strode into the lobby of the Newtonian Hotel. It had valets standing outside, wearing long burgundy coats with matching short-brimmed caps. One of them hurried to open the door for her and Olive swept in, never breaking stride.

"Does she intimidate everyone she meets?" I asked.

"Everyone," Jasper confirmed. "Tariq and I agree that if ever we're in a pub fight, we want Olive to have our backs."

I laughed. The mere idea of Olive in a bar brawl struck me as funny. I glanced at Jasper and his smile widened and I knew he had said what he did specifically to cheer me up.

"Try not to worry about the graveyard tonight," he said. "You don't have to do anything but be a lookout."

I shook my head. "I can be more help than that."

His gaze moved over my face, assessing my words. Then he nodded and said, "All right."

It was more than just assent. I felt as if he was agreeing that I had more value than just being an extra pair of eyes. I appreciated the confidence even as I had no idea what I had just agreed to do. Idiot.

Olive returned and Jasper opened the doors, letting a blast of cold air in with her. She stood on the steps and said, "Come on, Eloise, let's get you inside." She turned to Jasper. "We're booked in the penthouse, as it's a suite with four bedrooms. We'll see you two here when you're done."

Jasper nodded and I did, too. Eloise shuffled up the aisle and paused beside me. She patted my shoulder and with a worried expression she said, "Be careful, Zoe. Powerful beings lurk in cemeteries at night."

If she was trying to comfort me, this was not the thing to

say. I forced a smile and said, "I'm sure we'll be fine." I was sure of no such thing, but I didn't want to appear to be a doubter.

Eloise followed Olive into the hotel and Jasper started up the bus, leaving behind the penthouse suite, which was undoubtedly warm and had hot showers and room service. I tried not to pout.

The cemetery was well situated on the side of a hill. Jasper turned into the imposing entrance, which consisted of two stone pillars with a wrought iron arch over them. The name of the cemetery, Abiding Savior Green, was worked into the iron and lit by sconces on the pillars.

"These nighttime cemetery visits are becoming a habit for us," Jasper said.

I glanced at the dark headstones all around us and shivered. "At least we're not running for our lives this time."

"Not yet anyway."

I stared at the back of his head until he glanced up in the rearview and met my gaze. Our faces were illuminated by the blue glow of the dashboard and he looked apologetic and said, "Sorry, it was just a joke. I'm sure this will be nothing like the last time."

"No crazed Viking to trap in a tomb?" I asked. "That disappoints."

He laughed, it was deep and gravelly and it made me smile in return. Given the frazzled state of my nerves, it felt like a victory to be able to joke about the situation and get him to laugh. I'd take the win.

"How do we know where Moran's grave is?" I asked.

"I looked it up on the cemetery's website while we were sitting in traffic. His plot is on the west side next to one of the marble benches where visitors can sit and reflect."

"That narrows it down, I suppose." I moved from my seat to the bench diagonally across from his. "I'll look to the right if you want to take the left."

"Deal." He drove slowly, giving us plenty of time to try to spot the bench.

I tried to block Eloise's words from my mind, but the shadows that seemed to peer at me from around every tree and headstone made it impossible. Self-doubt crept in as thick and oppressive as the darkness. I didn't know what I was doing. I didn't know if I could help Eloise and I had no idea how I was going to figure out what had happened to my mother and grandmother. It all felt incredibly overwhelming but I was determined that my little black book and I would fake it until we could make it.

I patted the large inside pocket of my coat just to reassure myself that the grimoire was there. Its solid presence was strangely comforting.

"Hey, over there." Jasper pointed toward the side of the road. "Does that look like a memorial bench to you?"

I shook off the maudlin thoughts about my abilities and leaned forward. The headlights of the shuttle bus illuminated what was most definitely a marble bench.

"How do we know if it's the right bench?" I asked.

"Only one way to find out," Jasper said. He parked and pulled the lever for the doors. They opened and he grabbed a flashlight from the box under the dash. "Let's go."

Maybe it was a touch of post-traumatic stress disorder, but

I found I didn't want to step into the graveyard. I didn't want to run into anything my reasonable, fact-based brain couldn't explain.

"I can wait here if you want," I offered. "You know, to make sure no one steals the bus."

Jasper switched on his light and swept the area with the beam. "It doesn't seem like a hotbed of shuttle bus thievery, but by all means suit yourself." He glanced past me at the body bag in the back.

I followed his gaze and realized I had no interest in being left behind with the corpse. Nope. Nuh-uh. No thank you.

"Never mind, you're right," I said. "I'm sure the bus will be fine here."

Jasper handed me another flashlight from the box beneath the dashboard and we set out among the headstones. Jasper strode the uneven ground as if he were out on an afternoon hike. I wanted to snatch his calm and wrap it around myself like a blanket. Since I couldn't, I followed on his heels like a twitchy little squirrel expecting an owl to snatch it up at any moment.

"We can cover more ground if we split up," he said.

No, no, no. I didn't want to. Instead, not wanting to be perceived as the weakling I feared I was, I said, "Of course. I'll go this way."

I turned and took five steps when the ground disappeared beneath my feet and I tumbled into a deep, dark hole.

21

"Zoe!" Jasper cried, and I heard him run toward me. "Are you all right?"

I'd landed with a smack on a hard wooden surface, breaking the fall with an elbow and a hip. *Ouch!* It took me a second to realize I was in a grave and another moment to comprehend that I was lying on a casket. I let out a shriek and, despite the pain, scrambled to my feet.

Jasper's flashlight beam hit me full in the face and I held up my hand and turned away.

"Sorry!" He set the beam aside and reached a hand down. "Are you all right?"

"I don't think I broke anything except my spirit, if that's what you're asking," I said. He grunted a laugh and I clasped his wrist with my hand and he did the same with mine.

"Count of three," he said. "One, two, three . . ." He hauled me out of the hole as if I weighed no more than a sack of potatoes. I dropped to my knees on the cool grass and let the scent of the earth calm my beating heart.

Jasper knelt beside me and rested his hand on the center of my back. "On a positive note, I think you found it."

"Yay, me," I quipped. The heat of his hand helped to calm me even as it made me uncomfortably aware of him.

In my previous, quiet life, I hadn't run into men like Jasper often. Okay, ever. With his wavy dark hair, pale eyes, British accent, and impressive physique, he was so far out of my compatibility zone, I couldn't think of him as anything more than a colleague. To do otherwise would be disastrous for so many reasons, not the least of which was the inevitable heartbreak from unrequited love. Truly, there wasn't anything worse than that. I'd rather fall into ten more graves than suffer pining for someone who saw me as the plain Jane I was.

With that thought in mind, I pushed up to my feet and his hand dropped away. My elbow and my hip throbbed, but I took comfort in the fact that I hadn't landed on my face. Amazingly, I had kept my grip on my flashlight when I'd fallen and its beam still shone brightly. I moved it over the grave, pausing at the headstone. I couldn't make out the words, so I carefully picked my way around the hole until I could read it.

The headstone was a solid slab of granite, austere but softened by the words *Beloved Husband* and *Father*. I skipped over the dates and looked at the name: *Milton David Moran*. This was it. I moved the light beam down to the casket. The lid was obviously closed—*hallelujah!*—otherwise, I would have landed in the casket when I'd fallen and I didn't think my psyche was up for that.

"You're right," I said. "It's his."

"Excellent. Now we get him back inside and let him rest in peace." Jasper moved his flashlight across the piles of earth.

I frowned. "I just don't understand. Who did this and why? I mean, I get that it has to be a necromancer, but it seems like they went to an awful lot of trouble just to keep us from asking about my mother."

"More trouble than sending an undead Viking after you?"

"Fair. It just seems like a lot of effort to have him in place at Mystwood Manor if the intent was to keep us from asking about my mother's death."

"I think there is much more happening than trying to block your questions about your mum." Jasper's voice was low and cautious as if he didn't want to offend me. "Olive said that Moran reached across the desk and tried to strangle you."

"Or her," I protested. "It could have been her."

Jasper stared at me with his lips pressed together and gentle patience in his eyes. I glanced away. I was not enjoying the turn this conversation had taken.

"Let's get to it, then," I said. "I want to hear what Olive has discovered in the medical file."

"Fair enough," Jasper agreed. He took my uninjured elbow and guided me around the grave as if he feared I might fall in again. Not the unlikeliest of possibilities.

We arrived back at the bus to find it exactly as we'd left it. Jasper opened the back doors and there was the body bag with Moran. He hefted him back up over his shoulder and we returned to the grave.

Jasper laid him on the ground and we considered the casket below, the six-foot drop, and Moran's very heavy body.

"Can we lower him, using the body bag, and then remove it once we're down there?" I asked.

"It'd be easier to open the casket and just pop him in, body bag and all."

"His family most likely went to great expense to have him laid out just so," I said. "We can't disrespect that."

Jasper considered me for a long moment. I suspected he wanted to refuse, but finally he nodded. "All right, then."

He jumped down into the hole and opened the lid of the casket. This was no small endeavor, as the hole that had been dug—I tried not to picture Moran clawing his way out—was a tight squeeze.

Kneeling on the edge, I reached a hand down, offering to help Jasper out as he'd helped me. To my surprise, he took it and I had to clench my entire body to keep from dropping him back into the hole. I tried not to look at him, because I didn't want to be distracted.

As he used me to pull himself up, I slid across the grass to the edge of the hole. When his head cleared the grave, we were face-to-face and I found my brain shorting out as I noticed he had the thickest, darkest eyelashes of anyone I'd ever known. He reached past me and planted his hand on the ground and hauled himself out of the grave inch by inch. I should have helped, but he seemed to have it under control and I didn't think touching him would help me with my vow not to fall for him.

"Are you sure we can't just drop him in?" Jasper collapsed on the grass beside me.

The question brought me back to the situation at hand and I said, "Yes, very sure."

Jasper shrugged. "All right. I'll bring him down. You follow and you can help arrange him in the casket."

"Wait, if we're both down there, how will we get out?" I asked.

"I can lift you out from below and you can pull me out again," Jasper said. "Shine the light for me?"

He didn't wait for my response but pushed to his feet and hefted the body bag over his shoulder once again. I held the light steady while he slid down the side of the hole, barely keeping his balance when he landed in the bottom beside the casket. He placed the body bag inside and glanced up, waiting for me.

I half fell, half slid, just as he had, and together we unzipped the body bag and rolled what was left of Moran into the casket. The scent of lavender and whatever else Olive had used to mask the decay was still working, but the rotting flesh, which had begun to slide off his bones, made my knees weak and I thought I might be sick.

As Jasper rolled up the body bag and tossed it out of the grave onto the ground above, I gently tried to arrange Moran's arms as they would have been for his initial burial. I crossed them over his chest, hoping the look of peaceful repose would allow him to have just that.

I straightened his tie one last time. When I went to rise, Moran sat straight up in his coffin. I shrieked and his eyes flew open, one eyeball hanging a bit lower than the other, and he made a garbled sound in his throat as if he was trying to speak.

"Oy!" Jasper reached for me, but he was too late.

Moran clutched me by the throat with one bony-fingered hand and started to squeeze.

"She's too strong . . . I . . . don't . . . want . . . to . . . kill . . . you." Moran was muttering, clearly fighting to get every word out.

I grabbed at his arm, trying to break his grip. I felt Jasper lurch forward and his hands joined mine as he attempted to pry Moran away from me. My breath turned into a wheeze as my airway got smaller and smaller. I thrashed against Moran's hold as panic surged inside me. My vision went blurry and I felt myself start to black out.

I heard the sickening crunch of bones being crushed. My eyelids flickered as I fought unconsciousness. I was petrified that sound had been Jasper's bones and that this was to be our ill-fated end. Weird to think that right now I rather missed our homicidal Viking.

Focus, Zoe! I berated myself. I had to help Jasper!

"Corpus regressus ad mortem," I murmured, causing my throat to burn with pain. I didn't care. Whatever I had to do, I was willing if it meant we survived this. Inhaling through my nose, I forced the words out more emphatically this time. "Corpus regressus ad mortem."

The hand around my throat dropped away and Moran fell back into his coffin. I fell into the dirt on the side of the casket, no longer caring about arranging his limbs. Jasper reached around me and slammed the coffin shut.

He collapsed beside me and I turned to find his fierce gaze boring into mine, "Are you all right? Did he hurt you?"

"I'm okay," I said through chattering teeth. "Totally okay . . ." But I wasn't. I wanted to run, cry, scream, punch somebody—basically I was on the brink of a complete and total mental breakdown. "How did he rise again? I sent him back. He even wanted me to. How did he return?" My voice got higher with each word.

"I don't know." Jasper frowned and pulled me into his

arms. He hugged me tight until I stopped shaking. When he released me, I stepped back, feeling awkward and shy. I wasn't a hugger by nature and I was never clear on what I was supposed to do when the hug was over.

"He's gone now, but given that we don't know how he came back, I think it's best we get out of here as quickly as possible." Jasper took my hand and guided me to the side of the grave where I'd dropped my flashlight. He picked it up out of the dirt—it was still working—and handed it to me. He laced his fingers together and said, "Are you ready?"

I nodded. I wanted to get as far from this place as possible as fast as we could. I put the flashlight in my pocket and braced myself with a hand on his shoulder. I put my foot in his hands and he said, "Up you go!"

He hefted me as if I weighed nothing. My upper body was up out of the grave and I flopped against the grass as I tried to pull myself the rest of the way.

"Not to get too personal, love," Jasper said, "but I'm going to give you a push."

His hands cupped my ass and he gave me a hearty shove. I skidded across the ground and my coat took the brunt of the abuse, but I didn't care. I was free! I rolled onto my back and stared up at the night sky. The temperature had dropped and I suspected it was near freezing out, but I was so hot from my previous panic that I welcomed the chilly air against my feverish skin. I pulled the collar of my coat aside and tried to cool my neck where Moran's fingers had tried to squeeze the life out of me.

I closed my eyes for just a moment and then crawled back to the grave to offer Jasper my hand. He grabbed it, and I pulled while he dug his toes into the side of the grave wall. In moments he was up and out. I flopped back down and he fell back onto the cold, hard ground beside me.

"I think we need to ask for a raise," he said.

That surprised a chuckle out of me. "What's the going hourly rate for being almost strangled by the undead?"

"Not enough."

"Agreed."

"I'll admit this career path does take some getting used to," he said. "But I can say this, working for the BODO is never ever boring."

"Is that why you do it?" I pushed myself up to a seated position and Jasper followed.

"Among other reasons." He rose to stand and held his hand out to me. "Come on, let's get this bugger buried and get some food. I'm famished."

Jasper propped his flashlight on the headstone and stood with his arms wide. As I watched, he gestured to the mounds of dirt that surrounded the grave, and like a maestro conducting a symphony, he guided the piles of earth back into the grave, burying Mr. Milton David Moran for what I hoped was the last time.

We arrived at the penthouse looking rough. The doorman, upon hearing our destination, remained impassive, leading me to suspect that Olive had warned him that we would look worse for wear, or maybe that's just how doormen in posh hotels responded to people covered in leaves and mud with the lingering scent of a graveyard about their persons.

The elevator opened into a lobby that had only one door. We crossed the marble floor and Jasper turned the knob and pushed the door open. I froze in the doorway, taking in the opulence before me.

The floor-to-ceiling windows offered a view of the Boston skyline in the distance. The furniture was sleek and modern and mostly white. I glanced down at my dirt-encrusted clothes, afraid to step inside.

"There's a laundry bag in each of your rooms. Use them, and we'll have your clothes washed tonight and returned in the morning. I took the liberty of buying you each some clothes from the spa. They're nothing fancy, but they'll do." Olive was seated at a large table with a laptop in front of her. She was peering at the screen, not bothering to look at us.

"Brilliant, thank you," Jasper said. "I, for one, am going to take the longest, hottest shower of my life."

"You have thirty minutes. I've ordered room service for you," Olive said. "They'll be here in half an hour."

Jasper started across the room and, realizing I wasn't moving, paused and turned around. "All right, Zoe?" His tone was gentle, as if he expected the teeth-chattering disaster I'd been in the grave to return.

I nodded. "Yes, I'm just getting my bearings."

"Leave her with me," Olive said. "I want to talk to her."

Jasper glanced from me to Olive and back. He lifted his brows, silently asking if this was okay. I nodded.

"Bedrooms are up there." Olive gestured to the spiral

staircase at the end of the room. "Yours is the second on the right."

I watched Jasper climb the stairs and disappear down the hallway before I spoke. "Did you want to know how it went?"

"You're both here, so I assume it went well."

"Moran woke up." I strolled across the room and stood beside the table.

"Did he?" Olive turned away from the computer and glanced at me. Her gaze lingered on my neck. "I see there was a bit of a struggle."

I covered what I was certain were bruises with my hand. "How is it possible that he woke up? And, bigger concern, will he wake up again?"

Olive leaned back in her chair. "These are very good questions to which I have no answers."

"Why not?" I asked.

"Because necromancy is your gift, not mine."

"Surely you've come across this sort of thing before."

"Sorry, no." Olive looked very matter-of-fact about it. Why this irritated me so much, I had no idea, but it really peeved me.

"It's possible that the necromancer who raised Moran the first time raised him again in the cemetery," Olive said.

"You mean they were in the graveyard when we were there?" I asked.

Olive shrugged. "I have no other explanation for how he woke up."

"Then they could raise him again!" I was freaking out. I knew it. Olive knew it. There was no use trying to pretend I wasn't.

"Why would they when it seems they only raised Moran

to kill you and he failed?" Olive asked. "Now that you've sent him back and buried him, they'll likely raise another corpse to try to kill you."

She said this so matter-of-factly as she turned back to her computer that I wondered for a moment if the metaphorical heart encased in ice in *El Corazón* in the BODO collection wasn't Ariana Darkwood's but rather Olive's, because clearly she didn't have one.

"Where's Eloise?" I asked.

"She's resting. I think coming that close to a ghoul shook her up." Olive glanced back at the laptop. "She hasn't lost any more body parts, so that's something."

Weariness settled over me. I was tired all the way down to my soul. I wasn't used to nonanswers for answers and I really loathed not being able to find a case study or a dissertation or something that would help me comprehend this new reality I was living in. The only thing I could think to do was solve the problem at hand.

To that end, I asked, "Did you discover anything about my mother's death?"

Olive glanced back at me, considering. "Are you sure you want to hear it?"

"It's the assignment, isn't it?" I knew I sounded a bit snippy and I would have felt bad about it except that a corpse had tried to strangle me and I didn't have enough emotional bandwidth to feel regret for my tone.

Olive's lips actually turned up at the corners. "Very well, Ziakas."

If I didn't know better, I would have thought she was pleased with me. "I don't have definitive proof of murder."

I wasn't sure if I was relieved or not. I had no time to process as she continued.

"What I do have are some troubling medical records," she said.

I glanced at the chair near me. It was upholstered in white suede. I'd be an absolute ass to sit on it, but I was so exhausted. I pulled the chair out and sat—gingerly, but I sat.

"Have you ever heard of the Waning Curse?"

I frowned. "*Waning* as in a waning moon?"

Olive's eyebrows lifted in surprise. "Exactly. It coincides with the waning gibbous, third quarter, and waning crescent phases of the moon."

"What does it do?" I asked.

"Essentially, it's used on a witch or a mage to slowly kill them." A flicker of sympathy flashed in Olive's dark eyes. "I believe the curse was used on your mother."

"But why?" I asked.

"I suspect whoever did it wanted the grimoire, but your mother must have refused to tell them where it was," Olive said.

"It was hidden in time," I said.

Olive leaned forward. "What makes you say that?"

"It's a theory that Agatha has," I said. "She believes we could never figure out where my mother was because she was hiding in another time." I told her about my mother's sporadic visits and the strange antique gifts she always arrived with, like the dollhouse and the raven puppet.

"Which would explain why Eloise couldn't feel the grimoire and find Juliet," Olive said.

"What proof do you have that she had this Waning Curse?" I asked.

"The symptoms she had are what you'd expect—exhaustion, hallucinations, ravenous hunger but an inability to eat, difficulty in communicating, and her patient chart indicates a gradual slowing in the function of her body's organs with no indication of any known illness. Her magical powers would have gone dormant as well, meaning she couldn't even help herself with magic. Of course, human doctors wouldn't have known what was wrong with her or have the cure."

"So she just wasted away into nothing and no one helped her?" I asked.

Olive nodded. "Her official cause of death was cardiac arrest."

"That's what we were told."

"And it's probable that her heart gave out because of the curse," Olive said.

"And you're absolutely certain she was cursed?" I asked.

"I'd say, more accurately, your mother was magically murdered."

22

"Murdered." I needed to repeat it because my brain wanted to refute it totally and completely even though I'd suspected as much for weeks.

"Yes." Olive nodded. Then, as if it occurred to her belatedly to offer sympathy, she added, "Sorry."

I staggered to my feet and said, "I need some air."

"There's a balcony upstairs, feel free to step outside, but don't do anything dumb."

"Such as?"

"I don't know. You librarians are an overly emotional sort, so I feel compelled to caution you against being impulsive." Olive's focus returned to her laptop.

I blinked. "That's the first time I have ever been called too emotional because I'm a librarian." The mere suggestion almost made me smile as I thought of every overthinking, pragmatic librarian I had ever known during my years of service.

"Just stating facts."

"M'kay." I turned and headed for the upper floor.

"Your room is second on the left," Olive called after me. I

raised my hand in acknowledgment. Whether she saw it or not, I hadn't a clue nor did I care.

I pulled myself up the spiral staircase and saw the balcony doors. I turned the handle and stepped outside. The cold air hit my face like a slap. It felt good. Even as I shivered, I was grateful for the sting.

I stepped up to the waist-high railing and noted the stairs that led to the roof above. I wondered if it had a garden like the Museum of Literature did. When I hauled myself up, I was disappointed to see a barren landscape of roof. No garden beds, no chairs, no Miles and Tariq enjoying tea.

Why this gutted me, I had no idea, but I sank to the ground as tears blurred my vision. I sat on the ledge, letting my legs dangle. Then I dropped my head into my hands and sobbed.

The terror of the day, almost being strangled—twice!—the endless reveals about my family and the past, the probability that my mother had been murdered, combined with the overwhelming sense that I was failing at what I was supposed to be doing—figuring out who did it—all of it took me out at the knees and I indulged in a pity party of epic proportions.

I don't know how long I sat there or when exactly I felt another presence on the roof, but as my sobs diminished, I knew with a sudden clarity that I wasn't alone. I swiped at the wetness on my face with the sleeves of my coat. If it was Olive, I would never live down the humiliation of proving her right about the overly emotional state of librarians.

I dropped my hands and lifted my head. I put on my most disinterested expression, usually reserved for library patrons who offered scathing opinions about books they hadn't actually read, and prepared to face who or what was out there.

"Oh, hey, you."

Perched on the ledge mere feet from me was a raven. He was big, black, and boldly beautiful. His eyes were the same light blue that I remembered, which meant that he was young, probably a fledgling, as his eyes would change to a darker color when he matured. Yes, I'd looked it up.

I tipped my head to the side. Was he the raven who had taken up residence on my mailbox? We were in another state and more than two hundred miles from home. Ravens were known to fly up to thirty to forty miles from their roost to their feeding areas each day. It couldn't be him, could it?

"Are you following me?" I asked.

The raven tipped his head to the side as if he were listening. Weird. Was his appearance right here and now just a coincidence or did the bird have business here as well? Okay, that was ridiculous. What sort of business did a raven have on the top of a four-star hotel in the Boston suburbs in November?

"Apologies, I realize your life is not my business," I said. My voice was gruff from crying. I sniffed and sighed. "I'm not normally so impolite. It's just been a really rough day."

The raven turned to the view, then he very carefully began to sidle down the ledge toward me. He stopped when he was mere inches away. I wondered if he was a zombie raven that I'd inadvertently resurrected. He didn't look undead. If he wasn't a zombie bird—*oy!*—was he my familiar? If I did have the gift of necromancy, a raven would certainly be an on-the-nose choice.

My throat hurt, my eyes were swollen, and my nose wouldn't

stop running. I had no doubt I was the picture of misery. Perhaps having a designated magical buddy wouldn't be such a bad thing. Still, I didn't want to assume.

"Are you my familiar?" I asked. If the bird had talked back, I probably would have fallen right off the roof. He didn't. Instead, he inched closer to me and then he leaned in, pressing against my side.

It was then that I remembered my mother's words when she'd given me the raven puppet so many years ago. *I've had a vision about you and a raven. You need to trust the raven*, she'd said. Had the vision indicated that the raven was my familiar? I had so many questions and no way to get any answers.

I felt a sob bubble up, but I held it in my throat. I didn't want to scare my bird friend away. It was such an unexpected comfort to have this wild creature be so seemingly in tune with my emotions, which were all over the place at the moment.

There was nothing like being forced to confront my own mortality to make me realize I had so few connections in this life that practically no one would notice if I were suddenly gone.

Agatha. Agatha would miss me. A handful of people would notice I was no longer at work, mostly Bill, but the rest of the world would just sail on, going about their business as if Zoe Ziakas had never existed. I wasn't sure how I felt about that.

I didn't want to scare the raven, but the need to connect to another being was so strong that before I could overthink it, I reached out to stroke his feathers. I expected him to peck me and launch himself off the roof. Instead, he leaned more firmly into me while I rested my hand on his back, the silky softness of his feathers beneath my fingers the only thing locking me into this moment.

"I'm sorry I described you as pesky to my coworkers," I apologized, remembering my conversation with Tariq, Miles, and Jasper on the rooftop of the Museum of Literature. "You're not. In fact, you're really very lovely."

The raven ruffled his feathers and preened his outer wing a bit while still leaning into me. We sat on the roof ledge like that for a very long time.

The hot shower I took might have been the best of my entire life. By the time I'd left the roof, I couldn't feel my fingers or my nose. When I'd stood, my new friend had flown off into the night and I'd wondered if and when I'd see him again. I felt oddly certain that I would and I took comfort in that.

The clothes Olive had managed to acquire were actually very comfortable, even if they were the top and bottom of a tracksuit in an eye-watering shade of orange. I felt like a traffic cone. I wondered if Jasper had fared as well or worse. My curiosity and hunger propelled me downstairs to the main room.

Jasper, Eloise, and Olive were seated at the dining table and I could see they were in a video conference on Olive's laptop with Claire, Miles, and Tariq. Claire paused whatever she was saying to greet me.

"Zoe, good to see you," she said. "How are you feeling?"

"Fine." I winced, as my throat hurt when I spoke.

"Jasper told us what happened." Claire shook her head. "I would appreciate it if you'd see a doctor."

"Oh, no, that's not necessary." I pointed to my neck. "It looks worse than it is."

Claire didn't look convinced, but Olive took me at my word, which I appreciated.

"You look like hell, but you'll live. Eat." Olive nodded to me.

Jasper handed me a plate and I noted his tracksuit was a blistering shade of neon green. His gaze took in my suit and we shared chagrined expressions.

"If you say this is my color, I'll never forgive you," he said.

My lips twitched. "Same." His returning smile made a warmth unfurl inside me. At least I wasn't alone in this fashion catastrophe.

I perused the options on the loaded food cart while listening to the others talk. I chose a piece of cake. In my defense, it was coconut cake. Coconut was a fruit, so that made it practically a fruit salad.

"We have no idea who activated Moran," Miles said. He sounded exasperated. I glanced at the laptop screen as I took my seat and noted that his customary tufts of hair were higher than usual, as if he'd been running his fingers through them repeatedly.

"I checked the whereabouts of every known necromancer in the area and none of them was anywhere near Mystwood Manor," Tariq said. "Whoever brought Moran back is unknown to us."

"Is there any way to make them known?" Jasper asked. He was working his way through a plate of fish and chips, which looked excellent but wasn't what my body was craving.

"We're working on it," Miles said.

"I don't like it," Claire said. "If we don't know who it is, we can't protect you. I think you need to come back to New York."

I picked up my fork and went to stab a mouthful of cake. The tines hit the granite tabletop with a plink. Olive had whisked away the slice of cake and was shoving a plate of salad in its place, all while keeping her gaze on the laptop.

"Hey!"

"You can't fuel your potential with fat and sugar," Olive said. "Salad first, cake later."

"That's bullsh—" I began, but her scarred eyebrow went up and I took it as the warning it was. I stabbed a spinach leaf and stuffed it in my mouth to keep myself from saying anything else.

It occurred to me that Olive was even worse than Agatha. At least I wasn't afraid Agatha would turn me into a toadstool or a chair if I displeased her. I worked on the salad, eyeing the thick slice of cake and counting the seconds until it was mine.

"We're not coming back," Olive said. "Not right away. Instead, we're taking the ferry out to Hagshill Isle, off the coast of Rhode Island. It's where Toni Donadieu raised her daughter, Juliet. Eloise thinks someone there might remember something about Toni or Juliet."

That did it. I abandoned my salad and reached for the cake. I needed the decadent buttercream to soothe my jagged nerves. I hadn't been out to Hagshill Isle since the night my mother and I had fled after the terrible fight she'd had with Mamie.

I bit into the cake, ignoring Olive's exasperated glower.

"Are you all right with this, Zoe?" Jasper asked. "You don't have to come."

"Of course she does," Olive said. "If we don't find anyone who remembers Toni, then Zoe and her potential memories are the only lead we have."

Eloise glanced around the table. She seemed smaller to me. Was it my imagination? Was Eloise shrinking into herself with every day that passed and I couldn't help her to move on? The thought made me push aside my cake. I didn't like the weight of this responsibility. It was too much for a former skeptic like me to bear.

"It's fine," I said. "I'll go."

"Zoe, you—" Claire began, but Olive interrupted her.

"Now that it's settled, we've got to go. Big day tomorrow. We'll be in touch." Olive closed the laptop, cutting off the connection before anyone could say anything. She glanced at us. "What?"

"Mamie's been gone a long time," I said. "What if no one remembers her?"

"They will," Eloise said. "Island residents have long memories, especially for Toni. She did a lot of good in the community, working as a healer. An island community is fairly isolated and she cared for so many sick people who couldn't get medical attention. She saved many lives."

I didn't know what to say to that. No one had mentioned this part of Mamie's legacy before.

"That book of hers isn't just about raising the dead," Eloise continued. "She has centuries of knowledge passed down through generations of Donadieus in there."

Again, the weight of it felt like a cinder block on my chest. I had to figure out how to fully understand the grimoire. Maybe going to the island would help. Perhaps I would remember something. But the thought of being there again made me edgy. I hadn't ever planned to step foot on Hagshill Isle again.

I wondered if my raven friend would appear there. I had no knowledge about how familiars worked, but it seemed to me he should appear when I needed him. And I couldn't think of a time I would need him more than when I was confronting a place so fraught with emotion for me.

"We'll leave first thing in the morning." Olive rose from her seat and left the room without another word.

Eloise stood as well. "I'm heading to my room, too. I'm in the middle of season four of *The Office*. I want to see if I can finish the series before morning."

I frowned and then remembered Eloise didn't need sleep.

"Enjoy." I waved to her as she left the room.

"The British version is better," Jasper called after her.

Eloise smiled at him and started up the stairs.

"Is it crazy that I keep expecting a leg or an arm to fall off her?" I asked, keeping my voice low so Eloise couldn't hear me.

Jasper shook his head. "Not crazy, given her propensity for loose appendages."

I watched her until Eloise disappeared from sight.

"Here." Jasper handed me a spoon.

"What's this for?"

"Crème brûlée," he answered. He removed a small crock

from the rolling cart and put it on the table between us. "I was saving it for dessert, but I'm willing to share."

"I didn't share my coconut cake," I said.

"Understandable. That was your main course, wasn't it?"

"It was."

"Then consider this dessert."

I hesitated and he said, "It's pistachio."

"Pistachio crème brûlée? Why didn't you say so?" I leaned forward and cracked the caramelized sugar top.

He tucked in to the dessert and we were quiet as we savored the subtly sweet, velvety-rich goodness.

"This has been the longest day ever." Exhaustion had me slumping in my seat even as my brain was churning through everything that had happened and trying to parse out who had murdered my mother with a Waning Curse. Had they done the same thing to Mamie? And had it been the same witch or mage who had sent Moran to kill me so they could raise me from the dead and make me their Donadieu grimoire–wielding bitch? Weren't they in for a surprise when they discovered I couldn't even read the book.

"What are you thinking about?" Jasper put his spoon down and the intense look he gave me made my pulse skitter. I suspected he was using his innate charm and attractiveness to distract me.

"My potential as someone's undead magical minion when I don't even know how to use my magic for anything more than levitating myself or a book off the shelf. I can't even make a decent light orb." I tried to keep the panic out of my voice. I failed. "Everyone around me has effortless magic. I watched you move dirt, Olive shoots blue flames out of her fingers, and Tariq can make a potion for anything. I don't even know what Miles can do, but I bet it's significant."

Jasper pushed back from the table and stood, holding out his hand to me. "Come with me, love."

I felt my insides flutter at the endearment. He looked so calm and steady, standing beside me with his wavy black hair and stupefying good looks. Without overthinking it, I put my hand in his.

"Where are we going?" I asked.

"Where we won't be disturbed."

Well, that sounded hot. I cleared my throat. He couldn't possibly mean . . . nah.

Jasper led me out of the penthouse suite and into the elevator. He hit a button and we zipped down to the first floor. He never let go of my hand. I tried not to read too much into that, but my awareness of him—the bergamot-and-coffee scent of him, the warmth of his fingers around mine, the desire I felt to push him back against the wall and scale him like a mountain—was overriding my common sense. I shook my head.

The doors opened and Jasper and I stepped into a deserted hallway. The lights were dim and I could smell the astringent scent of . . . chlorine? We walked down the hallway to a pair of frosted glass doors. They were locked, but did this stop Jasper? No, it did not.

He let go of my hand and slipped his arm around my waist. Much like we did with the magicked doors at the BODO, we stepped forward, but instead of slamming into the glass, we were enveloped into a dark mist and my senses were muffled, almost as if I were underwater. When Jasper let me go, we were standing beside the hotel's indoor pool.

I glanced at him and said, "Fancied a late-night swim?"

"Ha . . . er . . . no." He ran a hand through his hair. "I thought you might appreciate some tutoring." I lifted my eyebrows in surprise. "Not to be too obvious with the metaphor, but you've been thrown into the deep end of the magical realm and I thought a quick lesson might help you . . ."

"Keep my head above water?" I said.

A laugh rumbled up inside him. "Precisely."

"And you chose this place because?"

"It's closed, dark, and very private."

Did I imagine that his voice dropped on that last word? Was the sudden sweat coating my skin because of the steam from the heated pool or him? Him. It was definitely him.

I cleared my throat and said, "Clearly you've forgotten about the exploding orange, but if you're willing, I'm all yours, Teach."

A small smile tipped his lips and I felt a flickering heat in my core at the same time a rivulet of sweat trickled down my neck.

"Let's start with something fun," he suggested. He took my hand and led me to the edge of the pool. "You mentioned how I moved the dirt at the grave. Water is the same principle."

He dropped my hand and then held his hands out over the water. I watched, entranced, as the water in the pool rippled as if awakening. He made a spiral with his right hand and the water started to spin. He lifted his left hand and a spout of water rose from the surface.

"How?" I whispered.

"The same way you retrieved Freya from the bookshelf and ripened the orange. You have to feel the magic inside you. You have to trust it and then focus on the outcome you want." He held his hands still and the water dropped and stopped moving. "You try."

I put my hands out over the water and closed my eyes. I thought about the warmth that infused me whenever I concentrated. Uninvited, an image of Jasper filling the grave with dirt flashed through my mind. I shook my head, trying to clear the image of him, but my brain was fixated as it flashed to the memory of him holding me after we contained the Viking. The attraction I had felt for this man from the moment I'd met him seemed to swirl up inside me, refusing to be ignored.

"Um . . . Zoe . . ." Jasper's voice broke through my muddled thoughts and I opened my eyes. And there he was, hovering over the water right in front of me, as I had obviously, albeit unintentionally, used magic to bring him to me. I gasped, breaking the spell, and he plunged right into the pool with an enormous splash.

"Jasper!" I pressed my hands to my mouth, horrified by what I'd done.

Jasper broke through the surface of the water, tossing his sodden hair out of his face. His gaze, when it locked on mine, had a mischievous glint. "So that's how it is, is it?"

He raised his hands in my direction and I felt my body rise and drift over the water. I held up my hands and said, "No! I didn't mean it. It was an accident."

"Tell me what you were thinking about when you tried to

move the water." His eyes smoldered and I knew he knew exactly what I'd been thinking about. Him. I felt a rush of embarrassed heat in my face and I knew I was blushing.

"Just the water," I fibbed.

"Really, love?" he asked.

Ugh, that damn endearment was going to be the death of me. I arched my back and stared at the ceiling overhead. He lowered me closer to the water. "All right, I was thinking about you. Are you satisfied?"

He held his arms still and I was held in place, suspended over the gently rippling surface while he considered the question. Then he grinned and said, "No."

He dropped his hands and I was plunged into the pool. I came up sputtering and furious. I had admitted the humiliating truth and he'd still dunked me! The nerve!

I broke the surface riding a wave of soggy indignation. Without even thinking about it, I moved my hands over the water's surface, creating two tall waves that came at him from both sides. He let out a pleased laugh and raised his arms, putting up a water wall that effectively blocked my waves. They crashed together in a tremendous splash that soaked us both.

I swiped at the water dripping down my face, then used both hands to push a spout of water up underneath Jasper, lifting him into the air. I could feel the heat of magic burning inside me and I was giddy from the power when he crafted the spout into a pair of wings and used them to fly by me. As he sailed past, he moved his hands as if fashioning a knot, and a rope made of water looped around my upper body, trapping my upper arms at my sides.

I thought I could shrug it off—it was only water after all—but no. I closed my eyes and lifted one hand, bending it at the elbow and focusing on the churning waves around me. A blade of water formed and slipped between my body and the water rope, slicing it. I was free. Jasper was standing in the shallows and I focused on the water between us, forming a bridge. I pulled myself up and strode toward him with all the swagger I was feeling. It was a lot, to be honest.

"Zoe, love, that was incredible!" Jasper dove at me, snatched me around the legs, lifted me off the bridge and held me high in the air. "Look at you! You're a natural."

His enthusiasm was infectious and I laughed, bracing my hands on his shoulders and feeling the afterglow of the magic that had unfurled inside me. I smiled down at him. "Is that how you teach all your students? By annoying them into retaliation?"

"I suppose so, given that you're my only student." He eased his grip and I slid down the front of his body. The warmth of the magic inside me was quickly replaced by a different sort of heat and it felt like the most natural thing in the world to slide my arms around his neck and kiss him.

It was supposed to be a simple kiss. An acknowledgment of the attraction I felt for him but also a thank-you. These moments in the pool were the first time I'd felt as if I could truly be the witch everyone assumed I was.

But his mouth fit mine perfectly and his lips were soft, while the kiss was firm, and I felt dizzy with the wave of want that swept me under more definitively than the water. I broke the kiss and pulled back. He wasn't having it.

Jasper locked me against him with one arm while the

other slid into the hair at the nape of my neck, then he lowered his mouth to mine and kissed me with a ruthless thoroughness that left me clinging to him. When his mouth left mine and slid across my jaw to the sensitive spot beneath my ear, my fingers flexed, digging into his shoulders and causing him to grunt with approval.

I cupped his face with my hands and brought his lips back to mine. I could feel the rough rub of his chin stubble against my skin as my mouth opened beneath his and his tongue tangled with mine as we tasted each other.

"Zoe, I—"

Whatever Jasper had been about to say was interrupted when the overhead lights snapped on and a voice said, "Oh for fuck's sake, the two of you are emitting enough magic to bring the local coven down on our heads."

Jasper and I broke apart to find Olive standing poolside with her arms crossed over her chest, looking like a dark thundercloud. Impatiently, she gestured to the pool, which was no longer blue but a swirling mix of black and red.

"Clean this up and go to bed. You need to be in top form tomorrow." With that, Olive turned and strode through the doors without opening them. Jasper watched her go with his eyebrows raised and an unrepentant smile on his lips.

I would have been embarrassed, but I was a grown woman and didn't have to answer to anyone but myself for my actions, including Olive. Also, I was too fascinated by the water lapping at our hips. "Did we do that?"

Jasper cupped a handful of water. It ran out of his palm in streams of red and black. "It would seem so."

"How?" I asked.

He grabbed my hand and pulled me back into the circle of his arms. "At a guess, I'd say want." He paused to kiss me. "Desire." He kissed me more deeply. "Lust." This time his lips trailed down my throat to nestle in the exposed skin above the V made by the zipper of my tracksuit. He pulled back. My ears were ringing and my brain fuzzy, but even I could see the water surrounding us was churning with whirlpools of black and red.

"I don't understand," I said. "I mean, I do." I paused and fanned my face, indicating my reaction to his kisses. Jasper laughed. "But I don't."

Jasper turned me around, pressing my back against his front, and I noted that we fit together perfectly as we surveyed the pool together. The underwater lights illuminated the ribbons of red among the black, and it was eerily beautiful.

"Every witch or mage has their own signature color. It enhances their powers and comes to light when they are in possession of deep feelings," he said. "Mine is black, so I'm confident we can say yours is red."

"Red." I skimmed my hand across the surface and crimson ribbons rose to the surface, twining around my fingers. I smiled. I'd always loved the color red.

23

Olive hadn't been kidding when she'd said we would leave at dawn. I barely had time to throw back a mug of coffee before we were headed to Hagshill. Thankfully, my clothes had been washed and dried and the shuttle bus returned to Mystwood Manor—I didn't ask—and we were now back in our rented SUV where I was happy to discover my backpack. I tucked the grimoire into it for safekeeping.

Jasper was driving, which was great, as it put some space between us. After we—meaning he—had returned the pool to its original state, he'd dried our clothes with a wave of his hand and walked me to my room, my fingers entwined with his the entire way.

The temptation to grab him by the front of his tracksuit and drag him into my room had been great, but Olive was right. Today was important and I didn't want to let a sex hangover impair my cognitive abilities. Jasper must have felt the same, because he'd cupped my face and kissed my forehead before opening my door and gently pushing me inside with a husky "Sleep well, love."

Olive navigated in the seat beside Jasper's while Eloise and I sat in the back. She seemed content to stare out the window, thinking about whatever the undead liked to think about. For me, it would probably be how much I missed eating chocolate cake. I respected her privacy and didn't ask.

The day was cold and drizzling, and I was dreading the ferry ride to the island. My stomach did not enjoy a choppy sea and I didn't want to add puking my guts out to the list of reasons Olive thought I was not up to snuff to work at the BODO. Not that I had decided I wanted to work there, but I didn't want to be disqualified for being weak. A professional woman has her pride after all.

We left Massachusetts behind and entered Rhode Island. It didn't take us long to get to the shore, and in no time, we were passing over the Newport Bridge. It felt as if we were driving straight up into the sky. Thankfully, I found a loose thread on my sweater and spent the ascent tying it off so my top wouldn't unravel.

When we reached the peak, Eloise rolled down her window and stuck her head and arm out. She waved enthusiastically at the seagulls soaring in the mist beyond the railing and yelled, "Hello! Hello, my darlings! I've missed you!"

"Eloise, get back in the car!" Olive snapped. "You're likely to lose an arm that way."

Eloise sighed and shut the window, ceasing the blast of cold, wet air that filled the vehicle.

"Sorry." Her eyes were large and filled with apology. "I'm just excited to be back."

"Try to contain it." Olive turned back to the front.

Eloise studied the back of Olive's head with a reproving expression and I suspected she didn't appreciate being bossed around any more than I did.

"How long did you live here?" I asked.

"When I was a child, I spent every summer here," Eloise said. "It's where I met Toni. We became instant friends. Too good of friends, perhaps."

There was a wistful note in her voice.

"Because when you died, she couldn't let you go?"

She nodded.

It occurred to me that I didn't know much about Eloise's life, other than her being born in Pennsylvania and spending time in New York, and I realized I'd been so preoccupied with learning about my own family, I had never asked about hers.

"What was your life like before . . . er . . . you came back?" I asked.

Eloise's smile was sweet and genuine, as if the mere thought of her early years brought her a special kind of joy.

"My parents were college professors," she said. "We lived in Wilkes-Barre, near King's College, where they taught. I loved living adjacent to the campus. There's such fantastic energy in places of learning, don't you think?"

I thought about my library. Given that a public library card provided users with a free self-directed education as far as they wanted to take it, I knew exactly what she meant about the energy. It was an amazing thing to help people pursue their passions.

"I do."

"But our summers on the island were magical," Eloise said. "There's just something about Hagshill. Well, you must remember it."

I shook my head. "It was a long time ago. My memories are hazy."

"It's a marvelous place. Toni loved it as much as I did. I really can't wait for you to experience it again, Zoe."

She turned back to the window and I stared at the side of her face. We were returning to a place from both our pasts. I could only hope that when I arrived, I remembered it as fondly as she did.

The sky had darkened with deep gray clouds, and the mist thickened until it coated everything, even my eyelashes. I blinked as we left the car in the belly of the ferry and took the narrow metal stairs to the passenger lounge above. I would have been happy to wait in the car and overthink the situation I was about to enter, but apparently that wasn't allowed.

Olive strode ahead. She stopped to speak with one of the ship's crew, and the next thing we knew, she was joining the captain on the bridge, because of course she was.

Eloise found a seat at the front by the windows. She looked out on the sea, staring at the horizon as if she could manifest Hagshill. I hoped her return wasn't a disappointment for her.

"Care for a cuppa?" Jasper gestured to the small food counter at the back of the lounge.

I nodded. "A coffee would be great." He placed his hand on my lower back and escorted me through the other passengers. I remembered the feel of his mouth on mine the night before and thought about where else I'd like to feel those lips. A warmth unfurled inside me not unlike how it felt when I called my magic.

"Zoe." Jasper leaned down and whispered in my ear, "Red streaks are appearing in your hair." He lifted a hank of hair from behind my back and held it over my shoulder for me to see.

Well, that was embarrassing. My hair was outing my fantasies about him as loudly as if I'd sexted him a naked photo. I tried to bluff, pulling my hair out of his fingers, while not meeting his gaze. "Imagine that."

"Yes, imagine." His laugh was deep and reverberated from his chest and into my spine and I could practically feel my hair changing color in response.

I quickly queued up behind a couple in matching Red Sox jackets. Baseball season was over, but their fan love lived on. Go Sox! I faced forward and pretended to read the limited menu, knowing full well that I was going to order a packet of Skittles and a Milky Way. Bad breakfast choices are the best breakfast choices.

I could feel Jasper looming behind me. Okay, more accurately, he was just standing, but given the unfinished state of things between us, it felt like looming.

"About last night," he said.

No, no, no. I didn't want to talk about this. The potential for more embarrassment was too high. Should I pretend I couldn't hear him? Interrupt him with some other talking point? Listen to him? Ugh, I was so bad at all this. This was why I was happily single and not dating, excluding short-lived hookups. Anything longer and I would inevitably humiliate myself.

"We should probably discuss it," he continued.

A motion outside the window in my peripheral vision drew my attention. I turned and felt my heart stop in my throat. It couldn't be. I squinted. It was!

"Given that my goal was to teach you to access your magic, I hope you don't feel that I took advantage—"

"Pirate!" I yelped.

"Well, I wouldn't go so far as to say that," Jasper protested.

I whipped around to face him and all thoughts of our previous evening's activities vanished. I glanced around the nearly empty lounge and pulled him down by the lapels of his freshly laundered coat.

His eyes went wide, his face mere inches from mine. "Zoe, I—"

"Listen, I don't want to panic the passengers, but, holy shitballs, there is a zombie pirate ship headed right for us."

Jasper turned his head slowly to the window. His eyebrows shot up and he muttered, "Bloody hell!"

"What do we do?" I asked.

"How strong of a swimmer are you?"

I stared at him. It would take a lot more than a ship of undead pirates to get me to jump into the freezing ocean.

"All right, we can commandeer a lifeboat," he said, correctly interpreting my expression. "Let's go."

"But what about the other passengers?" I asked. "We can't just leave them here."

He stared at me for a moment as if weighing his words,

then he said, "I don't think you understand. We're not abandoning them. We're saving them."

"How do you figure?" My voice was tight with panic as my gaze fixed on the battered wooden ship gliding *above* the choppy waves. It would be upon us in a matter of minutes. I could just make out the bodies of the men scattered aboard the ship. They did not look friendly or . . . alive.

"The pirates are after *you*, Zoe. You're what's putting the ship and passengers in jeopardy."

I whipped around and stared at Jasper in horror. He was right. The Viking and then Moran had come after me. It only made sense that whoever had sent them had also sent the pirates.

"Griffin. Ziakas." Olive strode across the lounge, her trench coat flapping and her dark glasses covering her eyes, looking a bit like a pirate herself. "Where's Eloise?"

I glanced around the room. Most of the passengers were staring at the screens of their phones or tablets and didn't see the horror headed our way. Eloise was exactly where we'd left her by the window.

I hurried across the lounge, not wanting to draw attention by shouting. I reached her side and noticed she was staring at the pirate ship with wide eyes. Her palms were pressed together in front of her chest and her lips were moving in what I suspected was a prayer to save us all.

"Come on, Eloise." I gently took her elbow and led her back toward Olive and Jasper. She reluctantly allowed me to lead her away.

"You saw that, didn't you?" she asked. "I wasn't hallucinating, was I?"

"We did and you weren't."

"I don't want to frighten you, but I think they're after you, my dear." She hugged her arms to her chest, looking fretful.

"Do you think the spell I used on Moran would work on the ship?" I asked.

She frowned. "It's a very big ship with a lot of men."

Given that I had barely managed to get Moran back in the ground, I knew what she was trying to say. I didn't have the chops for a job this big. I knew she was right.

"I think I need to try," I said as we joined Olive and Jasper. "What other choice do we have?"

"Lifeboat." Olive spun on her heel and led the way to the side door. "You can try your incantation while we launch plan B, which is to escape in a lifeboat."

"Oh, I like that plan." Eloise beamed. Of course she did. She was impervious to the cold and wet.

Jasper heaved open the side door and we stepped into the drizzling rain and gusting wind. I was instantly soaking wet and miserable.

"Give it a go," Olive ordered. "We'll prepare the boat."

Thankfully, the inclement weather kept everyone else inside. How my current associates thought they were going to launch a lifeboat without anyone noticing, I had no idea. I pressed myself against the railing. The wind whipped my face and the mist clouded my vision. I centered my gaze on the man with the long scraggly beard, the battered hat, and the lopsided grin sporting several missing teeth. He had the stance of a captain, so I went with the assumption.

Eloise was pressed up against my side like a trusted friend, offering her support much like the raven had last night. I immediately wondered where he was and hoped he didn't appear, as I didn't want him to get hurt by whatever was coming.

Using all the strength I could muster, I belted the words out from my core. "Corpus regressus ad mortem!"

I kept my gaze on the ship, hoping it would sink back down into the deep, taking its maniacal-looking crew with it. No dice.

"It didn't work." I turned to Eloise. She was staring at the pirates as if assessing them for weaknesses. Did she think we were going to have to fight them? My knowledge of swordplay was nonexistent beyond the historical romances I enjoyed on occasion.

"Try again!" Olive ordered from behind me. I glanced over my shoulder to see that she and Jasper had the lifeboat uncovered and were lowering it to the ferry's deck. How had no one seen them?

I glanced up at the captain's bridge. He was staring out the window, looking ahead at the island, which I could just see in the distance. He seemed completely unaware of the massive wooden ship headed for our starboard side with what appeared to be single-minded intent.

"What did you do to the crew?" I asked Olive.

"Never mind, just focus on your task."

I turned back to the railing. Eloise was watching the ship come nearer as if she didn't dare move for fear that they'd see her, which I understood completely. If I could have blended into the steel deck, I would have. The ship was close enough that I could see the sailors' faces now and there was not a kind one among them.

I glanced at the frigid water below, watching it churn and froth as the ferry plowed through the waves, and vowed to myself that this was not how I was going to go.

The ship was now mere yards away. I glanced at the pirate captain and I saw his eyes go wide. He lifted his arm high and I noted that in his fist he clutched a saber, identifiable by its short curved blade. My knees wobbled a bit at the grin he sent my way. I had the feeling he would slit my throat and not think twice about it.

"Steady," Eloise said.

I drew in a deep breath and focused my energy on the ship. The wind bit at my cheeks and the rain pelted my face but I didn't flinch. Instead, I bellowed, *"Corpus regressus ad mortem!"*

For a second, a nanosecond really, I expected the men to fall to the deck and the ship to sink back into the deep. It didn't. There was no crack of thunder, no flash of light, just the relentless rain and bone-chilling wind.

The captain, as if sensing my dismay, pointed his sword at me, threw back his head, and cackled. It was the most chilling noise I had ever heard. It froze my insides and made my brain flicker out like a candle.

"I'm Captain Cole Wener, and we're here for you, granddaughter of Toni Donadieu," he bellowed in a voice that boomed across the water as if punching through the rain to get to me. I stood staring stupidly at the terrifying specter in front of me. If I'd had a target on my chest, I was sure one of the cannons on the side of the ship would have blown a hole right through me.

"All right, ladies, come along, no time to sightsee." Jasper grabbed us by the arms and pulled us away from the railing.

We hurried to the side of the ship where one of the lifeboats was missing. I glanced over the side and Olive was sitting in the boat, which was dangling from the cables that held it. She looked completely calm, as if she were out for a leisurely ride in a canoe instead of being buffeted by the wind and rain and motion of the ferry as it sliced through the waves. Without hesitation, Eloise scrambled over the side and took a seat. I glanced quickly at Jasper and he nodded.

I clutched my backpack to my chest, holding the family grimoire close, and followed Eloise. As soon as I was seated, Jasper climbed aboard and lowered us into the water with a splash. Once the cables were disconnected, Jasper took control of the small outboard motor on the back of the boat.

We jetted away from the ferry as if . . . well, as if pirates were after us. Despite the cold, I felt my heart resume beating in my chest and I drew in a steadying breath. With the pirates trapped on the other side of the ferry, I felt confident we'd escaped. We were going to be all right.

Jasper opened up the small engine and we veered away from the ferry toward the island in the distance. I glanced back to confirm the pirates were gone. But they weren't.

Instead, much to my horror, the pirate ship passed right through the ferry. The pirates were not undead as I'd assumed. They were ghost pirates on a ghost ship.

24

"Bugger it! They're ghost pirates!" Jasper shouted. "Hang on tight!" He turned the motor on high and we bounced over the waves, smacking down on the surface of the water so hard my teeth clacked together. I clutched the boat's side, fearing I'd bounce right out of it.

Olive didn't flinch at the sight of the ship. Instead, she said, "Get us to shore. We'll be safe there."

"Safe from that?" I cried, gesturing wildly at the ship rapidly closing in on us. "They're saber-wielding ghosts!"

"Yes, I'm aware. Ghosts haunt the living either because they died a horrific death"—she paused to glance at the ship—"which in this case seems likely, or because they have unfinished business. Judging by the fact that none of them have jumped overboard to get to you, I suspect they're bound to their ship."

She lowered her sunglasses, which were suspiciously devoid of the water droplets that covered everything else, and studied the pirates with a narrowed gaze. Without looking away from the ship, she reached into the pocket of her overcoat and pulled out several small nutmeg shells that resembled mini conchs. She handed one to each of us. "Keep it on your person and the ghosts can't harm you."

I studied it, noting the thick red thread tied around the delicate brown-and-white shell. The scent of rosemary wafted up from the shell and I could see that a small sprig had been stuffed inside and secured by the thread.

Jasper pocketed his, as did Eloise. I followed suit, very doubtful that a shell the size of a walnut could protect me from a ship full of irate ghost pirates, but I wasn't about to quibble as we raced for our lives.

I wanted to keep my gaze on Hagshill Isle as it grew larger on the horizon, but I compulsively glanced back to track the progress of the ghost ship. Gliding unimpeded over the water, it was moving more swiftly than us. There was no way we were going to make landfall before they overtook us. I felt like throwing up my coffee, but there was no time.

"What else can we do?" I asked Olive, raising my voice to be heard over the engine's roar and the whipping wind.

She glanced at me and her dark eyes were solemn when she said, "Most likely, they're after that book of yours. If you throw it in the sea, they might go after it instead of us."

I felt a shiver from the backpack I'd put on backward to secure it to my chest. Was the book afraid? Instinctively, I clutched it closer and shook my head. "Unacceptable."

Olive's mouth tipped up in one corner a mere millimeter or two. I supposed it could have been a grimace from the impact the boat had on the water, but I preferred to believe it was approval.

"All right, then we have to scare them off," Olive declared.

"I don't think this boat has the fearsome quality you're looking for in a watercraft," Jasper shouted.

"It doesn't need it," Olive said. "It just needs an illusion."

I glanced at Eloise, who was watching Olive with a curious expression. As we watched, Olive tucked her sunglasses into her pocket and moved to stand in the center of our boat. Over her shoulder, she yelled, "Hold her steady."

Jasper nodded and turned toward the island. He slowed the speed just enough to keep the boat from slapping against the surface. I glanced at the pirate ship and noted it was closing the gap. Olive spread her arms wide, tipping her face up to the sky. The wind pulled at her coat and tugged her hair loose, letting it whip about her head and shoulders.

Fog appeared between her outstretched hands, materializing as if she'd fashioned it out of the air. As it was Olive, maybe she had. I would expect no less from her at this point. The fog mushroomed, enveloping our little boat in a thick bank. As I watched, it formed the shape of a dragon. I felt my mouth go slack as the head of the beast moved forward to loom over the ghost ship. We could hear shouts and curses from the ship, which appeared to have slowed as the body of the dragon spread out across the water, hiding us from view.

"That should do it." Olive sat down and Jasper revved the boat back into a driving pace.

I had no idea how he was navigating us to the island through the blanket of gray that enveloped us, but it was clear he knew what he was doing. A surge of relief for the competency of those around me filled me to the brim.

It was then that a cannonball landed in the water off the

starboard side of the boat, sending up a massive splash and taking my relief with it.

"Punch it, Griffin!" Olive ordered.

Jasper shoved the throttle into a higher gear and we went back to slamming our way across the water toward the island. I heard an eerie laugh behind us and a shiver of dread whispered down my spine. They were just ghosts, I told myself. Specters. They couldn't actually hurt us, could they?

"Wait!" I turned to Olive. "How could they be ghosts on a ghost ship that passed through another ship and have actual cannonballs that fire into the water? That makes no sense."

"How old do you suppose their ship is?" Olive asked me. It felt like a test.

"Judging by the rigging, it was built in the seventeen hundreds. Why?" I asked.

Her eyebrows went up and I might have thought she was impressed with my memory and random bits of knowledge, but she continued on before I could be sure. "Correct. Which means they've had almost three centuries to harness their ghostly powers."

"So they can manifest a ghost cannonball into a real one?" I asked.

"Precisely, the older the ghosts, the more powerful they are, and they do have the ability to harness energy and weaponize it."

"So ghosts can actually hurt you," I said.

"That's how I got this scar." Olive tapped the eyebrow with the slit in it. Having made her point, she slipped her sunglasses back on.

"Well, shit."

"Everyone, hang on," Jasper ordered. "I'm going to try to outmaneuver them."

We each grabbed a built-in handhold. Jasper veered to the right and then the left. He shot forward and dropped back. All the while, I heard the boom of the cannon and noted splashes of water breaking the surface all around us.

Suddenly, Jasper switched tactics and aimed straight for the island, which I could just make out in the thinning fog. The cannonballs landed all around us but never came close enough to cause any damage.

I leaned forward so I could see Jasper's face. His thoughtful expression indicated that he'd come to the same conclusion as me. "They're missing us on purpose."

He turned his head and his gaze met mine. "I think so, too, but why?"

I had no idea.

We glanced ahead and the island's marina appeared. Jasper turned to face the others and said, "Land ho!"

I turned back and saw the ghost ship stop. It hovered on the water, not moving. There had to be a ward or spell that kept it from the shore. Relief whooshed through me. There would be no ghosts stalking us on the island.

As I watched, Captain Cole raised his sword in the air. "Be wary, granddaughter of Toni Donadieu. All is not as it seems. We will await your return."

My return? Was he telling me we were going to do this dance again? No, no, no. I didn't care how I got off the island, I was not facing down a pirate ship again. No way, no how. I'd hire a helicopter if I had to.

Jasper slowed the boat to accommodate the no-wake zone as we entered the cove. With the pirates held firmly offshore, I found I could breathe again.

"They let us go. What a relief." Eloise sagged against her seat. "I'm surprised you didn't give them the book, Zoe."

"Me, too," I said. "But I couldn't. It wouldn't have been right."

Eloise smiled at me. Her eyes were kind and soulful when she said, "Your grandmother would have been proud of you."

I tried to wave her off, but a silly, sentimental part of me was pleased to hear it. Would Mamie have been proud? Or would she have thought I was an idiot? I had no way of knowing. She'd been gone for more years than I'd known her. I liked to think she'd have approved, but I didn't want to presume. I didn't want to be wrong.

Jasper pulled up to an open slip in the marina. The fog had lifted, leaving only the relentless rain. With a glance out at the ocean, I noticed the pirate ship had faded, much like the fog, leaving only the memory of its presence behind.

"Come on, let's tie up," Olive said. "We want to be out of here before the ferry lands and they realize they're missing a lifeboat."

Jasper lifted Eloise up and set her on the dock. He turned to do the same for Olive, but she climbed out of the boat, nimbly stepping onto the creaking boards and kneeling to tie the boat. I scrambled after her, tying the bow while Jasper propped up the engine on the back of the boat.

Olive led the way to the larger pier. Like good little soldiers, we fell into step behind her. Eloise was agog at the view of the town from the pier.

"Oh no, the ice cream parlor is gone!" she cried. "They've replaced it with a locally harvested seaweed shop. That's just wrong."

I kept glancing back at the ocean, expecting the pirates to appear.

"It's all right, Zoe." Jasper came up beside me. "As Olive said, the pirates can't leave their ship."

"You're right." I shook my head. "I'm just having a hard time processing . . ." I waved my hand at the water. "Whatever that was."

"Terrifying. It was bloody terrifying."

A surprised laugh burst out of me. "I thought I was the only one who thought so."

"Not at all. If I never see another pirate again in this life, I'm fine with it."

"Agreed."

"Where are we going first?" Eloise asked.

"We're going to Toni Donadieu's house," Olive said. She took out her phone and consulted the route. "It's only a ten-minute walk around the edge of the village."

"Is that the best idea?" I asked. Panic was thrumming through my veins. I realized I was scared to go to my grandmother's house. I hadn't been there since the night my mom and I had fled, and I was uneasy about returning.

Olive stopped walking and turned to face me. She lowered her sunglasses and peered over the top of them at me. I was getting accustomed to that look and found I wasn't as intimidated as usual. "Yes, it is."

"But what if the new owners don't like trespassers and call the police on us?" I asked.

Olive shrugged. "I don't care."

There were many things to admire about Olive Prendergast, but honestly, her zero-fucks-given attitude about what anyone else thought was my favorite.

"Griffin, the ferry will be docking soon," Olive said. "Can you slip on board and retrieve our vehicle?"

"Absolutely. Text me the address where you want me to meet you, and I'll be there." His gaze met mine briefly before he added, "Good luck."

He turned and walked away. I tried not to stare after him, but it was a struggle not to run after him and beg him to take me with him so I could avoid what I suspected would be a difficult emotional time for me when we arrived at Mamie's house.

"Now, that's a travesty!" Eloise drew my attention as she waved her hands in the direction of an organic smoothie shop with a giant blow-up pineapple in the front window. "The bakery where Toni and I used to get our morning coffee and pastry is now *this*. What even *is* a pineapple cleanse? Never mind. I don't want to know."

She looked distraught, so I stepped forward and walked beside her, falling in behind Olive. "How long has it been since you've visited the island?"

"Since Toni died," she said. "I had to follow the book, which meant tracking Juliet. I almost caught up to her a few times, but she was always out of reach."

I nodded. That checked out. My mom had popped in and out of my life so sporadically, I couldn't imagine trying to chase her down. It made Agatha's theory about my mom hiding in a different timeline very plausible.

"What did you do to get by?" I asked.

"I'd take odd jobs and work here and there, keeping busy while I waited. Time is rather inconsequential when you can't die." She sounded sad and I felt a flash of annoyance with my mom.

"Did my mother know about you?" I asked. "Did she know you were stranded without someone to help you move on?"

Eloise glanced away, looking anywhere but at me. It was answer enough and I didn't believe her when she said, "I don't think so."

"I promise, as soon as I figure out how to do it, I will send you on," I vowed.

"I appreciate that, my dear." She patted my arm.

It occurred to me that despite her propensity for having random body parts fall off, I'd gotten quite fond of Eloise and I would be sad to see her go.

As the cluster of shops fell behind us, Olive led us along a narrow paved walkway that followed the twists and turns of the shoreline. We passed house after house. I didn't recognize any of them. Then we turned down a narrow dirt hiking path, moving quietly through the seagrass and summer rosebushes now barren of blooms. When we turned the corner, Olive stopped abruptly, causing me to plow into her back.

She turned and glared at me, but I was too shocked to care. Rising up in front of us was a concrete, steel, and glass colossus. Olive glanced from her phone to the house and back three times before she said, "This is it."

Something fractured inside of me then. Gone was the quirky shingled cottage with the row of wind chimes hanging across the front porch. The sanctuary I remembered had been plowed down to make room for this modern monolithic structure. Anything that had been Mamie's was gone and there was no way for me to get it back. The feeling of loss was unbearable in its intensity.

A gravel shortcut led past the house to the beach beyond. "Excuse me," I muttered, and left them, not caring if the new owners saw me or not.

"Zoe," Eloise called after me.

"Let her go," Olive said. I appreciated the understanding or disinterest, whichever it was that motivated Olive. "I'm going to see if anyone's home. You stay here and keep watch."

"What am I watching for?" Eloise asked.

"Anything out of place," Olive answered.

I heard Eloise say something in return, but I couldn't make out the words over the sound of the wind and waves. It was just as well. I was too consumed with my churning emotions to participate in a meaningful way at the moment.

I stepped onto the beach and the size and shape of the boulders in front of me brought me right back to my childhood and the summer days I'd spent scrambling over these same rocks, pretending I was an adventurer, a superhero, a mythical creature of the sea, whatever my imagination conjured on any particular day.

The wind gusted across the sand by the water's edge and I hunkered into my coat. I pressed a hand against one of the rain-slick boulders and the memory of Mamie and me walking this beach together filled my mind. She'd always had time for me when we'd visited her. She taught me all sorts of things about the natural world: how to tell when rain was coming, the way the maple tree's leaves appear to turn upside down, or that honeybees actually spend two-thirds of their time doing nothing, so to her, being a busy bee meant giving herself plenty of downtime, usually with a good book.

I glanced at the ocean. The tide was coming in, although technically, as Mamie had explained it to me, the ocean doesn't actually move so much as Earth rotates through the bulge that the moon's gravitational pull on the ocean creates, producing the illusion of a tide that comes in and goes out. I shook my head. Mamie had taught me so many things. I glanced at the beach and remembered the day she had insisted I memorize some figures she drew in the sand. She told me someday I might need to use them.

I frowned. I found a piece of driftwood and started drawing in the sand, trying to remember. There was a triangular shape and then a swirly one, a cross, and a trapezoid sort of thing. What were the words she'd taught me to go with them? I hadn't thought of them in years. I mumbled the first two, couldn't remember the third, and stammered around the fourth.

"Mater matris *hmm-mm* ready." I frowned. When I was a kid, I'd thought it was just some silliness she'd made up to entertain me, but now with my own magic rising inside me, I knew she'd given me something more.

I didn't remember seeing any of these symbols in the book. Still, the memory strengthened my resolve. Maybe Mamie's house was gone, but there had to be someone on the island who remembered her, who could tell us something to help with the grimoire. I dropped the stick and strode back up the path.

Olive was coming around the corner from the house, a frown turning down the corners of her mouth.

"The owners were not accommodating?" Eloise asked.

"They're not there," Olive said. "No one is, which was easy to see, as their glass house is see-through, front to back, and there's practically nothing in it."

"It's such a shame." Eloise sighed. "Toni's cottage was so charming, with its front porch surrounded by hydrangea bushes and her collection of wind chimes."

"Now it's ornamental grasses and not a wind chime in sight," Olive said. "Quite depressing, actually."

We stood like the weary travelers we were, taking in a landscape that felt unduly harsh at the moment. A large black SUV rolled up beside us.

"Need a lift?" Jasper rolled down the driver's window and smiled at us.

"Yes, back to town." Olive gestured for Eloise and me to take the back seat.

"I take it the house didn't offer any insights?" Jasper asked.

"None other than the new residents have horrible taste," Olive said. "There was not a single book in sight." She shuddered and I felt a small smile tip my lips.

The rest of the car ride was silent until Jasper pulled into a spot in the center of town. "Where to next?"

Olive turned around in the passenger seat. "Eloise, you mentioned Toni might have some friends still on the island?"

"Potentially," Eloise confirmed.

"We can start there, then," Olive declared. I had another idea.

"I'm going to the library," I said. "I want to look up any local news articles there might be about Mamie."

Olive glanced at me, considering, and then nodded. "Suit

yourself. We'll meet you there in an hour. Griffin, you go with Ziakas. Don't get into trouble."

"Me?" Jasper's outraged expression was over the top. He was clearly teasing Olive, who unsurprisingly was not having it.

"Do you see anyone else named Griffin in here?" She didn't wait for his answer but popped her door open and stepped out. Eloise let out a small yip and hurried to keep up with her. I hoped she didn't lose a leg for her efforts.

"Shall we?" Jasper asked.

"We shall."

As we walked, I ignored him mostly, focusing instead on the figures I had remembered Mamie teaching me and trying to recall the name of the third symbol, which I had never seen before or since. Maybe it would come to me if I focused on something else.

The library was a small white clapboard cottage with green shutters nestled on a side street off the town square. Thankfully, it was open and Jasper held the door for me as we entered, stomping our feet on the doormat to get the excess rainwater off.

A just-past-middle-aged man wearing a cardigan and glasses—sometimes stereotypes are stereotypes for a reason—greeted us when we approached the reference desk.

"Hello, how can I help you?" he asked. I noted his name tag read *Roger*.

I stared at him, wondering for a moment if he might be undead. I wanted to reach out and pinch him. If he didn't respond, I'd know, but it seemed a bit pushy. Realizing I was suffering from some sort of undead post-traumatic stress, I glanced away, noting that there was a story time happening in the children's area on the other side of the library and several patrons were using the free-internet-access computers in the main part of the room. Other than that, all was quiet.

"Do you have an archive of the local newspaper?" Jasper asked. He glanced at me, no doubt wondering why I didn't identify myself as a fellow librarian, but I felt the less this man knew about us, the better for him. Jasper must have caught on, because his usual charming banter was kept to a minimum.

Roger pushed up his glasses and nodded. "Right this way. We keep them in the Hagshill History Room."

We followed him through the wooden shelving units to the back of the building where we entered a glassed-in room with two ancient microfilm readers, a large steel microfilm case, and a wooden study table with four chairs. The few bookshelves in the room held old school yearbooks from the island's only school, vintage phone directories, and a handful of books that I assumed were written by local residents.

"Do you know how to use microfilm?" Roger asked.

"I do," I said. "I do a lot of research in my line of work."

"Roger, Mrs. Chisholm is waiting at the reference desk." A woman poked her head into the room.

"Excuse me," Roger said. "I'll be at the service desk if you need help."

"Thank you," Jasper and I said together.

As soon as the door shut behind him, I turned to Jasper. He took one look at my expression and said, "No, I don't believe he is one of the undead."

"I didn't really think so." I shook my head.

"If it makes you feel any better, it took me a long time to get comfortable with the . . . unexpected," Jasper said.

"Why do I feel like that's a typical British understatement?" I asked.

He smiled at me and I tried really hard not to be dazzled by the deep dimples in his cheeks or the creases in the corners of his eyes or the way his thick dark hair fell back from his face in perfect waves. It was a struggle. I turned and went to the microfilm cabinet, looking for the roll that would include Mamie's obituary, assuming there had been one.

"Can you imagine living in such a quaint place that they haven't even digitized their collection?" I asked. Wessex was no hub of modernity, but we were fully digitized.

"I rather like it," Jasper said. "It feels calmer."

I paused and took a breath. He was right. There was a quietness here that soothed my soul. Was this why Mamie had loved island life so much? It made perfect sense to me.

I glanced down at the drawer and pulled out two rolls of microfilm. I handed one to Jasper, and we sat down at the two machines. It took me a moment to remember how to feed the film through the reader. As the front pages of old newspapers scrolled by, I was careful to keep the speed slow enough that I didn't give myself motion sickness.

"Antoinette Donadieu, that's her, right?" Jasper asked.

I scooted my chair in beside his and glanced at the grainy black-and-white photo. I recognized the same wavy brown hair and close-lipped smile that my mother and I shared.

"Yes, that's her." My throat was inexplicably tight.

"The resemblance is uncanny," Jasper said as he glanced from the photo to me and back. "She was a beauty."

Was that a compliment? It felt like a compliment. But I couldn't be sure. I studied Mamie's photo. It was a headshot taken when she was in her late twenties. She had a heart-shaped face with large eyes, a long nose that turned up slightly at the end, and full lips with the upper one slightly larger than the lower. These were the same features I saw in my own reflection every day. On her, they seemed much more attractive than they did on me.

I remembered being told once that confidence was the most attractive quality in a person. Was that why Mamie appeared to be so glamorous? She definitely looked more self-assured than I ever had. I shook my head, forcing myself to focus.

The date at the top of the page was November 21, 1999. I knew from what Eloise had told me that Mamie had died shortly after the night we had fled. I hit print on the machine, hoping something in the obit would give me a clue as to what had happened more than two decades ago.

I held the paper, and Jasper and I read the obituary silently together. It was a punch in the chest to see that my mother and I were listed as Mamie's only surviving relatives. Her many contributions to the community were also listed, but there was no cause of death, nothing that gave me any indication of how she died.

I opened my backpack and pulled out the grimoire. I carefully folded the printout of Mamie's obituary, planning to tuck it into the back of the grimoire for safekeeping. Before I could offer the book a drop of blood to open it, I felt a tear form in my eye and it plopped onto the book cover, right into the hexagonal medallion. The lock on the book turned and the cover flopped open. The pages began turning themselves and I jerked back in surprise. I glanced at Jasper to see if he was witnessing this, and when his gaze met mine, his eyes went wide with shock.

He snatched a tissue out of a nearby holder and handed it to me. "You have something in your eye."

I dabbed at the dampness that I felt, and when I pulled the tissue away, I noted it was bloody. "What the hell?"

"Precisely," Jasper agreed.

There was a rap on the door and Roger appeared. Jasper blocked me from view.

"Is everything all right in here?" Roger asked.

25

Jasper took the bloody tissue from my hand and held it to my nose, tipping my head back. He then shoved the grimoire and Mamie's obituary into my bag and thrust it into my arms. Then he hauled me to my feet and pulled me toward the door. "Let's go."

"But the film—" I protested. The librarian in me resisted leaving without putting away the materials we'd used.

"No time." Jasper steered me out of the room. "Roger, mate, so sorry! Have to dash. Nosebleed! We left the film in the machines, if you wouldn't mind taking care of it . . ."

"Not at all," Roger said. I don't think I imagined the sound of relief in his voice that my "nosebleed" was being ushered out of the building at top speed and would not be his problem.

Once we were out of sight of the library, Jasper stopped and removed the tissue from my nose. His forehead creased with lines of concern as he took in my face.

"What?" I asked.

"Nothing," he said quickly—too quickly. "Perhaps don't make eye contact with anyone."

"Ziakas, are you bleeding out of your eyeballs?" Olive appeared behind Jasper with Eloise in tow.

"No!" I protested, and then added, "Maybe?"

"The whites of your eyes are red," Eloise helpfully informed me. "You look like a vampire."

"Vampires are real?" I gasped. My brain was clearly avoiding acknowledging that I was crying blood tears, probably because I would absolutely faint if it did.

"Discussion for another day." Olive handed me her sunglasses. "Wear these."

"Thank you." I slid them on and immediately felt much less conspicuous, which was saying something given that I was wearing dark shades on a rainy day, knowing full well I did not have Olive's panache to carry it off.

"What happened?" Olive asked.

"We found Mamie's obituary," I said. "But when I took the grimoire out of my backpack to put the obit inside it, I was suddenly bleeding out of my eyes."

"The blood dropped onto the latch and the book unlocked and the pages started flipping," Jasper explained. "It was as if the book wanted to show her something."

"Did you note the pages?" Olive asked.

"Weirdly, with blood pouring out of my eyes, I didn't think to," I said.

Olive's lips pursed and I knew that if it was in her vernacular she would have called me lame. Whatever. I had bigger questions.

"Why would it do that?" I asked. "I mean, it's the book that made my eyes turn red and bleed, isn't it?"

"Probably." Olive glanced at my backpack. "I suspect it's getting impatient, waiting for you to translate it and handle the undead persons, like Eloise, who were left in limbo after your grandmother's passing."

"Did you know it could do something like this to me?" I asked, not even trying to keep the outrage out of my voice.

Olive shrugged. "Magic can be punitive."

I stared at her. "You might have mentioned that."

"Now you know," Olive said. "I suggest you expend your energy on translating the grimoire instead of being indignant with it."

"It's not the book I'm annoyed with, it's—" I began, but Olive cut me off.

"Was there anything of interest in the obituary?"

"There was no cause of death listed," Jasper answered.

It appeared we were skipping over my tantrum. Fine. "It listed her good works in the community and such, but that was it. Did you have any luck tracking down any of her old friends?" I asked.

"Not really." Eloise's eyes were filled with a deep sadness. "It seems most of the people we knew have either passed on or moved away."

"The one woman we did locate, Janet, mentioned that the island doctor, Dr. Hawthorne, relied on Toni's skills and was quite beside himself when she passed."

"Is he still practicing?" I asked.

"Yes, we're on our way to see him now," Olive said. The

wind tossed her dark hair around her handsome face. She lifted her eyebrows and added, "Maybe he can take a *look* at your eyes."

"Are you serious right now?" I asked. "You're actually making a joke when I resemble a vampire?"

Olive's mouth lifted in one corner. "If not now, when?" She turned on her heel and started walking. "Come on, then. The doctor is only going to be in the office for another thirty minutes. If we want to see him at all, we have to go now."

"But what about the grimoire?" I protested. If it wanted to show me something, I wanted to know what it was. Right now.

"It will keep for a half hour," Olive said. "Besides, opening the grimoire in the middle of town might cause attention we don't want. Let's go."

Frustrated, I followed Olive, hugging my backpack to my chest and mentally promising the grimoire that I'd get to it as soon as I could. I didn't think I was imagining the pouting coming from the book.

Dr. Hawthorne's office was tucked in another white clapboard cottage in the center of town. The island really was ridiculously picturesque. We entered the building and the scent of disinfectant with cold air greeted us, making it very clear that we were in a medical establishment.

Olive spoke to the woman at the front desk. The receptionist was shaking her head vigorously and Olive waved me forward. I had a feeling I knew what she wanted and was proved correct when Olive said, "Lower your glasses."

I glared at her, which was useless through the dark lenses, and reached up and lowered the shades just enough for the receptionist to see my eyes. Her gasp was not a delicate inhalation of surprise; rather it sounded like a sonic boom of shock.

She popped out of her seat and came around the counter. "This way. I'll tell Dr. Hawthorne it's an emergency."

She led Olive and me into the back while Jasper and Eloise, by unspoken agreement, stayed in the waiting room, keeping an eye out for anyone suspicious. As soon as the receptionist shut the door behind us, I turned to Olive and asked, "Was it really necessary to use me as bait?"

Olive held her arms wide. "We're here, aren't we?"

"How long will my eyes be like this?" I asked.

"No idea," she said. "But the sooner you figure out what the grimoire wants, the better. You don't want to start losing body parts like Eloise."

"If you're trying to freak me out, you can't possibly trip me out any more than I am right now," I said. "And believe me, if you'd given me a chance to see what the book was trying to show me, I'd be all over it. And yet, here we are."

A sharp rap on the door interrupted our conversation. Olive took the visitor's chair while I sat on the paper-covered exam table.

"Come in," I called.

The door was pushed open and a short, round man with neatly trimmed silver hair entered the room. There was a calmness and competency about him, as if he'd seen everything there was to see and could no longer be surprised by anything. Well, I was about to put that to the test.

"What can I do for you, Miss . . . ?"

"Zoe," I said. "Zoe Ziakas."

If he recognized my name, he didn't show it. I introduced

him to Olive and watched as the two big brains in the room squared off, taking each other's measure.

"Ms. Prendergast."

"Dr. Hawthorne."

"Would you be the same Olive Prendergast who works in the Books of Dubious Origin collection at the Museum of Literature?"

Olive's eyebrow, the one with the slit in it, rose. "You're familiar with the Books of Dubious Origin collection?"

"Miles and I went to Johns Hopkins medical school together," he said. "We keep in touch as time and distance allow."

Huh. I had not known that Miles had a medical degree. Interesting.

"In that case, yes, I am *that* Olive of whom I'm sure you've heard so much." Olive's eyebrow dropped and she looked chagrined.

"Only good things, I promise." An amused smile curved Dr. Hawthorne's lips. He turned back to me. "And what can I do for you?"

"I take it you haven't spoken to Miles recently?" I asked.

Dr. Hawthorne contemplated the ceiling while he tried to recall. "It's been about a month since we've talked."

I glanced at Olive and she nodded. I took this to mean I could show him my eyes and ask about Mamie, but I did not plan to tell him anything about the grimoire.

"I'm here for two things, actually." I closed my eyes as I removed my glasses, opening them when I added, "This is the first."

To his credit, Dr. Hawthorne didn't flutter an eyelash at

the sight of my vampire eyes. Instead, he took a small penlight out of the pocket of his white coat and said, "Look up." I did and felt him studying my eyes with the help of the light.

"Any itching, burning, stinging, or discomfort of any kind?" he asked.

"None."

"Normally, I would prescribe eye drops for an allergen or to flush an irritant out, but since you're Toni Donadieu's granddaughter, I suspect anything human I prescribe won't make a bit of difference to something caused by magic."

"You know who I am?" I lowered my head and met his gaze.

"You look just like her." His voice was gruff when he added, "Toni was a remarkable woman."

I tried to parse if there was some other deeper emotion between the doc and Mamie, but I didn't know him well enough to get a read on him. Either way, it was clear he held Mamie in high regard, which I found comforting.

"And if it is a magical injury?" I asked without admitting the truth.

Dr. Hawthorne glanced at Olive. "Suggestions?"

"She knows what she needs to do."

Dr. Hawthorne glanced between us. Clearly my red eyes weren't going to go away until I had a chance to look at the book.

"Fine." I put my glasses back on and addressed the doctor. "The second thing is that I'm following up on my own medical history and was wondering if you could answer some questions about Mamie . . . er . . . Toni's death."

"Oh, of course. I'll answer if I can," Dr. Hawthorne said.

"How did she die?" I asked. "My mother never told me and there's nothing in her obituary."

He stroked his chin and said, "Specifically, it was a cardiac arrest."

Just like my mother.

"Did she have a heart condition that you were aware of?" I asked.

"No." Dr. Hawthorne looked uneasy, as if he wasn't sure whether the vow of doctor-patient confidentiality extended to the grave.

"I promise there's a very good reason why we're asking." The paper that lined the exam table stuck to my palms. My stomach clenched with nerves. If Mamie had wasted away like my mother, then there was no doubt the same person had murdered them both and was likely coming for me.

"Your grandmother was as fit as could be until the last month of her life." Dr. Hawthorne crossed his arms over his chest, looking distinctly uncomfortable. "She just started to fade, losing her ability to communicate verbally or nonverbally. It was as if she was trapped inside her own body." He looked grim. "We did loads of tests, but I couldn't determine the cause of her sudden decline." He ran a hand over his face and his previously jovial expression became one of exhaustion. "I couldn't save her, and in the end, her body gave up the fight."

I glanced at Olive at the same moment that she turned to me. I took my phone out of my bag and did a quick search for the lunar phases during the last month of Mamie's life. When I read it, my heart sank even though I wasn't surprised. "The moon was waning."

Olive nodded and rose from her seat. "Thank you, Dr. Hawthorne. You've been very helpful."

He looked doubtful, but he turned to me and said, "Toni Donadieu was a brilliant woman with a generous heart. It was an honor to call her my friend."

If I were a touchy sort of person, I might have hugged him. Instead, I simply nodded and said, "Thank you for that."

I could feel him watching us as Olive pushed me out the door. Jasper and Eloise rose from their seats when we entered the waiting room. Olive shook her head ever so slightly, indicating that our conversation would wait.

When we reached the sidewalk, Olive glanced around. The rain had stopped and the sun was making a valiant effort to punch through the clouds. Locals and visitors clogged the sidewalk and she tapped her foot impatiently. "We need a place to look at the grimoire where we can't be overheard."

"The park?" Jasper indicated the town square. It was small and not busy at the moment.

"Anyone can see us there. I don't want to risk it." Olive shook her head.

"What about the Serenity Labyrinth?" Eloise suggested. "It's a meditation maze on the highest part of the island. It was one of Toni's favorite places. Zoe could open the grimoire without anyone observing her and we can talk on the way."

"I'd like to see a place that was special to Mamie," I said. Since Mamie's home was no longer in existence, maybe I could feel my grandmother's presence in the meditation maze. The longing to feel her here with me was so strong I'd visit anywhere if there was a chance of sensing her.

"That works for me." Olive and Jasper led the way to the car.

Eloise guided Jasper through town along a winding road that parted from the shore at the lighthouse and wound its way up to a peak on the north side of the island. While he drove, Olive shared what we'd learned from the doctor about Toni's death.

"She was cursed just like her daughter." Jasper's naturally deep voice went even lower with the gravity of the information.

"Whoever is after the grimoire is very powerful. A Waning Curse is one of the most complicated spells of dark magic," Olive said.

"It's just evil," Eloise said, her voice full of disgust. She went to tuck her hair behind her ear, but, of course, she had no ear. I imagined being stranded and losing body parts made her fury a bit keener than just her feeling of grief. Again, I felt the pressure to help her coupled with a righteous rage to hunt down whoever had done this to my family.

The sun had won its battle against the clouds and while it wasn't strong enough to make the day warmer, at least its rays were more cheerful than the dreary rain we'd been dealing with all day.

Jasper parked in the labyrinth's designated lot. He switched off the engine and said, "I'll wait here and keep watch just in case any pirates show up."

Eloise laughed. Her eyes glittered with humor and she said, "It would be a very long walk for the ghost pirates to make."

A fact that filled me with nothing but relief.

"Good thinking, Griffin. We'll call you if we need you." Olive and Eloise stepped out of the car.

I'd opened my door to follow when Jasper reached over the seat and grabbed my hand. I glanced up, meeting his pale gaze, and I felt my heart skitter in my chest at the concern I saw there.

"Remember what you learned last night, love," he said. "You're more powerful than you know. You can do this."

I smiled, bolstered by his confidence in me. Still, I couldn't help but ask, "Will you kiss me again if I manage to discover what the grimoire tried to show us?"

Jasper's eyes glinted as his gaze dropped to my mouth. "If Olive wasn't already glaring at me, I'd kiss you right now," he said.

I glanced out the front window and Olive was indeed glowering at us. I squeezed his hand and slipped out of the car.

Eloise and I followed Olive to the path that cut through a thick copse of beech trees. Judging by the size of their trunks, they'd probably been on the island since some of the earliest settlers had arrived. As we stepped out of the line of trees, I saw the circle in front of us. Made up of stones varying in size from rocks the size of gallon jugs to boulders that came up to mid-thigh, with precisely raked crushed seashells in between, the massive circle formed a large, intricate maze that was immaculately maintained. I paused, trying to get a sense of Mamie here, but there was nothing but the brisk breeze sweeping across the open area.

The labyrinth entrance was signified by an opening in the circle between the two largest boulders. I knew the maze's objective was for people to follow the various paths to the center while trying to clear their minds. With all that had happened, I knew this was a very tall order, as my brain currently felt like a hive of bees, and not the lazy ones either.

"Why don't you two walk the maze while I open the grimoire and see if it will show me the pages it wanted me to see," I said.

"Don't you want help?" Olive asked.

"I think this is between me and the grimoire."

"Fair enough." Olive nodded. She gestured to the maze and said to Eloise, "After you."

"All right." Eloise stepped into the opening. Olive waited a beat and then followed, choosing a different path and leaving me standing on the perimeter.

I pulled off my backpack and grabbed the zipper, but then hesitated. Something felt off. I shook my head. I was being ridiculous, probably because this entire trip to the island had been highly stressful and I had eyes that made me look like a sideshow freak, but whatever. I shook it off and stepped into the circle, planning to use one of the entrance boulders as a makeshift bookrest.

A wave of powerful emotion washed over me, then rose up inside me like a cresting wave, making me catch my breath as my knees buckled. I clutched the backpack to my chest, with the grimoire still inside, and tried to keep my legs beneath me. The closest thing I had ever felt to this was a rush of joy, but this wasn't that. There was no euphoria here. This, whatever it was, had darkness and a razor-sharp edge to it.

Olive and Eloise were deep in the circle, but neither of them seemed to notice the surging current that thrummed all around us. Was it just the energy of the circle? Were they both used to this sort of thing?

I stepped up to the boulder with intention, trying to be aware of the crunch of shells beneath my feet, the sun on the top of my head, and the scent of the briny sea beyond the trees in an effort to ground myself in this moment. I tried to clear my mind, but I kept getting pulled back to the symbols my grandmother had drawn in the sand and the words she had taught me. It felt imperative that I remember all of it.

Mater matris had been two of them. I knew it meant *mother's mother* or *grandmother* because it was the same in Latin, but what did the rest of the words mean? And why couldn't I, with my exemplary memory, remember all of them?

A shadow passed over me and I glanced up to see a raven in flight. The sight cheered me and I wondered if it was my friend even though I knew that was impossible. According to my research, ravens couldn't fly that far. We were miles offshore and ravens did not hitch rides on ferries. It had to be a coincidence, but it made me feel better nonetheless.

Glancing away from the raven, I reached for the zipper on my backpack. I could hear Eloise muttering under her breath and I wondered if she was using a visualization technique to clear her mind. I took a deep breath, determined to do the same. I knew I had to focus if I wanted to be able to communicate clearly with the grimoire.

The raven made a sudden dive right in front of me, forcing me back toward the entrance. I watched him soar back up to the sky again. What the hell? Mere moments passed and I watched him dive again, this time sending Eloise back on her heels. She let out an indignant cry of alarm and swatted at the bird. I couldn't blame her. It was no small thing to have a raven come straight at you at full speed.

Olive stopped walking and frowned when Eloise cried out. She glanced up at the raven and down at the circle. The raven swooped low in front of Olive, but it wasn't dive-bombing, rather it was as if Olive and the raven were communicating in some way Eloise and I couldn't understand. I would not have been at all surprised to find out that Olive could speak to birds—nonverbally, no less.

As I watched, Olive stepped out of her lane and darted across the circle toward me. "Ziakas, run!"

"What? Why?" I cried.

"Because this isn't a meditation maze," Olive said. "It's a summoning circle."

26

"What do you mean?" I cried. "Summoning what?"

As if in answer, a hand shot up from the dirt at our feet. It was bare of skin, and the bones clacked together as the fingers tried to grab us.

I let out a small shriek and stood locked in place as if it wouldn't find me if I didn't move.

"That! That's what's been summoned!" Olive shoved me, but she was too late, as the bony hand grabbed my foot in a tight grip. I tried to kick it off, but another dirt-encrusted skeletal hand snagged my other foot.

"Olive!" I reached for her but noticed she was in the same predicament, as her ankles had been caught by another pair of bony fingers.

"Eloise, go get Jasper!" I glanced up to see if Eloise had seen what was happening. She had. She was striding toward us with a look of purpose on her face and I felt my panic ebb. She would get Jasper and we'd get out of this. Except she didn't.

With her hand outstretched, Eloise ordered, "Give me the book."

I jerked back. Her hazel eyes had changed color to a vibrant green. They were so bright they almost glowed, and not in a friendly way either. I clutched my backpack more tightly to my chest. I glanced at Eloise's outstretched hand and noted that she'd removed her gloves, and her missing finger was back. "Eloise, what's happening to you?"

"I'm sorry, Zoe." Eloise's eyes flashed back to their original shade. "*She* watched me die and then brought me back and took possession of my body and my power."

"Who? Mamie?" I shook my head. "I don't understand. Eloise, what's happening? Why did you bring us here?"

An expression of anguish passed over Eloise's face. "I didn't want to leave this way. Goodbye, Zoe. Try to forgive me."

Her eyes rolled back in her head and her body began to slump to the ground, where greedy, bony hands were just waiting to snatch her.

"Eloise!" I tried to jerk my legs away from the skeletal hands that clutched me but had no success. "Hang on, Eloise, we're coming."

"My name is not Eloise." Eloise straightened back up with a jerk and strode toward me. With each step she took, stomping on the bony fingers reaching out of the dirt as she went, she began to transform. Gone were Eloise's camel coat and business casual attire. Now she was rocking a long black coat over an emerald silk blouse, a black wool skirt, and high-heeled black leather boots. Long reddish-brown hair sprouted out of the ash-blond bob, her figure changed from boxy to buxom, and the years that lined her face vanished, giving her a youthful dewy complexion, and her eyes flashed green. What the hell?!

"Well, well, well. Ariana Darkwood." Olive tipped her chin up in defiance, although I noticed her pale face was drained of all color, giving her an almost ghostly pallor. She didn't struggle against the hands holding her, as if she knew there was no way to fight them.

"Olive Prendergast. It's been a long time." Ariana's tone implied it hadn't been long enough.

I clapped a hand to my forehead. What was happening? Eloise was gone and in her place was this beautiful and yet absolutely terrifying woman. The same woman Miles had said Mamie helped to banish. Oh shit.

"I heard you were dead," Olive said.

"The report of my death was an exaggeration," Ariana said.

"Mark Twain." I didn't mean to say it out loud, but as a librarian, identifying famous quotes was kind of my kink.

"What?" Both Ariana and Olive glared at me.

"That's exactly what Twain said when he was mistakenly reported to be deceased. It gets misquoted all the time, but you were spot-on."

"Why are you so annoying?" Ariana asked me. "Do you have any idea how many times I had to fight to stay inside of Eloise and not reach out and slap you?"

"What happened to Eloise? Where did she go?" I asked.

"Eloise has finally crossed over," Olive explained. "Ariana has been a parasite, using Eloise as a host, and now Ariana's magic has transformed Eloise's vessel to resemble Ariana's former self."

"So, you aren't dead? What are you, then?" I asked the smirking woman in front of me.

"I'm the one who has returned." Ariana's smile made the hairs on the back of my neck stand on end. "This has been a long time in coming." She ran her hands over her body and through her hair as if reveling in being her own person again.

"You're a revenant." Horror made my voice low and gruff. "One who was dead but returns."

"That's right. Bound by vengeance, no necromancy required." Ariana reached for the book and I twisted away.

"Corpus regressus ad mortem!" The words flew out of me almost violently.

Ariana blinked and then she threw back her head and laughed and laughed. I glanced at Olive and she frowned and then looked deeply chagrined.

"You played us," Olive said.

Ariana stopped laughing and the malicious delight on her face was palpable. "You actually believed that you returned Moran to his grave? It was me. All of it was me."

"The Viking?" I asked.

"Me."

"The pirates?" I asked.

Ariana glanced away with a shrug. "What do you think?"

"How?" I asked. "Why?"

"How was easy," Ariana said. "I simply left the safe house Claire stuck Eloise—and me—in and followed you home. Using Eloise's power, impressive for a hedge witch, I reanimated the Viking from that very handy Eternal Shade Cemetery and sent him after you and the book." She glared at

Olive and then at me. "I wasn't aware that Jasper Griffin had been sent to guard you."

"And Moran?" I asked. "How did you get him in place at Mystwood Manor before we arrived?"

"I don't sleep," Ariana said. "I did tell you the truth about that."

"So you went to the cemetery the night before, raised him from his grave, and had him waiting for us at Mystwood the next day?" I asked. The fingers squeezing my foot tightened and I flinched. "Were you that desperate to keep us from finding out that my mother died from a Waning Curse?"

"No." Ariana shook her head. "I couldn't care less about that. I put Moran in place to kill you and steal the grimoire."

"That seems like a lot of work," Olive said. "Why didn't you just kill Ziakas yourself?"

I sent her an outraged glance, which she ignored.

"Because, as you know, my powers were stripped from me and trapped in *El Corazón*. I had nothing but a wisp of my ability left, and the only host I could find in that hellscape I was banished to was a very powerful but very lonely little hedge witch named Eloise Tate, who had been sent there to heal the earth but managed to get herself killed by the toxic fumes of the burning mine instead." She rolled her eyes, making it clear what she thought about that.

"You brought her back when she was freshly dead and took up residence inside her, leaving your own body behind," Olive clarified. "And Eloise losing her body parts had nothing to do with Toni Donadieu's necromancy magic fading, because she didn't bring Eloise back, you did. It was the power you were siphoning from Eloise that was weakening."

"You're not as slow as you look," Ariana said. Olive didn't rise to the bait. "Hedge witches, even the powerful ones, are not made for the long haul. Pity."

I swallowed, feeling nauseous. "Was it Eloise or you who killed Mamie and my mom with the Waning Curse?"

Ariana's eyes positively sparkled with delight. "Eloise was such a pathetic little thing; she would do anything I asked even if it went against her precious hedge witch ways. Once I convinced her to use her ability for murder, there was no turning back for her."

"None of this answers Olive's question. Why didn't you just have Eloise kill me, too?" I asked.

"Because you, my dear, were an unexpected gift," Ariana said. "I watched you over the years and knew you didn't use witchcraft. I feared you lacked the gift and had resigned myself to living within Eloise forever. But the night I followed the grimoire to your doorstep—hoping I was wrong about your abilities—you said you would take us to the Museum of Literature. I knew you were my pass into the Books of Dubious Origins department and all the delicious books there. I couldn't risk using Eloise to murder you for fear someone would figure it out and I'd lose my disguise.

"And it paid off. You gave me access to steal *El Corazón* and get my power back. And I did—as well as so many other wonderful items. Eloise really was the perfect disguise and I would have stayed within her and stolen every last one of the dark magic books in the collection. I would have been unstoppable. Oh, wait, I still am." She laughed and it chilled me to the core.

She reached into the pocket of her coat and pulled out the familiar small burgundy volume. *El Corazón*. When I glanced at it, I could feel the malevolence coming off it and the frozen heart inside. The feel of the clenching heart was fainter than when I'd first seen it in the BODO but still there.

She waved the book at Olive. "Before I can be fully realized and get all my power back, *El Corazón* needs a new witch's powers. It won't release me completely until I deliver, which is why I brought you here, Prendergast. Think you'll enjoy being imprisoned inside a book for eternity?" Olive stiffened, but Ariana slipped the book back into her pocket. "First things first, I am going to use the power I have regained to kill you, Zoe, the last Donadieu, and you are going to use all that untapped magic inside you to help me exchange Prendergast for me in *El Corazón*."

"You don't *have* to kill me," I protested. I felt the book tremble in my backpack and I clutched it close. I had no intention of giving it to Ariana but felt I needed to discourage her from murdering me.

Ariana threw back her head and laughed. It was as appealing as shattering glass. "Of course I do. Then I will raise you from the dead and you will use that grimoire to do my bidding. This is just the most perfect retribution for your grandmother stealing my powers and banishing me and for your mother eluding me for all these years. So many decades I spent tracking her as she slipped through time. It was supposed to be Juliet who became my undead servant with all the power of the Donadieu grimoire, but this is even better. Now it will be you, Zoe. You and the grimoire are all mine and everything your mother did to save you was for nothing. This revenge will be the sweetest I have ever known." Her eyes glowed with pure malice and I shivered.

I opened my mouth to fire more questions at her, but Ariana cut me off. "Give me the book, Zoe. Give me the book and I'll make your death painless."

"Don't do it." I felt Olive lean closer to me as if she would protect me or the book or both, and I was touched.

I glanced across the labyrinth, taking in the twitching fingers rising up from the dirt, and thought I might black out. But the reality that this woman had used Eloise to murder my mother and grandmother made a surge of fury obliterate every other feeling.

"You can murder me, but I won't come back and do your bidding." I had absolutely nothing to back this statement up except my rage.

Ariana simply stared at me. The sky had grown dark again as a second storm rolled in, dropping the temperature enough that I could see my breath. With her hair whipping about her face and her electric eyes fixed on me, Ariana looked lethal. I had the feeling that if she could break my neck with a snap of her fingers, she wouldn't hesitate. I refused to cower.

"You Donadieus are too weak to possess a grimoire with that much power. Do you have any idea of the spells contained in that book? A witch in possession of that book can do everything from traveling through time to seeing beyond the veil to mending souls."

It was Olive who laughed this time, and it was as cold as a winter wind. "You have to have a soul for it to be mended, Darkwood."

"Shut up! That grimoire belongs to me!" Ariana declared.

A flutter of fear came from inside the backpack. I hugged

it tighter, trying to calm the grimoire. The protective instinct to shield my family's legacy overrode any other emotion I was feeling at the moment, including terror.

"The hell it does," I snapped. I felt Olive staring at me and turned to find her color returning and, if I wasn't mistaken, a look of approval on her face.

Ariana strode even closer until she was a few feet away. "This conversation is tiresome. The book." She held out her hand.

"It won't open for you," I said. "You know that."

"Good thing I just need a bit of your blood." Ariana smiled. It was a terrifying display of perfect white teeth.

We were trapped. There was no escape for us. I felt the blood drain from my face. Everything went fuzzy except for a flash of blue in my peripheral vision. It was Olive, shooting blue fire out of her fingertips. Ariana darted back, but Olive wasn't aiming for her. Instead, she bent low and blasted the hands holding my feet and then her own.

"Run for the boulder, Ziakas!" Olive ordered, and we darted around one of the large stones that demarcated the entrance. Hands punched up out of the ground, trying to grab us or trip us, I had no idea which. When we reached the rock, Olive pushed me on top of it and moved to stand in front of me. She held her arms out in front of her and I knew she was trying to hold Ariana just as she had Moran. It didn't work. Ariana marched toward us with deliberate steps, her gaze unwavering on my backpack.

She was too close. If we ran, I knew she would just send her rising undead army after us. Why had we let Jasper stay in the car? We needed him.

The raven appeared above Ariana. He swooped low, diving at her head. I saw his beak make contact and she jumped and tried to smack him. She missed. He rose high again and dove straight at her like a bullet. At the last second, he turned and scratched her face with his talons.

The scream that came out of Ariana was unlike anything I had ever heard. It was a deep bellow of primal wrath that made everything in the vicinity of the labyrinth go completely still, except for the hair on my arms, which was standing at attention. Suddenly, the earth at Olive's feet was churning as more fists punched up through the dirt.

Olive whipped around where I crouched on the rock. "She's raising an army. We're going to have to run."

I jumped down from the rock just as the raven made another pass at Ariana. This time, she anticipated and reached down, then ripped an arm right out of the ground and threw it at the bird. My brain made a fritzing noise, clearly rejecting what it was seeing. It was a direct hit. The raven was knocked off course and headed straight for a nearby rock at the entrance of the circle. He slammed into it, and I ran forward, with Olive right behind me.

"No, no, no!" I moved to stand in front of the bird, shielding him from Ariana. "Don't be dead, don't be dead."

Olive stood shoulder to shoulder with me. "Look out!" Blue flames shot out of her fingers, and when a hand punched through the ground at our feet, she blasted it back under the surface. I made a mental note to ask her to teach me to make flames . . . later.

Ariana pivoted to face us. She positioned her arms wide with her fingers spread, and the ground beneath our feet became a frenzy of fists and arms clawing their way out. I could feel the earth churning with malice and I knew we were in deep, deep trouble.

Ariana looked invigorated by the rising horde. I had the brief thought that this was how I was going to die and then I immediately rejected it. Nope. Not today.

Olive was holding her hands in front of her. Her fingertips were alight in blue flame, but as helpful as it had been to release the hands that held us, I didn't think her fire wielding was enough to stop Ariana. Otherwise, she would have weaponized it by now.

"*Give. Me. The. Book.*" Ariana shouted each word. I clutched my backpack close and Olive assumed a defensive stance beside me as we huddled in the entrance of the labyrinth with the unconscious raven behind us.

"No." I tried to make my voice strong, but there was the tiniest quaver in it.

"So be it." Ariana stared at us, unblinking, as the heads and shoulders of her army began to appear, rising up from the dirt. There was no way we could hold back this number of undead.

Olive and I pressed closer together, bracing for impact as the first of her minions lurched out of the dirt and came at us at a run. The skeleton, which had a cracked skull, empty eye sockets, and a missing jaw, started to sprint and I felt my entire body clench. It was so close and then, *bam!* It was on the ground as if it had run into a thick wall of glass.

What the what?! I glanced from side to side, trying to figure out where the thick haze that separated us from Ariana and her minions had come from.

Olive glanced behind us at the path that cut through the copse of trees and said, "It's about time. Did you get lost?"

I followed her line of sight, expecting to see Jasper. Instead, it was Miles and Tariq. I almost sagged with relief. "Help!"

"Of course." Miles nodded. "You need to get the book out of here. Take the raven and get back to Jasper. Whatever you do, do not let any harm come to the bird. You must protect it and Jasper even if you have to take the car and get them out of here. Understand?"

"Yes." I didn't understand, not really. I was shaking and terrified. Running from here with an unconscious bird was fine with me, as I would leave the undead army behind, but it was also terrifying because I would be on my own.

"Here." Tariq handed me a small cloth pouch. "This will help you awaken the raven. You won't be able to rouse Jasper until the bird wakes up."

Rouse Jasper? At this point, I was going to kick him for not being here when I . . . we . . . needed him.

"They're coming through your shield, Miles," Olive said.

"Go!" Miles ordered. He turned back to face the horde with Olive and Tariq. I knelt down and gently scooped up the bird. I cradled him against the backpack I still wore on my front, then I sprinted through the trees for our SUV.

It was parked exactly where we'd left it. I opened the driver's-side door and found Jasper fully reclined and unconscious. I glanced from the raven to the man. I thought about the tattoos on his forearms and how he and the raven were never in the same place at the same time. They were connected!

"Jasper!" I used my free hand to shake him. He didn't

move. I remembered what Tariq had said and focused on the raven.

I hurried to the back and opened the hatch, then I gently laid the bird down. I opened the cloth pouch Tariq had given me. A small vial filled with purple flakes was inside.

Assuming it was like smelling salts for a bird, I unstoppered the vial and held it under the raven's beak. The bird didn't move, so I moved the bottle back and forth, hoping to get the scent moving out of the vial. Nothing. Was I supposed to sprinkle it on him? Make him eat the dried flakes inside the vial? Panicking, I glanced at where Jasper was asleep. *Come on*, I chided myself. *Think!* Or maybe don't think? What were my instincts telling me?

Somehow, Jasper and the raven were in some sort of mind meld. That's why Miles had been insistent that nothing happen to the bird. Could the bird's death cause Jasper's? I felt my anxiety spike all the way out of control and I hopped on my feet while a high whine came out of my mouth.

I had no idea what I was supposed to do, so I went with my gut and tipped the vial over the bird, sprinkling the purple flakes all over him. I held my breath until I saw his wing twitch ever so slightly. Slowly, as if he was coming out of a deep sleep, the bird ruffled his feathers. He popped up onto his feet and then blinked. He gave me a sideways glance from those familiar pale eyes and then spread his wings and launched himself out through the open hatch. I watched him soar, making certain he was okay and not headed back to the labyrinth.

"Zoe, are you all right?" Jasper appeared beside me, running his hands through his thick black hair as if he was trying to reorganize his brain. "I can't believe Eloise is Ariana Darkwood. She murdered your mother and your grandmother."

Relief that he was all right had me moving forward before I had the sense to check it. I threw my arms around his neck and hugged him hard. He clutched me close, squeezing me just as tightly. Then his words hit me, confirming what I'd suspected. The only way he could know those things was if he'd been there . . . in the form of a bird. Furious, I shoved him off me.

"You're a bird?" I cried. "You're a fucking bird?"

"A raven, actually." He jogged back to the driver's seat. "It's called aviankinesis. I have the ability to inhabit birds and control them, but ravens are my favorites."

"So the raven that attacked Ariana, the raven on the roof of the hotel, and the raven on my mailbox—all you?" I asked as I climbed into the passenger's seat.

"Yeah."

He'd seen me crying. He'd seen me at my most vulnerable. Anger that he hadn't told me sent my fist into his shoulder. "Why didn't you tell me?"

"Working *I can inhabit birds* into a conversation is not as seamless as one would think. I planned to tell you last night, but I got . . . distracted."

Well, what could I possibly say to that? "Fine, but we're talking about this later."

"I look forward to it." He flashed me a wicked grin just before he hit the gas, racing for the labyrinth. The beech trees didn't offer us entry, so we sped around the thick copse until we spotted an access road.

The sight of the now fully ambulatory teeming mass of

undead in various states of decay was worse than any horror movie I'd ever seen and if I could have scrubbed the image from my eyeballs, I would have.

"There they are!" I pointed to the large boulder by the entrance.

Miles, Olive, and Tariq were standing on top of it, trying to keep the undead scourge at bay. They were failing. Two of Ariana's minions were trying to pull Tariq off his perch. Miles was holding his shield around them, but the undead were slipping through the weak spots. And Olive was flaming anyone . . . rather, *anything* that came within striking distance, but even I could see from across the open space that the power of her blue flame was fading. Ariana stood watching from the center of the labyrinth with a smile of deep satisfaction, as if she knew all she had to do was bide her time.

"Can we run her over?" I shouted over the grunting, wailing, bone-clacking noise that filled the clearing.

"I wish. But given that she's undead, even hitting her with the car won't kill her. We have to save the others first."

I knew he was right, but as revenge for the murders of my mother and grandmother, I would gladly have torn Ariana apart with my bare hands.

Jasper sped around the circle. When we were close, he began to honk the horn. The foreign noise stunned the horde, and based on the centuries-old tatters of clothing that some of them wore, I suspected that most of them had been dead since long before the invention of the automobile. The maze must have been built on one of the island's early cemeteries.

Ariana whipped her head in our direction. I had no idea what sort of power was returning to her from *El Corazón*, but if she could raise this many corpses at half capacity, her full potential had to be significant. Jasper hit a few of the undead as he sped toward our people. One poor bastard bounced right over the roof of the car.

"Sorry, old chap." Jasper winced. "Nothing personal."

He braked hard, skidding right up to the boulder. He popped out and opened the back door. "Get in! Get in!"

Miles, Tariq, and Olive didn't hesitate. As one, they jumped off the boulder, shoving off the undead who grabbed at them, and slid into the car. Jasper got back into the driver's seat, slammed his door, and stomped on the gas.

The horde, sensing their prey was getting away, began to run after us.

"Hurry! They're gaining on us," Tariq cried. Then he let loose a scream of such a high pitch, I clapped my hands to my ears.

"What is it? Are you hurt?" Jasper demanded.

Tariq swatted at something as if he were slapping at a bug, and a bony-fingered hand flew across the car and landed on Olive's chest. Without altering her expression of mild boredom, she grasped the hand where it clutched at her jacket, rolled down the window, and tossed it outside. She closed the window, turned to Miles, and asked, "What's the plan?"

27

A crack of thunder boomed and a bolt of lightning ripped across the sky. Abruptly, torrential rain beat down on the car, and I glanced back to see that the horde was sliding in the mud as they tried to chase us. Jasper didn't slow down, putting distance between us and them, and I felt myself breathe for the first time in what felt like hours as the labyrinth and its inhabitants disappeared from view.

"With a storm like this, the ferry will be closed," Miles said. "We need to find a place to hide." He glanced at me. "Do you know of a place, Zoe?"

"I haven't been here in twenty-seven years," I said. "I remember Mamie's house, the beach, and picking blueberries at Berry Blue Acres . . . Wait." I paused. "There was a big barn there. It's the off season for berries. It might work as a hideout."

Tariq was searching for the location on his phone before I finished speaking.

"Perfect. It's only a few miles away. Keep following this road. We should be there in five minutes," Tariq said.

Berry Blue Acres was on the crest of a hill that, in daylight, would offer a sweeping view of blueberry bush–covered hills that led all the way to the ocean. At the moment, all we could do was crawl through the pouring rain, trying to see by the light of the lightning flashes to find the old barn that I remembered being on a side road before you reached the main farm.

"There! Through the trees!" Olive tapped the window on her side of the car.

Jasper cut the wheel to the right and the SUV bounced across the pitted old dirt road, stopping in front of a traditional red barn.

"This is exactly the sort of place where people get murdered in horror films," Tariq said.

"Who cares? We need to regroup," Olive countered.

"Olive is right," Miles said. "With Eloise . . . er . . . Ariana gathering her forces, we need to come up with a plan before we tangle with her again."

"You could just leave me, you know," I said. "It's the book she wants and my blood that she needs to open it."

"No!" They all responded at once, even Olive.

"I was hoping you'd feel that way." I sank against my seat in relief. "But good manners behooved me to offer."

"The BODO department does not leave anyone behind," Miles declared. He said it in a way that made me realize it must have come up before, because of course it had.

"Let's get inside," Olive ordered. "Park the car around the back, Griffin."

Jasper nodded and we all climbed out. The high grass surrounding the old barn was soggy and had thoroughly soaked my jeans before we reached the large sliding door. Tariq grabbed the handle and heaved the door to the side. It made a screech of protest before it finally moved just enough for us to squeeze inside.

Olive manifested a glowing orb between her hands, which she sent floating up above us. It illuminated the empty barn, with its decayed remnants of hay and vacant stalls.

"Ziakas, craft more light," Olive ordered. She gestured to Miles and Tariq. "We need a moment to recover."

"Oh, right," I said. I cupped my hands just as Olive had taught me and closed my eyes. In my mind, I pictured the same orb Olive had created and when I felt the warmth unfurl inside me, I opened my eyes and blinked.

Miles and Tariq were shielding their eyes from the glaringly bright red light shining through my fingers. "Sorry!" I closed my eyes and dimmed the light in my mind. When I opened them again, it was a gentle pink. I opened my hands and let it drift up to the ceiling.

"That'll do," Olive said. It felt like high praise.

There was no equipment in the barn, nothing to use to defend ourselves. I truly hoped Ariana couldn't find us. If we could just wait out the storm until the ferry was running again, maybe we could get off the island without her knowing. Then I thought of her pirates waiting for us and I felt queasy.

Was this what my mother's life had been like, always on the run? Had she chosen to hide from Ariana in a different timeline for all those years because it was the safest place she could find? I was heartsick at the thought. It occurred to me that everything she had done, she had done to keep me safe.

"All right, Zoe?" Jasper's sharp raven gaze—I couldn't think of it as anything else now—studied me.

"Yeah, I'm good." I opened my backpack and pulled out the book. "I need to know what the book was trying to show me."

"Absolutely," he said. I had lost Olive's sunglasses in the fray and I raised my eyebrows in silent question, to which he answered, "Yeah, still bloody."

I glanced away, relieved that I didn't have access to a mirror.

"Hey." Jasper cupped my chin with his hand and tipped my face up. "Don't feel bad. Just ask Tariq about the time he made a potion that turned Miles's hair into a flight of butterflies."

"Ha!" I heard a laugh from behind me and turned, pulling my chin away from Jasper's disturbing touch to find Tariq doubled over, slapping his knee. "That was a good one."

"And I once found my consciousness linked with a dove instead of a raven," Jasper said. "Doves are lovely to look at but quite thick."

"Don't forget the time Miles attempted time travel and caught himself in a loop where he glitched in and out of his office for three days." Olive joined in.

"I had vertigo for a week." Miles shook his head at the memory. "Why are we oversharing?"

"Zoe's got vampire eyes," Olive said. I noticed no one shared any mishaps from Olive. Either she was perfect—highly possible—or, more likely, they were afraid.

"Don't worry." Miles patted my hand. "When we get home, Tariq will brew a potion to set you right."

"Right," I agreed. I didn't correct him by saying *if* we got home.

"Ready to open the grimoire?" Jasper prompted me.

I glanced down at the volume in my hands. I studied its matte black cover and the hexagonal lock on the front. I paused, realizing I felt . . . *remorse?* . . . coming from the book. "Yes, even though it caused me to bleed out of my eyes . . . which was very, very wrong and it should never do that again . . . I forgive it and I'm ready." I felt a surge of relief coming from the book. It was so preposterously weird to have a book with *feelings* and yet it was beginning to seem normal. "Anyway, let's see if it will do it again."

"You two work on that and we'll see what we can do to shield this place," Miles said. "Ariana will be here soon. We need to be prepared to defend ourselves."

"Maybe she won't find us," I said.

"She will," Olive said.

"But how?" I persisted, not wanting to believe it.

"The book." They all said at once.

"Magical objects like your grimoire have their own auras. Anyone sensitive to them can track them," Miles explained.

Ariana was coming for us. Terrified, I sat on the filthy ground and placed the book on top of my backpack in front of me. I didn't care what might have scurried through this barn dirt before us. It was nothing compared to this day, the scariest of my life to date, and I'd certainly had some bangers during the past few weeks.

Without hesitating, I squeezed my eyes tight to form some tears. I didn't know if they'd still be bloody, but I figured it was easier than finding something unsterile to stab myself with. One, two, three drops fell into the tiny well in the center of the hexagon.

As soon as the hexagon turned and the latches popped, I wiped at my eyes with my sleeve. I leaned close to the book and said, "Show me again, please."

Immediately the cover flew open, as if the book was actually eager. The pages flipped with a dizzying speed. There was a pause, then the pages flipped back before it stopped. Lying face up and wide open was the second-to-last page of the section Mamie had written. And halfway down the page were the same symbols she'd taught me when she'd drawn them in the sand. They were in the book! Somehow I had missed them.

"Miles! I know these symbols!" I grabbed the book and jumped to my feet. I didn't wait for him to come to me but crashed into his conversation with Olive and Tariq. "These symbols here. Do you know them?"

Miles adjusted his glasses and glanced down at the page I was holding. He pursed his lips and then shook his head. "No, it's nothing I've ever seen before. I can't even come up with any frame of reference. Olive? Tariq? Jasper?"

In turn, they each examined the page. While they studied it, I said to Miles, "Mamie taught me those four symbols when I was a kid."

"You're sure?"

"Today on the beach by her house I remembered her drawing them in the sand and making me repeat their names, but I can't remember the third one. Or I couldn't until right now," I said.

Miles went very still. "You can verbalize those symbols?"

"I think so," I said. "Of course, I have no idea what will happen if I do."

There was a noise outside and Tariq hurried over to the gap between the sliding barn door and the wall. We had closed it but it was not a particularly snug fit.

"We have a problem," Tariq announced. "Two problems, actually."

"Do tell." Olive crossed her arms over her chest, expressionless as per usual.

"There is a small army of undead headed our way with Ariana in the lead, and the storm is strengthening and it looks to be a doozy."

"What do we do?" I asked.

"Use that incantation your grandmother taught you," Olive said. "We'll deal with the consequences, whatever they are."

I turned to Miles. He nodded. "Knowing Toni, if she taught you those symbols in particular, she did it for a reason. It might be our only hope."

"No pressure," I muttered.

"They're getting closer," Tariq said, his voice noticeably higher.

"Ziakas, work on your spell. Griffin, help her." Olive strode over to where Tariq stood and Miles followed.

I turned to Jasper. "What if I can't do it? What if it doesn't work? What if . . . ?"

He put his hands on my shoulders and met my gaze. "What if you can? What if it does? What if you just believe?"

Believe. And just like that, my anxiety spiral stopped.

"Try to remember the day your grandmother taught you

the words to go with those symbols. Allow yourself to be there fully and completely. I'll watch out for you."

Reassured, I closed my eyes and placed my hand on the page of the book right on top of the symbols. In my mind, I pictured that day at the beach. Mamie's thick, dark hair streaked with silver was in a loose knot on the crown of her head. She wore her usual long, flowing skirt with a formfitting top that complimented her lithe figure. Her eyes crinkled when she laughed as I showed her a cartwheel I was trying to perfect. She kissed my head, hugged me, and said, *You must believe, mon chaton.* Warmth bloomed in my chest and I felt a smile curve my lips. Mamie lifted me up in the air, making me laugh, and then we crouched in the sand and she began to draw her magic symbols. I could hear her voice in my head as if she were right here beside me, teaching me the words.

"Come on, Ziakas!" Olive cried. "Hurry."

"I am," I snapped.

"Easy, Olive. Give her a chance," Jasper said.

It was then that I heard the noise. The same unearthly cries and wails and the clacking of bones that I'd heard in the labyrinth. They were almost upon us.

"Okay, here goes," I said. I could feel the hum of the connection between me and the book. The whispers I had never understood before became clear and I repeated them. "Matris mater reditus ad me . . . no, wait . . . mater matris . . ." I shook my head. In my panic, the words were getting mixed-up and fuzzy.

"Zoe, I don't wish to rush you, but they are he—" The barn door boomed with the sound of bodies slamming against it, drowning Miles's voice out.

We all jumped back and I closed my eyes, put myself back in the moment on the beach, let the magic unfurl inside me, and bellowed, *"Mater matris ad me reditus!"*

There was a crack as if some celestial being had snapped open the sky and a blue light so bright it forced me to squint lit up the entire barn. As it faded, I blinked to find Mamie standing in front of us. She looked exactly as she had on that day on the beach, right down to her usual flowing skirt and formfitting top. I didn't hesitate but dropped the book and ran straight to her.

"Mamie!" I half expected her to disappear in my arms, but she didn't. Instead, she hugged me back just as tight.

"Mon chaton." She leaned back and cupped my face, studying it. "Look at you. You're all grown up, my brave girl."

"Toni!" Miles appeared at my side. "Sorry to interrupt your reunion but Ariana is just outside and we need you."

"Of course," Mamie said. She shoved me behind her as if I were still that nine-year-old girl. "I have a score to settle with that one."

"She murdered you." My voice cracked when I added, "And Mom, too."

Mamie turned back to me and grabbed my hands with hers. She felt so real. It was hard for me to accept that she was undead like the horde now banging incessantly on the barn doors.

"She did." An expression of devastation crossed over her face. "I took her power and the alliance exiled her. I thought that was the end of it, but she's a . . ."

Mamie paused and I said, "A revenant."

"Yes, we didn't know that Eloise Tate had been sent to

heal the land, that she would die and give Ariana an escape. Nor did we consider that she would harness the power of vengeance to become the one who was dead but returns. It was a grave mistake." She glanced at Miles and he nodded. "I think she wants to wipe out the Donadieu lineage for revenge upon me."

"She does," I agreed with Mamie. "She plans to finish us by murdering me and bringing me back to be her undead Donadieu minion using the spells in the grimoire for her nefarious purposes."

Mamie was already ghostly pale but still she blanched. Her grip on my hands tightened. "Your mother did not risk everything, hiding in time with the grimoire for all those years, only for me to let Ariana win now."

"How did the grimoire come to me? Was it . . . Mom?" I asked. "Did she deliver it to me?"

"No, mon chaton." Mamie cupped my cheek as if she knew the devastation I felt at the possibility that I could have seen my mother again. "The grimoire is spelled to appear to the next Donadieu in line one full lunar cycle after the last Donadieu has passed. That's why it showed up a month after your mother died."

"But the handwriting on the envelope was hers," I protested.

"And the envelope disappeared in green witch fire?" Mamie asked. "That's part of the spell. When you die, the grimoire will appear to the next Donadieu in an envelope with your handwriting and it will disappear in red witch fire—which is your magical color, yes?"

"Yes." I nodded. "Did Mom know that would happen?

She made me promise to never use magic. Why would she ask that of me if she knew the grimoire would come to me one day?"

"She believed she could find a way to break the grimoire's succession spell," Mamie said. "When it arrived in your mother's life a month after you two left me, she knew I had passed on. Ariana, disguised as Eloise, found you immediately, which was why your mother took you on the run. She knew Ariana had murdered me and that she was next. She used those years to perfect the spell in the grimoire that allows a witch to slip through time.

"Once she mastered it, your mother left you in Agatha's care, thinking you would be safe so long as she kept the grimoire and herself away from you. She'd hoped to find a way to defeat Ariana and be free of her, but Ariana managed to catch your mother coming to see you and cast the Waning Curse upon Juliet."

"That's why she ended up at Mystwood and never told us," I said. The thought of my mother choosing to die alone broke me.

As if reading my thoughts, Mamie said, "She didn't choose to die alone any more than I did. The Waning Curse takes away a witch's ability to communicate in any way. Trapped in her body as she wasted away, your mother had no way to reach out to you or warn you about Ariana, just as I'd had no way to warn her before I died."

That only made me feel worse.

"Your mother was afraid that Ariana would murder you and bring you back before you even had the grimoire in your possession. She realized she'd been wrong to ask you not to use magic and hoped you'd reconsider once the grimoire appeared. She trusted that Agatha would assist you in finding the help you needed." She glanced past me at the others. "And she did."

"How do you know all this?" I asked.

"Because your mother and I have talked about it."

I blinked at her. I had so many questions, not the least of which was what did she mean they had talked? *Recently?* I was about to barrage her with questions when one of the boards on the barn door was smashed and an arm appeared. The fingers on the bony hand twitched as it tried to grab for anything on the other side. I felt as if I were an expendable side character in every terrifying zombie movie ever created.

"What do we do, Toni?" Miles asked. "How do we stop her?"

"*We* don't," Toni said. "*I* do. The rest of you must protect Zoe and the grimoire. No matter what happens, she can't have that book. The spells in it would make her invincible."

I turned to retrieve the grimoire, but Jasper already had. He handed it to me and I clutched it to my chest. I felt the book press itself more firmly against me as if it knew I would do anything I could to protect it. When I glanced up, Olive, Miles, Tariq, and Jasper formed a circle around me. They were facing out and I knew without being told that they would sacrifice their lives to keep the book from Ariana.

A horrific crash sounded and I jumped. I peered over Miles's shoulder to see Ariana's undead horde in various states of decay spill into the barn like a ripped bag of beans. Surprisingly, they didn't attack. Instead, they moved into formation, creating an aisle, which Ariana strode down like a queen inspecting her troops.

"Darkwood." Mamie stood facing the door with her chin tipped up and not a bit of fear in her eyes. I was in awe.

At the sight of Mamie, Ariana faltered but caught herself. She glanced from Mamie to where I stood within the circle of the BODO staff. Then a terrifying smile spread across her lips. It was without mirth and full of malice. "I see your granddaughter finally managed to work a decent spell. Excellent." She practically purred the last word and it made goose bumps rise on my arms.

She flicked her wrist in the direction of Mamie, and her horde of undead attacked. Mamie stood no chance against so many. I tried to push out of the circle, but Jasper locked his arm around me, keeping me in place.

"No, Zoe, don't," he said. "Remember what your grandmother said. We have to protect the book."

Mamie held up her hand in a *stop* gesture but the undead ran right over whatever shield she was trying to contain them with. The smack of their bones colliding as they covered Mamie in a thrashing pile of limbs was a sound I knew I would never forget.

I strained against Jasper's hold and shouted at Miles, "Do something!"

He held up a finger, indicating that I should wait. I tried to twist my way out of the circle.

"Relax, Ziakas!" Olive ordered. "She's already dead. What do you think they can do to her?"

"Rip her apart?" I said as an arm—not Mamie's—was flung out of the mass of bodies.

"Toni can handle this," Miles said with complete confidence.

"We need to help her," I insisted. A leg was jettisoned out of the pile. Then a torso. The pieces came faster and faster, flung farther and farther, until the entire barn was littered with the dismantled bits of Ariana's army. Then, one by one, they simply went *poof* into a cloud of smoke and vanished.

Mamie emerged completely unharmed, not a hair out of place, standing right where she'd been all along.

We were all mesmerized by how Mamie had evaporated Ariana's army, so much so that we didn't notice when Ariana appeared right outside our circle. Tariq saw her first and let out a warning cry. It was too late.

Ariana grasped me by the hair and forcibly yanked me out of their protection. Jasper didn't let go of me, and as I was clutching the book to my chest with my right hand, I couldn't fight Ariana with anything more than a few blind punches with my left, which she deftly dodged.

"Let her go!" Jasper demanded.

Ariana laughed. "No." She grabbed my neck with her free hand and started to squeeze. "Release her."

I wanted to tell him not to, but Ariana's hand tightened, cutting off my air. I choked and Jasper dropped his arm from around my waist.

"That's better. I'm going to enjoy killing her and then I'll bring little Zoe back as my minion with her grandmother watching. How delicious."

"Don't. Even. Think. About. It." Mamie glowered. As if the storm outside was responding to the rager happening inside the barn, the wind picked up, the rain pelted through the cracks in the dried old boards overhead, lightning flashed, and thunder rumbled.

"You can't beat me," Ariana said. "Not anymore. And now that I have the book and your lovely granddaughter, there's nothing you can do to stop me."

"Isn't there?" Mamie asked.

"No, there isn't. I've waited a long time to be free," Ariana said. Her fingers clenched tighter around my throat and I started to panic, bucking against her hold, desperate to get some oxygen.

"Stop it!"

"Let her go!"

"Darkwood!"

"Enough!"

The last voice was Olive's and it left a chill in the air. "If you want freedom, we'll be happy to assist you onward in your journey."

Everything went gray, and I started to see spots when I was hit from the side by a truck—okay, it was Jasper—knocking me out of her hold and tucking me into his arms as we rolled across the barn floor, not stopping until we slammed into a half-rotten stable.

"All right, love?" he asked.

I spat a bit of moldy hay out of my mouth and sucked in a breath. "Yeah, I'm good."

Jasper rose to stand, pulling me up with him. I glanced up to see Ariana and Mamie squaring off. I wondered if this was going to be some magical duel where they each hit each other with spells until one of them won. It was not.

"Hold her," Mamie ordered.

As one, Jasper, Miles, Olive, and Tariq raised their hands, and colors, like the ones I'd seen in the pool that night with Jasper, shot out of their palms—black for Jasper, blue for Olive, silver for Tariq, and white for Miles. The streams of color twined around Ariana. She raised her arms to ward them off, but there were too many of them.

With her arms trapped at her sides, she hissed at Mamie. "Just like last time, it took the power of the alliance to hold me."

"Yes, but unlike last time, you're not getting exiled, you're being sent back beyond the veil."

I watched as Mamie placed her hand on Ariana's forehead and said, "Redire ad mortem."

I didn't need a translator to know it was a command to return to death. We collectively held our breath, waiting to see Ariana disappear beyond the veil, except she didn't. She broke through their hold, shoved Mamie's hand away, and said, "I told you, you can't control me anymore."

Ariana pulled *El Corazón* out of her pocket. Her smirk was pure evil when she said, "You really shouldn't have given Eloise full access to the BODO. I wonder what else, she—oops, I mean I—swiped from your collection. And I would have taken so much more had I not had to give up my host."

"That's it!" Olive started to glow. A bright blue light covered her entire body and glowing blue embers shone in her eyes.

"Try me, Fae witch," Ariana snapped.

Olive launched herself at Ariana, and there was an explosion of sparks and flames as Miles, Mamie, Jasper, and Tariq joined the fray. I didn't have that sort of power—not yet—but I desperately wanted to help.

Heat seared my hands and I yelped. The grimoire was

glowing bright red. My color! I held it on my open hands, blinked a few tears onto the lock, and said, "Show me."

The book popped open and the pages fluttered. It didn't go all the way to the end but rather stopped in the first section. I looked at the symbols and sighed. It was as incomprehensible . . . I closed my eyes. I heard Mamie's voice when I was a little girl. *Believe, mon chaton.* And Jasper's voice. *Belief is the fuel required for magic to exist.*

I opened my eyes. I glanced at the ancient page in front of me. The symbols that had been impossible to decipher just hours before started to rewrite themselves on the page in words I could actually read. They were Latin-based, but that was okay. I could work with that.

A yell sounded and I glanced up to see Tariq sail across the barn and crash against a far wall while Miles went down in a poof of white smoke. It was not going well for my team.

I glanced down at the book and scanned the page. According to the grimoire, there was only one way to rid ourselves of the revenant of a dark witch who was bound by vengeance. Following the instructions, I placed my hand palm up on the open page and concentrated on the words I'd read. *Mihi pugionem mortis trade.*

When I felt the weight of cool metal, I opened my eyes to find a lethal-looking dagger resting on my hand. The Dagger of Death had been delivered per my request. I felt its weight in my soul. I scanned the page one more time, ignoring the shouts as my grandmother and friends fought for their lives.

I closed the grimoire and its lock snapped shut. "Trust me," I said as I clutched it close. I held the dagger at my back, then rushed forward just as Ariana dropped Olive to her knees and looked to be about to finish her off with a magical strike.

"Stop!" I slid across the dirt floor to stand in front of her. "Stop! I'll give you the book. I'll be yours to command. Just stop!"

"Zoe, no!" Jasper yelled at the same time Mamie cried, "Mon chaton, no!"

Ariana held *El Corazón* in one hand and with the sweep of her other arm, blasted a shot of green fire at everyone but me, which spread to the far corners of the barn. Then she threw up a shield much like the one Miles had used at the maze.

"I'm listening." Ariana tipped her head to the side. Her green eyes were glowing with unchecked power. I swallowed, trying to steady my nerves.

"The Donadieu grimoire. You can have it and me as your servant. Just don't hurt them." I didn't have to manufacture the wobble in my voice.

"Now, why would I let them go when I can trap their powers in my book?" Ariana asked. "I can be what I was supposed to be before your grandmother ruined everything."

I felt a trembling start in my legs. I wasn't going to be able to outmaneuver her. She was going to steal all of our magic. A thrum of power rippled against my side. I knew without looking that it was the grimoire. A trickle of warmth, the same feeling I had when I used magic, was pouring from the book into me, giving me its strength and power.

How had I ever resisted this world, this book, and my ancestry? I would not let Ariana take it from me when I had just discovered it. And there was no way in hell I was going to let her get away with murdering Mamie and my mom.

Newly resolved, I clutched the book closer. I made my voice quake as if I were afraid. "That's not the bargain." I lowered my head, pretending to sob. "You have to set them free."

"Do I?" Ariana reached out with her free hand and cupped my chin, pulling me in close as she forced me to meet her gaze. "Do I really?"

I blinked, forcing some blood tears to fall. When Ariana reached out to catch a tear on her fingertip, I thrust the Dagger of Death straight into the faintly clenching heart of the book she held.

Ariana staggered back. The shield she had placed around us vanished, and my friends raced forward just in time to see Ariana's form turn to ash and fall to the ground. The book with the dagger in it dropped to the ground with a thud.

"You did it, Zoe!" Miles snatched up the book. "You have vanquished Ariana Darkwood once and for all."

"Mon chaton!" Mamie stood outside the group, looking around as if she couldn't see. "Are you all right?"

"Mamie, I'm here!" I rushed to her. When I grabbed her hand in mine, she blinked and then smiled. "There you are. You look so much like your mother, even she thinks so."

My heart thumped against my chest and I scanned the dark barn. "Is she—?"

Mamie turned her head as if she was listening to a conversation only she could hear.

"Mamie?"

"I have to go, mon chaton."

"But why?" I cried. "You just got here and I haven't seen you in decades. I have so many questions."

"I know, but you have discovered the most important part of being a witch . . . belief," Mamie said, but her voice sounded more like an echo and when I looked at her, she was less substantial, as if she was fading.

"Are you leaving me?" I asked. My throat was tight and tears burned my eyes. I couldn't believe that I had her back only to lose her in a matter of minutes. "Please don't leave."

"I can't stay," she said. "Your magic is not yet strong enough to hold me."

"But will you come back?"

"You know how to call for me," she said. "Practice, mon chaton. Practice very hard and we will see each other again."

Her hand in mine faded, feeling as insubstantial as mist.

"Don't go, Mamie." I couldn't keep the pleading out of my voice. I went for a plea of help, hoping that could anchor her. "We have ghost pirates circling the island waiting for us. What do we do?"

Her laugh was a soft chuckle. "Before I died, I tasked the pirates with protecting the island and you, should you ever return, from Ariana. They were quite peeved that you showed up with her in disguise, which is why they tried to overtake you but couldn't risk harming you. They aren't there to hurt you but to watch over you. Have no fear."

Well, hell, there went my last argument. "I need you, Mamie."

"I'm always with you," she said. She was glittery mist shimmering on the air now, barely visible. I wanted to cry and wail and demand that she stay, but I didn't. And then she was gone.

28

"Zoe! Your eyes! Were you bitten by a vampire?" Agatha gasped as she walked into Miles's office, where I'd been sitting alone, trying to process the events of the past few days.

When Mamie had disappeared, I'd shut down. Incapable of speech, I'd climbed into the back of the SUV, and other than the time I'd spent on the ferry, staring morosely out at the sea, where we did not see the ghost pirates, I'd slept all the way to New York. Tariq and Jasper had tried to talk to me, but I simply hadn't had the reserves to talk about what had happened, what I'd learned, or what I'd lost.

I didn't know who'd called Agatha—I suspected Claire—but I was grateful to have her here. My throat got tight and I let out a small sob. Agatha swooped across the room, sank onto the couch beside me, and swept me into a hug.

"It's all right, Zoe," she crooned. I rested my head on her shoulder and she held me and rocked me as if I were six instead of thirty-six. "You've been through so much and you've been so brave. I'm very proud of you."

That was one of the many reasons why I valued Agatha.

She was always there for me and she always knew exactly what to say. I let her comforting kitchen witch warmth wash over me like a balm.

When I felt as if the broken bits of me were slowly knitting themselves back together, I pulled back and met her warm brown gaze. "Have I ever told you how much I appreciate you?"

Agatha cupped my cheek with one hand and said, "Not often enough."

I laughed but then sobered and continued, "You've been a bonus mom to me all these years, and you didn't have to be. I *don't* tell you often enough how much you mean to me. I love you, Agatha." And for the first time since I was a child, I initiated a hug.

"Oh Lord, you are a vampire, aren't you?" she cried, hugging me close.

Another laugh burst out of me and I leaned back and said, "No, I promise. I'm okay." I gestured to the table in front of us where I'd placed the grimoire. "The book and I have developed a relationship. Yeah, there's no way I can explain what happened without it sounding super weird."

Agatha patted my hand. "Oh good, I love weird—"

"Zoe, I have your remedy." Tariq entered the room with a determined stride that faltered as he took in Agatha and me sitting on the couch, clearly having a moment.

"Sorry." He put his hand on his heart. "So sorry. I didn't mean to interrupt."

"No." I waved him into the room. "Your treatment for my eyes is priority number one."

He looked at Agatha, who nodded. "Come in, Tariq. It's fine."

Agatha rose from her seat and moved to a chair, letting Tariq take her place.

"Lean your head back," he instructed. "These eye drops should work immediately."

"Are they going to sting or burn?" I wanted to be prepared.

"No, they should feel soothing," he answered. "I'll put three drops in each eye and then I want you to close them for a few minutes."

"All right." I tipped my head, resting it on the back of the couch. I heard the door open and the footsteps of someone or multiple someones entering the room, but Tariq squeezed the dropper before I could glance up. I felt the liquid when it hit. I didn't blink or flinch and when he was done, I just closed my eyes, letting the solution settle.

"Is she—?" a woman whispered and I recognized the voice as belonging to Claire.

"I'm fine," I said. "Just following Tariq's instructions for my eyes."

"Let's hope he doesn't turn them a different color," another female voice said. It was Olive. I knew because only Olive gave Tariq such a hard time.

"That only happened once," Tariq said. His Nigerian accent got thicker as he defended himself.

"Now, now, we're not here to bicker," Miles said. "We need to catch Claire up on what happened.

I felt my lips curve up as I listened. After the past few

weeks, I'd come to understand that the staff of the BODO really were a found family, much like Agatha and I were, and I was a part of it. The certainty of this made me feel warm inside, much like my magic did.

"Yes, I'm eager to hear everything, but first I need to follow up," Claire said. "Jasper, what has happened to the Viking being held in the Lively tomb?"

"It's sorted." His voice was a deep, rough rasp that made my insides flutter.

"How?" Claire asked.

"When Zoe sent Ariana irrevocably beyond the veil by destroying *El Corazón*, he, as a remnant of her magic, went as well."

"And Moran stayed interred?"

"Yes, I had a colleague in Boston follow up," Tariq said. "He remains undisturbed."

Miles took over the telling of the story with added bits and tangents from Olive and Jasper and Tariq.

With my eyes shut, it was disconcerting to have so many voices coming from all directions in the room. I felt a solid weight sit on the armrest to my right and I knew without opening my eyes that it was Jasper. There was something both disturbing and comforting about his nearness. I tried to breathe myself into a state of calm with marginal success.

When they got to the part about Mamie appearing in the barn, they all went quiet. I knew they were waiting for me to finish the tale. I could have passed and let Miles finish, but that would have been the coward's way out.

Instead, I sat up and opened my eyes. I turned to Tariq

first, trusting that if his potion hadn't worked, he'd come up with something else. Instead, a wide smile parted his lips and he said, "There she is."

I turned back to the group and saw Agatha's shoulders drop in relief. When I glanced at Jasper, he winked at me, and I glanced away before my flustered reaction was obvious to everyone.

"You don't have to talk about this if you're not ready." Claire's voice was gentle with understanding.

"No, it's okay." I swallowed around the knot in my throat. The sadness of losing Mamie all over again was going to take some time to fade.

I cleared my throat and described the events that had brought Mamie back and what had happened when she and Ariana had faced each other. I told them that in that final showdown, I had managed to unlock the grimoire and it had showed me how to call up the Dagger of Death.

"About that. Why did you stab the book and not Ariana?" Tariq asked.

"The grimoire specifically stated that I was to use the dagger on whatever the dark witch used for her power, which for Ariana was *El Corazón*. What happened to it, by the way?"

"We removed the dagger, and the book turned to ash just like Ariana. It is no more," Miles said.

"How extraordinary." Claire glanced at me. "Your family is very talented."

"Apparently." I nodded.

"I suggest you all take a few days off to recuperate from your ordeal," Claire said.

"Or . . ." Olive swept a quelling glance around the room. "We could go out to the collection and do inventory to determine what other books that revenant stole."

Tariq sighed and stood up. "I knew you were going to say that. Not even a near-death experience gets us a day off."

Olive followed him out of Miles's office. "If you knew, then why are you complaining?"

Claire rose and said, "We'd better mediate."

I grabbed the grimoire off the table and followed the others into the main room to find Tariq and Olive still bickering.

I glanced at the three stories of dubious books surrounding me and felt the same stirring sensation of being home that I'd experienced the very first time I'd entered the BODO.

"What are your plans now, Zoe?" Miles asked. "Since your situation is resolved, we could take charge of the grimoire and keep it here for you if you'd like."

I felt the book go still as if awaiting my answer. "Thank you, Miles, but I'm going to hang on to it."

"If you're sure?"

"I'm sure."

The corner of his mouth curved up and he said, "The job offer still stands."

I felt all their eyes on me, waiting to hear what I'd say.

"About that." I cleared my throat. "What's the vacation situation?"

"Are you accepting?" Miles asked.

I glanced at the group. Both Claire and Agatha looked hopeful, Tariq encouraging, and Jasper—well, the man simply smoldered. I couldn't look at him too long or I'd lose the entire thread of the conversation. Olive's expression was bored, as per usual, while Miles seemed pensive.

"Yes," I said. "I'm accepting."

"That's the first sensible thing you've ever said, Ziakas." Olive clapped her hands. "We have an inventory to do, people. Let's get to it."

And so we did.

ACKNOWLEDGMENTS

Being an author is a strange occupation. I spend a lot of time wandering around in my own head, thinking about make-believe people, places, and things. All of this would be for nothing if I didn't have so many amazing readers out there willing to follow along on my mysteries, rom-coms, and now fantasy novels. I am one very lucky author, and I can't ever thank my readers enough. You complete me!

I am also incredibly fortunate to have an exemplary team. They make me a much better writer than I actually am by sharing their insights and wisdom, helping me to craft the best stories possible. They also support and encourage me when I have a new *idea* and want to jump genres. Thank you, Kate Seaver, Amanda Maurer, Christina Hogrebe, and Jessica Errera. You are all so talented and brilliant. I am extremely grateful for all that you do and your willingness to explore new genres with me.

Thank you to my publicity and marketing team, Kaila Mundell-Hill and Kim-Salina I. Your tireless work on behalf of my books is much appreciated.

To the behind the scenes crew, Christine Legon and Kristin del Rosario, I appreciate your talents and gifts so much in presenting my work in its best possible light.

Special thanks to the artist Brandon Dorman. I am absolutely besotted with this gorgeous cover. Thank you so much for creating such a stunning visual for the book.

Many thanks to my writer friends who also encourage my need to try new things: Kate Carlisle, Paige Shelton, Hannah Dennison, and the lovely Jungle Red Writers: Hallie Ephron, Hank Phillippi Ryan, Rhys Bowen, Deborah Crombie, Lucy Burdette, and Julia Spencer-Fleming.

Special shout-out to my assistants Christie Conlee, who administers the Facebook group McKinlay Mavens, and Jenel Looney, who runs the BookTalk group on social media—you're both just amazing! Cheers to the Xuni Team who manage my website and for making it so darn pretty!

Lastly, I want to thank my people—my friends and family—who know and understand that I won't answer the phone or come out of my office while on deadline and frequently miss things because writing isn't a 9-5 job, at least for me. And saving the best for last, I want to give hugs and high fives to my squad: Chris Hansen Orf, Wyatt Orf, Beckett Orf, and Catherine Pettycrew. Your input on my ideas and support for my work means so much to me. I love you all and look forward to many more outings and adventures together.

Keep reading for an excerpt from
Jenn McKinlay's novel . . .

Love at First Book

1

"Em, are you all right?" Samantha Gale, my very best friend, answered her phone on the fourth ring. Her voice was rough with sleep and it belatedly occurred to me that nine o'clock in the morning in Finn's Hollow, Ireland, was four o'clock in the morning in Oak Bluffs, Martha's Vineyard.

"Oh, I'm sorry. Damn it, I woke you up, didn't I?" I asked, feeling awful about it.

"No, it's fine," Sam said. "I told you when you left that I'm always here for you." There was a low grumbling in the background and she added, "And Ben says he's here for you, too."

That made me laugh. Sam and Ben had become couple goals for me. Not that I thought I'd ever find anything like the connection they'd made, but they kept the pilot light of my innermost hope aflame.

"Thank you and Ben," I said. "I'm going to hang up now. Forget I ever called."

"Emily Allen, don't you dare," Sam said. Now she sounded fully awake. *Oops.*

"No, really I—" I began but she interrupted me.

"Tell me why you're calling, otherwise I'll worry." There was more grumbling in the background. Sam laughed and said, "Ben says he's begging you to tell me so that I don't drive him crazy with speculation."

I grinned. She would, too. Then I grew serious.

Glancing around the Last Chapter, the quaint bookshop in which I was presently standing, I noted objectively that it was a booklover's dream come true. A three-story stone building chock-full of books with a small café, where the scent of fresh-brewed coffee, berry-filled scones, and cinnamon pastry permeated the air. I felt myself lean in that direction as if the delicious aromas were reeling me in.

One of the employees had unlocked the front door of the shop, and I had trailed in behind a handful of customers who'd been waiting. I'd been agog ever since.

This was it. The bookshop where I'd be working for the next year. My heart was pounding and my palms were sweaty. The black wool turtleneck sweater I was wearing, in an attempt to defeat the early November chill, felt as if it were choking me and I was quite sure the pain spearing through my head meant I was having an aneurysm.

"I'm supposed to meet my boss in a few minutes, and I think I'm having a heart attack or potentially a stroke," I said.

There was a beat of silence then Sam said, "Tell me your symptoms."

I listed them all and she noted each one with an "uh-huh," which told me nothing whatsoever as to what she thought about my condition. I was three thousand miles away and starting a new job in a bookshop, having put my career as a librarian on Martha's Vineyard on hold to chase some crazy fantasy where I traveled to a foreign destination and lived a life full of adventure.

"I think I'm going to throw up," I groaned.

"Inhale," Sam said. "You know the drill—in for eight seconds, hold for four, out for eight."

I sucked in a breath. *Ouch.* "I can't. It makes my head throb. See? Aneurysm."

"Or a lack-of-caffeine headache," she said. "Have you had coffee yet?"

Come to think of it, I had not. I'd been too nervous to make any before I left my cottage this morning so the potential for this skull splitter to be from coffee deprivation seemed likely.

"No," I said. "And I see where you're going, but I still have brutal nausea and I'm sweating. I bet I have a fever. Maybe it's food poisoning from the airplane food last night. I had the beef stroganoff."

"You ate airplane food?" Sam sounded as incredulous as if I'd confessed to eating ice cream off the bathroom floor. She was a professional chef, so not a big surprise.

"I know, I know," I said. "It's pure preservatives. I'll likely be dead within the hour."

There was a lengthy pause where I imagined Sam was practicing her last words to me, wanting to get them just right.

"Em, you know I love you like a sister, right?" she asked.

Well, that didn't sound like the beginning of a vow of friendship into the afterlife.

"I do," I said. "I also know that's how you'd start a sentence I'm not going to like."

"You're panicking, Em," Sam said. Her voice was full of empathy. "And you and I both know that bout of hypochondria you dealt with last summer was how you coped with your unhappiness."

"But I'm not unhappy," I protested. "I'm living the dream in a quaint village in County Kerry where the green is the greenest green I've ever seen and there's a sheep staring at me over the top of every stone wall. Seriously, I'm drowning in picturesque charm, which is probably why I'm about to keel over dead."

A sound came from my phone that resembled someone stepping on a duck.

"Are you laughing at me?" I asked. Rude but understandable.

"No, never," Sam said. She cleared her throat. "I just think you might be freaking out because it's your first day at your new job."

"I'm not," I protested. I was. I absolutely was. "I just think I need to come home before they discover I have some highly contagious pox or plague and I'm quarantined in a thatched stone cottage to live out my days in a fairy-infested forest, talking to the trees and hedgehogs while farming for potatoes."

"Have you ever considered that you read too much?" Sam asked.

"No!" I cried and I heard Ben, also a librarian and formerly my boss, protest as well.

Sam laughed. She enjoyed goading us.

"Just think, if I leave now, we can meet for coffee and pastries at the Grape tomorrow morning."

"While I'd love to see you, you know that, you have to stay in Ireland and see your journey through," Sam said. "If you go home now your mother will guilt you into never leaving again, not to mention clobber you with the dreaded 'I told you so.'"

"Fair point." I sighed. I glanced at the display on my phone. My mother had already called five times and texted twelve and I hadn't even been in Ireland for twenty-four hours yet. I'd let her know I'd arrived safely, but I knew that wasn't what her messages were about.

My mother had made it clear that she expected me to continue in the role of her caregiver, a position I'd assumed when my father left several years ago. Were she incapable of caring for herself, I'd understand, but there was absolutely nothing wrong with her except a scorching case of toxic narcissism. I tabled the mom problem to deal with the one at hand.

"I still think I might pass out and then I'll likely lose the job and this entire conversation becomes moot," I said.

"You won't," Sam said. "Find a place to sit down. Can you do that?"

"Okay." I was standing in the stacks—well, more accurately, hiding. The shelves were dark wood, long and tall and stuffed with books. They comforted me. Scattered randomly amid the shelving units were step stools. I found one and sat down.

"Are you sitting?" Sam asked.

"Yes."

"Good, now put your head between your knees," she ordered.

"Um." I was wearing a formfitting, gray wool pencil skirt.

I tried to maneuver my head down. No luck. The skirt was too snug. The closest I could get was to look over my knees at my very cute black ankle boots. "Sorry, Sam, nothing is getting between these knees. Not even a hot Irishman."

Sam chuckled, but over that I heard a strangled noise behind me and I straightened up and turned around to see a man in jeans and an Aran sweater, holding his fist to his mouth, looking as if he was choking. He had thick, wavy black hair and blue eyes so dark they were almost the same shade as his hair. Also, if I wasn't mistaken, he was my new boss.

2

"Um, Sam, I have to go," I said.

"The breathing helped, right?" she asked.

"Totally. Call you later." I ended the call and stood up. The man cleared his throat and dropped his fist. Now that I could see his face, it was indeed my new boss, Kieran Murphy. He appeared to be trying to figure out what to say, so I jumped in and asked, "You didn't happen to hear what I just said, did you?"

My long auburn hair was pinned at the nape of my neck in a loose bun and I pushed my large wire-framed glasses up on my nose. Suddenly, I was overly warm and not in a good way. I paused to consider it. I was only twenty-nine. This could not be a hot flash . . . could it?

"Just the last little bit," he said. His voice was deep and his brogue was thick and it curled around me as if it were a magic spell being cast. He tipped his head to the side and said, "Should I take it as a warning?"

"Oh, no, it wasn't meant that way," I protested. "I'd be

happy to have a hot Irishman . . . er . . ." I paused and shook my head. "That's not going to come out right either."

I wanted to smack my forehead. I didn't. Instead I stood there, feeling my face heat up with extreme self-consciousness, which no doubt would turn my pasty complexion the shade of an overripe tomato. I probably looked like I had a horrible skin condition.

Mr. Murphy's unwavering gaze had me completely rattled. Not just because he was my boss but because he *was* a hot Irishman and I was sure that penetrating stare of his could see into my very soul. What a sorry impression I was making. I felt like the human embodiment of embarrassment wrapped in mortification dipped in humiliation.

"Yes, well." He cleared his throat and said, "I think we can just leave that to be sorted another time, all right?"

"Absolutely. No need to talk about it." I pressed my lips into a tight line, determined to do just that. But being me, I couldn't. "Unless you wanted to discuss that bit of awkwardness right now, which would alleviate me from stressing about the first impressions I made, because I totally will—all day."

He looked surprised and then he laughed. It was a rich rumble that came from his chest and I felt it reverberate in my spine. It was a good laugh. When I smiled in return, he abruptly grew serious, as if he'd caught himself being amused by me and shut it right down. Huh.

"How about we just start over?" He held out his hand. "Emily Allen, I presume?"

"Yes." I clasped his hand in mine a bit too enthusiastically and he winced. I immediately let go. "Sorry."

"No need, fingers are overrated," he assured me while he wiggled the blood back into his. "I'm Kieran Murphy."

"It's nice to meet you, Mr. Murphy," I said.

"Just call me Murphy," he said. "Everyone does."

"All right, Mr. . . . uh . . . Murphy," I agreed. He didn't seem like a Murphy to me. In my mind, he was Kieran, or Kier for short, a romance-hero-worthy name for a man who certainly looked the part. I could picture him on a seaside cliff, the wind tousling his thick dark curls and lifting the ends of a red cashmere scarf he'd casually draped around his neck, while he stood with his legs braced and his broad shoulders squared, daring the wind to knock him down as he squinted out at the ocean, looking for, well, obviously his long-lost love.

He was watching me as if waiting for something. It belatedly occurred to me to invite him to use my first name.

"And please call me Emily or Em, that's what my friends call me, you know, if they're close friends, or Red, some people call me Red, well actually, no, only strangers who couldn't be bothered to learn my name have called me Red." I was babbling. I shut my mouth.

Murphy nodded. "So noted . . . Red."

Was he saying we'd remain strangers? Well, that wasn't very friendly.

He turned and we left the shelves behind us. I followed him feeling like an idiot—why the hell had I told him strangers call me Red? But was it really my fault? The man was insanely attractive. If I could have managed it, I would've taken a stealth picture of him and sent it to Sam. She would die. We'd noted he was good-looking from the picture on the bookshop's website but the live-action Kieran Murphy was next level.

I was completely unprepared for this contingency. Why couldn't he be a much older man with thinning hair, a beer gut, and a roguish twinkle in his eye?

"Why don't I show you around a bit before you meet Siobhan." He glanced over his shoulder at me. His expression was shuttered, adding one more layer to his perfection as a brooding romance hero.

No, no, no. I hadn't been on a date in forever but there was no way I was going to start crushing on my new boss. Not when I was on a mission of self-discovery. I had to keep my priorities straight. The only relationship I was having on this trip was with myself.

"That would be lovely." I sounded entirely too eager. I cleared my throat and asked, "How did you know who I was?" I didn't mean to be so blunt, but my curiosity was highly verbal and very direct.

"Deductive reasoning," he said. He gestured to the customers with whom I'd entered the building. "You're the only person I didn't recognize so I figured you must be our new hire."

"Oh." There was no faulting that logic. "Mystery fan, are you?"

He glanced at me with one eyebrow raised slightly higher than the other. It was a dead sexy look. I tried to blink it away like those spots that blur your vision when you inadvertently glance at the sun.

"Indeed I am," he said. "Mostly noir but a bit of traditional as well. And you?"

"Agatha and Dorothy are my girls," I said. He nodded in what I hoped was approval or at the very least acceptance. Mystery readers could be so judgy about the cozy subgenre.

I glanced at the signs over the shelving units. We'd moved from fiction, through books of Irish interest, and now we were standing beside the history section.

"Here's a hypothetical," Murphy said. "A lad comes in and asks for books on magic. Where do you direct him?"

"I'd tell him they all disappeared." I waved my hands in the air like a magician and grinned. His right eyebrow ticked up again. He didn't smile. I immediately grew serious. "Just kidding, you know, to break the ice with the boy." He continued to stare, clearly waiting for my answer. Okay, then. "I'd ask him what he wanted to know about magic specifically."

"Stories about magicians."

"Real or fictional?"

"Fictional."

I started to hum the theme to the Harry Potter movies and the corner of his mouth twitched, which felt like quite a victory until Murphy shook his head and said, "He's read those."

"Ah, well, then I'd show him *The Golden Compass*, *The Magicians*, *Shadow and Bone*, and the Simon Snow series."

Murphy made a *humph* sound, which I believed meant he was grudgingly impressed. He turned and continued walking through the shop. It had that delightful smell unique to bookshops and libraries that was earthy and woody with notes of vanilla and chocolate. The pragmatic librarian in me knew that the smell was caused by the organic compounds in the paper pages breaking down but the booklover in me thought it was just one more aspect of the allure of books. I was soaking it in, using it to calm my nerves, when my new boss spun around so quickly I almost slammed into him.

"An older gentleman asks you for books about Egypt. Where do you direct him?"

I paused. Another question? Was this a test? Was he quizzing me? Had the man forgotten that I was a librarian? I'd thought part of the reason I'd been hired was for my research skills. As I understood from the job offer, I'd be the assistant to the writer in residence for part of the day and a shop clerk for the rest. I was overqualified for both positions but the former was, quite frankly, the reason I'd accepted the job.

I felt a tiny prickle of unease. Was this hot Irishman looking for a reason to get rid of me? Well, I wasn't going to make it easy for him.

Jenn McKinlay is the award-winning *New York Times*, *USA Today*, and *Publishers Weekly* bestselling author of several mystery and romance series. Her work has been translated into multiple languages in countries all over the world. She lives in sunny Arizona in a house that is overrun with books, pets, and her husband's guitars.

VISIT JENN MCKINLAY ONLINE

JennMcKinlay.com
JennMcKinlayAuthor
McKinlayJenn

**Learn more about this book
and other titles from
New York Times Bestselling Author**

JENN McKINLAY

SCAN ME
or visit
prh.com/jennmckinlay

PRH collects and processes your personal information on scan. See prh.com/notice/